FRANCIS BRET HARTE was born in Albany, New York, in 1836. Confined by ill health from the time he was six until he was ten, he read widely in the library of his father, a schoolteacher, who encouraged his literary interests. His first poem, written when he was eleven, was published in the *New York Sunday Atlas*. During his early teens he worked in a lawyer's office and in the accounting room of a merchant. At about the age of sixteen he moved to California, worked as a printer, schoolteacher, and finally in a mint. He also began to publish stories and poems in various magazines. In 1857 he became a typesetter for the *Golden Era* in San Francisco and contributed short sketches to this publication. *The Californian* published his *Condensed Novels and Other Papers,* which were parodies of current fiction. By 1868 he had achieved local fame and was made editor of a new magazine, the *Overland Monthly*. His story "The Luck of Roaring Camp" was published in its second issue and his reputation quickly spread across the continent. In 1871, at the request of Eastern editors, he returned to New York. After great initial success, he became a literary idol and subsequently fell into financial difficulties. He was glad to accept a position as a U. S. consular agent in Crefeld, Germany, in 1878, leaving his wife and four children behind in America. Two years later he was transferred to Glasgow and eventually settled in London, where he continued writing stories and was welcomed into literary circles. He died in Camberley, England, in 1902.

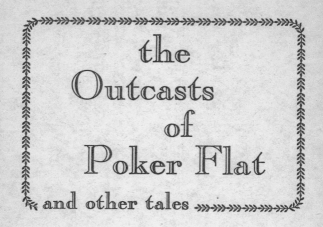

the Outcasts of Poker Flat
and other tales

by BRET HARTE

With an Introduction by
WALLACE STEGNER

A SIGNET CLASSIC from
NEW AMERICAN LIBRARY
TIMES MIRROR
New York and Scarborough, Ontario
The New English Library Limited, London

SIGNET CLASSIC TRADEMARK REG. U.S. PAT. OFF. AND FOREIGN COUNTRIES
REGISTERED TRADEMARK—MARCA REGISTRADA
HECHO EN CHICAGO, U.S.A.

SIGNET, SIGNET CLASSICS, MENTOR, PLUME AND MERIDIAN BOOKS
are published *in the United States* by
The New American Library, Inc.,
1301 Avenue of the Americas, New York, New York 10019,
in Canada by The New American Library of Canada Limited,
81 Mack Avenue, Scarborough, Ontario M1L 1M8,
in the United Kingdom by The New English Library Limited,
Barnard's Inn, Holborn, London, E.C. 1, England

9 10 11 12 13 14 15 16 17

PRINTED IN THE UNITED STATES OF AMERICA

Contents ⋙⋙⋙⋙⋙⋙⋙⋙

Introduction ≫≫≫≫≫≫≫≫≫≫≫

There are some writers who, no matter how great their living reputations, reveal themselves after their deaths—sometimes long after—to have been greater than their contemporaries thought them. New meanings come pushing up through them like stones pushed upward by the frost; or to take a figure from the Gold Rush, readers panning the tailings and gravel heaps of these old literary placers sometimes find more gold than the original Argonauts found. Bret Harte, it must be said at once, does not seem to be one of these writers. Though the critics have been out in Chinese hordes panning the worked-over gravels of American literature, no critic has made a new strike in him. The consensus on Harte is approximately what it was at the time of his death: that he was a skillful but not profound writer who made a lucky strike in subject matter and for a few heady months enjoyed a fabulous popularity; that once the artifice, narrowness, and shallowness of his work began to be perceived, he fell out of public favor; and that through the last twenty-four years of his life, while he lived abroad, he went on tiredly repeating himself in potboiler after potboiler, turning over his own tailings in a pathetic attempt to recapture what had first made him.

That estimate is not true in all its details or in all its implications, but it is broadly true. Harte *was* lucky, he *was* limited, he *did* swiftly lose his popularity in America, he *did* go on repeating himself. Of the scores of stories that he wrote during his years in Germany, Scotland, and England, all but a small handful return to the picturesque gulches of the Sierra foothills from which, in one blazing strike, he had extracted the nugget of his reputation. Now, no critic takes him very seriously; he is read principally by children and students. And yet he cannot be dismissed. More than a hundred years after his first sketches and poems began to appear in *The Golden Era* in the late 1850's, he remains embedded in the American literary tradition, and it looks as if he will stay. It is worth trying to discover what is keeping him there.

Whatever virtues he had, they were not the virtues of realism. His observation of Gold Rush country, character, and society was neither very accurate nor very penetrating; neither was much of it firsthand. Despite persistent legends of Harte's mining experiences, his Indian fighting, and his stint as a Wells-Fargo gun guard, George Stewart and others have demonstrated that his actual experience in the mines was probably limited to a season of schoolteaching near La Grange, plus a brief "picnic," as Harte called it, in the diggings, plus a later tour with Anton Roman in frank search of literary material. The literary tourists who make pilgrimages to the "Bret Harte country" are seeing it nearly as intimately as Harte did. He was a city man, a bit of a dandy, literary from a precocious age (he published his first poem at the age of eleven), and though he arrived in California as early as 1854, at the age of eighteen, and thereafter lived in the swirling fringe of the Gold Rush and the Comstock silver rush, he managed to get into his writing just about as much Irving and Dickens and Dumas as authentic Jackass Hill.

His geography sounds authentic, but when one attempts to pin it down to locality it swims and fades into the outlines of Never-Never Land. Harte had no such personal familiarity with the Sierra as his contemporaries Clarence King and John Muir had, and no such scientific accuracy of observation. There are a hundred firsthand accounts that give a more faithful picture of life in the mines than his stories do. Some of them, in fact, he used: the *Shirley Letters,* finest of all Gold Rush books, gave him two of the best touches his stories provide: the birth of a child in an unregenerate camp on the Feather River, used as the basis for "The Luck of Roaring Camp," and the silent mounding of snow on the shoulders of a man hanged by vigilantes, used to soften the death of Piney and the Duchess in "The Outcasts of Poker Flat." But he did not always have an observer as acute as Louise Amelia Knapp Smith Clappe to draw on, and not all his situations and effects are that good.

He did not have, as the great fiction writers have, the fac-

ulty of realizing real characters on the page in terms more
vivid than reality. His practice was to select occupations
and turn them into types; and though individual models
were sometimes present, as in the case of the gambler-duelist
prototype of Jack Hamlin, the gamblers, schoolmarms, stage
drivers, and miners of the stories are usually predictable.
Harte dealt many times with the character of the "Pike," the
"Anglo-Saxon reverted to barbarism" who was one of the
stand-by's of California literature, but even that type character he did not do as well as Clarence King did him in
"The Newtys of Pike"—and as for Mark Twain's definitive
portrait in Pap Finn, that is of another and higher order of
literature entirely.

Harte was at a disadvantage. He could not draw, as Mark
Twain could, on a rich and various experience as small-
town frontier boy, jour printer, river pilot, territorial secre-
tary, reporter, and pocket miner. He could not say of almost any eccentric character, "I know him—knew him on
the river." Unlike Mark Twain's human swarm, Harte's characters do not strike us with their lifelikeness. They are self-
consistent, they have clear outlines and logical coherence,
and they speak a lingo that sounds suitably rough and crude.
Yet they look *made,* and they are.

These are, in fact, early forms of some of our most venerable literary stereotypes. Since Harte it has been next to
impossible for a writer to present a Western gambler who
has not some of the self-contained poise, readiness, and
chivalry of Jack Hamlin and John Oakhurst. Even Stephen
Crane, in his superb short story "The Blue Hotel," suc-
cumbed to the pattern that Harte had laid down. Since Harte
showed the world how, every horse-opera stage driver has
driven with the picturesque recklessness and profanity of
Yuba Bill. The schoolmarms of our movie and television
westerns owe about as much to Harte's Miss Mary, in "The
Idyl of Red Gulch," as to Molly Wood in Owen Wister's
The Virginian—and it should be noted, in Harte's favor, that
"The Idyl of Red Gulch" came thirty-two years before *The
Virginian.*

Harte's geography seems vague because he did not know
the real geography of the Sierra well, and didn't feel that he
needed to. His characters seem made because they *were*
made, according to a formula learned from Dickens: the
trick of bundling together apparently incompatible qualities
to produce a striking paradox. Thus Harte's gamblers, though

Lotharios with ladies of easy virtue, are chivalry itself when Innocence makes its call on them, as in "A Protégée of Jack Hamlin's." Thus the virulent Mother Shipton starves herself to death to give her rations to Piney in "The Outcasts." Thus the best shots have only one eye, the strongest men only three fingers, the most dangerous men the gentlest manner, the roughest men the softest center, the most pompous men the most forthright bravery at twenty paces. Characters are not only built to a pattern, but they repeat. Having developed the limited perfection of Jack Hamlin in "Brown of Calaveras," Harte was tempted into re-using him in twenty different stories. Colonel Starbottle accounts for another twenty, Yuba Bill appears in sixteen, John Oakhurst in four. The effect, repetitious as it is, is to emphasize the clear outlines of the little artificial world of Harte's creation—to make it, however artificial, indelible.

The world of the Gold Rush proper, that first blooming of mushroom camps in the gulches, where every man worked his own claim with pan, rocker, or sluice box, where a hotel was canvas over a frame, and a saloon a keg and a tin cup under a tree, was of course gone before Harte began writing of it. Many camps were ghosts within a year or two of their establishment, and the whole first phase of the mines lasted only from the Sutter's Mill strike of 1848 to the Comstock strike ten years later that stampeded all the loose miners over the Sierra and left behind mainly the big mines, the monitors, and the quartz leads. But when Harte's first mining camp stories appeared there were still plenty of people around who had "seen the elephant," and who did not wholeheartedly respond to the fictional variety. Harte's popularity, as a matter of fact, was always greatest in direct proportion to the reader's distance from and ignorance of the mines. By a happy chance of lagging factual reports, his stories reached Eastern readers when they were still titillated by rumor but unsatisfied in detail. As in the Currier and Ives prints about the buffalo plains, art passed for fact until fact overtook it, whereupon it began to lose its currency even as art. Then, after his popularity had dwindled on the Eastern seaboard, Harte found still another audience, even more remote from the Mother Lode, in England, and that audience stuck loyally with him until his death and after. In a way, it was the worst thing that could have happened to him, for it helped keep him from becoming anything more than the writer he already was.

The writer that he was a product of a long and diligent apprenticeship, a lucky accident, and the publishing acuteness of Anton Roman, who had hired him as editor of the new *Overland Monthly* and had enthusiastically talked up the mines as literary material. With characteristic dilatoriness, Harte missed the first issue, but publication of "The Luck of Roaring Camp" in the second, in August, 1868, demonstrated Roman's foresight and Harte's gift. Though there were local objections to a story written about a prostitute's baby, as well as to such language as Kentuck's admiring "the d—d little cuss!", the response from the East, when it came, was one long joyous outcry. By the end of two years, Harte had published and collected in a book seven stories under the title *The Luck of Roaring Camp, and Other Sketches,* and in September, 1870, he slipped into the *Overland* almost casually, as filler, the dialect poem called "Plain Language from Truthful James," generally known as "The Heathen Chinee." That went off in the public's face like a firecracker; it shook men down in laughter all across the country, was reprinted in numberless newspapers, pasted in barbershop windows, committed to memory. It has been seriously suggested that no single work ever made a writer so famous. And when Harte decided in 1871 to follow his popularity eastward, his progress was like the passage of a public hero or a president.

Probably the sudden elevation to fame, the familiarity with the literary great, the universal admiration, went to his head. He appears to have fallen somewhat short of the twelve stories and poems he agreed to supply the *Atlantic,* for a fee of $10,000, during the year. Though he charmed many people—Mark Twain called him the most charming of men, also the least charming—he disappointed others by not turning out to be a hairy man in boots and a blue flannel shirt. His popularity began to wane. He went on three separate lecture tours, at considerable cost in fatigue and with diminishing financial return. His hopes of writing assignments and editorial posts came to nothing; he sold less, and to less profitable journals. The play *Ah Sin,* a collaboration with Mark Twain dramatizing "The Heathen Chinee," was only a modest success. Burdened with debts, grabbing at any straw, he accepted an appointment as consular assistant in the silk town of Crefeld, Germany, near Düsseldorf, and in 1878 left behind him his family, his country, and his collapsing reputation. None of them was ever restored to him.

Bret Harte represented two very common American literary phenomena. For one thing he was victimized, as many of our writers have been, by the boom-and-bust freakishness of public favor. For another, he was that American type, the local writer whom fame has drawn away from the local, and who now has a choice between developing new themes and a literary manner more suitable for a sophisticated audience, or repeating from exile, with increasing thinness and unreality, the localism he has left behind.

The very perfection of Harte's little world of the local picturesque made it all but impossible for him to break out of it. Mark Twain, who had never been so typed or so limited, was freed by the variety of his own life and by the vitality with which he welcomed new experience; he escaped into travel literature, into history, into causes, into his rich nostalgia for boyhood and the river. But Harte was imprisoned in his own creation. Pressed for money as he always was, he dared not vary locale or tone. He was bound to his desk by poverty, illnesses, the monthly draft—usually late but never evaded—to his family. Temperamentally, too, he was incapable of mean living, shabby dressing, the avoidance of expensive friends. "I grind out the old tunes on the old organ and gather up the coppers," he wrote his wife in 1879, "but I never know whether my audience behind the window blinds are wishing me to 'move on' or not."

It was the American audience on which he could no longer depend. In 1885 he wrote, "Unfortunately, while my stuff is held at a premium here, it is falling off in America. Dana gives *less than half* what he gave me at first; my publishers, Houghton, Mifflin and Company, scarcely anything." Quite apart from his ambiguous relations with his wife, he could hardly have returned to America if he had wanted to. "As far as I can judge hastily, my chances, for the present at least, are better *here*. I have never stood so well in regard to the *market value* of my works in any other country as here; with all my patriotism I am forced to confess that I do not stand as high in my own country . . . I was told that Mr. Sargent, of California, while Minister to Germany, intimated . . . that he was surprised at my German reputation, as I was completely 'played out' in America."

And so, from necessity, timidity, incapacity, or whatever, Harte made hardly a gesture toward discovering new sources of stories. He did now and then turn to poetry, but "only as a change to my monotonous romances. Perhaps it is very *little change,* for my poetry, I fear, is coming from the same spring as my prose, only the tap is nearer the fountain—and filtered." He also tried several plays, hoping for a success that would relieve his constant financial anxiety ("I am quite content if the papers abuse the play so long as the audience like it, and the thing pays"); but the only half-successful one, *Sue,* never made enough to give him the independence he wanted. And it is doubtful that by 1896, when that play was produced, he could have altered his writing habits in the slightest. He could go on working painfully hard against many handicaps; he could hike his daily production from 600 to 1,000 words, "Sundays and holidays, sick or well"; he could retain a rather pathetic professional pride in not doing shoddy work; but he knew better than to respect most of what he wrote, and he had no other sort of thing to write.

Or thought he hadn't. Yet in the *Letters* there is a more personal Bret Harte, one who makes us realize almost with a shock how little Harte's personality shows in the stories. There he is as scrupulously aloof and "indifferent," as "refined out of existence," as the most rigorous dramatic ideal could ask. His characters, whatever else they are, are never made in Harte's image, but are themselves, creations, clean of any taint of their creator. Like the perfect little world of picturesque localism and romantic paradox that they inhabit, they eventually controlled their creator as much as he controlled them; they were a thing he hid behind.

Reading the *Letters,* one wishes that Harte had let himself be revealed more: he is himself more interesting than his gallery of types. For one thing, the letters give evidence that if he had chosen to, he might have become a lively, biased, and outrageous travel reporter in the jingoist tradition of Mark Twain. "The Californian mountains and Coast ranges are vastly superior to these famous Alps—in every respect. As the Rhine is inferior to the Hudson, so is Switzerland to California, and even to the Catskills in New York. The snow peaks visible from my window are fine, but I have seen finer views from a wayside hotel in California country."

That tone alone might have restored him his American audience, always happy to come out ahead in comparisons with Europe. And the mingling of complaint with humor, the casting of criticism into exaggerated form, was in the best vein of the bumptious American visiting the old home.

As with Switzerland, so with the Swiss, "with their sham sentiments, their sham liberty, their sham chamois (an ugly cross between a goat and a jackass), their sham jödel—that awful falsetto as musical as a cat's serenade; and nothing real about them but their hideous *goiters*." Or consider Glasgow, where Harte was unhappily consul from 1880 to 1885: "I cannot help feeling that I am living by gaslight in a damp cellar with an occasional whiff from a drain, from a coal heap, from a moldy potato bin, and from dirty washtubs."

As nostalgic and unhappy as that, yet he never went back. Lonely as his letters show him to have been, he neither sent for his family nor returned to them, and when, twenty years after their separation, they visited England, he did not live with them. It is probable that intimate passages have been edited out of Harte's letters to his wife. Certainly what remains is so cool, so oddly confiding and courteous and responsible, yet so transparently determined that circumstances will not permit a reunion, that one itches to know more. Harte was his own best paradox. In his self-imposed exile he enjoyed at once the consolations of poverty, hard work, and self-pity, and the companionship of lords, ladies, and international celebrities. This driven hack was one of the most honored of expatriate American writers. Max Nordau called him "the Columbus of American fiction"; he was invited to respond to the toast to literature at the Royal Academy; he influenced Kipling and delighted young Chesterton; his life fluctuated between hard hours at his desk and luxurious holidays with the Marquess of Northhampton or the Duchess of St. Albans.

It is one of the great unwritten books—the revelation of what lay behind that self-indulgent and laborious, that miserable and flattering, that lonely and cherished, exile. Harte wrote not a word of it, and all we know of his desolation we read between the lines of the *Letters*. That is enough to make us regret that temperament and circumstances kept him away from a more personal sort of writing and held him to the controlled play-acting of Red Dog and Poker Flat. Almost until his death of throat cancer on May 5, 1902, Harte went on producing diffuse variants of the laconic and startling stories that had made his reputation more than thirty years before.

The stories, ultimately, are all he has to be judged by; if anything tangible is keeping him in the textbooks, they are.

Admitting that there is in them little honest observation

of people or of nature, no real character, no accurate picture of a society however fleeting, no true ear for the lingo, no symbolic depth, no valid commentary upon the human condition, no inadvertent self-revelation, and no real weight of mind, there is still something. There is humor—pervasive, unprudish, often still fresh and natural. There is good prose, and this is nearly unfailing. He was master of a flexible instrument, and if his language was rather more literary than native, if he leaned toward the King's English and never made of his dialect much more than a sort of decoration, he can hardly be blamed. Of all his contemporaries, only Mark Twain managed to make the vernacular do everything a true literary language has to do. Harte's prose was sometimes inflated and self-conscious, but more often it was markedly clean and direct. He was capable of a notable economy, passages and sometimes whole stories of a striking nervous compactness in which character, situation, and realized place come off the page instantly visual. Try the opening of "A Protégée of Jack Hamlin's," a story written as late as 1893.

Economy and a formal precision were part both of his temperament and his training. In *Condensed Novels,* a series of parodies written during the sixties, he had learned to boil whole novelists down to a few pages of essence. But it was his adaptation of the short story to Californian materials that created something like a revolution. His example emancipated writers in every region, confirming them in their subject matter and confirming them in their preference for the short-story form. So great was Harte's influence upon the whole local color school that in 1894 he modestly felt compelled to deny, in an article for *Cornhill,* that he had invented the short story itself. Invent it he did not, but no historian of the short story can overlook his shaping influence upon it or his enormous influence in popularizing it through the expanding magazines.

Humor, economy, mastery of a prose instrument and a compact fictional form, a trick of paradox and color, a chosen (later compulsive) subject matter full of romantic glamor, a faculty for creating types that have become the stock in trade of a whole entertainment industry—these are surely enough to account for Harte's lasting. But there is something more. He made a world.

Admittedly it was a world insufficiently rooted in fact to have realistic validity, and even such facts as it contained were mainly anachronisms already outlived. Yet it was at once recognizable as plausible, cohesive, self-contained; it is as much a world as Faulkner's Yoknapatawpha County, and it is peopled by creatures of a simple and enduring kind. The pilgrims who visit the "Bret Harte country," and the chambers of commerce along Highway 49 who set their traps for them, have a surer instinct than the critics; they recognize valid myths when they see them.

For Harte succeeded more than some better writers at creating American archetypes. In his Yuba Bills and Jack Hamlins he made trial syntheses of the American character in local western terms. Despite gross simplifications and despite a failure of superficial realism, his creations have lasted and become stereotypes precisely because they *do* approximate myths. They are all of them—rough but sentimental miners, dishonest but loyal partners, wicked but chivalrous gamblers, virtuous but tender schoolmarms, unvirtuous but tender prostitutes—shapes of the essential American Innocence that Mark Twain, James, Howells, and many more have asserted and personified. With all their faults upon them, the inhabitants of Red Dog and Poker Flat belong somewhere in the same literary tradition with Leatherstocking and Huckleberry Finn.

Wallace Stegner
Stanford University

The Right Eye of the
>>>->>>->>>->>>->>>->>>->>> Commander >>>->>>->>>->>>->>>

>>>->>>->>> The year of grace 1797 passed away on the coast of California in a southwesterly gale. The little bay of San Carlos, albeit sheltered by the headlands of the Blessed Trinity, was rough and turbulent; its foam clung quivering to the seaward wall of the mission garden; the air was filled with flying sand and spume, and as the Señor Comandante, Hermenegildo Salvatierra, looked from the deep embrasured window of the presidio guardroom, he felt the salt breath of the distant sea buffet a color into his smoke-dried cheeks.

The commander, I have said, was gazing thoughtfully from the window of the guardroom. He may have been reviewing the events of the year now about to pass away. But, like the garrison at the presidio, there was little to review. The year, like its predecessors, had been uneventful—the days had slipped by in a delicious monotony of simple duties, unbroken by incident or interruption. The regularly recurring feasts and saints' days, the half-yearly courier from San Diego, the rare transport ship and rarer foreign vessel, were the mere details of his patriarchal life. If there was no achievement, there was certainly no failure. Abundant harvests and patient industry amply supplied the wants of presidio and mission. Isolated from the family of nations, the wars which shook the world concerned them not so much as the last earthquake; the struggle that emancipated their sister colonies on the other side of the continent to them had no suggestiveness. In short, it was that glorious Indian summer of Californian history around which so much poetical haze still lingers—that bland, indolent autumn of Spanish rule, so soon to be followed by the wintry storms of Mexican independence and the reviving spring of American conquest.

The commander turned from the window and walked toward the fire that burned brightly on the deep ovenlike hearth. A pile of copybooks, the work of the presidio school, lay on the table. As he turned over the leaves with a paternal interest and surveyed the fair round Scripture text, the first pious pothooks of the pupils of San Carlos, an audible commentary fell from his lips: " 'Abimelech took her from Abraham'—ah, little one, excellent!—'Jacob sent to see his brother'—body of Christ! that upstroke of thine, Paquita, is marvelous; the governor shall see it!" A film of honest pride dimmed the commander's left eye—the right, alas! twenty years before had been sealed by an Indian arrow. He rubbed it softly with the sleeve of his leather jacket, and continued, " 'The Ishmaelites having arrived—' "

He stopped, for there was a step in the courtyard, a foot upon the threshold, and a stranger entered. With the instinct of an old soldier, the commander, after one glance at the intruder, turned quickly toward the wall, where his trusty Toledo hung, or should have been hanging. But it was not there, and as he recalled that the last time he had seen that weapon it was being ridden up and down the gallery by Pepito, the infant son of Bautista, the tortilio-maker, he blushed, and then contented himself with frowning upon the intruder.

But the stranger's air, though irreverent, was decidedly peaceful. He was unarmed, and wore the ordinary cape of tarpaulin and sea-boots of a mariner. Except a villainous smell of codfish, there was little about him that was peculiar.

His name, as he informed the commander in Spanish that was more fluent than elegant or precise—his name was Peleg Scudder. He was master of the schooner General Court, of the port of Salem, in Massachusetts, on a trading voyage to the South Seas, but now driven by stress of weather into the bay of San Carlos. He begged permission to ride out the gale under the headlands of the Blessed Trinity, and no more. Water he did not need, having taken in a supply at Bodega. He knew the strict surveillance of the Spanish port regulations in regard to foreign vessels, and would do nothing against the severe discipline and good order of the settlement. There was a

slight tinge of sarcasm in his tone as he glanced toward
the desolate parade ground of the presidio and the open
unguarded gate. The fact was that the sentry, Felipe
Gomez, had discreetly retired to shelter at the beginning
of the storm, and was then sound asleep in the corridor.

The commander hesitated. The port regulations were
severe, but he was accustomed to exercise individual authority, and beyond an old order issued ten years before,
regarding the American ship Columbia, there was no
precedent to guide him. The storm was severe, and a
sentiment of humanity urged him to grant the stranger's
request. It is but just to the commander to say that his
inability to enforce a refusal did not weigh with his decision. He would have denied with equal disregard of con-
sequences that right to a seventy-four-gun ship which he
now yielded so gracefully to this Yankee trading schooner.
He stipulated only that there should be no communication between the ship and shore. "For yourself, Señor
Captain," he continued, "accept my hospitality. The fort
is yours as long as you shall grace it with your distinguished presence," and with old-fashioned courtesy he
made the semblance of withdrawing from the guardroom.

Master Peleg Scudder smiled as he thought of the half-
dismantled fort, the two moldy brass cannon, cast in
Manila a century previous, and the shiftless garrison. A
wild thought of accepting the commander's offer literally,
conceived in the reckless spirit of a man who never let
slip an offer for trade, for a moment filled his brain, but
a timely reflection of the commercial unimportance of
the transaction checked him. He only took a capacious
quid of tobacco, as the commander gravely drew a settle
before the fire, and in honor of his guest untied the black
silk handkerchief that bound his grizzled brows.

What passed between Salvatierra and his guest that
night it becomes me not, as a grave chronicler of the
salient points of history, to relate. I have said that Master Peleg Scudder was a fluent talker, and under the influence of divers strong waters, furnished by his host, he
became still more loquacious. And think of a man with
a twenty years' budget of gossip! The commander
learned, for the first time, how Great Britain lost her
colonies; of the French Revolution; of the great Na-

poleon, whose achievements, perhaps, Peleg colored more highly than the commander's superiors would have liked. And when Peleg turned questioner, the commander was at his mercy. He gradually made himself master of the gossip of the mission and presidio, the "small beer" chronicles of that pastoral age, the conversion of the heathen, the presidio schools, and even asked the commander how he had lost his eye. It is said that at this point of the conversation Master Peleg produced from about his person divers small trinkets, kickshaws and new-fangled trifles, and even forced some of them upon his host. It is further alleged that under the malign influence of Peleg and several glasses of aguardiente the commander lost somewhat of his decorum, and behaved in a manner unseemly for one in his position, reciting high-flown Spanish poetry, and even piping in a thin high voice divers madrigals and heathen canzonets of an amorous complexion, chiefly in regard to a "little one" who was his, the commander's, "soul." These allegations, perhaps unworthy the notice of a serious chronicler, should be received with great caution, and are introduced here as simple hearsay. That the commander, however, took a handkerchief and attempted to show his guest the mysteries of the sembi cuacua, capering in an agile but indecorous manner about the apartment, has been denied. Enough for the purposes of this narrative, that at midnight Peleg assisted his host to bed with many protestations of undying friendship, and then, as the gale had abated, took his leave of the presidio, and hurried aboard the General Court. When the day broke the ship was gone.

I know not if Peleg kept his word with his host. It is said that the holy Fathers at the mission that night heard a loud chanting in the plaza, as of the heathens singing psalms through their noses; that for many days after an odor of salt codfish prevailed in the settlement; that a dozen hard nutmegs, which were unfit for spice or seed, were found in the possession of the wife of the baker, and that several bushels of shoe-pegs, which bore a pleasing resemblance to oats, but were quite inadequate to the purposes of provender, were discovered in the stable of the blacksmith. But when the reader reflects upon the sacredness of a Yankee trader's word, the stringent discipline of the Spanish port regulations, and the proverbial indisposition of my countrymen to impose upon the confidence of a simple people, he will at once reject this part of the story.

A roll of drums, ushering in the year 1798, awoke the commander. The sun was shining brightly, and the storm had ceased. He sat up in bed, and through the force of habit rubbed his left eye. As the remembrance of the previous night came back to him, he jumped from his couch and ran to the window. There was no ship in the bay. A sudden thought seemed to strike him, and he rubbed both of his eyes. Not content with this, he consulted the metallic mirror which hung beside his crucifix. There was no mistake; the commander had a visible second eye—a right one—as good, save for the purposes of vision, as the left.

Whatever might have been the true secret of this transformation, but one opinion prevailed at San Carlos. It was one of those rare miracles vouchsafed a pious Catholic community as an evidence to the heathen, through the intercession of the blessed San Carlos himself. That their beloved commander, the temporal defender of the Faith, should be the recipient of this miraculous manifestation was most fit and seemly. The commander himself was reticent; he could not tell a falsehood—he dared not tell the truth. After all, if the good folk of San Carlos believed that the powers of his right eye were actually restored, was it wise and discreet for him to undeceive them? For the first time in his life the commander thought of policy—for the first time he quoted that text which has been the lure of so many well-meaning but easy Christians, of being "all things to all men." Infeliz Hermenegildo Salvatierra!

For by degrees an ominous whisper crept through the little settlement. The right eye of the commander, although miraculous, seemed to exercise a baleful effect upon the beholder. No one could look at it without winking. It was cold, hard, relentless, and unflinching. More than that, it seemed to be endowed with a dreadful prescience—a faculty of seeing through and into the inarticulate thoughts of those it looked upon. The soldiers

of the garrison obeyed the eye rather than the voice of
their commander, and answered his glance rather than
his lips in questioning. The servants could not evade the
ever-watchful but cold attention that seemed to pursue
them. The children of the presidio school smirched their
copybooks under the awful supervision, and poor Paquita,
the prize pupil, failed utterly in that marvelous upstroke
when her patron stood beside her. Gradually distrust,
suspicion, self-accusation, and timidity took the place of
trust, confidence, and security throughout San Carlos.
Wherever the right eye of the commander fell, a shadow
fell with it.

Nor was Salvatierra entirely free from the baleful influence of his miraculous acquisition. Unconscious of its
effect upon others, he only saw in their actions evidence
of certain things that the crafty Peleg had hinted on that
eventful New Year's Eve. His most trusty retainers stammered, blushed, and faltered before him. Self-accusations,
confessions of minor faults and delinquencies, or extravagant excuses and apologies met his mildest inquiries. The
very children that he loved—his pet pupil, Paquita—
seemed to be conscious of some hidden sin. The result of
this constant irritation showed itself more plainly. For the
first half-year the commander's voice and eye were at
variance. He was still kind, tender, and thoughtful in
speech. Gradually, however, his voice took upon itself
the hardness of his glance and its skeptical, impassive
quality, and as the year again neared its close it was
plain that the commander had fitted himself to the eye,
and not the eye to the commander.

It may be surmised that these changes did not escape
the watchful solicitude of the Fathers. Indeed, the few
who were first to ascribe the right eye of Salvatierra to
miraculous origin and the special grace of the blessed
San Carlos now talked openly of witchcraft and the agency
of Luzbel, the evil one. It would have fared ill with Hermenegildo Salvatierra had he been aught but commander
or amenable to local authority. But the reverend Father,
Friar Manuel de Cortes, had no power over the political
executive, and all attempts at spiritual advice failed sig-
nally. He retired baffled and confused from his first interview with the commander, who seemed now to take a

grim satisfaction in the fateful power of his glance. The holy Father contradicted himself, exposed the fallacies of his own arguments, and even, it is asserted, committed himself to several undoubted heresies. When the commander stood up at mass, if the officiating priest caught that skeptical and searching eye, the service was inevitably ruined. Even the power of the Holy Church seemed to be lost, and the last hold upon the affections of the people and the good order of the settlement departed from San Carlos.

As the long dry summer passed, the low hills that surrounded the white walls of the presidio grew more and more to resemble in hue the leathern jacket of the commander, and Nature herself seemed to have borrowed his dry, hard glare. The earth was cracked and seamed with drought; a blight had fallen upon the orchards and vineyards, and the rain, long delayed and ardently prayed for, came not. The sky was as tearless as the right eye of the commander. Murmurs of discontent, insubordination, and plotting among the Indians reached his ear; he only set his teeth the more firmly, tightened the knot of his black silk handkerchief, and looked up his Toledo.

The last day of the year 1798 found the commander sitting, at the hour of evening prayers, alone in the guardroom. He no longer attended the services of the Holy Church, but crept away at such times to some solitary spot, where he spent the interval in silent meditation. The firelight played upon the low beams and rafters, but left the bowed figure of Salvatierra in darkness. Sitting thus, he felt a small hand touch his arm, and looking down, saw the figure of Paquita, his little Indian pupil, at his knee. "Ah! littlest of all," said the commander, with something of his old tenderness, lingering over the endearing diminutives of his native speech—"sweet one, what doest thou here? Art thou not afraid of him whom everyone shuns and fears?"

"No," said the little Indian readily, "not in the dark. I hear your voice—the old voice; I feel your touch—the old touch; but I see not your eye, Señor Comandante. That only I fear—and that, O señor, O my father," said the child, lifting her little arms towards his—"that I know is not thine own!"

The commander shuddered and turned away. Then, recovering himself, he kissed Paquita gravely on the forehead and bade her retire. A few hours later, when silence had fallen upon the presidio, he sought his own couch and slept peacefully.

At about the middle watch of the night a dusky figure crept through the low embrasure of the commander's apartment. Other figures were flitting through the parade ground, which the commander might have seen had he not slept so quietly. The intruder stepped noiselessly to the couch and listened to the sleeper's deep-drawn respiration. Something glittered in the firelight as the savage lifted his arm; another moment and the sore perplexities of Hermenegildo Salvatierra would have been over, when suddenly the savage started and fell back in a paroxysm of terror. The commander slept peacefully, but his right eye, widely opened, fixed and unaltered, glared coldly on the would-be assassin. The man fell to the earth in a fit, and the noise awoke the sleeper.

To rise to his feet, grasp his sword, and deal blows thick and fast upon the mutinous savages who now thronged the room, was the work of a moment. Help opportunely arrived, and the undisciplined Indians were speedily driven beyond the walls; but in the scuffle the commander received a blow upon his right eye, and lifting his hand to that mysterious organ, it was gone. Never again was it found, and never again, for bale or bliss, did it adorn the right orbit of the commander.

With it passed away the spell that had fallen upon San Carlos. The rain returned to invigorate the languid soil, harmony was restored between priest and soldier, the green grass presently waved over the sere hillsides, the children flocked again to the side of their martial preceptor, a *Te Deum* was sung in the mission church, and pastoral content once more smiled upon the gentle valleys of San Carlos. And far southward crept the General Court with its master, Peleg Scudder, trafficking in beads and peltries with the Indians, and offering glass eyes, wooden legs, and other Boston notions to the chiefs.

M'liss: An Idyl of
>>>->>>->>>->>>->>>->>>->>> Red Mountain >>>->>>->>>->>>

CHAPTER ONE
Smith's Pocket

>>>->>>->>> Just where the Sierra Nevada begins to subside in gentle undulations, and the rivers grow less rapid and yellow, on the side of a great red mountain stands Smith's Pocket. Seen from the red road at sunset, in the red light and the red dust, its white houses look like the outcroppings of quartz on the mountainside. The red stage, topped with red-shirted passengers, is lost to view half a dozen times in the tortuous descent, turning up unexpectedly in out-of-the-way places, and vanishing altogether within a hundred yards of the town. It is probably owing to this sudden twist in the road that the advent of a stranger at Smith's Pocket is usually attended with a peculiar circumstance. Dismounting from the vehicle at the stage office the too-confident traveler is apt to walk straight out of town under the impression that it lies in quite another direction. It is related that one of the tunnel men, two miles from town, met one of these self-reliant passengers with a carpetbag, umbrella, "Harper's Magazine," and other evidences of "civilization and refinement," plodding along over the road he had just ridden, vainly endeavoring to find the settlement of Smith's Pocket.

Had he been an observant traveler he might have found some compensation for his disappointment in the weird aspect of that vicinity. There were huge fissures on the hillside, and displacements of the red soil, resembling more the chaos of some primary elementary upheaval than the work of man; while, halfway down, a long flume straddled its narrow body and disproportionate legs over the chasm, like an enormous fossil of some forgotten antediluvian. At every step smaller ditches crossed the road, hiding in their shallow depths unlovely streams that crept away to a clandestine union with the great yellow torrent below. Here and there the ruins of some cabin, with the chimney alone left intact and the hearth-stone open to the skies, gave such a flat contradiction to the poetic delusion of Lares and Penates that the heart of the traveler must have collapsed as he gazed, and even the barroom of the National Hotel have after-ward seemed festive and invested with preternatural comfort and domesticity.

The settlement of Smith's Pocket owed its origin to the finding of a "pocket" on its site by a veritable Smith. Five thousand dollars were taken out of it in one half hour by Smith. Three thousand dollars were expended by Smith and others in erecting a flume and in tunneling. And then Smith's Pocket was found to be only a pocket, and subject like other pockets to depletion. Although Smith pierced the bowels of the great red mountain, that five thousand dollars was the first and the last return of his labor. The mountain grew reticent of its golden secrets, and the flume steadily ebbed away the remainder of Smith's fortune. Then Smith went into quartz mining. Then into quartz milling. Then into hydraulics and ditching, and then by easy degrees into saloon keeping. Presently it was whispered that Smith was drinking a good deal; then it was known that Smith was an habitual drunkard; and then people began to think, as they are apt to, that he had never been anything else. But the settlement of Smith's Pocket, like that of most discoveries, was happily not dependent on the fortune of its pioneer, and other parties projected tunnels and found pockets. So Smith's Pocket became a settlement with its two fancy stores, its two hotels, its one express office, and its two first families. Occasionally its one long straggling street was overawed by the assumption of the latest San Francisco fashions, imported per express exclusively to the first families; making outraged nature, in the ragged outline of her furrowed surface, look still more homely, and putting personal insult on that greater portion of the population to whom the Sabbath, with a change of linen, brought merely the necessity of cleanliness without the luxury of adornment. Then there was a Methodist church, and hard by a monte bank, and a little beyond, on the mountainside, a graveyard; and then a little schoolhouse.

"The master," as he was known to his little flock, sat alone one night in the schoolhouse with some open copybooks before him, carefully making those bold and full characters which are supposed to combine the extremes of chirographical and moral excellence, and had got as far as "Riches are deceitful," and was elaborating the noun with an insincerity of flourish that was quite in the spirit of his text, when he heard a gentle tapping. The woodpeckers had been busy about the roof during the day, and the noise did not disturb his work. But the opening of the door, and the tapping continuing from the inside, caused him to look up. He was slightly startled by the figure of a young girl, dirty and shabbily clad. Still her great black eyes, her coarse uncombed lusterless black hair falling over her sunburned face, her red arms and feet streaked with the red soil, were all familiar to him. It was Melissa Smith—Smith's motherless child.

"What can she want here?" thought the master. Everybody knew "M'liss," as she was called, throughout the length and height of Red Mountain. Everybody knew her as an incorrigible girl. Her fierce, ungovernable disposition, her mad freaks and lawless character, were in their way as proverbial as the story of her father's weakness, and as philosophically accepted by the townsfolk. She wrangled with and fought the schoolboys with keener invective and quite as powerful arm. She followed the trails with woodman's craft, and the master had met her before, miles away, shoeless, stockingless, and bareheaded on the mountain road. The miners' camps along the stream supplied her with subsistence during these voluntary pilgrimages, in freely offered alms. Not but that a larger protection had been previously extended to M'liss. The Rev. Joshua McSnagley, "stated" preacher, had placed her in the hotel as servant, by way of preliminary refinement, and had introduced her to his scholars at Sunday school. But she threw plates occasionally at the landlord, and quickly retorted to the cheap witticisms of the guests, and created in the Sabbath school a sen-

sation that was so inimical to the orthodox dullness and
placidity of that institution that, with a decent regard
for the starched frocks and unblemished morals of the
two pink-and-white-faced children of the first families,
the reverend gentleman had her ignominiously expelled.
Such were the antecedents and such the character of
M'liss as she stood before the master. It was shown in
the ragged dress, the unkempt hair and bleeding feet,
and asked his pity. It flashed from her black fearless
eyes, and commanded his respect.

"I come here tonight," she said rapidly and boldly,
keeping her hard glance on his, "because I knew you
was alone. I wouldn't come here when them gals was here.
I hate 'em and they hates me. That's why. You keep
school—don't you? I want to be teached!"

If to the shabbiness of her apparel and uncomeliness
of her tangled hair and dirty face she had added the
humility of tears the master would have extended to her
the usual moiety of pity, and nothing more. But with the
natural though illogical instincts of his species, her boldness awakened in him something of that respect which all
original natures pay unconsciously to one another in any
grade. And he gazed at her the more fixedly as she went
on still rapidly, her hand on the doorlatch and her eyes
on his.

"My name is M'liss—M'liss Smith! You can bet your
life on that. My father's Old Smith—Old Bummer Smith
—that's what's the matter with him. M'liss Smith—and
I'm comin' to school!"

"Well?" said the master.

Accustomed to be thwarted and opposed, often wan-
tonly and cruelly, for no other purpose than to excite
the violent impulses of her nature, the master's phlegm
evidently took her by surprise. She stopped. She began to
twist a lock of her hair between her fingers; and the rigid
line of upper lip, drawn over the wicked little teeth, relaxed and quivered slightly. Then her eyes dropped, and
something like a blush struggled up to her cheek and
tried to assert itself through the splashes of redder soil
and the sunburn of years. Suddenly she threw herself forward, calling on God to strike her dead, and fell quite

weak and helpless, with her face on the master's desk, crying and sobbing as if her heart would break.

The master lifted her gently, and waited for the paroxysm to pass. When, with face still averted, she was repeating between her sobs the *mea culpa* of childish penitence—that "she'd be good, she didn't mean to," etc., it came to him to ask her why she had left Sabbath school.

Why had she left Sabbath school? Why? Oh, yes. What did he (McSnagley) want to tell her she was wicked for? What did he tell her that God hated her for? If God hated her, what did she want to go to Sabbath school for? *She* didn't want to be beholden to anybody who hated her.

Had she told McSnagley this?

Yes, she had.

The master laughed. It was a hearty laugh and echoed so oddly in the little schoolhouse, and seemed so inconsistent and discordant with the sighing of the pines without, that he shortly corrected himself with a sigh. The sigh was quite as sincere in its way, however, and after a moment of serious silence he asked about her father.

Her father. What father? Whose father? What had he ever done for her? Why did the girls hate her? Come, now! What made the folks say, "Old Bummer Smith's M'liss" when she passed? Yes; oh, yes. She wished he was dead—she was dead—everybody was dead; and her sobs broke forth anew.

The master then, leaning over her, told her, as well as he could, what you or I might have said after hearing such unnatural theories from childish lips; only bearing in mind perhaps better than you or I the unnatural facts of her ragged dress, her bleeding feet, and the omnipresent shadow of her drunken father. Then raising her to her feet, he wrapped his shawl around her, and bidding her come early in the morning he walked with her down the road. Then he bade her "good night." The moon shone brightly on the narrow path before them. He stood and watched the bent little figure as it staggered down the road, and waited until it had passed the little graveyard and reached the curve of the hill, where it turned and stood for a moment, a mere atom of suffering outlined against the far-off patient stars. Then he went back to his work. But the lines of the copybook thereafter faded into long parallels of never-ending road, over which childish figures seemed to pass sobbing and crying to the night. Then, the little schoolhouse seeming lonelier than before, he shut the door and went home.

The next morning M'liss came to school. Her face had been washed, and her coarse black hair bore evidence of recent struggles with the comb, in which both had evidently suffered. The old defiant look shone occasionally in her eyes, but her manner was tamer and more subdued. Then began a series of little trials and self-sacrifices in which master and pupil bore an equal part, and which increased the confidence and sympathy between them. Although obedient under the master's eye, at times during recess, if thwarted or stung by a fancied slight, M'liss would rage in ungovernable fury, and many a palpitating young savage, finding himself matched with his own weapons of torment, would seek the master with torn jacket and scratched face, and complaints of the dreadful M'liss. There was a serious division among the townspeople on the subject; some threatening to withdraw their children from such evil companionship, and others as warmly upholding the course of the master in his work of reclamation. Meanwhile, with a steady persistence that seemed quite astonishing to him on looking back afterward, the master drew M'liss gradually out of the shadow of her past life, as though it were but her natural progress down the narrow path on which he had set her feet the moonlight night of their first meeting. Remembering the experience of the evangelical McSnagley, he carefully avoided that Rock of Ages on which that unskillful pilot had shipwrecked her young faith. But if in the course of her reading she chanced to stumble upon those few words which have lifted such as she above the level of the older, the wiser, and the more prudent—if she learned something of a faith that is symbolized by suffering, and the old light softened in her eyes, it did not take the shape of a lesson. A few of the plainer people had made up a little sum by which the ragged M'liss was enabled to assume the garments of respect and civilization, and often a rough shake of the hand and words of commendation from a red-shirted and burly figure sent a glow to the cheek of the young master and set him to thinking if it was altogether deserved.

Three months had passed from the time of their first meeting, and the master was sitting late one evening over the moral and sententious copies, when there came a tap at the door, and again M'liss stood before him. She was neatly clad and clean-faced, and there was nothing perhaps but the long black hair and bright black eyes to remind him of his former apparition. "Are you busy?" she asked; "can you come with me?" and on his signifying his readiness, in her old willful way she said, "Come, then, quick!"

They passed out of the door together and into the dark road. As they entered the town, the master asked her whither she was going. She replied, "to see her father."

It was the first time he had heard her use that filial expression, or indeed, allude to him in any other way than "Old Smith" or the "Old Man." It was the first time in many weeks that she had spoken of him at all. He had been missed from the settlement for the past fortnight, and the master had credited the rumors of the townsfolk that Smith had "struck something rich" on the "North Fork," about ten miles from the village. As they neared the settlement, the master gathered from M'liss that the rumor was untrue, and that she had seen her father that day. As she grew reticent to further questioning, and as the master was satisfied from her manner that she had some definite purpose beyond her usual willfulness, he passively resigned himself and followed her.

Through remote groggeries, restaurants, and saloons; in gambling hells and dance houses, the master, preceded by M'liss, passed and repassed. In the reeking smoke and blasphemous outcries of noisome dens, the child, holding the master's hand, pursued her search with a strange familiarity, perfect self-possession, and implied protection of himself, that even in his anxiety seemed ludicrous. Some of the revelers, recognizing M'liss, called to her to sing and dance for them, and would have forced liquor upon her but for the master's interference. Others mutely made way for them. So an hour slipped by, and as yet their search was fruitless. The master had yawned once

or twice and whistled—two fatal signs of failing interest—
and finally came to a full stop.

"It's half past eleven, Melissa," said he, consulting his
watch by a broad pencil of light from an open shutter—
"half past eleven; and it strikes me that our old friends,
the woodpeckers, must have gone to bed some hours ago,
unless they are waiting up for us. I'm much obliged to
you for the evening's entertainment, but I'm afraid that
even the pretext of looking for a parent won't excuse
further dissipation. We'd better put this off till tomorrow.
What do you say, Melissa? Why! what ails the child?
What's that noise? Why, a pistol!—You're not afraid of
that?"

Few children brought up in the primeval seclusion of
Smith's Pocket were unfamiliar with those quick and
sharp notes which usually rendered the evening zephyrs
of that locality vocal; certainly not M'liss, to have started
when that report rang on the clear night air. The echoes
caught it as usual, and carried it round and round Red
Mountain, and set the dogs to barking all along the
streams. The lights seemed to dance and move quickly on
the outskirts of the town for a few moments afterward,
the stream suddenly rippled quite audibly behind them,
a few stones loosened themselves from the hillside and
splashed into the stream, a heavy wind seemed to suage
the branches of the funereal pines, and then the silence
fell again, heavier, deadlier than ever.

When the last echo had died away, the master felt his
companion's hand relax its grasp. Taking advantage of
this outward expression of tractability, he drew her gently
with him until they reached the hotel, which—in her
newer aspect of a guest whose board was secured by responsible parties—had forgivingly opened its hospitable
doors to the vagrant child. Here the master lingered a
moment to assure her that she might count upon his
assistance tomorrow; and having satisfied his conscience
by this anticipated duty, bade her good night. In the
darkness of the road—going astray several times on his
way home and narrowly escaping the yawning ditches in
the trail—he had reason to commend his foresight in dis-
suading M'liss from a further search that night, and in

this pleasant reflection went to bed and slept soundly.

For some hours after a darkness thick and heavy brooded over the settlement. The somber pines encompassing the village seemed to close threateningly about it as if to reclaim the wilderness that had been wrested from them. A low rustling as of dead leaves, and the damp breath of forest odors filled the lonely street. Emboldened by the darkness other shadows slipped by, leaving strange footprints in the moist ditches for people to point at next day, until the moon, round and full, was lifted above the crest of the opposite hill, and all was magically changed.

The shadows shrank away, leaving the straggling street sleeping in a beauty it never knew by day. All that was unlovely, harsh, and repulsive in its jagged outlines was subdued and softened by that uncertain light. It smoothed the rough furrows and unsightly chasms of the mountain with an ineffable love and tenderness. It fell upon the face of the sleeping M'liss, and left a tear glittering on her black lashes and a smile on her lip, which would have been rare to her at any other time; and fell also on the white upturned face of "Old Smith," with a pistol in his hand and a bullet in his heart, lying dead beside his empty pocket.

CHAPTER TWO

Which Contains A Dream of the Just Aristides

The opinion which McSnagley expressed in reference to a "change of heart," as experienced by M'liss, was more forcibly described in the gulches and tunnels. It was thought there that M'liss had struck a "good lead." And when there was a new grave added to the little enclosure and—at the expense of the master—a little board and inscription put above it, the *Red Mountain Banner* came out quite handsomely and did the correct thing for the memory of one of "our oldest pioneers," alluding gracefully to that "bane of noble intellects," touching slightly on the "vicissitudes of fortune," and otherwise assisting our dear brother into genteel obscurity. "He leaves an only child to mourn his loss," said the *Banner,* "who is now an exemplary scholar, thanks to the efforts of the Rev. J. McSnagley." That reverend gentleman, in fact, made a strong point of M'liss's conversion, and indirectly attributing to her former bad conduct the suicide of her father, made affecting allusions in Sunday school to the beneficial effects of the "silent tomb," and in that cheerful contemplation froze most of the children into speechless horror, and caused the fair-complexioned scions of the first families to howl dismally and refuse to be comforted.

Of the homes that were offered to M'liss when her conversion became known, the master had preferred that of Mrs. Morpher, a womanly and kind-hearted specimen of Southwestern efflorescence, known in her maidenhood as the "Per-ra-rie Rose." By a steady system of struggle and self-sacrifice, she had at last subjugated her naturally careless disposition to principles of "order," which as a pious woman she considered, with Pope, as "Heaven's first law." But she could not entirely govern the orbits of her satellites, however regular her own movements, and her old nature asserted itself in her children. Lycurgus dipped in the cupboard "between meals," and Aristides came home from school without shoes, leaving those important articles at the threshold, for the delights of a barefooted walk down the ditches. Octavia and Cassandra were "keerless" of their clothes. So that with but one exception, however the "Prairie Rose" might have trimmed, pruned, and trained her own natural luxuriance, the little shoots came up defiantly wild and straggling. That one exception was Clytemnestra Morpher, aged fifteen. She was the realization of her mother's most extravagant dream. I stay my hand with difficulty at this moment, for I long to describe this model of deportment; but the progress of my story just as present supplants Clytemnestra in the larger prominence it gives to another member of the family —the just Aristides.

The long dry summer had come. As each fierce day seemed to burn itself out in little whiffs of pearl gray smoke on the mountain summits, and as the upspringing breeze scattered what might have been its red embers

over the landscape, the green wave which in early spring
had upheaved above Smith's grave grew sere and dry
and hard. In those days, the master, strolling in the little
churchyard of a Sabbath afternoon, was sometimes surprised to find a few wild flowers, plucked from the damp
pine forest, scattered there, and oftener rude wreaths
hung upon the little pine cross. Most of these wreaths
were formed of a sweet-scented grass which the children
loved to keep in their desks, entwined with the pompon-
like plumes of the buckeye and syringa, the wood anem-
one, and here and there the master noticed the dark blue
cowl of the monkshood or deadly aconite. One day during a walk, in crossing a wooded ridge, he came upon
M'liss in the heart of the forest, perched upon a prostrate
pine, on a fantastic throne, formed by the hanging plumes
of lifeless branches, her lap full of grasses and pine burrs,
and crooning to the just Aristides, who sat humbly at
her feet, one of the Negro melodies of her younger life.
It was perhaps the influence of the season, or the memory
of this sylvan enjoyment, which caused Aristides, one midsummer day, to have a singular vision.

The just Aristides had begun that morning with a
serious error. Loitering on his way to school, occasionally
stopping to inspect the footprints of probable bears, or
indulging in cheerful badinage with the tunnel men—to
whom the apparition of a shortlegged boy weighed down
by a preternaturally large satchel was an object of boisterous solicitude—Aristides suddenly found that he was an
hour and a half too late for school. Whether this circumstance was purely accidental or not is a question of
some uncertainty, for Aristides, on finding himself occupying this criminal position, at once resolved to play
truant. I shall not stop to inquire by what system of logic
this result presented itself to that just youth as a consistent deduction, or whether some indistinct apprehen-
sion of another and a better world beyond the settlement,
where there were no schools and blackberries were plenty,
had not influenced him in taking this fatal step. Enough
that he entered on his rash career by instantly eating
the dinner which he carried with him, and having pro-
pitiated that terrible god whose seat is every small boy's
stomach, with a feeling of inexpressible guiltiness creeping

over him, he turned his back upon the schoolhouse and ran into the woods.

Away from the glare of the red road, how deliciously cool was the damp breath and twilight dimness of the stately pines. How they seemed to welcome him in their deepest recesses, ranging themselves silently around him as he ran, shutting out the world and its schoolhouses, and the pursuit of indignant parents and vindictive teachers. How in the forest depths the blue jay called to him mockingly, and the kingbird, spreading his tail like a crimson pennant, beckoned him onward. How there was recognition and greeting even in the squirrel that scampered past him, mischievously whisking his ridiculous tail within an inch of his outstretched fingers. And how Aristides, at last flinging away hat, shoes, and satchel, uttered a shrill whoop and dashed forward like a youthful savage. But are not these things written in the dog-eared pages of every boy's memory, even though they seemed afterward to the just Aristides a part and parcel of his own strange vision?

Yet even such delights had their hour of culmination, and Aristides found himself at high noon back on the road again in a state of feverish excitement, carrying a ravished jay's nest, two pine cones, a dead hare, and a plume of the white syringa. Somewhat overpowered by the weight of these trophies, which he had collected in the vague belief that they would be of future service to him, he began to look about for some convenient place to bestow his booty. It was nearly time for the great Wingdam stage to go by, and when it came at last with a sharp rattle of wheels and prancing of horses, and a red pillar of dust hanging over it that partook of both the fiery and cloudy attributes of the Israelitish sign, Aristides exchanged epithets with the driver, and although standing knee-deep in red dust, felt a thrill of joy in the recognition which no future honor or dignity might ever give him.

Retracing his steps, the truant presently came to a semicircular opening in the side of Red Mountain, which enclosed, like the walls of some vast amphitheater, what had been the arena of the early struggles of the gladiators of fortune. There were terrible traces of that struggle still—in the rock blasted by fire—in the bank furrowed by water—and in the débris of Red Mountain scattered along the gulch two miles in extent. Their forgotten engines were lying half buried in the ditches—the primeval structure which had served them for a banking house was roofless, and held the hoards of field mice and squirrels. The unshapely stumps of ancient pines dotted the ground, and Aristides remembered that under the solitary redwood, which of all its brothers remained still standing, one of those early pioneers lay buried. No wonder that as the gentle breeze of that summer day swept through its branches, the just Aristides might have heard, as part of his wonderful dream, some echo of its far-off brothers of Lebanon, saying, "Since thou art fallen, no feller has risen up against us!"

But the short legs of Aristides were aching, and he was getting thirsty. There was a rough cavern close at hand; and as most of these openings condensed their general dampness somewhere in quiet pools, Aristides turned into the first one. When he had slaked his thirst, he looked around him and recognized Smith's Pocket.

It had undergone little change in the last two years. The winter rains had detached those portions of the wall which were not upheld by decaying timbers. It was certainly a dirty pocket—a pocket filled with rubbish—a shabby pocket—a worn-out and ragged pocket. It was so unpromising in its present exterior, so graphic in its story of misfortune, and so terrible in its recent memories, that the most sanguine prospector would have passed it by, as though the hopeless sentence of Dante had been written over its ragged portal.

The active mind of Aristides, however, saw in the lurking shadows of its arches much promise as a future playroom, to which he intended to induct hereafter his classical brother Lycurgus. In this reflection he threw himself on the ground, and luxuriously burying his bare feet in the cool, loose soil, gave himself up to serene meditation. But the heat and exertion were beginning to exert a certain influence over him, and once or twice his eyes closed. The water rippled beside him with a sleepy sound. The sunlight on the hill without made him wink. The long-drawn cawing of a crow on the opposite hillside, and the buzzing of a bluebottle fly who had sought retreat in the cavern, had a like effect, and he felt himself falling asleep. How long he slept, or if he slept at all, he could not remember, for he started suddenly, and listening a moment, sprang to his feet.

The low, heavy blows of a pick came deadened and muffled from the extremity of the cavern.

At first a terrible fear took possession of him; for an instant the white, rigid face of Smith, as he had seen it on the day of the inquest, when an irresistible curiosity led him to creep into the room where the dead man was lying—for an instant only, this fearful remembrance seemed to rise before him out of the gloom of the pit. The terror passed away.

Ghosts were historically unknown to Aristides, and even had his imaginative faculty been more prominent, the education of Smith's Pocket was not of a kind to foster such weaknesses. Except a twinge of conscience, a momentary recollection of the evil that comes to bad boys through the severe pages of Sunday-school books— with this exception, Aristides was not long in recovering his self-possession. He did not run away, for his curiosity was excited. The same instinct which prompted an examination of bear tracks gave a fascination to the situation and a nervous energy to his frame.

The regular blows of the pick still resounded through the cavern. He crept cautiously to the deepest recesses of the pocket, and held his breath and listened. The sound seemed to come from the bowels of the mountain. There was no sign of opening or ingress; an impenetrable veil of quartz was between him and the mysterious laborer. He was creeping back between the displaced rafters when a light glanced suddenly in his face, and flashed on the wet roof above him. Looking fearfully down, Aristides beheld between the interstices of the rafters, which formed a temporary flooring, that there was another opening below, and in that opening a man was working. In the queer fantasy of Aristides's dream, it took the aspect of a second pocket and a duplicate Smith!

He had no time to utter his astonishment, for at that moment an ominous rattling of loose soil upon his back made him look up, and he had barely time to spring away before a greater portion of the roof of Smith's Pocket, loosened by the displacement of its supports in his search, fell heavily to the ground. But in the fall a long-handled shovel which had been hidden somewhere in the crevices of the rock above came rattling down with it, and seizing this as a trophy, Aristides emerged from Smith's Pocket at a rate of speed which seemed singularly disproportionate with his short legs and round stomach.

When he reached the road the sun was setting. Inspecting his prize by that poetic light, he found that the shovel was a new one, and bore neither mark of use nor exposure. Shouldering it again, with the intention of presenting it as a peace offering to propitiate the just wrath of his parents, Aristides had gone but a few rods when an unexpected circumstance occurred which dashed his fond hope, and to the conscientious child seemed the shadow of an inevitable Nemesis. At the curve of the road, as the settlement of Smith's Pocket came into view with its straggling street and its church spire that seemed a tongue of flame in the setting sun, a broad-shouldered figure sprang, apparently from out of the bank, and stood in the path of that infelix infant.

"Where are you going with that shovel, you young devil?"

Aristides looked up and saw that his interlocutor was a man of powerful figure, whose face, though partially concealed by a red handkerchief, even in that uncertain light was not prepossessing. Children are quick physiognomists, and Aristides, feeling the presence of evil, from the depths of his mighty little soul then and there took issue with the giant.

"Where are you going with that shovel; d—n you, do you hear?" said he of the red handkerchief impatiently.

"Home," said Aristides stoutly.

"Home, eh!" said the stranger sneeringly. "And where did you steal it, you young thief?"

The Morpher stock not being of a kind to receive opprobrious epithets meekly, Aristides slowly and with an evident effort lifted the shovel in a menacing attitude.

A single step was all that separated six feet of Strength from three feet of Valor. The stranger eyed Aristides with an expression of surly amazement, and hesitated. The elephant quailed before the gadfly. As that precocious infant waved the threatening shovel, his youthful lips slowly fashioned this tremendous sentence:

"You let me pass and I won't hit you!"

And here I must pause. I would that for the sake of poetry I could leave my hero, bathed in that heroic light, erect and menacing. But alas, in this practical world of ours, the battle is too often to the strong. And I hasten over the humiliating spectacle of Aristides, spanked, cuffed, and kicked, and pick him from the ditch into which he was at last ignominiously tossed, a defeated but still struggling warrior, and so bring him, as the night closes charitably around him, in contrite tears and muddy garments to his father's door.

When the master stopped at Mrs. Morpher's to inquire after his errant pupil that night, he found Aristides in bed, smelling strongly of soap and water, and sinking into a feverish sleep. As he muttered from time to time some incoherent sentence, tossing restlessly in his cot, the master turned to those about him and asked what it was he said.

It was nothing. Aristides had been dreaming, and that was his dream.

That was all. Yet a dream that foreshadowed a slow-coming but unerring justice, that should give the little dreamer in after years some credit to the title of Aristides the Just.

CHAPTER THREE

Under the Greenwood Tree

It was an amiable weakness of Mrs. Morpher to imagine that of all her classical progeny Clytemnestra was particularly the model for M'liss. Following this fallacy she threw "Clytie" at the head of M'liss when she was "bad," and set her up before the child for adoration in her penitential moments. It was not therefore surprising to the master to hear that Clytie was coming to school, obviously as a favor to the master and as an example for M'liss and others. For Clytie was quite a young lady. Inheriting her mother's physical peculiarities, and in obedience to the climatic laws of the Red Mountain region, she was an early bloomer. The youth of Smith's Pocket, to whom this kind of flower was rare, sighed for her in April and languished in May. Enamored swains haunted the schoolhouse at the hour of dismissal. A few were jealous of the master.

Perhaps it was this latter circumstance that opened the master's eyes to another. He could not help noticing that Clytie was romantic; that in school she required a great deal of attention; that her pens were uniformly bad and wanted fixing; that she usually accompanied the request with a certain expectation in her eye that was somewhat disproportionate to the quality of service she verbally required; that she sometimes allowed the curves of a round plump white arm to rest on his when he was writing her copies; that she always blushed and flung back her blond curls when she did so. I don't remember whether I have stated that the master was a young man —it's of little consequence, however. He had been severely educated in the school in which Clytie was taking her first lesson, and on the whole withstood the flexible curves and facetious glance like the fine young Spartan that he was. Perhaps an insufficient quality of food may have tended to this asceticism. He generally avoided Clytie; but one evening when she returned to the schoolhouse after something she had forgotten—and did not find it until the master walked home with her—I hear that he endeavored to make himself particularly agreeable, partly from the fact, I imagine, that his conduct was adding gall and bitterness to the already overcharged hearts of Clytemnestra's admirers.

The morning after this affecting episode, M'liss did not come to school. Noon came, but not M'liss. Questioning Clytie on the subject, it appeared that they had left for school together, but the willful M'liss had taken another road. The afternoon brought her not. In the evening he called on Mrs. Morpher, whose motherly heart was really alarmed. Mr. Morpher had spent all day in search of her, without discovering a trace that might lead to her discovery. Aristides was summoned as a probable accomplice, but that equitable infant succeeding in impressing the household with his innocence, Mrs. Morpher entertained a vivid impression that the child would yet be found drowned in a ditch, or—what was almost as terrible—mud-dyed and soiled beyond the redemption of soap and water. Sick at heart, the master returned to the schoolhouse. As he lit his lamp and seated himself at his desk, he found a note lying before him, addressed to himself in M'liss's handwriting. It seemed to be written on a leaf torn from some old memorandum book, and to prevent sacrilegious trifling, had been sealed with six broken wafers. Opening it almost tenderly, the master read as follows:

RESPECTED SIR: When you read this, I am run away. Never to come back. *Never* NEVER NEVER. You can give my beeds to Mary Jennings, and my Amerika's Pride [a highly colored lithograph from a tobacco box] to Sally Flanders. But don't you give anything to Clytie Morper. Don't you dair to. Do you know what my opinnion is of her, it is this, she is perfekly disgustin. That is all and no more at present from

                                        MELISSA SMITH

The master mused for some time over this characteristic epistle. As he was mechanically refolding it his eye caught a sentence written on the back in pencil, in another handwriting, somewhat blurred and indistinct from the heavy incisive strokes of M'liss's pen on the other side. It seemed to be a memorandum belonging to the book from which the leaf was originally torn:

July 17th. 5 hours in drift—dipping west—took out 20 oz.; cleaned up 40 oz. Mem.—saw M. S.

"July 17th," said the master, opening his desk and taking out a file of the *Red Mountain Banner*. "July 17th," he repeated, running over the pages till he came to a paragraph headed "DISTRESSING SUICIDE." "July 17th—why, that's the day Smith killed himself. That's funny!"

In a strict etymological sense there was nothing so very ludicrous in this coincidence, nor did the master's face betray any expression of the kind. Perhaps the epithet was chosen to conceal the vague uneasiness which it produced in his mind. We are all of us more affected by these coincidences than we care to confess to one another. If the most matter-of-fact reader of these pages were to find a hearse standing in front of his door for three consecutive mornings, although the circumstance might be satisfactorily explained—shall I go further and say, *because* the circumstance might be satisfactorily explained—he would vaguely wish it hadn't happened. Philosophize as we may, the simple fact of two remote lines crossing each other always seems to us of tremendous significance and quite overshadows the more important truth that the real parallels of life's journey are the lines that never meet. It will do us good to remember these things, and look more kindly on our brothers of Borrioboola-Gha and their fetich superstitions when we drop our silver in the missionary box next Sabbath.

"I wonder where that memorandum came from," said the master, as he rose at last and buttoned up his coat. "Who is 'M. S.'? M. S. stands for manuscript and Melissa Smith. Why don't—" But checking an impulsive query as to why people don't make their private memoranda generally intelligible, the master put the letter in his pocket and went home.

At sunrise the next morning he was picking his way through the palmlike fern and thick underbrush of the pine forest, starting the hare from its form, and awakening a querulous protest from a few dissipated crows, who had evidently been making a night of it, and so came to the wooded ridge where he had once found M'liss. There he found the prostrate pine and tessellated branches, but the throne was vacant. As he drew nearer, what might have been some frightened animal started through the crackling limbs. It ran up the tossed arms of the fallen monarch, and sheltered itself in some friendly foliage. The master, reaching the old seat, found the nest still warm; looking up in the intertwining branches, he met the black eyes of the errant M'liss. They gazed at each other without speaking. She was first to break the silence.

"What do you want?" she asked curtly.

The master had decided on a course of action. "I want some crab apples," he said humbly.

"Shan't have 'em! go away! Why don't you get 'em of Clytemnerestera?" It seemed to be a relief to M'liss to express her contempt in additional syllables to that classical young woman's already long-drawn title. "Oh, you wicked thing!"

"I am hungry, Lissy. I have eaten nothing since dinner yesterday. I am famished!" and the young man, in a state of remarkable exhaustion, leaned against the tree.

Melissa's heart was touched. In the bitter days of her gypsy life she had known the sensation he so artfully simulated. Overcome by his heartbroken tone, but not entirely divested of suspicion, she said:

"Dig under the tree near the roots, and you'll find lots: but mind you don't tell," for M'liss had *her* hoards as well as the rats and squirrels.

But the master of course was unable to find them, the effects of hunger probably blinding his senses. M'liss grew uneasy. At length she peered at him through the leaves in an elfish way, and questioned:

"If I come down and give you some, you'll promise you won't touch me?"

The master promised.

"Hope you'll die if you do?"

The master accepted instant dissolution as a forfeit. M'liss slid down the tree. The duties of hospitality fulfilled, she seated herself at a little distance and eyed the master with extreme caution.

"Why didn't you eat your breakfast, you bad man?"

"Because I've run away."

"Where to?" said M'liss, her eyes twinkling.

"Anywhere—anywhere away from here!" responded that deceitful wretch with tragic wildness of demeanor.

"What made you?—bad boy!" said M'liss, with a sudden respect of conventionalities, and a rare touch of tenderness in her tones. "You'd better go back where your vittals are."

"What are victuals to a wounded spirit?" asked the young man dramatically. He had reached the side of M'liss during this dialogue, and had taken her unresisting hand. He was too wise to notice his victory, however; and drawing Melissa's note from his pocket, opened it before her.

"Couldn't you find any paper in the schoolhouse without tearing a leaf out of my memorandum book, Melissa?" he asked.

"It ain't out of your memorandum book," responded M'liss fiercely.

"Indeed," said the master, turning to the lines in pencil; "I thought it was my handwriting."

M'liss, who had been looking over his shoulder, suddenly seized the paper and snatched it out of his hand.

"It's father's writing!" she said after a pause, in a softer tone.

"Where did you get it, M'liss?"

"Aristides gave it to me."

"Where did he get it?"

"Don't know. He had the book in his pocket when I told him I was going to write to you, and he tore the leaf out. There now—don't bother me any more." M'liss had turned her face away, and the black hair had hid her downcast eyes.

Something in her gesture and expression reminded him of her father. Something, and more that was characteristic to her at such moments, made him fancy another resemblance, and caused him to ask impulsively, and less cautiously than was his wont:

"Do you remember your mother, M'liss?"

"No."

"Did you never see her?"

"No—didn't I tell you not to bother, and you're a-goin' and doin' it," said M'liss savagely.

The master was silent a moment. "Did you ever think you would like to have a mother, M'liss?" he asked again.

"No-o-o-o!"

The master rose; M'liss looked up.

"Does Aristides come to school today?"

"I don't know."

"Are you going back? You'd better," she said.

"Well!—perhaps I may. Good-by!"

He had proceeded a few steps when, as he expected, she called him back. He turned. She was standing by the tree with tears glistening in her eyes. The master felt the right moment had come. Going up to her, he took both her hands in his, and looking in her tearful eyes, said gravely:

"M'liss, do you remember the first evening you came to see me?"

M'liss remembered.

"You asked me if you might come to school, and I said—"

"Come!" responded the child softly.

"If I told you I was lonely without my little scholar, and that I wanted her to come, what would you say?"

The child hung her head in silence. The master waited patiently. Tempted by the quiet, a hare ran close to the couple, and raising her bright eyes and velvet forepaws, gazed at them fearlessly. A squirrel ran halfway down the furrowed bark of the fallen tree, and there stopped.

"*We* are waiting, Lissy," said the master in a whisper, and the child smiled. Stirred by a passing breeze, the tree-tops rocked, and a slanting sunbeam stole through their interlaced boughs and fell on the doubting face and irresolute little figure. But a step in the dry branches and a rustling in the underbrush broke the spell.

A man dressed as a miner, carrying a long-handled shovel, came slowly through the woods. A red handkerchief tied around his head under his hat, with the loose ends hanging from beneath, did not add much favor to his unprepossessing face. He did not perceive the master and M'liss until he was close upon them. When he did, he stopped suddenly and gazed at them with an expression of lowering distrust. M'liss drew nearer to the master.

"Good mornin'—picknickin', eh?" he asked, with an attempt at geniality that was more repulsive than his natural manner.

"How are you—prospecting, eh?" said the master

quietly, after the established colloquial formula of Red Mountain.

"Yes—a little in that way."

The stranger still hesitated, apparently waiting for them to go first, a matter which M'liss decided by suddenly taking the master's hand in her quick way. What she said was scarcely audible, but the master, parting her hair over her forehead, kissed her, and so, hand in hand, they passed out of the damp aisles and forest odors into the open sunlit road. But M'liss, looking back, saw that her old seat was occupied by the hopeful prospector, and fancied that in the shadows of her former throne something of a gratified leer overspread his face. "He'll have to dig deep to find the crab apples," said the child to the master, as they came to the Red Mountain road.

When Aristides came to school that day he was confronted by M'liss. But neither threats nor entreaties could extract from that reticent youth the whereabout of the memorandum book nor where he got it. Two or three days afterward, during recess, he approached M'liss, and beckoned her one side.

"Well," said M'liss impatiently.

"Did you ever read the story of 'Ali Baba'?"

"Yes."

"Do you believe it?"

"No."

"Well," said that sage infant, wheeling around on his stout legs, *"it's true!"*

CHAPTER FOUR

Which Has A Good Moral Tendency

Somewhat less spiteful in her intercourse with the other scholars, M'liss still retained an offensive attitude toward Clytemnestra. Perhaps the jealous element was not entirely stilled in her passionate little breast. Perhaps it was that Clytemnestra's round curves and plump outlines afforded an extensive pinching surface. But while these ebullitions were under the master's control, her enmity occasionally took a new and irresponsible form.

In his first esimate of the child's character he could not
conceive that she had ever possessed a doll. But the master, like many other professed readers of character, was
safer in *a posteriori* than *a priori* reasoning, for M'liss
had a doll. But then it was a peculiar doll—a frightful per-
version of wax and sawdust—a doll fearfully and won-
derfully made—a smaller edition of M'liss. Its unhappy
existence had been a secret discovered accidentally by
Mrs. Morpher. It had been the old-time companion of
M'liss's wanderings, and bore evident marks of suffering.
Its original complexion was long since washed away by
the weather and anointed by the slime of ditches. It
looked very much as M'liss had in days past. Its one
gown of faded stuff was dirty and ragged as hers had been.
M'liss had never been known to apply to it any childish
term of endearment. She never exhibited it in the presence
of other children. It was put severely to bed in a hollow
tree near the schoolhouse, and only allowed exercise during M'liss's rambles. Fulfilling a stern duty to her doll—
as she would to herself—it knew no luxuries.

Now, Mrs. Morpher, obeying a commendable impulse,
bought another doll and gave it to M'liss. The child received it gravely and curiously. The master, on looking at
it one day, fancied he saw a slight resemblance in its
round red cheeks and mild blue eyes to Clytemnestra.
It became evident before long that M'liss had also noticed
the same resemblance. Accordingly she hammered its wax-
en head on the rocks when she was alone, and sometimes dragged it with a string round its neck to and from
school. At other times, setting it up on her desk, she made
a pincushion of its patient and inoffensive body. Whether
this was done in revenge of what she considered a second
figurative obtrusion of Clytie's excellencies upon her; or
whether she had an intuitive appreciation of the rites of
certain other heathens, and indulging in that "fetish" ceremony imagined that the original of her wax model would
pine away and finally die, is a metaphysical question I
shall not now consider.

In spite of these moral vagaries, the master could not
help noticing in her different tasks the workings of a quick,
restless, and vigorous perception. She knew neither the
hesitancy nor the doubts of childhood. Her answers in

class were always slightly dashed with audacity. Of course she was not infallible. But her courage and daring in venturing beyond her own depth and that of the floundering little swimmers around her, in their minds outweighed all errors of judgment. Children are no better than grown people in this respect, I fancy; and whenever the little red hand flashed above her desk, there was a wondering silence, and even the master was sometimes oppressed with a doubt of his own experience and judgment.

Nevertheless, certain attributes which at first amused and entertained his fancy began to affect him with grave doubts. He could not but see that M'liss was revengeful, irreverent, and willful. But there was one better quality which pertained to her semi-savage disposition—the faculty of physical fortitude and self-sacrifice, and another —though not always an attribute of the noble savage— truth. M'liss was both fearless and sincere—perhaps in such a character the adjectives were synonymous.

The master had been doing some hard thinking on this subject, and had arrived at that conclusion quite common to all who think sincerely, that he was generally the slave of his own prejudices, when he determined to call on the Rev. Mr. McSnagley for advice. This decision was somewhat humiliating to his pride, as he and McSnagley were not friends. But he thought of M'liss and the evening of their first meeting; and perhaps with a pardonable superstition that it was not chance alone that had guided her willful feet to the schoolhouse, and perhaps with a complacent consciousness of the rare magnanimity of the act, he choked back his dislike and went to McSnagley.

The reverend gentleman was glad to see him. Moreover, he observed that the master was looking "peartish" and hoped he had got over the "neuralgy" and "rheumatiz." He himself had been troubled with a dumb "ager" since last conference. But he had learned to "rastle and pray."

Pausing a moment to enable the master to write this certain method of curing the dumb "ager" upon the book and volume of his brain, Mr. McSnagley proceeded to inquire after Sister Morpher. "She is an adornment to Christewanity, and has a likely, growin' young family," added Mr. McSnagley; "and there's that mannerly young gal—so well behaved—Miss Clytie." In fact, Clytie's perfections seemed to affect him to such an extent that he dwelt for several minutes upon them. The master was doubly embarrassed. In the first place, there was an enforced contrast with poor M'liss in all this praise of Clytie. Secondly, there was something unpleasantly confidential in his tone of speaking of Morpher's earliest born. So that the master, after a few futile efforts to say something natural, found it convenient to recall another engagement and left without asking the information required, but in his after reflections somewhat unjustly giving the Rev. Mr. McSnagley the full benefit of having refused it.

But the master obtained the advice in another and unexpected direction.

The resident physician of Smith's Pocket was a Dr. Duchesne, or as he was better known to the locality, "Dr. Doochesny." Of a naturally refined nature and liberal education, he had steadily resisted the aggressions and temptations of Smith's Pocket, and represented to the master a kind of connecting link between his present life and the past. So that an intimacy sprang up between the two men, involving prolonged interviews in the doctor's little back shop, often to the exclusion of other suffering humanity and their physical ailments. It was in one of these interviews that the master mentioned the coincidence of the date of the memoranda on the back of M'liss's letter and the day of Smith's suicide.

"If it were Smith's own handwriting, as the child says it is," said the master, "it shows a queer state of mind that could contemplate suicide and indite private memoranda within the same twenty-four hours."

Dr. Duchesne removed his cigar from his lips and looked attentively at his friend.

"The only hypothesis," continued the master, "is that Smith was either drunk or crazy, and the fatal act was in a measure unpremeditated."

"Every man who commits suicide," returned the doctor gravely, "is in my opinion insane, or what is nearly the same thing, becomes through suffering an irresponsible agent. In my professional experience I have seen most of the forms of mental and physical agony, and know what sacrifices men will make to preserve even an existence that to me seemed little better than death, so long as their intellect remained unclouded. When you come to reflect on the state of mind that chooses death as a preferable alternative, you generally find an exaltation and enthusiasm that differs very little from the ordinary diagnosis of delirium. Smith was not drunk," added the doctor in his usual careless tone; "I saw his body."

The master remained buried in reflection. Presently the doctor removed his cigar.

"Perhaps I might help you to explain the coincidence you speak of."

"How?"

"Very easily. But this is a professional secret, you understand."

"Yes, I understand," said the master hastily, with an ill-defined uneasiness creeping over him.

"Do you know anything of the phenomena of death by gunshot wounds?"

"No!"

"Then you must take certain facts as granted. Smith, you remember, was killed *instantly!* The nature of his wound and the manner of his death were such as would have caused an instantaneous and complete relaxation of *all* the muscles. Rigidity and contraction would have supervened of course, but only after life was extinct and consciousness fled. Now Smith was found with his hand tightly grasping a pistol."

"Well?"

"Well, my dear boy, he must have grasped it after he was dead, or have prevailed on some friend to stiffen his fingers round it."

"Do you mean that he was murdered?"

Dr. Duchesne rose and closed the door. "We have different names for these things in Smith's Pocket. I mean to say that he didn't kill himself—that's all."

"But, doctor," said the master earnestly; "do you think you have done right in concealing this fact? Do you think it just—do you think it consistent with your duty to his orphan child?"

"That's why I have said nothing about it," replied the

doctor coolly—"because of my consideration for his orphan child."

The master breathed quickly, and stared at the doctor.

"Doctor! you don't think that M'liss—"

"Hush!—don't get excited, my young friend. Remember I am not a lawyer—only a doctor."

"But M'liss was with me the very night he must have been killed. We were walking together when we heard the report—that is—a report—which must have been the one—" stammered the master.

"When was that?"

"At half past eleven. I remember looking at my watch."

"Humph!—when did you meet her first?"

"At half past eight. Come, doctor, you have made a mistake here at least," said the young man with an assumption of ease he was far from feeling. "Give M'liss the benefit of the doubt."

Dr. Duchesne replied by opening a drawer of his desk. After rummaging among the powders and mysterious looking instruments with which it was stored, he finally brought forth a longitudinal slip of folded white paper. It was appropriately labeled *"Poison."*

"Look here," said the doctor, opening the paper. It contained two or three black coarse hairs. "Do you know them?"

"No."

"Look again!"

"It looks something like Melissa's hair," said the master, with a fathomless sinking of the heart.

"When I was called to look at the body," continued the doctor with the deliberate cautiousness of a professional diagnosis, "my suspicions were aroused by the circumstance I told you of. I managed to get possession of the pistol, and found these hairs twisted around the lock as though they had been accidentally caught and violently disentangled. I don't think that anyone else saw them. I removed them without observation, and—they are at your service."

The master sank back in his seat and pressed his hand to his forehead. The image of M'liss rose before him with flashing eye and long black hair, and seemed to beat down and resist defiantly the suspicion that crept slowly over his heart.

"I forbore to tell you this, my friend," continued the doctor slowly and gravely, "because when I learned that you had taken this strange child under your protection I did not wish to tell you that which—though I contend does not alter her claims to man's sympathy and kindness —still might have prejudiced her in your eyes. Her improvement under your care has proven my position correct. I have, as you know, peculiar ideas of the extent to which humanity is responsible. I find in my heart—looking back over the child's career—no sentiment but pity. I am mistaken in you if I thought this circumstance aroused any other feeling in yours."

Still the figure of M'liss stood before the master as he bent before the doctor's words, in the same defiant attitude, with something of scorn in the great dark eyes, that made the blood tingle in his cheeks, and seemed to make the reasoning of the speaker but meaningless and empty words. At length he rose. As he stood with his hand on the latch he turned to Dr. Duchesne, who was watching him with careful solicitude.

"I don't know but that you have done well to keep this from me. At all events it has not—cannot, and should not alter my opinion toward M'liss. You will of course keep it a secret. In the meantime you must not blame me if I cling to my instincts in preference to your judgment. I still believe that you are mistaken in regard to her."

"Stay, one moment," said the doctor; "promise me you will not say anything of this, nor attempt to prosecute the matter further till you have consulted with me."

"I promise. Good night."

"Good night"; and so they parted.

True to that promise and his own instinctive promptings the master endeavored to atone for his momentary disloyalty by greater solicitude for M'liss. But the child had noticed some change in the master's thoughtful manner, and in one of their long post-prandial walks she stopped suddenly, and mounting a stump, looked full in his face with big searching eyes.

"You ain't mad?" said she, with an interrogative shake of the black braids.

"No."

"Nor bothered?"

"No."

"Nor hungry?" (Hunger was to M'liss a sickness that might attack a person at any moment.)

"No."

"Nor thinking of her?"

"Of whom, Lissy?"

"That white girl." (This was the latest epithet invented by M'liss, who was a very dark brunette, to express Clytemnestra.)

"No."

"Upon your word?" (A substitute for "Hope you'll die!" proposed by the master.)

"Yes."

"And sacred honor?"

"Yes."

Then M'liss gave him a fierce little kiss, and hopping down, fluttered off. For two or three days after that she condescended to appear like other children and be, as she expressed it, "good."

When the summer was about spent, and the last harvest had been gathered in the valleys, the master bethought him of gathering in a few ripened shoots of the young idea, and of having his Harvest Home, or Examination. So the savans and professionals of Smith's Pocket were gathered to witness that time-honored custom of placing timid children in a constrained position, and bullying them as in a witness box. As usual in such cases, the most audacious and self-possessed were the lucky recipients of the honors. The reader will imagine that in the present instance M'liss and Clytie were pre-eminent and divided public attention: M'liss with her clearness of material perception and self-reliance, and Clytie with her placid self-esteem and saintlike correctness of deportment. The other little ones were timid and blundering. M'liss's readiness and brilliancy, of course, captivated the greatest number and provoked the greatest applause, and M'liss's antecedents had unconsciously awakened the strongest sympathies of the miners, whose athletic forms were ranged against the walls, or whose handsome bearded faces looked in at the window. But M'liss's popularity was overthrown by an unexpected circumstance.

McSnagley had invited himself, and had been going through the pleasing entertainment of frightening the more timid pupils by the vaguest and most ambiguous questions, delivered in an impressive, funereal tone; and M'liss had soared into astronomy, and was tracking the course of our "spotted ball" through space, and defining the "tethered orbits" of the planets, when McSnagley deliberately arose.

"Meelissy, ye were speaking of the revolutions of this yer yearth and its movements with regard to the sun, and I think you said it had been a-doin' of it since the creation, eh?"

M'liss nodded a scornful affirmative.

"Well, was that the truth?" said McSnagley, folding his arms.

"Yes," said M'liss, shutting up her little red lips tightly.

The handsome outlines at the windows peered further into the schoolroom, and a saintly, Raphael-like face, with blond beard and soft blue eyes, belonging to the biggest scamp in the diggings, turned toward the child and whispered:

"Stick to it, M'liss! It's only a big bluff of the parson."

The reverend gentleman heaved a deep sigh, and cast a compassionate glance at the master, then at the children, and then rested his eye on Clytemnestra. That young woman softly elevated her round, white arm. Its seductive curves were enhanced by a gorgeous and massive specimen bracelet, the gift of one of her humblest worshipers, worn in honor of the occasion. There was a momentary pause. Clytie's round cheeks were very pink and soft. Clytie's big eyes were very bright and blue. Clytie's low-necked white book muslin rested softly on Clytie's white, plump shoulders. Clytie looked at the master, and the master nodded. Then Clytie spoke softly:

"Joshua commanded the sun to stand still, and it obeyed him."

There was a low hum of applause in the schoolroom, a triumphant expression on McSnagley's face, a grave shadow on the master's, and a comical look of disappointment reflected from the windows. M'liss skimmed rapidly over her astronomy, and then shut the book with a loud snap. A groan burst from McSnagley, an expression of astonishment from the schoolroom, and a yell from the windows, as M'liss brought her red fist down on the desk, with the emphatic declaration:

"It's a d—n lie. I don't believe it!"

CHAPTER FIVE

"Open Sesame"

The long wet season had drawn near its close. Signs of spring were visible in the swelling buds and rushing torrents. The pine forests exhaled a fresher spicery. The azaleas were already budding; the ceanothus getting ready its lilac livery for spring. On the green upland which climbed the Red Mountain at its southern aspect, the long spike of the monkshood shot up from its broadleaved stool and once more shook its dark blue bells. Again the billow above Smith's grave was soft and green, its crest just tossed with the foam of daisies and buttercups. The little graveyard had gathered a few new dwellers in the past year, and the mounds were placed two by two by the little paling until they reached Smith's grave, and there, there was but one. General superstition had shunned the enforced companionship. The plot beside Smith was vacant.

It was the custom of the driver of the great Wingdam stage to whip up his horses at the foot of the hill, and so enter Smith's Pocket at that remarkable pace which the woodcuts in the hotel barroom represented to credulous humanity as the usual rate of speed of that conveyance. At least, Aristides Morpher thought so as he stood one Sunday afternoon, uneasily conscious of his best jacket and collar, waiting its approach. Nor could anything shake his belief that regularly on that occasion the horses ran away with the driver, and that that individual from motives of deep policy pretended not to notice it until they were stopped.

"Anybody up from below, Bill?" said the landlord as the driver slowly descended from his perch.

"Nobody for you," responded Bill shortly. "Dusenberry kem up as usual, and got off at the old place. You can't make a livin' off him, I reckon."

"Have you found out what his name is yet?" continued the landlord, implying that "Dusenberry" was simply a playful epithet of the driver.

"He says his name is Waters," returned Bill. "Jake said he saw him at the North Fork in '50—called himself Moore then. Guess he ain't no good, nohow. What's he doin' round here?"

"Says he's prospectin'," replied the landlord. "He has a claim somewhere in the woods. Gambles a little too, I reckon. He don't travel on his beauty anyhow."

"If you had seen him makin' up to a piece of calico inside, last trip, and she a-makin' up to him quite confidential-like, I guess you'd think he was a lady-killer. My eye, but wasn't she a stunner! Clytie Morpher wasn't nowhere to begin with her."

"Who was she, Bill?" asked half a dozen masculine voices.

"Don't know. We picked her up this side of 'Coyote.' Fancy? I tell you!—pretty little hat and pink ribbings— eyes that ud bore you through at a hundred yards— white teeth—brown gaiters, and such an ankle! She didn't want to show it—oh, no!" added the sarcastic Bill with deep significance.

"Where did you leave her, Bill?" asked a gentle village swain who had been fired by the glowing picture of the fair unknown.

"That's what's the matter. You see after we picked her up, she said she was goin' through to Wingdam. Of course there wasn't anything in the stage or on the road too good to offer her. Old Major Spaffler wanted to treat her to lemonade at every station. Judge Plunkett kep' a-pullin' down the blinds and a-h'istin' of them up to keep out the sun and let in the air. Blest if old McSnagley didn't want to carry her travelin' bag. There wasn't any attention, boys, she didn't get—but it wasn't no use—bless you! She never so much as passed the time of day with them."

"But where did she go?" inquired another anxious auditor.

"Keep your foot off the drag, and I'll tell you. Arter we left Ring Tail Canyon, Dusenberry, as usual, got on. Presently one of the outsides turned round to me, and says he, 'D——d if Ugly Mug ain't got the inside track of all of you this time!' I looked down, and dern my skin if there wasn't Dusenberry a-sittin' up alongside of the lady, quite comfortable, as if they had ben children together. At the next station Dusenberry gets off. So does the lady. 'Ain't you goin' on to Wingdam,' says I. 'No,' says she. 'Mayn't we have the pleasure of your kempany further?' says the judge, taking off his hat. 'No, I've changed my mind,' says she, and off she got, and off she walked arm in arm with him as cool as you please."

"Wonder if that wa'n't the party that passed through here last July?" asked the blacksmith, joining the loungers in front of the stage office. "Waters brought up a buggy to get the axle bolted. There was a woman setting in the buggy, but the hood was drawn down, and I didn't get to see her face."

During this conversation Aristides, after a long, lingering glance at the stage, had at last torn himself away from its fascinations, and was now lounging down the long straggling street in a peculiarly dissipated manner, with his hat pushed on the back part of his head, his right hand and a greater portion of his right arm buried in his trousers pocket. This might have been partly owing to the shortness of his legs and the comparative amplitude of his trousers, which to the casual observer seemed to obviate the necessity of any other garment. But when he reached the bottom of the street, and further enlivened his progress by whistling shrilly between his fingers, and finally drew a fragment of a cigar from his pocket and placed it between his teeth, it was evident that there was a moral as well as physical laxity in his conduct. The near fact was that Aristides had that afternoon evaded the Sunday school, and was open to any kind of infant iniquity.

The main street of Smith's Pocket gradually lost its civilized character, and after one or two futile attempts at improvement at its lower extremity, terminated impotently in a chaos of ditches, races, and trailings. Out of this again a narrow trail started along the mountainside, and communicated with that vast amphitheater which still exhibited the pioneer efforts of the early settlers. It was this trail that Aristides took that Sunday afternoon, and which he followed until he reached the hillside a few rods below the yawning fissure of Smith's Pocket. After a careful examination of the vicinity, he cleared away the underbrush beside a fallen pine that lay near, and sat down in the attitude of patient and deliberate expectancy.

Five minutes passed—ten, twenty—and finally a half-hour was gone. Aristides threw away his cigar, which he had lacked determination to light, and peeled small slips from the inner bark of the pine tree, and munched them gravely. Another five, ten, and twenty minutes passed, and the sun began to drop below the opposite hillside. Another ten minutes, and the whole of the amphitheater above was in heavy shadow. Ten minutes more, and the distant windows in the settlement flamed redly. Five minutes, and the spire of the Methodist church caught the glow—and then the underbrush crackled.

Aristides, looking up, saw the trunk of the prostrate pine slowly lifting itself before him.

A second glance showed the fearless and self-possessed boy that the apparent phenomenon was simply and easily explained. The tree had fallen midway and at right angles across the trunk of another prostrate monarch. So accurately and evenly was it balanced that the child was satisfied, from a liberal experience of the application of these principles to the game of "seesaw," that a very slight impulse to either end was sufficient to destroy the equilibrium. That impulse proceeded from his end of the tree, as he saw when the uplifted trunk disclosed an opening in the ground beneath it and the head and shoulders of a man emerging therefrom.

Aristides threw himself noiselessly on his stomach. The thick clump of an azalea hid him from view, though it did not obstruct his survey of the stranger, whom he at once recognized as his former enemy—the man with the red handkerchief—the hopeful prospector of Red Mountain, and the hypothetical "Dusenberry" of the stage driver.

The stranger looked cautiously round, and Aristides shrank close behind the friendly azalea.

Satisfied that he was unobserved, the subterranean proprietor returned to the opening and descended, reappear-
ing with a worn black enameled traveling bag which he
carried with difficulty. This he again enveloped in a blanket and strapped tightly on his back, and a long-handled
shovel, brought up from the same mysterious storehouse,
completed his outfit. As he stood for a moment leaning
on the shovel, it was the figure of the hopeful prospector
in the heart of the forest. A very slight effort was sufficient to replace the fallen tree in its former position.
Raising the shovel to his shoulder, he moved away, brush-
ing against the azalea bush which hid the breathless
Aristides. The sound of his footsteps retreating through
the crackling brush presently died out, and a drowsy
Sabbath stillness succeeded.

Aristides rose. There was a wonderful brightness in his
gray eyes, and a flush on his sunburned cheek. Seizing a
root of the fallen pine he essayed to move it. But it defied
his endeavors. Aristides looked round.

"There's some trick about it, but I'll find it yet," said
that astute child.

Breaking off the limb of a buckeye, he extemporized a
lever. The first attempt failed. The second succeeded,
and the long roots of the tree again ascended. But as it
required prolonged effort to keep the tree up, before
the impetus was lost Aristides seized the opportunity to
jump into the opening. At the same moment the tree
slowly returned to its former position.

In the sudden change from the waning light to complete
darkness, Aristides was for a moment confounded. Recovering himself, he drew a match from his capacious
pocket, and striking it against the sole of his shoe, by the
upspringing flash perceived a candle stuck in the crevices of the rock beside him. Lighting it, he glanced curiously around him. He was at the entrance of a long
gallery at the further extremity of which he could faintly
see the glimmering of the outer daylight. Following this
gallery cautiously he presently came to an antechamber,
and by the glimmering of the light above him at once saw
that it was the same he had seen in his wonderful dream.

The antechamber was about fourteen feet square with
walls of decomposed quartz, mingling with flaky mica that

reflected here and there the gleam of Aristides's candle with a singular brilliancy. It did not need much observation on his part to determine the reason of the stranger's lonely labors. On a rough rocker beside him were two fragments of ore taken from the adjacent wall, the smallest of which the two arms of Aristides could barely clasp. To his dazzled eyes they seemed to be almost entirely of pure gold. The great strike of '56 at Ring Tail Canyon had brought to the wonderful vision of Smith's Pocket no such nuggets as were here.

Aristides turned to the wall again, which had been apparently the last scene of the stranger's labors and from which the two masses of ore were taken. Even to his inexperienced eye it represented a wealth almost incalculable. Through the loose, red soil everywhere glittering star points of the precious metal threw back the rays of his candle. Aristides turned pale and trembled.

Here was the realization of his most extravagant fancy. Ever since his strange dream and encounter with the stranger, he had felt an irresistible desire to follow up his adventure and discover the secrets of the second cavern. But when he had returned to Smith's Pocket a few days after, the wreck of the fallen roof had blocked up that part of the opening from which he had caught sight of the hidden workman below. During his visit he had picked up from among the rubbish the memorandum book which had supplied M'liss with letter paper. Still haunting the locality after school hours, he had noticed that regularly at sunset the man with the red handkerchief appeared in some mysterious way from the hillside below Smith's Pocket, and went away in the direction of the settlement. By careful watching, Aristides had fixed the location of his mysterious appearance to a point a few rods below the opening of Smith's Pocket. Flushed by this discovery, he had been betrayed from his usual discretion so far as to intimate a hinting of the suspicion that possessed him in the few mysterious words he had whispered to M'liss at school. The accident we have described above determined the complete discovery of the secret.

Who was the stranger, and why did he keep the fact of this immense wealth hidden from the world? Suppose he,

Aristides, were to tell? Wouldn't the schoolboys look up at him with interest as the hero and discoverer of this wonderful cavern, and wouldn't the stage driver feel proud of his acquaintance and offer him rides for nothing? Why hadn't Smith discovered it—who was poor and wanted money, whom Aristides had liked, who was the father of M'liss, for whom Aristides confessed a secret passion, who belonged to the settlement and helped to build it up—instead of the stranger? Had Smith never a suspicion that gold was so near him, and if so, why had he killed himself? But did Smith kill himself? And at this thought and its correlative fancy, again the cheek of Aristides blanched, and the candle shook in his nerveless fingers.

Apart and distinct from these passing conjectures one idea remained firm and dominant in his mind: the man with the red handkerchief had no right to this treasure! The mysterious instinct which directed this judicial ruling of Aristides had settled this fact as indubitably as though proven by the weight of the strongest testimony. For an instant a wild thought sprang up in his heart, and he seized the nearest mass of ore with the half-formed intention of bearing it directly to the feet of M'liss as her just and due inheritance. But Aristides could not lift it, and the idea passed out of his mind with the frustrated action.

At the further end of the gallery a few blankets were lying, and with some mining implements, a kettle of water, a few worn flannel shirts, were the only articles which this subterranean habitation possessed. In turning over one of the blankets Aristides picked up a woman's comb. It was a tortoise shell, and bright with some fanciful ornamentation. Without a moment's hesitation Aristides pocketed it as the natural property of M'liss. A pocketbook containing a few old letters in the breast pocket of one of the blue shirts was transferred to that of Aristides with the same coolness and sentiment of instinctive justice.

Aristides wisely reflected that these unimportant articles would excite no suspicion if found in his possession. A fragment of the rock, which if he had taken it as he felt impelled, would have precipitated the discovery that

Aristides had decided to put off until he had perfected a certain plan.

The light from the opening above had gradually faded, and Aristides knew that night had fallen. To prevent suspicion he must return home. He re-entered the gallery and reached the opening of the egress. One of the roots of the tree projected into the opening.

He seized it and endeavored to lift it, but in vain. Panting with exertion, he again and again exerted the fullest power of his active sinews, but the tree remained immovable—the opening remained sealed as firmly as with Solomon's signet. Raising his candle towards it, Aristides saw the reason of its resistance. In his hurried ingress he had allowed the tree to revolve sufficiently to permit one of its roots to project into the opening, which held it firmly down. In the shock of the discovery the excitement which had sustained him gave way, and with a hopeless cry the just Aristides fell senseless on the floor of the gallery.

CHAPTER SIX

The Trials of Mrs. Morpher

"Now, where on earth can that child be?" said Mrs. Morpher, shading her eyes with her hand as she stood at the door of the "Mountain Ranch," looking down the Wingdam road at sunset. "With his best things on, too. Goodness!—what *were* boys made for?"

Mr. Morpher, without replying to this question, apparently addressed to himself as an adult representative of the wayward species, appeared at the door and endeavored to pour oil on the troubled waters.

"Oh, *he's* all right, Sue! Don't fuss about *him*," said Mr. Morpher with an imbecile sense of conveying comfort in the emphasized pronoun. "He's down the gulch, or in the tunnel, or over to the claim. He'll turn up by bedtime. Don't you worry about *him*. I'll look him up in a minit," and Mr. Morpher, taking his hat, sauntered down the road in the direction of the National Hotel.

Mrs. Morpher gazed doubtfully after her liege. "Look-

ing up" Aristides, in her domestic experience, implied a
prolonged absence in the barroom of the hotel, the
tedium whereof was beguiled by seven-up or euchre. But
she only said: "Don't be long, James," and sighed hopelessly as she turned back into the house.

Once again within her own castle walls Mrs. Morpher
dropped her look of patient suffering and glanced defiantly around for a fresh grievance.

The decorous little parlor offered nothing to provoke
the hostility of her peculiar instincts. Spotless were the
white curtains; the bright carpet guiltless of stain or dust.
The chairs were placed arithmetically in twos, and added
up evenly on the four sides with nothing to carry over.
Two bunches of lavender and fennel breathed an odor
of sanctified cleanliness through the room. Five daguerreo-
types on the mantelpiece represented the Morpher family in the progressive stages of petrifaction, and had the
Medusa-like effect of freezing visitors into similar atti-
tudes in their chairs. The walls were further enlivened
with two colored engravings of scenes in the domestic
history of George Washington, in which the Father of his
Country seemed to look blandly from his own correct
family circle into Morpher's, and to breathe quite audibly
from his gilt frame a dignified blessing.

Lingering a moment in this sacred enclosure to readjust
the tablecloth, Mrs. Morpher passed into the dining
room, where the correct Clytie presided at the supper
table at which the rest of the family were seated. Mrs.
Morpher's quick eyes caught the spectacle of M'liss with
her chin resting on her hands and her elbows on the
table, sardonically surveying the model of deportment
opposite to her.

"M'liss!"

"Well?"

"Where's your elbows?"

"Here's one and there's the other," said M'liss quietly,
indicating their respective localities by smartly tapping
them with the palm of her hand.

"Take them off the table instantly, you bold, forward
girl—and you, sir, quit that giggling and eat your supper,
if you don't want to be put to bed without it!" added
Mrs. Morpher to Lycurgus, to whom M'liss's answer had

afforded boundless satisfaction. "You're getting to be just as bad as her, and mercy knows you never were a seraphim!"

"What's a seraphim, mother, and what do they do?" asked Lycurgus with growing interest.

"They don't ask questions when they should be eating their supper, and thankful for it," interposed Clytie authoritatively, as one to whom the genteel attributes and social habits of the seraphim had been a privileged revelation.

"But, mother—"

"Hush—and don't be a heathen—run and see who is coming in," said Mrs. Morpher, as the sound of footsteps was heard in the passage.

The door opened and McSnagley entered.

"Why, bless my soul—how do you do?" said Mrs. Morpher, with genteel astonishment. "Quite a stranger, I declare."

This was a polite fiction. M'liss knew the fact to be that Mrs. Morpher was reputed to "set the best table" in Smith's Pocket, and McSnagley always called in on Sunday evenings at supper to discuss the current gossip, and "nag" M'liss with selected texts.

The verbal McSnagley as usual couldn't stop a moment —and just dropped in "in passin'." The actual McSnagley deposited his hat in the corner, and placed himself, in the flesh, on a chair by the table.

"And how's Brother James, and the fammerly?"

"They're all well—except 'Risty'; he's off again—as if my life weren't already pestered out with one child," and Mrs. Morpher glanced significantly at M'liss.

"Ah, well, we all of us have our trials," said McSnagley. "I've been ailin' again. That ager must be in my bones still. I've been rather onsettled myself today."

There was the appearance of truth in this statement; Mr. McSnagley's voice had a hollow resonant sound, and his eyes were nervous and fidgety. He had an odd trick, too, of occasionally stopping in the middle of a sentence, and listening as though he heard some distant sound. These things, which Mrs. Morpher recalled afterwards, did not, in the undercurrent of uneasiness about Aristides which she felt the whole of that evening, so particularly attract her notice.

"I know something," said Lycurgus, during one of these pauses, from the retirement of his corner.

"If you dare to—Kerg!" said M'liss.

"M'liss says she knows where Risty is, but she won't tell," said the lawgiver, not heeding the warning. The words were scarcely uttered before M'liss's red hand flashed in the air and descended with a sounding box on the traitor's ear. Lycurgus howled, Mrs. Morpher darted into the corner, and M'liss was dragged defiant and struggling to the light.

"Oh, you wicked, wicked child—why don't you say where, if you know?" said Mrs. Morpher, shaking her, as if the information were to be dislodged from some concealed part of her clothing.

"I didn't say I knew for sure," at last responded M'liss. "I said I thought I knew."

"Well, where do you think he is?"

But M'liss was firm. Even the gloomy picture of the future state devised by McSnagley could not alter her determination. Mrs. Morpher, who had a wholesome awe for this strange child, at last had recourse to entreaty. Finally M'liss offered a compromise.

"I'll tell the master, but I won't tell you—partikerly him," said M'liss, indicating the parson with a bodkin-like dart of her forefinger.

Mrs. Morpher hesitated. Her maternal anxiety at length overcame her sense of dignity and discipline.

"Who knows where the master is, or where he is to be found tonight?" she asked hastily.

"He's over to Dr. Duchesne's," said Clytie eagerly; "that is," she stammered, a rich color suddenly flushing from her temples to her round shoulders, "he's usually there in the evenings, I mean."

"Run over, there's a dear, and ask him to come here," said Mrs. Morpher, without noticing a sudden irregularity of conduct in her first-born. "Run quick!"

Clytie did not wait for a second command. Without availing herself of the proffered company of McSnagley she hastily tied the strings of her school hat under her plump chin, and slipped out of the house. It was not far to the doctor's office, and Clytie walked quickly, overlooking in her haste and preoccupation the admiring glances which several of the swains of Smith's Pocket cast after her as she passèd. But on arriving at the doctor's door, so out of breath and excited was this usual model of deportment that, on finding herself in the presence of the master and his friend, she only stood in embarrassed silence, and made up for her lack of verbal expression by a succession of eloquent blushes.

Let us look at her for a moment as she stands there. Her little straw hat, trimmed with cherry-colored ribbons, rests on the waves of her blonde hair. There are other gay ribbons on her light summer dress, clasping her round waist, girdling her wrist, and fastening her collar about her white throat. Her large blue eyes are very dark and moist—it may be with excitement or a tearful thought of the lost Aristides—or the tobacco smoke, with which I regret to say the room is highly charged. But certainly as she stands leaning against the doorway, biting her moist scarlet lip, and trying to pull down the broad brim of her hat over the surging waves of color that *will* beat rhythmically up to her cheeks and temples, she is so dangerously pretty that I am glad for the master's sake he is the philosopher he has just described himself to his friend the doctor, and that he prefers to study human physiology from the inner surfaces.

When Clytie had recovered herself sufficiently to state her message, the master offered to accompany her back. As Clytie took his arm with some slight trepidation Dr. Duchesne, who had taken sharp notes of these "febrile" symptoms, uttered a prolonged whistle and returned thoughtfully to his office.

Although Clytie found the distance returning no further than the distance going, with the exhaustion of her first journey it was natural that her homeward steps should be slower, and that the master should regulate his pace to accommodate her. It was natural, too, that her voice should be quite low and indistinct, so that the master was obliged to bring his hat nearer the cherry-colored ribbons in the course of conversation. It was also natural that he should offer the sensitive young girl such comfort as lay in tenderly modulated tones and playful epithets.

And if in the irregularities of the main street it was necessary to take Clytie's hand or to put his arm around her
waist in helping her up declivities, that the master saw no
impropriety in the act was evident from the fact that he
did not remove his arm when the difficulty was surmounted. In this way Clytie's return occupied some moments more than her going, and Mrs. Morpher was waiting
anxiously at the door when the young people arrived.

As the master entered the room, M'liss called him to
her. "Bend down your head," she said, "and I'll whisper.
But mind, now, I don't say I know for truth where Risty
is, I only reckon."

The master bent down his head. As usual in such cases,
everybody else felt constrained to listen, and McSnagley's
curiosity was awakened to its fullest extent. When the
master had received the required information, he said
quietly:

"I think I'll go myself to this place which M'liss wishes
to make a secret of and see if the boy is there. It will
save trouble to anyone else, if she should be mistaken."

"Hadn't you better take someone with you?" said Mrs.
Morpher.

"By all means. I'll go!" said Mr. McSnagley, with feverish alacrity.

The master looked inquiringly at M'liss.

"He can go if he wants to, but he'd better not," said
M'liss, looking directly into McSnagley's eyes.

"What do you mean by that, you little savage?" said
McSnagley quickly.

M'liss turned scornfully away. "Go," she said—"go
if you want to," and resumed her seat in the corner.

The master hesitated. But he could not withstand the
appeal in the eyes of the mother and daughter, and after
a short inward struggle he turned to McSnagley and bade
him briefly "Come."

When they had left the house and stood in the road
together, McSnagley stopped.

"Where are you goin'?"

"To Smith's Pocket."

McSnagley still lingered. "Do you ever carry any weppings?" he at length asked.

"Weapons? No. What do you want with weapons to

go a mile on a starlit road to a deserted claim. Nonsense, man, what are you thinking of? We're hunting a lost child, not a runaway felon. Come along," and the master dragged him away.

Mrs. Morpher watched them from the door until their figures were lost in the darkness. When she returned to the dining room, Clytie had already retired to her room, and Mrs. Morpher, overruling M'liss's desire to sit up until the master returned, bade her follow that correct example. "There's Clytie now, gone to bed like a young lady, and do you do like her," and Mrs. Morpher, with this one drop of balm in the midst of her trials, trimmed the light and sat down in patience to wait for Aristides, and console herself with the reflection of Clytie's excellence. "Poor Clytie!" mused that motherly woman; "how excited and worried she looks about her brother. I hope she'll be able to get to sleep."

It did not occur to Mrs. Morpher that there were seasons in the life of young girls when younger brothers ceased to become objects of extreme solicitude. It did not occur to her to go upstairs and see how her wish was likely to be gratified. It was well in her anxiety that she did not, and that the crowning trial of the day's troubles was spared her then. For at that moment Clytie was lying on the bed where she had flung herself without undressing, the heavy masses of her blonde hair tumbled about her neck, and her hot face buried in her hands.

Of what was the correct Clytie thinking?

She was thinking, lying there with her burning cheeks pressed against the pillow, that she loved the master! She was recalling step by step every incident that had occurred in their lonely walk. She was repeating to herself his facile sentences, wringing and twisting them to extract one drop to assuage the strange thirst that was growing up in her soul. She was thinking—silly Clytie!— that he had never appeared so kind before, and she was thinking—sillier Clytie!—that no one had ever before felt as she did then.

How soft and white his hands were! How sweet and gentle were the tones of his voice! How easily he spoke— so unlike her father, McSnagley, or the young men whom she met at church or on picnics! How tall and handsome he looked as he pressed her hand at the door! Did he press her hand, or was it a mistake? Yes, he must have pressed her hand, for she remembers now to have pressed his in return. And he put his arm around her waist once, and she feels it yet, and the strange perfume as he drew her closer to him. (Mem.—The master had been smoking. Poor Clytie!)

When she had reached this point she raised herself and sat up, and began the process of undressing, mechanically putting each article away in the precise, methodical habit of her former life. But she found herself soon sitting again on the bed, twisting her hair, which fell over her plump white shoulders, idly between her fingers, and patting the carpet with her small white foot. She had been sitting thus some minutes when she heard the sound of voices without, the trampling of many feet, and a loud rapping at the door below. She sprang to the door and looked out in the passage. Something white passed by her like a flash and crouched down at the head of the stairs. It was M'liss.

Mrs. Morpher opened the door.

"Is Mr. Morpher in?" said a half dozen strange, hoarse voices.

"No!"

"Where is he?"

"He's at some of the saloons. Oh, tell me, has anything happened? Is it about Aristides? Where is he—is he safe?" said Mrs. Morpher, wringing her hands in agony.

"He's all right," said one of the men, with Mr. Morpher's old emphasis; "but—"

"But what?"

M'liss moved slowly down the staircase, and Clytie from the passage above held her breath.

"There's been a row down to Smith's old Pocket—a fight—a man killed."

"Who?" shouted M'liss from the stairs.

"McSnagley—shot dead."

CHAPTER SEVEN

The People   }
      vs.   } *Before Chief Justice Lynch*
John Doe Waters }

The hurried statement of the messenger was corroborated in the streets that night. It was certain that Mc-Snagley was killed. Smith's Pocket, excited but skeptical, had seen the body, had put its fingers in the bullethole, and was satisfied. Smith's Pocket, albeit hoarse with shouting and excitement, still discussed details with infinite relish in barrooms and saloons, and in the main street in clamorous knots that in front of the jail where the prisoner was confined seemed to swell into a mob. Smith's Pocket, bearded, blue shirted, and belligerent, crowding about this locality, from time to time uttered appeals to justice that swelled on the night wind, not infrequently coupling these invocations with the name of that eminent jurist—Lynch.

Let not the simple reader suppose that the mere taking off of a fellow mortal had created this uproar. The tenure of life in Smith's Pocket was vain and uncertain at the best, and as such philosophically accepted, and the blowing out of a brief candle here and there seldom left a permanent shadow with the survivors. In such instances, too, the victims had received their quietus from the hands of brother townsmen, socially, as it were, in broad day, in the open streets, and under other mitigating circumstances. Thus, when Judge Starbottle of Virginia and "French Pete" exchanged shots with each other across the plaza until their revolvers were exhausted, and the luckless Pete received a bullet through the lungs, half the town witnessed it, and were struck with the gallant and chivalrous bearing of these gentlemen, and to this day point with feelings of pride and admiration to the bulletholes in the door of the National Hotel, as they explain how narrow was the escape of the women in the parlor. But here was a man murdered at night, in a lonely place,

and by a stranger—a man unknown to the saloons of
Smith's Pocket—a wretch who could not plead the excitement of monte or the delirium of whiskey as an excuse. No wonder that Smith's Pocket surged with virtuous
indignation beneath the windows of his prison, and clam-
ored for his blood.

And as the crowd thickened and swayed to and fro, the
story of his crime grew exaggerated by hurried and frequent repetition. Half a dozen speakers volunteered to give
the details with an added horror to every sentence. How
one of Morpher's children had been missing for a week
or more. How the schoolmaster and the parson were
taking a walk that evening, and coming to Smith's Pocket
heard a faint voice from its depths which they recognized
as belonging to the missing child. How they had succeeded in dragging him out and gathered from his infant
lips the story of his incarceration by the murderer, Waters, and his enforced labors in the mine. How they
were interrupted by the appearance of Waters, followed
by a highly colored and epithet-illustrated account of the
interview and quarrel. How Waters struck the schoolmaster, who returned the blow with a pick. How
Waters thereupon drew a derringer and fired, missing the
schoolmaster, but killing McSnagley behind him. How it
was believed that Waters was one of Joaquin's gang, that
he had killed Smith, etc., etc. At each pause the crowd
pushed and panted, stealthily creeping around the doors
and windows of the jail like some strange beast of prey,
until the climax was reached, and a hush fell, and two
men were silently dispatched for a rope, and a critical
examination was made of the limbs of a pine tree in the
vicinity.

The man to whom these incidents had the most terrible
significance might have seemed the least concerned as he
sat that night but a few feet removed from the eager
crowd without, his hands lightly clasped together between
his knees, and the expression on his face of one whose
thoughts were far away. A candle stuck in a tin sconce on
the wall flickered as the night wind blew freshly through a
broken pane of the window. Its uncertain light revealed
a low room whose cloth ceiling was stained and ragged,
and from whose boarded walls the torn paper hung in

strips; a lumber room partitioned from the front office, which was occupied by a justice of the peace. If this temporary dungeon had an appearance of insecurity, there was some compensation in the spectacle of an armed sentinel who sat upon a straw mattress in the doorway, and another who patrolled the narrow hall which led to the street. That the prisoner was not placed in one of the cells in the floor below may have been owing to the fact that the law recognized his detention as only temporary, and while providing the two guards as a preventive against the egress of crime within, discreetly removed all unnecessary and provoking obstacles to the ingress of justice from without.

Since the prisoner's arrest he had refused to answer any interrogatories. Since he had been placed in confinement he had not moved from his present attitude. The guard, finding all attempts at conversation fruitless, had fallen into a reverie, and regaled himself with pieces of straw plucked from the mattress. A mouse ran across the floor. The silence contrasted strangely with the hum of voices in the street.

The candlelight, falling across the prisoner's forehead, showed the features which Smith's Pocket knew and recognized as Waters, the strange prospector. Had M'liss or Aristides seen him then they would have missed that sinister expression which was part of their fearful remembrance. The hard, grim outlines of his mouth were relaxed, the broad shoulders were bent and contracted, the quick, searching eyes were fixed on vacancy. The strong man—physically strong only—was breaking up. The fist that might have felled an ox could do nothing more than separate its idle fingers with childishness of power and purpose. An hour longer in this condition and the gallows would have claimed a figure scarcely less limp and impotent than that it was destined to ultimately reject.

He had been trying to collect his thoughts. Would they hang him? No, they must try him first, legally, and he could prove—he could prove— But what could he prove? For whenever he attempted to consider the uncertain chances of his escape, he found his thoughts straying wide of the question. It was of no use for him to clasp his fingers or knit his brows. Why did the recollection of a schoolfellow long since forgotten blot out all the fierce and feverish memories of the night and the terrible certainty of the future? Why did the strips of paper hanging from the wall recall to him the pattern of a kite he had flown forty years ago. In a moment like this, when all his energies were required and all his cunning and tact would be called into service, could he think of nothing better than trying to match the torn paper on the wall, or to count the cracks in the floor? And an oath rose to his lips, but from very feebleness died away without expression.

Why had he ever come to Smith's Pocket? If he had not been guided by that hellcat, this would not have happened. What if he were to tell *all* he knew? What if he should accuse *her?* But would they be willing to give up the bird they had already caught? Yet he again found himself cursing his own treachery and cowardice, and this time an exclamation burst from his lips and attracted the attention of the guard.

"Hello, there! easy, old fellow; thar ain't any good in that," said the sentinel, looking up. "It's a bad fix you're in, *sure,* but rarin' and pitchin' won't help things. 'T ain't no use cussin'—leastways, 't ain't that kind o' swearing that gets a chap out o' here," he added, with a conscientious reservation. "Now, ef I was in your place, I'd kinder reflect on my sins, and make my peace with God Almighty, for I tell you the looks o' them people outside ain't pleasant. You're in the hands of the law, and the law will protect you as far as it can—as far as two men can stand agin a hundred; sabe? That's what's the matter; and it's as well that you knowed that now as any time."

But the prisoner had relapsed into his old attitude, and was surveying the jailor with the same abstraced air as before. That individual resumed his seat on the mattress, and now lent his ear to a colloquy which seemed to be progressing at the foot of the stairs. Presently he was hailed by his brother turnkey from below.

"Oh, Bill," said fidus Achates from the passage, with the usual Californian prefatory ejaculation.

"Well?"

"Here's M'liss! Says she wants to come up. Shall I let her in?"

The subject of inquiry, however, settled the question of admission by darting past the guard below in this moment of preoccupation, and bounded up the stairs like a young fawn. The guards laughed.

"Now, then, my infant phenomenon," said the one called Bill, as M'liss stood panting before him, "wot's up? and nextly, wot's in that bottle?"

M'liss whisked the bottle which she held in her hand smartly under her apron, and said curtly, "Where's him that killed the parson?"

"Yonder," replied the man, indicating the abstracted figure with his hand. "Wot do *you* want with him? None o' your tricks here, now," he added threateningly.

"I want to see him!"

"Well, look! make the most of your time, and *his* too, for the matter of that; but mind, now, no nonsense, M'liss, he won't stand it!" repeated the guard with an emphasis in the caution.

M'liss crossed the room until opposite the prisoner. "Are you the chap that killed the parson?" she said, addressing the motionless figure.

Something in the tone of her voice startled the prisoner from the reverie. He raised his head and glanced quickly, and with his old sinister expression, at the child.

"What's that to you?" he asked, with the grim lines setting about his mouth again, and the old harshness of his voice.

"Didn't I tell you he wouldn't stand any of your nonsense, M'liss?" said the guard testily.

M'liss only repeated her question.

"And what if I did kill him?" said the prisoner savagely; "what's that to you, you young hellcat? Guard! —damnation!—what do you let her come here for? Do you hear? Guard!" he screamed, rising in a transport of passion, "take her away! fling her downstairs! What the h—ll is she doing here?"

"If you was the man that killed McSnagley," said M'liss, without heeding the interruption, "I've brought you something;" and she drew the bottle from under her apron and extended it to Waters, adding, "It's brandy— Cognac—A-1."

"Take it away, and take yourself with it," returned

Waters, without abating his angry accents. "Take it away! do you hear?"

"Well, that's what I call ongrateful, doggone my skin if it ain't," said the guard, who had been evidently struck with M'liss's generosity. "Pass the licker this way, my beauty, and I'll keep it till he changes his mind. He's naturally a little flustered just now, but he'll come round after you go."

But M'liss didn't accede to this change in the disposition of the gift, and was evidently taken aback by her reception and the refusal of the proffered comfort.

"Come, hand the bottle here!" repeated the guard. "It's agin rules to bring the pris'ner anything, anyway, and it's confiscated to the law. It's agin the rules, too, to ask a pris'ner any question that'll criminate him, and on the whole you'd better go, M'liss," added the guard, to whom the appearance of the bottle had been the means of provoking a spasm of discipline.

But M'liss refused to make over the coveted treasure. Bill arose half jestingly and endeavored to get possession of the bottle. A struggle ensued, good-naturedly on the part of the guard, but characterized on the part of M'liss by that half-savage passion which any thwarted whim or instinct was sure to provoke in her nature. At last with a curse she freed herself from his grasp, and seizing the bottle by the neck aimed it with the full strength of her little arm fairly at his head. But he was quick enough to avert that important object, if not quick enough to save his shoulder from receiving the strength of the blow, which shattered the thin glass and poured the fiery contents of the bottle over his shirt and breast, saturating his clothes, and diffusing a sharp alcoholic odor through the room.

A forced laugh broke from his lips, as he sank back on the mattress, not without an underlying sense of awe at this savage girl who stood panting before him, and from whom he had just escaped a blow which might have been fatal. "It's a pity to waste so much good licker," he added, with affected carelessness, narrowly watching each movement of the young pythoness, whose rage was not yet abated.

"Come, M'liss," he said at last, "we'll say quits. You've

lost your brandy, and I've got some of the pieces of yonder bottle sticking in my shoulder yet. I suppose brandy is good for bruises, though. Hand me the light!"

M'liss reached the candle from the sconce and held it by the guard as he turned back the collar of his shirt to lay bare his shoulder. "So," he muttered, "black and blue; no bones broken, though no fault of yours, eh? my young cherub, if it wasn't. There—why, what are you looking at in that way, M'liss, are you crazy?—hell's furies, don't hold the light so near! What are you doing; hell—ho, there! Help!"

Too late, for in an instant he was a sheet of living flame. When or how the candle had touched his garments, saturated with the inflammable fluid, Waters, the only inactive spectator in the room, could never afterward tell. He only knew that the combustion was instantaneous and complete, and before the cry had died from his lips, not only the guard, but the straw mattress on which he had been sitting, and the loose strips of paper hanging from the walls, and the torn cloth ceiling above were in flames.

"Help! Help! Fire! Fire!"

With a superhuman effort, M'liss dragged the prisoner past the blazing mattress, through the doorway into the passage, and drew the door, which opened outwardly, against him. The unhappy guard, still blazing like a funeral pyre, after wildly beating the air with his arms for a few seconds, dashed at the broken window, which gave way with his weight and precipitated him, still flaming, into the yard below. A column of smoke and a licking tongue of flame leaped from the open window at the same moment, and the cry of fire was re-echoed from a hundred voices in the street. But scarcely had M'liss closed the open door against Waters, when the guard from the doorway mounted the stairs in time to see a flaming figure leap from the window. The room was filled with smoke and fire. With an instinct of genius, M'liss, pointing to the open window, shouted hoarsely in his ear:

"Waters has escaped!"

A cry of fury from the guard was echoed from the stairs, even now crowded by the excited mob, who feared the devastating element might still cheat them of their intended victim. In another moment the house was emptied, and the front street deserted, as the people rushed to the rear of the jail—climbing fences and stumbling over ditches in pursuit of the imagined runaway. M'liss seized the hat and coat of the luckless "Bill," and dragging the prisoner from his place of concealment hurriedly equipped him, and hastened through the blinding smoke of the staircase boldly on the heels of the retiring crowd. Once in the friendly darkness of the street, it was easy to mingle with the pushing throng until an alley crossing at right angles enabled them to leave the main thoroughfare. A few moments' rapid flight, and the outskirts of the town were reached, the tall pines opened their abysmal aisles to the fugitives, and M'liss paused with her companion. Until daybreak, at least, here they were safe!

From the time they had quitted the burning room to that moment, Waters had passed into his listless, abstracted condition, so helpless and feeble that he retained the grasp of M'liss's hand more through some instinctive prompting rather than the dictates of reason. M'liss had found it necessary to almost drag him from the main street and the hurrying crowd, which seemed to exercise a strange fascination over his bewildered senses. And now he sat down passively beside her, and seemed to submit to the guidance of her superior nature.

"You're safe enough now till daylight," said M'liss, when she had recovered her breath, "but you must make the best time you can through these woods tonight, keeping the wind to your back, until you come to the Wingdam road. There! do you hear?" said M'liss, a little vexed at her companion's apathy.

Waters released the hand of M'liss, and commenced mechanically to button his coat around his chest with fumbling, purposeless fingers. He then passed his hand across his forehead as if to clear his confused and bewildered brain; all this, however, to no better result than to apparently root his feet to the soil and to intensify the stupefaction which seemed to be creeping over him.

"Be quick, now! You've no time to lose! Keep straight on through the woods until you see the stars again before you, and you're on the other side of the ridge.

What are you waiting for?" And M'liss stamped her little foot impatiently.

An idea which had been struggling for expression at last seemed to dawn in his eyes. Something like a simpering blush crept over his face as he fumbled in his pocket. At last, drawing forth a twenty-dollar piece, he bashfully offered it to M'liss. In a twinkling the extended arm was stricken up, and the bright coin flew high in the air, and disappeared in the darkness.

"Keep your money! I don't want it. Don't do that again!" said M'liss, highly excited, "or I'll—I'll—bite you!"

Her wicked little white teeth flashed ominously as she said it.

"Get off while you can. Look!" she added, pointing to a column of flame shooting up above the straggling mass of buildings in the village, "the jail is burning; and if that goes, the block will go with it. Before morning these woods will be filled with people. Save yourself while you can!"

Waters turned and moved away in the darkness. "Keep straight on, and don't waste a moment," urged the child, as the man seemed still disposed to linger. "Trot now!" and in another moment he seemed to melt into the forest depths.

M'liss threw her apron around her head, and coiled herself up at the root of a tree in something of her old fashion. She had prophesied truly of the probable extent of the fire. The fresh wind, whirling the sparks over the little settlement, had already fanned the single flame into the broad sheet which now glowed fiercely, defining the main street along its entire length. The breeze which fanned her cheek bore the crash of falling timbers and the shouts of terrified and anxious men. There were no engines in Smith's Pocket, and the contest was unequal. Nothing but a change of wind could save the doomed settlement.

The red glow lit up the dark cheek of M'liss and kindled a savage light in her black eyes. Relieved by the background of the somber woods, she might have been a red-handed Nemesis looking over the city of Vengeance. As the long tongues of flame licked the broad colonnade of the National Hotel and shot a wreathing pillar of fire and smoke high into the air, M'liss extended her tiny fist and shook it at the burning building with an inspiration that at the moment seemed to transfigure her.

So the night wore away until the first red bars of morning light gleamed beyond the hill, and seemed to emulate the dying embers of the devastated settlement. M'liss for the first time began to think of the home she had quitted the night before, and looked with some anxiety in the direction of "Mountain Ranch." Its white walls and little orchard were untouched, and looked peacefully over the blackened and deserted village. M'liss rose, and stretching her cramped limbs, walked briskly toward the town. She had proceeded but a short distance when she heard the sound of cautious and hesitating footsteps behind her, and facing quickly about, encountered the figure of Waters.

"Are you drunk?" said M'liss passionately, "or what do you mean by this nonsense?"

The man approached her with a strange smile on his face, rubbing his hands together and shivering as with cold. When he had reached her side he attempted to take her hand. M'liss shrank away from him with an expression of disgust.

"What are you doing here again?" she demanded.

"I want to go with you. It's dark in there," he said, motioning to the wood he had just quitted, "and I don't like to be alone. You'll let me be with you, won't you? I won't be any trouble;" and a feeble smile flickered on his lips.

M'liss darted a quick look into his face. The grim outlines of his mouth were relaxed, and his lips moved again impotently. But his eyes were bright and open—bright with a look that was new to M'liss—that imparted a strange softness and melancholy to his features—the incipient gleam of insanity!

CHAPTER EIGHT

The Author to the Reader—Explanatory

If I remember rightly, in one of the admirable tragedies of Tsien Tsiang at a certain culminating point of interest an innocent person is about to be sacrificed. The knife is raised and the victim meekly awaits the stroke. At this moment the author of the play appears on the stage, and delivering an excellent philosophical dissertation on the merits of the "situation," shows that by the purest principles of art the sacrifice is necessary, but at the same time offers to the audience the privilege of changing the dénouement. Such, however, is the nice aesthetic sense of a Chinese auditory, and so universal the desire of bloodshed in the heathen breast, that invariably at each representation of this remarkable tragedy the cause of humanity gives way to the principles of art.

I offer this precedent as an excuse for digressing at a moment when I have burned down a small settlement, dispatched a fellow being, and left my heroine alone in the company of an escaped convict who has just developed insanity as a new social quality. My object in thus digressing is to confer with the reader in regard to the evolution of this story—a familiarity not without precedent, as I might prove from most of the old Greek comedies, whose *parabasis* permits the poet to mingle freely with the *dramatis personæ,* to address the audience and descant at length in regard to himself, his play, and his own merits.

The fact is that during the progress of this story I have received many suggestions from intimate friends in regard to its incidents and construction. I have also been in the receipt of correspondence from distant readers, one letter of which I recall signed by an "Honest Miner," who advises me to "do the right thing by M'liss," or intimates somewhat obscurely that he will "bust my crust for me," which, though complimentary in its abstract expression of interest and implying a taste for euphonism, evinces an innate coarseness which I fear may blunt his perceptions of delicate shades and Greek outlines.

Again, the practical nature of Californians and their familiarity with scenes and incidents which would be novel to other people have occasioned me great uneasiness. In the course of the last three chapters of M'liss I have received some twenty or thirty communications from different parts of the State corroborating incidents of my story, which I solemnly assure the reader is purely fictitious. Someone has lately sent me a copy of an interior paper containing an old obituary of Smith of Smith's Pocket. Another correspondent writes to me that he was acquainted with the schoolmaster in the fall of '49, and that they "grubbed together." The editors of the serial in which this story appears assure me that they have received an advertisement from the landlord of the "National Hotel" contingent upon an editorial notice of its having been at one time the abode of M'liss; while an aunt of the heroine, alluding in excellent terms to the reformed character of her niece M'liss, clenches her sincerity by requesting the loan of twenty dollars to buy clothes for the desolate orphan.

Under these circumstances I have hesitated to go on. What were the bodiless creatures of my fancy—the pale phantoms of thought, evoked in the solitude of my chamber, and sometimes even midst the hum of busy streets—have suddenly grown into flesh and blood, living people, protected by the laws of society, and having their legal right to actions for slander in any court. Worse than that, I have sometimes thought with terror of the new responsibility which might attach to my development of their characters. What if I were obliged to support and protect these Frankenstein monsters? What if the original of the principal villain of my story should feel impelled through aesthetic principles of art to work out in real life the supposititious dénouement I have sketched for him?

I have therefore concluded to lay aside my pen for this week, leaving the catastrophe impending, and await the suggestion of my correspondents. I do so the more cheerfully as it enables the editors of this weekly to publish twenty-seven more columns of Miss Braddon's "Outcasts of Society" and the remainder of the "Duke's Motto"—two works which in the quiet simplicity of their homelike pictures and household incidents are attended with none of the difficulties which beset my unhappy story.

CHAPTER NINE

Cleaning Up

As the master, wan-eyed and unrefreshed by slumber, strayed the next morning among the blackened ruins of the fire, he was conscious of having undergone some strange revulsion of sentiment. What he remembered of the last evening's events, though feverish and indistinct as a dream, and though, like a dream, without coherency or connected outline, had nevertheless seriously impressed him. How frivolous and trifling his past life and its pursuits looked through the lightning vista opened to his eyes by the flash of Waters's pistol! "Suppose I had been killed," ruminated the master, "what then? A paragraph in the *Banner,* headed 'Fatal Affray,' and my name added to the already swollen list of victims to lawless violence and crime! Humph! A pretty scrape, truly!" And the master ground his teeth with vexation.

Let not the reader judge him too hastily. In the best regulated mind, thankfulness for deliverance from danger is apt to be mingled with some doubts as to the necessity of the trial.

In this frame of mind the last person he would have cared to meet was Clytie. That young woman's evil genius, however, led her to pass the burnt district that morning. Perhaps she had anticipated the meeting. At all events, he had proceeded but a few steps before he was confronted by the identical round hat and cherry-colored ribbons. But in his present humor the cheerful color somehow reminded him of the fire and of a ruddy stain over McSnagley's heart, and invested the innocent Clytie with a figurative significance. Now Clytie's reveries at that moment were pleasant, if the brightness of her eyes and the freshened color on her cheeks were any sign,

and as she had not seen the master since then, she
naturally expected to take up the thread of romance
where it had been dropped. But it required all her feminine tact to conceal her embarrassment at his formal
greeting and constrained manner.

"He is bashful," reasoned Clytie to herself.

"This girl is a tremendous fool," growled the master
inwardly.

An awkward pause ensued. Finally, Clytie *loquitur:*
"M'liss has been missing since the fire!"

"Missing?" echoed the master in his natural tone.

Clytie bit her lip with vexation. "Yes, she's always
running away. She'll be back again. But you look interested. Do you know," she continued with exceeding
archness, "I sometimes think, Mr. Gray, if M'liss were a
little older—"

"Well?"

"Well, putting this and that together, you know!"

"Well?"

"People will talk, you know," continued Clytie, with
that excessive fondness weak people exhibit in envelop-
ing in mystery the commonest affairs of life.

"People are d——d fools!" roared the master.

The correct Clytie was a little shocked. Perhaps under-
neath it was a secret admiration of the transgressor.
Force even of this cheap quality goes a good way with
some natures.

"That is," continued the master, with an increase of
dignity in inverse proportion to the lapse he had made,
"people are apt to be mistaken, Miss Morpher, and without meaning it, to do infinite injustice to their fellow
mortals. But I see I am detaining you. I will try and
find Melissa. I wish you good morning." And Don Whisk-
erandos stalked solemnly away.

Clytie turned red and white by turns, and her eyes
filled with tears. This dénouement to her dreams was
utterly unexpected. While a girl of stronger character
and active intelligence would have employed the time in
digesting plans of future retaliation and revenge, Clytie's
dull brain and placid nature were utterly perplexed and
shaken.

"Dear me!" said Clytie to herself, as she started home, "if he don't love me, why don't he say so?"

The master, or Mr. Gray, as we may now call him as he draws near the close of his professional career, took the old trail through the forest, which led to M'liss's former hiding place. He walked on briskly, revolving in his mind the feasibility of leaving Smith's Pocket. The late disaster, which would affect the prosperity of the settlement for some time to come, offered an excuse to him to give up his situation. On searching his pockets he found his present capital to amount to ten dollars. This increased by forty dollars due him from the trustees would make fifty dollars; deduct thirty dollars for liabilities, and he would have twenty dollars left to begin the world anew. Youth and hope added an indefinite number of ciphers to the right hand of these figures, and in this sanguine mood our young Alnaschar walked on until he had reached the old pine throne in the bank of the forest. M'liss was not there. He sat down on the trunk of the tree, and for a few moments gave himself up to the associations it suggested. What would become of M'liss after he was gone? But he quickly dropped the subject as one too visionary and sentimental for his then fiercely practical consideration, and to prevent the recurrence of such distracting fancies, began to retrace his steps toward the settlement. At the edge of the woods, at a point where the trail forked toward the old site of Smith's Pocket, he saw M'liss coming toward him. Her ordinary pace on such occasions was a kind of Indian trot; to his surprise she was walking slowly, with her apron thrown over her head—an indication of meditation with M'liss and the usual way in which she excluded the outer world in studying her lessons. When she was within a few feet of him he called her by name. She started as she recognized him. There was a shade of seriousness in her dark eyes, and the hand that took his was listless and totally unlike her old frank, energetic grasp.

"You look worried, M'liss," said Mr. Gray soothingly, as the old sentimental feeling crept over his heart. "What's the matter now?"

M'liss replied by seating herself on the bank beside

the road, and pointed to a place by her side. Mr. Gray took the proffered seat. M'liss then, fixing her eyes on some distant part of the view, remained for some moments in silence. Then, without turning her head or moving her eyes, she asked:

"What's that they call a girl that has money left her?"

"An heiress, M'liss?"

"Yes, an heiress."

"Well?" said Mr. Gray.

"Well," said M'liss, without moving her eyes, "I'm one —I'm a heiress!"

"What's that, M'liss?" said Mr. Gray laughingly.

M'liss was silent again. Suddenly turning her eyes full upon him, she said:

"Can you keep a secret?"

"Yes," said Mr. Gray, beginning to be impressed by the child's manner.

"Listen, then."

In short quick sentences, M'liss began. How Aristides had several times hinted of the concealed riches of Smith's Pocket. How he had last night repeated the story to her of a strange discovery he had made. How she remembered to have heard her father often swear that there was money "in that hole," if he only had means to work it. How, partly impressed by this statement and partly from curiosity and pity for the prisoner, she had visited him in confinement. An account of her interview, the origin of the fire, her flight with Waters. (*Questions* by Mr. Gray: What was your object in assisting this man to escape? *Ans.* They were going to kill him. *Ques.* Hadn't he killed McSnagley. *Ans.* Yes, but McSnagley ought to have been killed long ago.) How she had taken leave of him that morning. How he had come back again "silly." How she had dragged him on toward the Wingdam road, and how he had told her that all the hidden wealth of Smith's Pocket had belonged to her father. How she had found out from some questions that he had known her father. But how all his other answers were "silly."

"And where is he now?" asked Mr. Gray.

"Gone," said M'liss. "I left him at the edge of the wood to go back and get some provisions, and when I returned he was gone. If he had any senses left, he's miles away by this time. When he was off I went back to Smith's Pocket. I found the hidden opening and saw the gold."

Mr. Gray looked at her curiously. He had, in his more intimate knowledge of her character, noticed the unconcern with which she spoke of the circumstances of her father's death and the total lack of any sentiment of filial regard. The idea that this man whom she had aided in escaping had ever done her injury had not apparently entered her mind, nor did Mr. Gray think it necessary to hint the deeper suspicion he had gathered from Dr. Duchesne that Waters had murdered her father. If the story of the concealed treasures of Smith's Pocket were exaggerated he could easily satisfy himself on that point. M'liss met his suggestion to return to the Pocket with alacrity, and the two started away in that direction.

It was late in the afternoon when Mr. Gray returned. His heightened color and eager inquiry for Dr. Duchesne provoked the usual hope from the people that he met "that it was nothing serious." No, nothing was the matter, the master answered with a slight laugh, but would they send the doctor to his schoolhouse when he returned? "That young chap's worse than he thinks," was one sympathizing suggestion; "this kind of life's too rough for his sort."

To while away the interim, Mr. Gray stopped on his way to the schoolhouse at the stage office as the Wingdam stage drew up and disgorged its passengers. He was listlessly watching the passengers as they descended when a soft voice from the window addressed him, "May I trouble you for your arm as I get down?" Mr. Gray looked up. It was a singular request, as the driver was at that moment standing by the door, apparently for that purpose. But the request came from a handsome woman, and with a bow the young man stepped to the door. The lady laid her hand lightly on his arm, sprang from the stage with a dexterity that showed the service to have been merely ceremonious, thanked him with an elaboration of acknowledgment which seemed equally gratuitous, and disappeared in the office.

"That's what I call a dead set," said the driver, drawing a long breath, as he turned to Mr. Gray, who stood in some embarrassment. "Do you know her?"

"No," said Mr. Gray laughingly, "do you?"

"Nary time! But take care of yourself, young man; she's after you, sure!"

But Mr. Gray was continuing his walk to the schoolhouse, unmindful of the caution. From the momentary glimpse he had caught of this woman's face, she appeared to be about thirty. Her dress, though tasteful and elegant, in the present condition of California society afforded no criterion of her social status. But the figure of Dr. Duchesne waiting for him at the schoolhouse door just then usurped the place of all others, and she dropped out of his mind.

"Now then," said the doctor, as the young man grasped his hand, "you want me to tell you why your eyes are bloodshot, why your cheeks burn, and your hand is dry and hot?"

"Not exactly! Perhaps you'll understand the symptoms better when you've heard my story. Sit down here and listen."

The doctor took the proffered seat on top of a desk, and Mr. Gray, after assuring himself that they were entirely alone, related the circumstances he had gathered from M'liss that morning.

"You see, doctor, how unjust were your surmises in regard to this girl," continued Mr. Gray. "But let that pass now. At the conclusion of her story, I offered to go with her to this Ali Baba cave. It was no easy job finding the concealed entrance, but I found it at last, and ample corroboration of every item of this wild story. The pocket is rich with the most valuable ore. It has evidently been worked for some time since the discovery was made, but there is still a fortune in its walls, and several thousand dollars of ore sacked up in its galleries. Look at that!" continued Mr. Gray, as he drew an oblong mass of quartz and metal from his pocket. "Think of a secret of this kind having been entrusted for three weeks to a penniless orphan girl of twelve and an eccentric schoolboy of ten, and undivulged except when a proper occasion offered."

Dr. Duchesne smiled. "And Waters is really clear?"

"Yes," said Mr. Gray.

"And M'liss assisted him to escape?"

"Yes."

"Well, you are an innocent one! And you see nothing in this but an act of thoughtless generosity? No assisting of an old accomplice to escape?"

"I see nothing but truth in her statement," returned Mr. Gray stoutly. "If there has been any wrong committed, I believe her to be innocent of its knowledge."

"Well, I'm glad at least the money goes to her and not to him. But how are you to establish her right to this property?"

"That was my object in conferring with you. At present the claim is abandoned. I have taken up the ground in my own name (for her), and this afternoon I posted up the usual notice."

"Go on. You are not so much of a fool, after all."

"Thank you! This will hold until a better claim is established. Now, if Smith had discovered this lead, and was, as the lawyers say, 'seized and possessed' of it at the time of his death, M'liss, of course, as next of kin, inherits it."

"But how can this be proved? It is the general belief that Smith committed suicide through extreme poverty and destitution."

Mr. Gray drew a letter from his pocket.

"You remember the memorandum I showed you, which came into my possession. Here it is; it is dated the day of his death."

Dr. Duchesne took it and read:

"July 17th. Five hours in drift—dipping west. Took out 20 oz.—cleaned up 40 oz.—Mem. Saw M. S."

"This evidently refers to actual labor in the mine at the time," said Dr. Duchesne. "But is it legally sufficient to support a claim of this magnitude? That is the only question now. You say this paper was the leaf of an old memorandum, torn off and used for a letter by M'liss; do you know where the original book can be found?"

"Aristides has it, or knows where it is," answered Mr. Gray.

"Find it by all means. And get legal advice before you do anything. Go this very evening to Judge Plunkett and

state your case to him. The promise of a handsome contingent fee won't hurt M'liss's prospects any. Remember,
our ideas of abstract justice and the letter of the law in
this case may be entirely different. Take Judge Plunkett
your proofs; that is," said the doctor, stopping and eying his friend keenly, "if you have no fears for M'liss if
this matter should be thoroughly ventilated."

Mr. Gray did not falter.

"I go at once," said he gaily, "if only to prove the
child's claim to a good name if we fail in getting her
property."

The two men left the schoolhouse together. As they
reached the main street, the doctor paused:

"You are still determined?"

"I am," responded the young man.

"Good night, and God speed you, then," and the doctor
left him.

The fire had been particularly severe on the legal
fraternity in the settlement, and Judge Plunkett's office,
together with those of his learned brethren, had been
consumed with the courthouse on the previous night. The
judge's house was on the outskirts of the village, and
thither Mr. Gray proceeded. The judge was at home, but
engaged at that moment. Mr. Gray would wait, and was
ushered into a small room evidently used as a kitchen,
but just then littered with law books, bundles of papers,
and blanks that had been hastily rescued from the burning building. The sideboard groaned with the weight of
several volumes of New York Reports, that seemed to
impart a dusty flavor to the adjoining victual. Mr. Gray
picked up a volume of supreme court decisions from the
coal scuttle, and was deep in an interesting case, when
the door of the adjoining room opened and Judge
Plunkett appeared.

He was an oily man of about fifty, with spectacles. He
was glad to see the schoolmaster. He hoped he was not
suffering from the excitement of the previous evening.
For his part, the spectacle of sober citizens rising in a
body to vindicate the insulted majesty of the laws of society and of man had always something sublime in it.
And the murderer had really got away after all. And it

was a narrow escape the schoolmaster had, too, at Smith's Pocket.

Mr. Gray took advantage of the digression to state his business. He briefly recounted the circumstances of the discovery of the hidden wealth of Smith's Pocket, and exhibited the memorandum he had shown the doctor. When he had concluded, Judge Plunkett looked at him over his spectacles, and rubbed his hands with satisfaction.

"You apprehend," said the judge eagerly, "that you will have no difficulty in procuring this book from which the leaf was originally torn?"

"None," replied Mr. Gray.

"Then, sir, I should give as my professional opinion that the case was already won."

Mr. Gray shook the hand of the little man with great fervor, and thanked him for his belief. "And so this property will go entirely to M'liss?" he asked again.

"Well—ah—no—not exactly," said Judge Plunkett, with some caution. "She will benefit by it undoubtedly—undoubtedly," and he rubbed his hands again.

"Why not M'liss alone? There are no other claimants!" said Mr. Gray.

"I beg your pardon—you mistake," said Judge Plunkett, with a smile. "You surely would not leave out the widow and mother?"

"Why, M'liss is an orphan," said Mr. Gray in utter bewilderment.

"A sad mistake, sir—a painful though natural mistake. Mr. Smith, though separated from his wife, was never divorced. A very affecting history—the old story, you know—an injured and loving woman deserted by her natural protector, but disdaining to avail herself of our legal aid. By a singular coincidence that I should have told you, I am anticipating you in this very case. Your services, however, I feel will be invaluable. Your concern for her amiable and interesting daughter Narcissa—ah, no, Melissa—will, of course, make you with us. You have never seen Mrs. Smith? A fine-looking, noble woman, sir—though still disconsolate—still thinking of the departed one. By another singular coincidence that I should have told you, she is here now. You shall see her, sir. Pray, let me introduce you;" and still rubbing his hands, Judge Plunkett led the way to the adjoining room.

Mr. Gray followed him mechanically. A handsome woman rose from the sofa as they entered. It was the woman he assisted to alight from the Wingdam stage.

CHAPTER TEN

The Red Rock

In the strong light that fell upon her face, Mr. Gray had an opportunity to examine her features more closely. Her eyes, which were dark and singularly brilliant, were half closed, either from some peculiar conformation of the lids, or an habitual effort to conceal expression. Her skin was colorless with that satinlike luster that belongs to some brunettes, relieved by one or two freckles that were scarcely blemishes. Her face was squared a little at the lower angles, but the chin was round and soft, and the curves about the mouth were full and tender enough to destroy the impression left by contemplation of those rigid outlines. The effect of its general contour was that of a handsome woman of thirty. In detail, as the eye dwelt upon any particular feature, you could have added a margin of ten years either way.

"Mrs. Smith—Mr. Gray," said the lawyer briskly. "Mr. Gray is the gentleman who, since the decease of your husband, has taken such a benevolent interest in our playful Narcissa—Melissa, I should say. He is the preceptor of our district school, and beside his relation as teacher to your daughter has, I may say in our legal fashion, stood *in loco parentis*—in other words, has been a parent, a—a—father to her."

At the conclusion of this speech Mrs. Smith darted a quick glance at Mr. Gray, which was unintelligible to any but a woman. As there were none of her own keen-witted sex present to make an ungracious interpretation of it, it passed unnoticed, except the slight embarrassment and confusion it caused the young man from its apparent gratuity.

"We have met before, I believe," said Mrs. Smith, with her bright eyes half hid and her white teeth half disclosed. "I can easily imagine Mr. Gray's devotion to a friend from his courtesy to a stranger. Let me thank you again for both my daughter and myself."

In the desperate hope of saying something natural, Mr. Gray asked if she had seen Melissa yet.

"Oh, dear, no! Think how provoking! Judge Plunkett says it is absolutely impossible till some tiresome formalities are over. There are so many stupid forms to go through with first. But how is she? You have seen her, have you not? you will see her again tonight, perhaps? How I long to embrace her again! She was a mere baby when she left me. Tell her how I long to fly to her."

Her impassioned utterance and the dramatic gestures that accompanied these words afforded a singular contrast to the cool way with which she rearranged the folds of her dress when she had finished, folding her hands over her lap and settling herself unmistakably back again on the sofa. Perhaps it was this that made Mr. Gray think she had, at some time, been an actress. But the next moment he caught her eye again and felt pleased—and again vexed with himself for being so—and in this mental condition began to speak in favor of his old pupil. His embarrassment passed away as he warmed with his subject, dwelling at length on M'liss's better qualities, and did not return until in a breathless pause he became aware that this woman's bright eyes were bent upon him. The color rose in his cheek, and with a half-muttered apology for his prolixity he offered his excuses to retire.

"Stay a moment, Mr. Gray," said the lawyer. "You are going to town, and will not think it a trouble to see Mrs. Smith safely back to her hotel. You can talk these things over with our fair friend on the way. Tomorrow at ten I trust to see you both again."

"Perhaps I am taxing Mr. Gray's gallantry too much," interposed the lady with a very vivid disclosure of eyes and teeth. "Mr. Gray would be only too happy." After he had uttered this civility, there was a slight consciousness of truth about it that embarrassed him again. But Mrs. Smith took his proffered arm, and they bade the lawyer good night and passed out in the starlit night together.

Four weeks have elapsed since the advent of Mrs. Smith to the settlement—four weeks that might have been years in any other but a California mining camp, for the wonderful change that has been wrought in its physical aspect. Each stage has brought its load of fresh adventurers; another hotel, which sprang up on the site of the National, has its new landlord, and a new set of faces about its hospitable board, where the conventional bean appears daily as a modest vegetable or in the insincerer form of coffee. The sawmills have been hard at work for the last month, and huge gaps appear in the circling files of redwood where the fallen trees are transmuted to a new style of existence in the damp sappy tenements that have risen over the burnt district. The "great strike" at Smith's Pocket has been heralded abroad, and above and below, and on either side of the crumbling tunnel that bears that name, as other tunnels are piercing the bowels of the mountain, shafts are being sunk, and claims are taken up even to the crest of Red Mountain, in the hope of striking the great Smith lead. Already an animated discussion has sprung up in the columns of the *Red Mountain Banner* in regard to the direction of the famous lead—a discussion assisted by correspondents who have assumed all the letters of the alphabet in their anonymous arguments, and have formed the opposing "angle" and "dip" factions of Smith's Pocket. But whatever be the direction of the lead, the progress of the settlement has been steadily onward, with an impetus gained by the late disaster. That classical but much abused bird, the phoenix, has been invoked from its ashes in several editorials in the *Banner* to sit as a type of resuscitated Smith's Pocket, while in the homelier phrase of an honest miner "it seemed as if the fire kem to kinder clean out things for a fresh start."

Meanwhile the quasi-legal administration of the estate of Smith is drawing near a termination that seems to credit the prophetic assertion of Judge Plunkett. One fact has been evolved in the process of examination, viz., that Smith had discovered the new lead before he was murdered. It was a fair hypothesis that the man who assumed the benefit of his discovery was the murderer, but as this did not immediately involve the settlement of the estate it excited little comment or opposition. The probable murderer had escaped. Judicial investigations even in the hands of the people had been attended with disastrous public results, and there was no desire on the part of justice to open the case and deal with an abstract principle when there was no opportunity of making an individual example. The circumstances were being speedily forgotten in the new excitement; even the presence of Mrs. Smith lost its novelty. The *Banner,* when alluding to her husband, spoke of him as the "late J. Smith, Esq.," attributing the present activity of business as the result of his lifelong example of untiring energy, and generally laid the foundation of a belief, which thereafter obtained, that he died comfortably in the bosom of his family, surrounded by disconsolate friends. The history of all pioneer settlements has this legendary basis, and M'liss may live to see the day when her father's connection with the origin of the settlement shall become apocryphal, and contested like that of Romulus and Remus and their wolfish wet nurse.

It is to the everlasting credit and honor of Smith's Pocket that the orphan and widow meet no opposition from the speculative community, and that the claim's utmost boundaries are liberally rendered. How far this circumstance may be owing to the rare personal attractions of the charming widow or to M'liss's personal popularity, I shall not pretend to say. It is enough that when the brief of Judge Plunkett's case is ready there are clouds of willing witnesses to substantiate and corroborate doubtful points to an extent that is more creditable to their generosity than their veracity.

M'liss has seen her mother. Mr. Gray, with his knowledge of his pupil's impulsiveness, has been surprised to notice that the new relationship seems to awaken none of those emotions in the child's nature that he confidently looked for. On the occasion of their first meeting, to which Mr. Gray was admitted, M'liss maintained a guarded shyness totally different from her usual frank boldness—a shyness that was the more remarkable from its contrast with the unrepressed and somewhat dramatic emotions of Mrs. Smith. Now, under her mother's protection and care, he observes another radical change in M'liss's appearance. She is dressed more tastefully and neatly—not entirely the result of a mother's influence, but apparently the result of some natural instinct now for the first time indulged, and exhibited in a ribbon or a piece of jewelry, worn with a certain air of consciousness. There is a more strict attention to the conventionalities of life; her speech is more careful and guarded; her walk, literally, more womanly and graceful. Those things Mr. Gray naturally attributes to the influence of the new relation, though he cannot help recalling his meeting with M'liss in the woods on the morning of the fire, and of dating many of these changes from thence.

It is a pleasant morning, and Mr. Gray is stirring early. He has been busied in preparation the night previous, for this is his last day in Smith's Pocket. He lingers for some time about the schoolhouse, gathering up those little trifles which lie about his desk, which have each a separate history in his experience of Smith's Pocket, and are a part of the incrustations of his life. Lastly, a file of the *Red Mountain Banner* is taken from the same receptacle and packed away in his bag. He walks to the door and turns to look back. Has he forgotten anything? No, nothing. But still he lingers. He wonders who will take his place at the desk, and for the first time in his pedagogue experience, perhaps, feels something of an awful responsibility as he thinks of his past influence over the wretched little beings who used to tremble at his nod, and whose future, ill or good, he may have helped to fashion. At last he closes the door, almost tenderly, and walks thoughtfully down the road. He has to pass the cabin of an Irish miner, whose little boy is toddling in the ditch, with a pinafore, hands, and face in a chronic state of untidiness. Mr. Gray seizes him with an hilarious impulse, and after a number of rapid journeys to Banbury Cross, in search of an old woman who mounted a mythical white horse, he kisses the cleanest place on his broad expanse of cheek, presses some silver into his chubby fist, tells him to be a good boy, and deposits him in the ditch again. Having in this youthful way atoned for certain sins of omission a little further back, he proceeds with a sense of perfect absolution on his way to the settlement.

A few hours lie between him and his departure, to be employed in friendly visits to Mrs. Morpher, Dr. Duchesne, M'liss, and her mother. The Mountain Ranch is nearest, and thither Mr. Gray goes first. Mrs. Morpher, over a kneading trough with her bare arm whitened with flour, is genuinely grieved at parting with the master, and in spite of Mr. Gray's earnest remonstrances, insists upon conducting him into the chill parlor, leaving him there until she shall have attired herself in a manner becoming to "company." "I don't want you to go at all—no more I don't," says Mrs. Morpher, with all sincerity, as she seats herself finally on the shining horsehair sofa. "The children will miss you. I don't believe that anyone will do for Risty, Kerg, and Clytie what you have done. But I suppose you know best what's best. Young men like to see the world, and it ain't expected one so young as you should settle down yet. That's what I was telling Clytie this morning. That was just the way with my John afore he was married. I suppose you'll see M'liss and *her* before you go. They say that she is going to San Francisco soon. Is it so?"

Mr. Gray understands the personal pronoun to refer to Mrs. Smith, a title Mrs. Morpher has never granted M'liss's mother, for whom she entertains an instinctive dislike. He answers in the affirmative, however, with the consciousness of uneasiness under the inquiry; and as the answer does not seem to please Mrs. Morpher, he is constrained to commend M'liss's manifest improvement under her mother's care.

"Well," says Mrs. Morpher, with a significant sigh, "I hope it's so; but bless us, where's Clytie? You mustn't go without saying 'good-by' to her," and Mrs. Morpher starts away in search of her daughter.

The dining room door scarcely closes before the bedroom door opens, and Clytie crosses the parlor softly with something in her hands. "You are going now?" she says hurriedly.

"Yes."

"Will you take this?" putting a sealed package into his hand, "and keep it without opening it until—"

"Until when, Clytie?"

"Until you are married."

Mr. Gray laughs.

"Promise me," repeats Clytie.

"But I may expire in the meantime, through sheer curiosity."

"Promise!" says Clytie gravely.

"I promise, then."

Mr. Gray receives the package. "Good-by," says Clytie softly.

Clytie's rosy cheek is very near Mr. Gray. There is nobody by. He is going away. It is the last time. He kisses her just before the door opens again to Mrs. Morpher.

Another shake of hands all around, and Mr. Gray passes out of the Mountain Ranch forever.

Dr. Duchesne's office is near at hand; but for some reason that Mr. Gray cannot entirely explain to himself he prefers to go to Mrs. Smith's first. The little cottage which they have taken temporarily is soon reached, and as the young man stands at the door he reknots the bow of his cravat and passes his fingers through his curls —trifles that to Dr. Duchesne or any other critical, middle-aged person might look bad.

M'liss and Mrs. Smith were both at home. They have been waiting for him so long. Was it that pretty daughter of Mrs. Morpher—the fair young lady with blond curls —who caused the detention? Is not Mr. Gray a sly young fellow for all his seeming frankness? So he must go today? He cannot possibly wait a few days and go with them? Thus Mrs. Smith, between her red lips and white teeth, and under her half-closed eyes; for M'liss stands quietly apart without speaking. Her reserve during the interview contrasts with the vivacity of her mother as though they had changed respective places in relationship. Mr. Gray is troubled by this, and as he rises to go, he takes M'liss's hand in his.

"Have you nothing to say to me before I go?" he asks.

"Good-by," answers M'liss.

"Nothing more?"

"That's enough," rejoins the child simply.

Mr. Gray bites his lips. "I may never see you again, you know, Melissa," he continues.

"You will see us again," says M'liss quietly, raising her great dark eyes to his.

The blood mounted to his cheek and crimsoned his forehead. He was conscious, too, that the mother's face had taken fire at his own, as she walked away toward the window.

"Good-by, then," said Mr. Gray pettishly, as he stooped to kiss her.

M'liss accepted the salute stoically. Mr. Gray took Mrs. Smith's hand; her face had resumed its colorless, satinlike sheen.

"M'liss knows the strength of your good will, and makes her calculations accordingly. I hope she may not be mistaken," she said, with a languid tenderness of voice and eye. The young man bent over her outstretched hand, and withdrew as the Wingdam stage noisily rattled up before the National Hotel.

There was but little time left to spend with Dr. Duchesne, so the physician walked with him to the stage office. There were a few of the old settlers lounging by the stage, who had discerned, just as the master was going away, how much they liked him. Mr. Gray had gone through the customary bibulous formula of leave-taking; with a hearty shake of the doctor's hand, and a promise to write, he climbed to the box of the stage. "All aboard!" cried the driver, and with a preliminary bound, the stage rolled down Main Street.

Mr. Gray remained buried in thought as they rolled through the town, each object in passing recalling some incident of his past experience. The stage had reached the outskirts of the settlement when he detected a well-known little figure running down a bytrail to intersect the road before the stage had passed. He called the driver's attention to it, and as they drew up at the crossing Aristides's short legs and well-known features were plainly discernible through the dust. He was holding in his hand a letter.

"Well, my little man, what is it?" said the driver impatiently.

"A letter for the master," gasped the exhausted child.

"Give it here!—Any answer?"

"Wait a moment," said Mr. Gray.

"Look sharp, then, and get your billet-duxis before you go next time."

Mr. Gray hurriedly broke the seal and read these words:

Judge Plunkett has just returned from the county seat. Our case is won. We leave here next week.   J. S.

P. S. Have you got my address in San Francisco?

"Any answer?" said the driver.

"None."

"Get up!"

And the stage rolled away from Smith's Pocket, leaving the just Aristides standing in the dust of its triumphal wheels.

The Luck of
>>>>>>>>>>>>>>>>>>>>>>Roaring Camp >>>>>>>>>>>>>>

>>>>>>>>> There was commotion in Roaring Camp. It could not have been a fight, for in 1850 that was not novel enough to have called together the entire settlement. The ditches and claims were not only deserted, but "Tuttle's grocery" had contributed its gamblers, who, it will be remembered, calmly continued their game the day that French Pete and Kanaka Joe shot each other to death over the bar in the front room. The whole camp was collected before a rude cabin on the outer edge of the clearing. Conversation was carried on in a low tone, but the name of a woman was frequently repeated. It was a name familiar enough in the camp—"Cherokee Sal."

Perhaps the less said of her the better. She was a coarse and, it is to be feared, a very sinful woman. But at that time she was the only woman in Roaring Camp, and was just then lying in sore extremity, when she most needed the ministration of her own sex. Dissolute, abandoned, and irreclaimable, she was yet suffering a martyrdom hard enough to bear even when veiled by sympathizing womanhood, but now terrible in her loneliness. The primal curse had come to her in that original isolation which must have made the punishment of the first transgression so dreadful. It was, perhaps, part of the expiation of her sin that, at a moment when she most lacked her sex's intuitive tenderness and care, she met only the half-contemptuous faces of her masculine associates. Yet a few of the spectators were, I think, touched by her sufferings. Sandy Tipton thought it was "rough on Sal," and in the contemplation of her condition, for a moment rose superior to the fact that he had an ace and two bowers in his sleeve.

It will be seen also that the situation was novel. Deaths were by no means uncommon in Roaring Camp, but a birth was a new thing. People had been dismissed the camp effectively, finally, and with no possibility of return; but this was the first time that anybody had been introduced *ab initio*. Hence the excitement.

"You go in there, Stumpy," said a prominent citizen known as "Kentuck," addressing one of the loungers. "Go in there, and see what you kin do. You've had experience in them things."

Perhaps there was a fitness in the selection. Stumpy, in other climes, had been the putative head of two families; in fact, it was owing to some legal informality in these proceedings that Roaring Camp—a city of refuge—was indebted to his company. The crowd approved the choice, and Stumpy was wise enough to bow to the majority. The door closed on the extempore surgeon and midwife, and Roaring Camp sat down outside, smoked its pipe, and awaited the issue.

The assemblage numbered about a hundred men. One or two of these were actual fugitives from justice, some were criminal, and all were reckless. Physically they exhibited no indication of their past lives and character. The greatest scamp had a Raphael face, with a profusion of blond hair; Oakhurst, a gambler, had the melancholy air and intellectual abstraction of a Hamlet; the coolest and most courageous man was scarcely over five feet in height, with a soft voice and an embarrassed, timid manner. The term "roughs" applied to them was a distinction rather than a definition. Perhaps in the minor details of fingers, toes, ears, etc., the camp may have been deficient, but these slight omissions did not detract from their aggregate force. The strongest man had but three fingers on his right hand; the best shot had but one eye.

Such was the physical aspect of the men that were dispersed around the cabin. The camp lay in a triangular valley between two hills and a river. The only outlet was a steep trail over the summit of a hill that faced the cabin, now illuminated by the rising moon. The suffering woman might have seen it from the rude bunk whereon she lay—seen it winding like a silver thread until it was lost in the stars above.

A fire of withered pine boughs added sociability to the gathering. By degrees the natural levity of Roaring Camp returned. Bets were freely offered and taken regarding the result. Three to five that "Sal would get through with it"; even that the child would survive; side bets as to the sex and complexion of the coming stranger. In the midst of an excited discussion an exclamation came from those nearest the door, and the camp stopped to listen. Above the swaying and moaning of the pines, the swift rush of the river, and the crackling of the fire rose a sharp, querulous cry—a cry unlike anything heard before in the camp. The pines stopped moaning, the river ceased to rush, and the fire to crackle. It seemed as if Nature had stopped to listen too.

The camp rose to its feet as one man! It was proposed to explode a barrel of gunpowder; but in consideration of the situation of the mother, better counsels prevailed, and only a few revolvers were discharged; for whether owing to the rude surgery of the camp, or some other reason, Cherokee Sal was sinking fast. Within an hour she had climbed, as it were, that rugged road that led to the stars, and so passed out of Roaring Camp, its sin and shame, forever. I do not think that the announcement disturbed them much, except in speculation as to the fate of the child. "Can he live now?" was asked of Stumpy. The answer was doubtful. The only other being of Cherokee Sal's sex and maternal condition in the settlement was an ass. There was some conjecture as to fitness, but the experiment was tried. It was less problematical than the ancient treatment of Romulus and Remus, and apparently as successful.

When these details were completed, which exhausted another hour, the door was opened, and the anxious crowd of men, who had already formed themselves into a queue, entered in single file. Beside the low bunk or shelf, on which the figure of the mother was starkly outlined below the blankets, stood a pine table. On this a candle-box was placed, and within it, swathed in staring red flannel, lay the last arrival at Roaring Camp. Beside the candlebox was placed a hat. Its use was soon indicated. "Gentlemen," said Stumpy, with a singular mixture of authority and *ex officio* complacency—"gentlemen will please pass in at the front door, round the table, and out at the back door. Them as wishes to contribute anything toward the orphan will find a hat handy." The first man

entered with his hat on; he uncovered, however, as he
looked about him, and so unconsciously set an example
to the next. In such communities good and bad actions
are catching. As the procession filed in comments were
audible—criticisms addressed perhaps rather to Stumpy
in the character of showman: "Is that him?" "Mighty small
specimen;" "Hasn't more'n got the color;" "Ain't bigger
nor a derringer." The contributions were as characteristic:
A silver tobacco box; a doubloon; a navy revolver, silver
mounted; a gold specimen; a very beautifully embroidered
lady's handkerchief (from Oakhurst the gambler); a diamond breastpin; a diamond ring (suggested by the pin,
with the remark from the giver that he "saw that pin and
went two diamonds better"); a slung shot; a Bible (con-
tributor not detected); a golden spur; a silver teaspoon
(the initials, I regret to say, were not the giver's); a pair
of surgeon's shears; a lancet; a Bank of England note for
£5; and about $200 in loose gold and silver coin.
During these proceedings Stumpy maintained a silence as
impassive as the dead on his left, a gravity as inscrutable
as that of the newly born on his right. Only one incident
occurred to break the monotony of the curious procession. As Kentuck bent over the candlebox half curiously, the child turned, and, in a spasm of pain, caught at his
groping finger and held it fast for a moment. Kentuck
looked foolish and embarrassed. Something like a blush
tried to assert itself in his weather-beaten cheek. "The
d—d little cuss!" he said, as he extricated his finger, with
perhaps more tenderness and care than he might have
been deemed capable of showing. He held that finger a
little apart from its fellows as he went out, and examined
it curiously. The examination provoked the same original
remark in regard to the child. In fact, he seemed to
enjoy repeating it. "He rastled with my finger," he remarked to Tipton, holding up the member, "the d—d little
cuss!"

It was four o'clock before the camp sought repose. A
light burnt in the cabin where the watchers sat, for Stumpy
did not go to bed that night. Nor did Kentuck. He drank
quite freely, and related with great gusto his experience,
invariably ending with his characteristic condemnation of
the newcomer. It seemed to relieve him of any unjust im-

plication of sentiment, and Kentuck had the weaknesses of the nobler sex. When everybody else had gone to bed, he walked down to the river and whistled reflectingly. Then he walked up the gulch past the cabin, still whistling with demonstrative unconcern. At a large redwood tree he paused and retraced his steps, and again passed the cabin. Halfway down to the river's bank he again paused, and then returned and knocked at the door. It was opened by Stumpy. "How goes it?" said Kentuck, looking past Stumpy toward the candlebox. "All serene!" replied Stumpy. "Anything up?" "Nothing." There was a pause —an embarrassing one—Stumpy still holding the door. Then Kentuck had recourse to his finger, which he held up to Stumpy. "Rastled with it—the d—d little cuss," he said, and retired.

The next day Cherokee Sal had such rude sepulture as Roaring Camp afforded. After her body had been committed to the hillside, there was a formal meeting of the camp to discuss what should be done with her infant. A resolution to adopt it was unanimous and enthusiastic. But an animated discussion in regard to the manner and feasibility of providing for its wants at once sprang up. It was remarkable that the argument partook of none of those fierce personalities with which discussions were usually conducted at Roaring Camp. Tipton proposed that they should send the child to Red Dog—a distance of forty miles—where female attention could be procured. But the unlucky suggestion met with fierce and unanimous opposition. It was evident that no plan which entailed parting from their new acquisition would for a moment be entertained. "Besides," said Tom Ryder, "them fellows at Red Dog would swap it, and ring in somebody else on us." A disbelief in the honesty of other camps prevailed at Roaring Camp, as in other places.

The introduction of a female nurse in the camp also met with objection. It was argued that no decent woman could be prevailed to accept Roaring Camp as her home, and the speaker urged that "they didn't want any more of the other kind." This unkind allusion to the defunct mother, harsh as it may seem, was the first spasm of propriety— the first symptom of the camp's regeneration. Stumpy advanced nothing. Perhaps he felt a certain delicacy in interfering with the selection of a possible successor in office. But when questioned, he averred stoutly that he and "Jinny"—the mammal before alluded to—could manage to rear the child. There was something original, independent, and heroic about the plan that pleased the camp. Stumpy was retained. Certain articles were sent for to Sacramento. "Mind," said the treasurer, as he pressed a bag of gold dust into the expressman's hand, "the best that can be got—lace, you know, and filigree work and frills— d—n the cost!"

Strange to say, the child thrived. Perhaps the invigorating climate of the mountain camp was compensation for material deficiencies. Nature took the foundling to her broader breast. In that rare atmosphere of the Sierra foothills—that air pungent with balsamic odor, that ethereal cordial at once bracing and exhilarating—he may have found food and nourishment, or a subtle chemistry that transmuted ass's milk to lime and phosphorus. Stumpy inclined to the belief that it was the latter and good nursing. "Me and that ass," he would say, "has been father and mother to him! Don't you," he would add, apostrophizing the helpless bundle before him, "never go back on us."

By the time he was a month old the necessity of giving him a name became apparent. He had generally been known as "The Kid," "Stumpy's Boy," "The Coyote" (an allusion to his vocal powers), and even by Kentuck's endearing diminutive of "The d—d little cuss." But these were felt to be vague and unsatisfactory, and were at last dismissed under another influence. Gamblers and adventurers are generally superstitious, and Oakhurst one day declared that the baby had brought "the luck" to Roaring Camp. It was certain that of late they had been successful. "Luck" was the name agreed upon, with the prefix of Tommy for greater convenience. No allusion was made to the mother, and the father was unknown. "It's better," said the philosophical Oakhurst, "to take a fresh deal all round. Call him Luck, and start him fair." A day was accordingly set apart for the christening. What was meant by this ceremony the reader may imagine who has already gathered some idea of the reckless irreverence of Roaring Camp. The master of ceremonies was one "Boston," a noted wag, and the occasion seemed to promise the greatest facetiousness. This ingenious satirist had spent two days in preparing a burlesque of the Church service, with pointed local allusions. The choir was properly trained, and Sandy Tipton was to stand god-father. But after the procession had marched to the grove with music and banners, and the child had been deposited before a mock altar, Stumpy stepped before the expectant crowd. "It ain't my style to spoil fun, boys," said the little man, stoutly eying the faces around him, "but it strikes me that this thing ain't exactly on the squar. It's playing it pretty low down on this yer baby to ring in fun on him that he ain't goin' to understand. And ef there's goin' to be any godfathers round, I'd like to see who's got any better rights than me." A silence followed Stumpy's speech. To the credit of all humorists be it said that the first man to acknowledge its justice was the satirist thus stopped of his fun. "But," said Stumpy, quickly following up his advantage, "we're here for a christening, and we'll have it. I proclaim you Thomas Luck, according to the laws of the United States and the State of California, so help me God." It was the first time that the name of the Deity had been otherwise uttered than profanely in the camp. The form of christening was perhaps even more ludicrous than the satirist had conceived; but strangely enough, no-body saw it and nobody laughed. "Tommy" was chris-tened as seriously as he would have been under a Chris-tian roof, and cried and was comforted in as orthodox fashion.

And so the work of regeneration began in Roaring Camp. Almost imperceptibly a change came over the settlement. The cabin assigned to "Tommy Luck"—or "The Luck," as he was more frequently called—first showed signs of improvement. It was kept scrupulously clean and whitewashed. Then it was boarded, clothed, and papered. The rosewood cradle, packed eighty miles by mule, had, in Stumpy's way of putting it, "sorter killed the rest of the furniture." So the rehabilitation of the camp became a necessity. The men who were in the habit of lounging in at Stumpy's to see "how 'The Luck' got on" seemed to appreciate the change, and in self-defense the rival establishment of "Tuttle's grocery" bestirred itself and imported a carpet and mirrors. The reflections of the

latter on the appearance of Roaring Camp tended to produce stricter habits of personal cleanliness. Again Stumpy
imposed a kind of quarantine upon those who aspired to
the honor and privilege of holding The Luck. It was a
cruel mortification to Kentuck—who, in the carelessness
of a large nature and the habits of frontier life, had begun
to regard all garments as a second cuticle, which, like a
snake's, only sloughed off through decay—to be debarred
this privilege from certain prudential reasons. Yet such
was the subtle influence of innovation that he thereafter
appeared regularly every afternoon in a clean shirt and
face still shining from his ablutions. Nor were moral and
social sanitary laws neglected. "Tommy," who was supposed to spend his whole existence in a persistent attempt
to repose, must not be disturbed by noise. The shouting
and yelling, which had gained the camp its infelicitous
title, were not permitted within hearing distance of
Stumpy's. The men conversed in whispers or smoked
with Indian gravity. Profanity was tacitly given up in these
sacred precincts, and throughout the camp a popular form
of expletive, known as "D—n the luck!" and "Curse the
luck!" was abandoned, as having a new personal bearing.
Vocal music was not interdicted, being supposed to have
a soothing, tranquilizing quality; and one song, sung by
"Man-o'-War Jack," an English sailor from her Majesty's
Australian colonies, was quite popular as a lullaby. It was
a lugubrious recital of the exploits of "the Arethusa,
Seventy-four," in a muffled minor, ending with a prolonged dying fall at the burden of each verse, "On b-oo-o-
ard of the Arethusa." It was a fine sight to see Jack holding The Luck, rocking from side to side as if with the
motion of a ship, and crooning forth this naval ditty.
Either through the peculiar rocking of Jack or the length
of his song—it contained ninety stanzas, and was continued with conscientious deliberation to the bitter end—
the lullaby generally had the desired effect. At such times
the men would lie at full length under the trees in the soft
summer twilight, smoking their pipes and drinking in the
melodious utterances. An indistinct idea that this was
pastoral happiness pervaded the camp. "This 'ere kind o'
think," said the Cockney Simmons, meditatively reclining

on his elbow, "is 'evingly." It reminded him of Greenwich.

On the long summer days The Luck was usually carried to the gulch from whence the golden store of Roaring Camp was taken. There, on a blanket spread over pine boughs, he would lie while the men were working in the ditches below. Latterly there was a rude attempt to decorate this bower with flowers and sweet-smelling shrubs, and generally some one would bring him a cluster of wild honeysuckles, azaleas, or the painted blossoms of Las Mariposas. The men had suddenly awakened to the fact that there were beauty and significance in these trifles, which they had so long trodden carelessly beneath their feet. A flake of glittering mica, a fragment of variegated quartz, a bright pebble from the bed of the creek, became beautiful to eyes thus cleared and strengthened, and were invariably put aside for The Luck. It was wonderful how many treasures the woods and hillsides yielded that "would do for Tommy." Surrounded by playthings such as never child out of fairyland had before, it is to be hoped that Tommy was content. He appeared to be serenely happy, albeit there was an infantine gravity about him, a contemplative light in his round gray eyes, that sometimes worried Stumpy. He was always tractable and quiet, and it is recorded that once, having crept beyond his "corral"—a hedge of tessellated pine boughs, which surrounded his bed—he dropped over the bank on his head in the soft earth, and remained with his mottled legs in the air in that position for at least five minutes with unflinching gravity. He was extricated without a murmur. I hesitate to record the many other instances of his sagacity, which rest, unfortunately, upon the statements of prejudiced friends. Some of them were not without a tinge of superstition. "I crep' up the bank just now," said Kentuck one day, in a breathless state of excitement, "and dern my skin if he wasn't a-talking to a jay bird as was a-sittin' on his lap. There they was, just as free and sociable as anything you please, a-jawin' at each other just like two cherrybums." Howbeit, whether creeping over the pine boughs or lying lazily on his back blinking at the leaves above him, to him the birds sang, the squirrels chattered, and the flowers bloomed. Nature was his nurse and playfellow. For him she would let slip between the leaves golden shafts of sunlight that fell just within his grasp; she would send wandering breezes to visit him with the balm of bay and resinous gum; to him the tall redwoods nodded familiarly and sleepily, the bumblebees buzzed, and the rooks cawed a slumbrous accompaniment.

Such was the golden summer of Roaring Camp. They were "flush times," and the luck was with them. The claims had yielded enormously. The camp was jealous of its privileges and looked suspiciously on strangers. No encouragement was given to immigration, and, to make their seclusion more perfect, the land on either side of the mountain wall that surrounded the camp they duly pre-empted. This, and a reputation for singular proficiency with the revolver, kept the reserve of Roaring Camp in-violate. The expressman—their only connecting link with the surrounding world—sometimes told wonderful stories of the camp. He would say, "They've a street up there in 'Roaring' that would lay over any street in Red Dog. They've got vines and flowers round their houses, and they wash themselves twice a day. But they're mighty rough on strangers, and they worship an Ingin baby."

With the prosperity of the camp came a desire for further improvement. It was proposed to build a hotel in the following spring, and to invite one or two decent families to reside there for the sake of The Luck, who might perhaps profit by female companionship. The sacri-fice that this concession to the sex cost these men, who were fiercely skeptical in regard to its general virtue and usefulness, can only be accounted for by their affec-tion for Tommy. A few still held out. But the resolve could not be carried into effect for three months, and the minority meekly yielded in the hope that something might turn up to prevent it. And it did.

The winter of 1851 will long be remembered in the foothills. The snow lay deep on the Sierras, and every mountain creek became a river, and every river a lake. Each gorge and gulch was transformed into a tumultuous watercourse that descended the hillsides, tearing down giant trees and scattering its drift and debris along the plain. Red Dog had been twice under water, and Roaring Camp had been forewarned. "Water put the gold into them gulches," said Stumpy. "It's been here once and will be here again!" And that night the North Fork suddenly leaped over its banks and swept up the triangular valley of Roaring Camp.

In the confusion of rushing water, crashing trees, and crackling timber, and the darkness which seemed to flow with the water and blot out the fair valley, but little could be done to collect the scattered camp. When the morning broke, the cabin of Stumpy, nearest the river-bank, was gone. Higher up the gulch they found the body of its unlucky owner; but the pride, the hope, the joy, The Luck, of Roaring Camp had disappeared. They were returning with sad hearts when a shout from the bank recalled them.

It was a relief-boat from down the river. They had picked up, they said, a man and an infant, nearly exhausted, about two miles below. Did anybody know them, and did they belong here?

It needed but a glance to show them Kentuck lying there, cruelly crushed and bruised, but still holding The Luck of Roaring Camp in his arms. As they bent over the strangely assorted pair, they saw that the child was cold and pulseless. "He is dead," said one. Kentuck opened his eyes. "Dead?" he repeated feebly. "Yes, my man, and you are dying too." A smile lit the eyes of the expiring Kentuck. "Dying!" he repeated; "he's a-taking me with him. Tell the boys I've got The Luck with me now;" and the strong man, clinging to the frail babe as a drowning man is said to cling to a straw, drifted away into the shadowy river that flows forever to the unknown sea.

The Outcasts of
⋙⋙⋙⋙⋙⋙⋙ Poker Flat ⋙⋙⋙⋙⋙⋙⋙

⋙⋙⋙ As Mr. John Oakhurst, gambler, stepped into the main street of Poker Flat on the morning of the 23d of November, 1850, he was conscious of a change in its moral atmosphere since the preceding night. Two or three men, conversing earnestly together, ceased as he approached, and exchanged significant glances. There was a Sabbath lull in the air, which, in a settlement unused to Sabbath influences, looked ominous.

Mr. Oakhurst's calm, handsome face betrayed small concern in these indications. Whether he was conscious of any predisposing cause was another question. "I reckon they're after somebody," he reflected; "likely it's me." He returned to his pocket the handkerchief with which he had been whipping away the red dust of Poker Flat from his neat boots, and quietly discharged his mind of any further conjecture.

In point of fact, Poker Flat was "after somebody." It had lately suffered the loss of several thousand dollars, two valuable horses, and a prominent citizen. It was experiencing a spasm of virtuous reaction, quite as lawless and ungovernable as any of the acts that had provoked it. A secret committee had determined to rid the town of all improper persons. This was done permanently in regard of two men who were then hanging from the boughs of a sycamore in the gulch, and temporarily in the banishment of certain other objectionable characters. I regret to say that some of these were ladies. It is but due to the sex, however, to state that their impropriety was professional, and it was only in such easily established standards of evil that Poker Flat ventured to sit in judgment.

Mr. Oakhurst was right in supposing that he was included in this category. A few of the committee had urged hanging him as a possible example and a sure method of reimbursing themselves from his pockets of the sums he had won from them. "It's agin justice," said Jim Wheeler, "to let this yer young man from Roaring Camp—an entire stranger—carry away our money." But a crude sentiment of equity residing in the breasts of those who had been fortunate enough to win from Mr. Oakhurst overruled this narrower local prejudice.

Mr. Oakhurst received his sentence with philosophic calmness, none the less coolly that he was aware of the hesitation of his judges. He was too much of a gambler not to accept fate. With him <u>life was at best an uncertain game, and he recognized the usual percentage in favor of the dealer.</u>

A body of armed men accompanied the deported wickedness of Poker Flat to the outskirts of the settlement. Besides Mr. Oakhurst, who was known to be a coolly desperate man, and for whose intimidation the armed escort was intended, the expatriated party consisted of a young woman familiarly known as "The Duchess"; another who had won the title of "Mother Shipton"; and "Uncle Billy," a suspected sluice-robber and confirmed drunkard. The cavalcade provoked no comments from the spectators, nor was any word uttered by the escort. Only when the gulch which marked the uttermost limit of Poker Flat was reached, the leader spoke briefly and to the point. The exiles were forbidden to return at the peril of their lives.

As the escort disappeared, their pent-up feelings found vent in a few hysterical tears from the Duchess, some bad language from Mother Shipton, and a Parthian volley of expletives from Uncle Billy. The philosophic Oakhurst alone remained silent. He listened calmly to Mother Shipton's desire to cut somebody's heart out, to the repeated statements of the Duchess that she would die in the road, and to the alarming oaths that seemed to be bumped out of Uncle Billy as he rode forward. With the easy good humor characteristic of his class, he insisted upon exchanging his own riding-horse, "Five-Spot," for the sorry mule which the Duchess rode. But even this act did not draw the party into any closer sympathy. The young woman readjusted her somewhat draggled plumes with a feeble, faded coquetry; Mother Shipton eyed the pos-

sessor of "Five-Spot" with malevolence, and Uncle Billy
included the whole party in one sweeping anathema.

The road to Sandy Bar—a camp that, not having as yet
experienced the regenerating influences of Poker Flat,
consequently seemed to offer some invitation to the emi-
grants—lay over a steep mountain range. It was distant a
day's severe travel. In that advanced season the party
soon passed out of the moist, temperate regions of the
foothills into the dry, cold, bracing air of the Sierras.
The trail was narrow and difficult. At noon the Duchess,
rolling out of her saddle upon the ground, declared her
intention of going no farther, and the party halted.

The spot was singularly wild and impressive. A wooded
amphitheatre, surrounded on three sides by precipitous
cliffs of naked granite, sloped gently toward the crest of
another precipice that overlooked the valley. It was, undoubtedly, the most suitable spot for a camp, had camp-
ing been advisable. But Mr. Oakhurst knew that scarcely
half the journey to Sandy Bar was accomplished, and the
party were not equipped or provisioned for delay. This
fact he pointed out to his companions curtly, with a
philosophic commentary on the folly of "throwing up
their hand before the game was played out." But they
were furnished with liquor, which in this emergency stood
them in place of food, fuel, rest, and prescience. In spite
of his remonstrances, it was not long before they were
more or less under its influence. Uncle Billy passed
rapidly from a bellicose state into one of stupor, the
Duchess became maudlin, and Mother Shipton snored.
Mr. Oakhurst alone remained erect, leaning against a
rock, calmly surveying them.

Mr. Oakhurst did not drink. It interfered with a profession which required coolness, impassiveness, and presence of mind, and in his own language, he "couldn't
afford it." As he gazed at his recumbent fellow exiles,
the loneliness begotten of his pariah trade, his habits of
life, his very vices, for the first time seriously oppressed
him. He bestirred himself in dusting his black clothes,
washing his hands and face, and other acts characteristic
of his studiously neat habits, and for a moment forgot
his annoyance. The thought of deserting his weaker and
more pitiable companions never perhaps occurred to

him. Yet he could not help feeling the want of that excitement which, singularly enough, was most conducive to that calm equanimity for which he was notorious. He looked at the gloomy walls that rose a thousand feet sheer above the circling pines around him, at the sky ominously clouded, at the valley below, already deepening into shadow; and doing so, suddenly he heard his own name called.

A horseman slowly ascended the trail. In the fresh, open face of the newcomer Mr. Oakhurst recognized Tom Simson, otherwise known as "The Innocent," of Sandy Bar. He had met him some months before over a "little game," and had, with perfect equanimity, won the entire fortune—amounting to some forty dollars—of that guileless youth. After the game was finished, Mr. Oakhurst drew the youthful speculator behind the door and thus addressed him: "Tommy, you're a good little man, but you can't gamble worth a cent. Don't try it over again." He then handed him his money back, pushed him gently from the room, and so made a devoted slave of Tom Simson.

There was a remembrance of this in his boyish and enthusiastic greeting of Mr. Oakhurst. He had started, he said, to go to Poker Flat to seek his fortune. "Alone?" No, not exactly alone; in fact (a giggle), he had run away with Piney Woods. Didn't Mr. Oakhurst remember Piney? She that used to wait on the table at the Temperance House? They had been engaged a long time, but old Jake Woods had objected, and so they had run away, and were going to Poker Flat to be married, and here they were. And they were tired out, and how lucky it was they had found a place to camp, and company. All this the Innocent delivered rapidly, while Piney, a stout, comely damsel of fifteen, emerged from behind the pine tree, where she had been blushing unseen, and rode to the side of her lover.

Mr. Oakhurst seldom troubled himself with sentiment, still less with propriety; but he had a vague idea that the situation was not fortunate. He retained, however, his presence of mind sufficiently to kick Uncle Billy, who

was about to say something, and Uncle Billy was sober
enough to recognize in Mr. Oakhurst's kick a superior
power that would not bear trifling. He then endeavored
to dissuade Tom Simson from delaying further, but in
vain. He even pointed out the fact that there was no
provision, nor means of making a camp. But, unluckily,
the Innocent met this objection by assuring the party
that he was provided with an extra mule loaded with
provisions, and by the discovery of a rude attempt at a
log house near the trail. "Piney can stay with Mrs. Oakhurst," said the Innocent, pointing to the Duchess, "and
I can shift for myself."

Nothing but Mr. Oakhurst's admonishing foot saved
Uncle Billy from bursting into a roar of laughter. As it
was, he felt compelled to retire up the canyon until he
could recover his gravity. There he confided the joke to
the tall pine trees, with many slaps of his leg, contortions
of his face, and the usual profanity. But when he returned to the party, he found them seated by a fire—
for the air had grown strangely chill and the sky over-
cast—in apparently amicable conversation. Piney was
actually talking in an impulsive girlish fashion to the
Duchess, who was listening with an interest and anima-
tion she had not shown for many days. The Innocent
was holding forth, apparently with equal effect, to Mr.
Oakhurst and Mother Shipton, who was actually relaxing into amiability. "Is this yer a d—d picnic?" said
Uncle Billy, with inward scorn, as he surveyed the sylvan
group, the glancing firelight, and the tethered animals in
the foreground. Suddenly an idea mingled with the alcoholic fumes that disturbed his brain. It was apparently
of a jocular nature, for he felt impelled to slap his leg
again and cram his fist into his mouth.

As the shadows crept slowly up the mountain, a slight
breeze rocked the tops of the pine trees and moaned
through their long and gloomy aisles. The ruined cabin,
patched and covered with pine boughs, was set apart
for the ladies. As the lovers parted, they unaffectedly exchanged a kiss, so honest and sincere that it might have
been heard above the swaying pines. The frail Duchess
and the malevolent Mother Shipton were probably too
stunned to remark upon this last evidence of simplicity,

and so turned without a word to the hut. The fire was replenished, the men lay down before the door, and in a few minutes were asleep.

Mr. Oakhurst was a light sleeper. Toward morning he awoke benumbed and cold. As he stirred the dying fire, the wind, which was now blowing strongly, brought to his cheek that which caused the blood to leave it—snow!

He started to his feet with the intention of awakening the sleepers, for there was no time to lose. But turning to where Uncle Billy had been lying, he found him gone. A suspicion leaped to his brain, and a curse to his lips. He ran to the spot where the mules had been tethered —they were no longer there. The tracks were already rapidly disappearing in the snow.

The momentary excitement brought Mr. Oakhurst back to the fire with his usual calm. He did not waken the sleepers. The Innocent slumbered peacefully, with a smile on his good-humored, freckled face; the virgin Piney slept beside her frailer sisters as sweetly as though attended by celestial guardians; and Mr. Oakhurst, drawing his blanket over his shoulders, stroked his mustaches and waited for the dawn. It came slowly in a whirling mist of snowflakes that dazzled and confused the eye. What could be seen of the landscape appeared magically changed. He looked over the valley, and summed up the present and future in two words, "Snowed in!"

A careful inventory of the provisions, which, fortunately for the party, had been stored within the hut, and so escaped the felonious fingers of Uncle Billy, disclosed the fact that with care and prudence they might last ten days longer. "That is," said Mr. Oakhurst *sotto voce* to the Innocent, "if you're willing to board us. If you ain't —and perhaps you'd better not—you can wait till Uncle Billy gets back with provisions." For some occult reason, Mr. Oakhurst could not bring himself to disclose Uncle Billy's rascality, and so offered the hypothesis that he had wandered from the camp and had accidentally stampeded the animals. He dropped a warning to the Duchess and Mother Shipton, who of course knew the facts of their associate's defection. "They'll find out the truth about us *all* when they find out anything," he added significantly, "and there's no good frightening them now."

Tom Simson not only put all his worldly store at the disposal of Mr. Oakhurst, but seemed to enjoy the prospect of their enforced seclusion. "We'll have a good camp for a week, and then the snow'll melt, and we'll all go back together." The cheerful gayety of the young man and Mr. Oakhurst's calm infected the others. The Innocent, with the aid of pine boughs, extemporized a thatch for the roofless cabin, and the Duchess directed Piney in the rearrangement of the interior with a taste and tact that opened the blue eyes of that provincial maiden to their fullest extent. "I reckon now you're used to fine things at Poker Flat," said Piney. The Duchess turned away sharply to conceal something that reddened her cheeks through their professional tint, and Mother Shipton requested Piney not to "chatter." But when Mr. Oakhurst returned from a weary search for the trail, he heard the sound of happy laughter echoed from the rocks. He stopped in some alarm, and his thoughts first naturally reverted to the whiskey, which he had prudently cached. "And yet it don't somehow sound like whiskey," said the gambler. It was not until he caught sight of the blazing fire through the still blinding storm, and the group around it, that he settled to the conviction that it was "square fun."

Whether Mr. Oakhurst had cached his cards with the whiskey as something debarred the free access of the community, I cannot say. It was certain that, in Mother Shipton's words, he "didn't say 'cards' once" during that evening. Haply the time was beguiled by an accordion, produced somewhat ostentatiously by Tom Simson from his pack. Notwithstanding some difficulties attending the manipulation of this instrument, Piney Woods managed to pluck several reluctant melodies from its keys to an accompaniment by the Innocent on a pair of bone castanets. But the crowning festivity of the evening was reached in a rude camp-meeting hymn, which the lovers, joining hands, sang with great earnestness and vociferation. I fear that a certain defiant tone and covenanter's swing to its chorus, rather than any devotional quality, caused it speedily to infect the others, who at last joined in the refrain:

> "I'm proud to live in the service of the Lord,
> And I'm bound to die in His army."

The pines rocked, the storm eddied and whirled above the miserable group, and the flames of their altar leaped heavenward, as if in token of the vow.

At midnight the storm abated, the rolling clouds parted, and the stars glittered keenly above the sleeping camp. Mr. Oakhurst, whose professional habits had enabled him to live on the smallest possible amount of sleep, in dividing the watch with Tom Simson somehow managed to take upon himself the greater part of that duty. He excused himself to the Innocent by saying that he had "often been a week without sleep." "Doing what?" asked Tom. "Poker!" replied Oakhurst sententiously. "When a man gets a streak of luck—nigger-luck—he don't get tired. The luck gives in first. Luck," continued the gambler reflectively, "is a mighty queer thing. All you know about it for certain is that it's bound to change. And it's finding out when it's going to change that makes you. We've had a streak of bad luck since we left Poker Flat—you come along, and slap you get into it, too. If you can hold your cards right along you're all right. For," added the gambler, with cheerful irrelevance—

> " 'I'm proud to live in the service of the Lord,
> And I'm bound to die in His army.' "

The third day came, and the sun, looking through the white-curtained valley, saw the outcasts divide their slowly decreasing store of provisions for the morning meal. It was one of the peculiarities of that mountain climate that its rays diffused a kindly warmth over the wintry landscape, as if in regretful commiseration of the past. But it revealed drift on drift of snow piled high around the hut—a hopeless, uncharted, trackless sea of white lying below the rocky shores to which the castaways still clung. Through the marvelously clear air the smoke of the pastoral village of Poker Flat rose miles away. Mother Shipton saw it, and from a remote pinnacle of her rocky fastness hurled in that direction a final malediction. It was her last vituperative attempt, and perhaps for that reason was invested with a certain degree of sublimity. It did her good, she privately informed the Duchess. "Just you go out there and cuss, and see." She then set herself to the task of amusing "the child," as she and the Duchess were pleased to call Piney. Piney was no chicken, but it was a soothing and original theory of the pair thus to account for the fact that she didn't swear and wasn't improper.

When night crept up again through the gorges, the reedy notes of the accordion rose and fell in fitful spasms and long-drawn gasps by the flickering campfire. But music failed to fill entirely the aching void left by insufficient food, and a new diversion was proposed by Piney—storytelling. Neither Mr. Oakhurst nor his female companions caring to relate their personal experiences, this plan would have failed too, but for the Innocent. Some months before he had chanced upon a stray copy of Mr. Pope's ingenious translation of the Iliad. He now proposed to narrate the principal incidents of that poem—having thoroughly mastered the argument and fairly forgotten the words—in the current vernacular of Sandy Bar. And so for the rest of that night the Homeric demigods again walked the earth. Trojan bully and wily Greek wrestled in the winds, and the great pines in the canyon seemed to bow to the wrath of the son of Peleus. Mr. Oakhurst listened with quiet satisfaction. Most especially was he interested in the fate of "Ash-heels," as the Innocent persisted in denominating the "swift-footed Achilles."

So, with small food and much of Homer and the accordion, a week passed over the heads of the outcasts. The sun again forsook them, and again from leaden skies the snowflakes were sifted over the land. Day by day closer around them drew the snowy circle, until at last they looked from their prison over drifted walls of dazzling white that towered twenty feet above their heads. It became more and more difficult to replenish their fires, even from the fallen trees beside them, now half hidden in the drifts. And yet no one complained. The lovers turned from the dreary prospect and looked into each other's eyes, and were happy. Mr. Oakhurst settled himself coolly to the losing game before him. The Duchess, more cheerful than she had been, assumed the care of Piney. Only Mother Shipton—once the strongest of the party—seemed to sicken and fade. At midnight on the tenth day she called Oakhurst to her side. "I'm going," she said, in a voice of querulous weakness, "but don't say anything about it. Don't waken the kids. Take the bundle from under my head, and open it." Mr. Oakhurst did so. It contained Mother Shipton's rations for the last week, untouched. "Give 'em to the child," she said, pointing to the sleeping Piney. "You've starved yourself," said the gambler. "That's what they call it," said the woman querulously, as she lay down again, and turning her face to the wall, passed quietly away.

The accordion and the bones were put aside that day, and Homer was forgotten. When the body of Mother Shipton had been committed to the snow, Mr. Oakhurst took the Innocent aside, and showed him a pair of snow-shoes, which he had fashioned from the old pack-saddle. "There's one chance in a hundred to save her yet," he said, pointing to Piney; "but it's there," he added, pointing toward Poker Flat. "If you can reach there in two days she's safe." "And you?" asked Tom Simson. "I'll stay here," was the curt reply.

The lovers parted with a long embrace. "You are not going, too?" said the Duchess, as she saw Mr. Oakhurst apparently waiting to accompany him. "As far as the canyon," he replied. He turned suddenly and kissed the Duchess, leaving her pallid face aflame, and her trembling limbs rigid with amazement.

Night came, but not Mr. Oakhurst. It brought the storm again and the whirling snow. Then the Duchess, feeding the fire, found that someone had quietly piled beside the hut enough fuel to last a few days longer. The tears rose to her eyes, but she hid them from Piney.

The women slept but little. In the morning, looking into each other's faces, they read their fate. Neither spoke, but Piney, accepting the position of the stronger, drew near and placed her arm around the Duchess's waist. They kept this attitude for the rest of the day. That night the storm reached its greatest fury, and rending asunder the protecting vines, invaded the very hut.

Toward morning they found themselves unable to feed the fire, which gradually died away. As the embers slowly blackened, the Duchess crept closer to Piney, and broke the silence of many hours: "Piney, can you pray?" "No, dear," said Piney simply. The Duchess, without knowing exactly why, felt relieved, and putting her head upon Piney's shoulder, spoke no more. And so reclining, the younger and purer pillowing the head of her soiled sister upon her virgin breast, they fell asleep.

The wind lulled as if it feared to waken them. Feathery drifts of snow, shaken from the long pine boughs, flew like white winged birds, and settled about them as they slept. The moon through the rifted clouds looked down upon what had been the camp. But all human stain, all trace of earthly travail, was hidden beneath the spotless mantle mercifully flung from above.

They slept all that day and the next, nor did they waken when voices and footsteps broke the silence of the camp. And when pitying fingers brushed the snow from their wan faces, you could scarcely have told from the equal peace that dwelt upon them which was she that had sinned. Even the law of Poker Flat recognized this, and turned away, leaving them still locked in each other's arms.

But at the head of the gulch, on one of the largest pine trees, they found the deuce of clubs pinned to the bark with a bowie knife. It bore the following, written in pencil in a firm hand:

†

BENEATH THIS TREE
LIES THE BODY
OF
JOHN OAKHURST,
WHO STRUCK A STREAK OF BAD LUCK
ON THE 23D OF NOVEMBER, 1850,
AND
HANDED IN HIS CHECKS
ON THE 7TH DECEMBER, 1850.

↓

And pulseless and cold, with a derringer by his side and a bullet in his heart, though still calm as in life, beneath the snow lay he who was at once the strongest and yet the weakest of the outcasts of Poker Flat.

Tennessee's
≫≫≫≫≫≫≫≫≫≫≫ Partner ≫≫≫≫≫≫≫≫≫

≫≫≫≫≫ I do not think that we ever knew his real name. Our ignorance of it certainly never gave us any social inconvenience, for at Sandy Bar in 1854 most men were christened anew. Sometimes these appellatives were derived from some distinctiveness of dress, as in the case of "Dungaree Jack"; or from some peculiarity of habit, as shown in "Saleratus Bill," so called from an undue proportion of that chemical in his daily bread; or from some unlucky slip, as exhibited in "The Iron Pirate," a mild, inoffensive man, who earned that baleful title by his unfortunate mispronunciation of the term "iron pyrites." Perhaps this may have been the beginning of a rude heraldry; but I am constrained to think that it was because a man's real name in that day rested solely upon his own unsupported statement. "Call yourself Clifford, do you?" said Boston, addressing a timid newcomer with infinite scorn; "hell is full of such Cliffords!" He then introduced the unfortunate man, whose name happened to be really Clifford, as "Jaybird Charley"—an unhallowed inspiration of the moment that clung to him ever after.

But to return to Tennessee's Partner, whom we never knew by any other than this relative title. That he had ever existed as a separate and distinct individuality we only learned later. It seems that in 1853 he left Poker Flat to go to San Francisco, ostensibly to procure a wife. He never got any farther than Stockton. At that place he was attracted by a young person who waited upon the table at the hotel where he took his meals. One morning he said something to her which caused her to smile not unkindly, to somewhat coquettishly break a plate of toast over his upturned, serious, simple face, and to retreat to the kitchen. He followed her, and emerged a few moments later, covered with more toast and victory. That

124

day week they were married by a justice of the peace,
and returned to Poker Flat. I am aware that something
more might be made of this episode, but I prefer to tell it
as it was current at Sandy Bar—in the gulches and barrooms—where all sentiment was modified by a strong
sense of humor.

Of their married felicity but little is known, perhaps for
the reason that Tennessee, then living with his partner, one
day took occasion to say something to the bride on his
own account, at which, it is said, she smiled not unkindly
and chastely retreated—this time as far as Marysville,
where Tennessee followed her, and where they went to
housekeeping without the aid of a justice of the peace.
Tennessee's Partner took the loss of his wife simply and
seriously, as was his fashion. But to everybody's surprise, when Tennessee one day returned from Marysville,
without his partner's wife—she having smiled and retreated with somebody else—Tennessee's Partner was the
first man to shake his hand and greet him with affection.
The boys who had gathered in the canyon to see the
shooting were naturally indignant. Their indignation might
have found vent in sarcasm but for a certain look in
Tennessee's Partner's eye that indicated a lack of humor-
ous appreciation. In fact, he was a grave man, with a
steady application to practical detail which was unpleasant in a difficulty.

Meanwhile a popular feeling against Tennessee had
grown up on the Bar. He was known to be a gambler; he
was suspected to be a thief. In these suspicions Tennessee's Partner was equally compromised; his continued intimacy with Tennessee after the affair above quoted could
only be accounted for on the hypothesis of a copartner-
ship of crime. At last Tennessee's guilt became flagrant.
One day he overtook a stranger on his way to Red Dog.
The stranger afterward related that Tennessee beguiled
the time with interesting anecdote and reminiscence, but
illogically concluded the interview in the following words:
"And now, young man, I'll trouble you for your knife,
your pistols, and your money. You see your weppings
might get you into trouble at Red Dog, and your money's
a temptation to the evilly disposed. I think you said your
address was San Francisco. I shall endeavor to call." It

may be stated here that Tennessee had a fine flow of humor, which no business preoccupation could wholly subdue.

This exploit was his last. Red Dog and Sandy Bar made common cause against the highwayman. Tennessee was hunted in very much the same fashion as his prototype, the grizzly. As the toils closed around him, he made a desperate dash through the Bar, emptying his revolver at the crowd before the Arcade Saloon, and so on up Grizzly Canyon; but at its farther extremity he was stopped by a small man on a gray horse. The men looked at each other a moment in silence. Both were fearless, both self-possessed and independent, and both types of a civilization that in the seventeenth century would have been called heroic, but in the nineteenth simply "reckless." *5 thought*

"What have you got there?—I call," said Tennessee quietly. *2 jacks*   *card game*

"Two bowers and an ace," said the stranger as quietly, showing two revolvers and a bowie knife.

"That takes me," returned Tennessee; and with this gambler's epigram, he threw away his useless pistol and rode back with his captor.

It was a warm night. The cool breeze which usually sprang up with the going down of the sun behind the chaparral-crested mountain was that evening withheld from Sandy Bar. The little canyon was stifling with heated resinous odors, and the decaying driftwood on the Bar sent forth faint sickening exhalations. The feverishness of day and its fierce passions still filled the camp. Lights moved restlessly along the bank of the river, striking no answering reflection from its tawny current. Against the blackness of the pines the windows of the old loft above the express office stood out staringly bright; and through their curtainless panes the loungers below could see the forms of those who were even then deciding the fate of Tennessee. And above all this, etched on the dark firmament, rose the Sierra, remote and passionless, crowned with remoter passionless stars.

The trial of Tennessee was conducted as fairly as was consistent with a judge and jury who felt themselves to some extent obliged to justify, in their verdict, the previous irregularities of arrest and indictment. The law of

Sandy Bar was implacable, but not vengeful. The excitement and personal feeling of the chase were over; with Tennessee safe in their hands, they were ready to listen patiently to any defense, which they were already satisfied was insufficient. There being no doubt in their own minds, they were willing to give the prisoner the benefit of any that might exist. Secure in the hypothesis that he ought to be hanged on general principles, they indulged him with more latitude of defense than his reckless hardihood seemed to ask. The Judge appeared to be more anxious than the prisoner, who, otherwise unconcerned, evidently took a grim pleasure in the responsibility he had created. "I don't take any hand in this yer game," had been his invariable but good-humored reply to all questions. The Judge—who was also his captor—for a moment vaguely regretted that he had not shot him "on sight" that morning, but presently dismissed this human weakness as unworthy of the judicial mind. Nevertheless, when there was a tap at the door, and it was said that Tennessee's Partner was there on behalf of the prisoner, he was admitted at once without question. Perhaps the younger members of the jury, to whom the proceedings were becoming irksomely thoughtful, hailed him as a relief.

For he was not, certainly, an imposing figure. Short and stout, with a square face, sunburned into a preternatural redness, clad in a loose duck "jumper" and trousers streaked and splashed with red soil, his aspect under any circumstances would have been quaint, and was now even ridiculous. As he stooped to deposit at his feet a heavy carpetbag he was carrying, it became obvious, from partially developed legends and inscriptions, that the material with which his trousers had been patched had been originally intended for a less ambitious covering. Yet he advanced with great gravity, and after shaking the hand of each person in the room with labored cordiality, he wiped his serious perplexed face on a red bandana handkerchief, a shade lighter than his complexion, laid his powerful hand upon the table to steady himself, and thus addressed the Judge:

"I was passin' by," he began, by way of apology, "and I thought I'd just step in and see how things was gittin' on with Tennessee thar—my pardner. It's a hot night. I disremember any sich weather before on the Bar."

He paused a moment, but nobody volunteering any other meteorological recollection, he again had recourse to his pocket handkerchief, and for some moments mopped his face diligently.

"Have you anything to say on behalf of the prisoner?" said the Judge finally.

"Thet's it," said Tennessee's Partner, in a tone of relief. "I come yar as Tennessee's pardner—knowing him nigh on four year, off and on, wet and dry, in luck and out o' luck. His ways ain't aller my ways, but thar ain't any p'ints in that young man, thar ain't any liveliness as he's been up to, as I don't know. And you sez to me, sez you—confidential-like, and between man and man—sez you, 'Do you know anything in his behalf?' and I sez to you, sez I—confidential-like, as between man and man—'What should a man know of his pardner?' "

"Is this all you have to say?" asked the Judge impatiently, feeling, perhaps, that a dangerous sympathy of humor was beginning to humanize the court.

"Thet's so," continued Tennessee's Partner. "It ain't for me to say anything agin' him. And now, what's the case? Here's Tennessee wants money, wants it bad, and doesn't like to ask it of his old pardner. Well, what does Tennessee do? He lays for a stranger, and he fetches that stranger; and you lays for *him*, and you fetches *him;* and the honors is easy. And I put it to you, bein' a fa'r-minded man, and to you, gentlemen all, as fa'r-minded men, ef this isn't so."

"Prisoner," said the Judge, interrupting, "have you any questions to ask this man?"

"No! no!" continued Tennessee's Partner hastily. "I play this yer hand alone. To come down to the bedrock, it's just this: Tennessee thar has played it pretty rough and expensivelike on a stranger, and on this yer camp. And now, what's the fair thing? Some would say more, some would say less. Here's seventeen hundred dollars in coarse gold and a watch—it's about all my pile—and call it square!" And before a hand could be raised to prevent him, he had emptied the contents of the carpetbag upon the table.

For a moment his life was in jeopardy. One or two men sprang to their feet, several hands groped for hidden weapons, and a suggestion to "throw him from the window" was only overridden by a gesture from the Judge. Tennessee laughed. And apparently oblivious of the excitement, Tennessee's Partner improved the opportunity to mop his face again with his handkerchief.

When order was restored, and the man was made to understand by the use of forcible figures and rhetoric that Tennessee's offense could not be condoned by money, his face took a more serious and sanguinary hue, and those who were nearest to him noticed that his rough hand trembled slightly on the table. He hesitated a moment as he slowly returned the gold to the carpetbag, as if he had not yet entirely caught the elevated sense of justice which swayed the tribunal, and was perplexed with the belief that he had not offered enough. Then he turned to the Judge, and saying, "This yer is a lone hand, played alone, and without my pardner," he bowed to the jury and was about to withdraw, when the Judge called him back:

"If you have anything to say to Tennessee, you had better say it now."

For the first time that evening the eyes of the prisoner and his strange advocate met. Tennessee smiled, showed his white teeth, and saying, "Euchred, old man!" held out his hand. Tennessee's Partner took it in his own, and saying, "I just dropped in as I was passin' to see how things was gettin' on," let the hand passively fall, and adding that "it was a warm night," again mopped his face with his handkerchief, and without another word withdrew.

The two men never again met each other alive. For the unparalleled insult of a bribe offered to Judge Lynch—who, whether bigoted, weak, or narrow, was at least incorruptible—firmly fixed in the mind of that mythical personage any wavering determination of Tennessee's fate; and at the break of day he was marched, closely guarded, to meet it at the top of Marley's Hill.

How he met it, how cool he was, how he refused to say anything, how perfect were the arrangements of the committee, were all duly reported, with the addition of a

warning moral and example to all future evildoers, in the
Red Dog Clarion by its editor, who was present, and to
whose vigorous English I cheerfully refer the reader. But
the beauty of that midsummer morning, the blessed amity
of earth and air and sky, the awakened life of the free
woods and hills, the joyous renewal and promise of Nature, and above all, the infinite serenity that thrilled
through each, was not reported, as not being a part of
the social lesson. And yet, when the weak and foolish
deed was done, and a life, with its possibilities and responsibilities, had passed out of the misshapen thing that dan-
gled between earth and sky, the birds sang, the flowers
bloomed, the sun shone, as cheerily as before; and possibly the *Red Dog Clarion* was right.

Tennessee's Partner was not in the group that surrounded the ominous tree. But as they turned to disperse,
attention was drawn to the singular appearance of a
motionless donkey cart halted at the side of the road. As
they approached, they at once recognized the venerable
Jenny and the two-wheeled cart as the property of Tennessee's Partner, used by him in carrying dirt from his
claim; and a few paces distant the owner of the equipage
himself, sitting under a buckeye tree, wiping the perspiration from his glowing face. In answer to an inquiry, he said
he had come for the body of the "diseased," "if it was
all the same to the committee." He didn't wish to "hurry
anything;" he could "wait." He was not working that day;
and when the gentlemen were done with the "diseased,"
he would take him. "Ef thar is any present," he added,
in his simple, serious way, "as would care to jine in the
fun'l, they kin come." Perhaps it was from a sense of
humor, which I have already intimated was a feature of
Sandy Bar—perhaps it was from something even better
than that, but two thirds of the loungers accepted the
invitation at once.

It was noon when the body of Tennessee was delivered
into the hands of his partner. As the cart drew up to the
fatal tree, we noticed that it contained a rough oblong
box—apparently made from a section of sluicing—and
half filled with bark and the tassels of pine. The cart was
further decorated with slips of willow and made fragrant
with buckeye blossoms. When the body was deposited in

the box, Tennessee's Partner drew over it a piece of tarred canvas, and gravely mounting the narrow seat in front, with his feet upon the shafts, urged the little donkey forward. The equipage moved slowly on, at that decorous pace which was habitual with Jenny even under less solemn circumstances. The men—half curiously, half jestingly, but all good-humoredly—strolled along beside the cart, some in advance, some a little in the rear of the homely catafalque. But whether from the narrowing of the road or some present sense of decorum, as the cart passed on, the company fell to the rear in couples, keeping step, and otherwise assuming the external show of a formal procession. Jack Folinsbee, who had at the outset played a funeral march in dumb show upon an imaginary trombone, desisted from a lack of sympathy and appreciation—not having, perhaps, your true humorist's capacity to be content with the enjoyment of his own fun.

The way led through Grizzly Canyon, by this time clothed in funereal drapery and shadows. The redwoods, burying their moccasined feet in the red soil, stood in Indian file along the track, trailing an uncouth benediction from their bending boughs upon the passing bier. A hare, surprised into helpless inactivity, sat upright and pulsating in the ferns by the roadside as the cortége went by. Squirrels hastened to gain a secure outlook from higher boughs; and the blue jays, spreading their wings, fluttered before them like outriders, until the outskirts of Sandy Bar were reached, and the solitary cabin of Tennessee's Partner.

Viewed under more favorable circumstances, it would not have been a cheerful place. The unpicturesque site, the rude and unlovely outlines, the unsavory details, which distinguish the nest-building of the California miner, were all here with the dreariness of decay superadded. A few paces from the cabin there was a rough enclosure, which, in the brief days of Tennessee's Partner's matrimonial felicity, had been used as a garden, but was now overgrown with fern. As we approached it, we were surprised to find that what we had taken for a recent attempt at cultivation was the broken soil about an open grave.

The cart was halted before the enclosure, and rejecting the offers of assistance with the same air of simple self-

reliance he had displayed throughout, Tennessee's Partner
lifted the rough coffin on his back, and deposited it un-
aided within the shallow grave. He then nailed down the
board which served as a lid, and mounting the little
mound of earth beside it, took off his hat and slowly
mopped his face with his handkerchief. This the crowd
felt was a preliminary to speech, and they disposed themselves variously on stumps and boulders, and sat expectant.

"When a man," began Tennessee's Partner slowly, "has
been running free all day, what's the natural thing for
him to do? Why, to come home. And if he ain't in a condition to go home, what can his best friend do? Why,
bring him home. And here's Tennessee has been running
free, and we brings him home from his wandering." He
paused and picked up a fragment of quartz, rubbed it
thoughtfully on his sleeve, and went on: "It ain't the first
time that I've packed him on my back, as you see'd
me now. It ain't the first time that I brought him to this
yer cabin when he couldn't help himself; it ain't the first
time that I and Jinny have waited for him on yon hill, and
picked him up and so fetched him home, when he
couldn't speak and didn't know me. And now that it's
the last time, why"——he paused and rubbed the quartz
gently on his sleeve——"you see it's sort of rough on his
pardner. And now, gentlemen," he added abruptly, picking up his long-handled shovel, "the fun'l's over; and my
thanks, and Tennessee's thanks, to you for your trouble."

Resisting any proffers of assistance, he began to fill in
the grave, turning his back upon the crowd, that after a
few moments' hesitation gradually withdrew. As they
crossed the little ridge that hid Sandy Bar from view, some,
looking back, thought they could see Tennessee's Partner,
his work done, sitting upon the grave, his shovel between
his knees, and his face buried in his red bandana handkerchief. But it was argued by others that you couldn't
tell his face from his handkerchief at that distance, and
this point remained undecided.

In the reaction that followed the feverish excitement
of that day, Tennessee's Partner was not forgotten. A
secret investigation had cleared him of any complicity
in Tennessee's guilt, and left only a suspicion of his gen-

eral sanity. Sandy Bar made a point of calling on him, and proffering various uncouth but well-meant kindnesses. But from that day his rude health and great strength seemed visibly to decline; and when the rainy season fairly set in, and the tiny grass blades were beginning to peep from the rocky mound above Tennessee's grave, he took to his bed.

One night, when the pines beside the cabin were swaying in the storm and trailing their slender fingers over the roof, and the roar and rush of the swollen river were heard below, Tennessee's Partner lifted his head from the pillow, saying, "It is time to go for Tennessee; I must put Jinny in the cart;" and would have risen from his bed but for the restraint of his attendant. Struggling, he still pursued his singular fancy: "There, now, steady, Jinny, steady, old girl. How dark it is! Look out for the ruts, and look out for him, too, old gal. Sometimes, you know, when he's blind drunk, he drops down right in the trail. Keep on straight up to the pine on the top of the hill. Thar! I told you so!—thar he is—coming this way, too—all by himself, sober, and his face a-shining. Tennessee! Pardner!"

And so they met.

The Idyl of
>>>-->>>-->>>-->>>-->>>-->>>-->>>-->>> Red Gulch >>>-->>>-->>>-->>>

>>>-->>>-->>> Sandy was very drunk. He was lying under an azalea bush, in pretty much the same attitude in which he had fallen some hours before. How long he had been lying there he could not tell, and didn't care; how long he should lie there was a matter equally indefinite and unconsidered. A tranquil philosophy, born of his physical condition, suffused and saturated his moral being.

The spectacle of a drunken man, and of this drunken man in particular, was not, I grieve to say, of sufficient novelty in Red Gulch to attract attention. Earlier in the day some local satirist had erected a temporary tombstone at Sandy's head, bearing the inscription, "Effects of McCorkle's whiskey—kills at forty rods," with a hand pointing to McCorkle's saloon. But this, I imagine, was, like most local satire, personal; and was a reflection upon the unfairness of the process rather than a commentary upon the impropriety of the result. With this facetious exception, Sandy had been undisturbed. A wandering mule, released from his pack, had cropped the scant herbage beside him, and sniffed curiously at the prostrate man; a vagabond dog, with that deep sympathy which the species have for drunken men, had licked his dusty boots and curled himself up at his feet, and lay there, blinking one eye in the sunlight, with a simulation of dissipation that was ingenious and doglike in its implied flattery of the unconscious man beside him.

Meanwhile the shadows of the pine trees had slowly swung around until they crossed the road, and their trunks barred the open meadow with gigantic parallels of black and yellow. Little puffs of red dust, lifted by the plunging hoofs of passing teams, dispersed in a grimy shower upon the recumbent man. The sun sank lower and lower, and still Sandy stirred not. And then the repose of this philosopher was disturbed, as other philosophers have been, by the intrusion of an unphilosophical sex.

"Miss Mary," as she was known to the little flock that she had just dismissed from the log schoolhouse beyond the pines, was taking her afternoon walk. Observing an unusually fine cluster of blossoms on the azalea bush opposite, she crossed the road to pluck it, picking her way through the red dust, not without certain fierce little shivers of disgust and some feline circumlocution. And then she came suddenly upon Sandy!

Of course she uttered the little staccato cry of her sex. But when she had paid that tribute to her physical weakness she became overbold and halted for a moment—at least six feet from this prostrate monster—with her white skirts gathered in her hand, ready for flight. But neither sound nor motion came from the bush. With one little foot she then overturned the satirical headboard, and muttered "Beasts!"—an epithet which probably, at that moment, conveniently classified in her mind the entire male population of Red Gulch. For Miss Mary, being possessed of certain rigid notions of her own, had not, perhaps, properly appreciated the demonstrative gallantry for which the Californian has been so justly celebrated by his brother Californians, and had, as a newcomer, perhaps fairly earned the reputation of being "stuck up."

As she stood there she noticed, also, that the slant sunbeams were heating Sandy's head to what she judged to be an unhealthy temperature, and that his hat was lying uselessly at his side. To pick it up and to place it over his face was a work requiring some courage, particularly as his eyes were open. Yet she did it and made good her retreat. But she was somewhat concerned, on looking back, to see that the hat was removed, and that Sandy was sitting up and saying something.

The truth was that in the calm depths of Sandy's mind he was satisfied that the rays of the sun were beneficial and healthful; that from childhood he had objected to lying down in a hat; that no people but condemned fools, past redemption, ever wore hats; and that his right to dispense with them when he pleased was inalienable. This was the statement of his inner consciousness. Un-

fortunately, its outward expression was vague, being limited to a repetition of the following formula: "Su'shine
all ri'! Wasser maär, eh? Wass up, su'shine?"

Miss Mary stopped, and taking fresh courage from her
vantage of distance, asked him if there was anything that
he wanted.

"Wass up? Wasser maär?" continued Sandy, in a
very high key.

"Get up, you horrid man!" said Miss Mary, now thoroughly incensed; "get up and go home."

Sandy staggered to his feet. He was six feet high, and
Miss Mary trembled. He started forward a few paces and
then stopped.

"Wass I go home for?" he suddenly asked, with great
gravity.

"Go and take a bath," replied Miss Mary, eying his
grimy person with great disfavor.

To her infinite dismay, Sandy suddenly pulled off his
coat and vest, threw them on the ground, kicked off
his boots, and plunging wildly forward, darted headlong
over the hill in the direction of the river.

"Goodness heavens! the man will be drowned!" said
Miss Mary; and then, with feminine inconsistency, she
ran back to the schoolhouse and locked herself in.

That night, while seated at supper with her hostess, the
blacksmith's wife, it came to Miss Mary to ask, demurely,
if her husband ever got drunk. "Abner," responded Mrs.
Stidger reflectively—"let's see! Abner hasn't been tight
since last 'lection." Miss Mary would have liked to ask if
he preferred lying in the sun on these occasions, and if a
cold bath would have hurt him; but this would have in-
volved an explanation, which she did not then care to
give. So she contented herself with opening her gray
eyes widely at the red-cheeked Mrs. Stidger—a fine
specimen of Southwestern efflorescence—and then dismissed the subject altogether. The next day she wrote to
her dearest friend in Boston: "I think I find the intoxi-
cated portion of this community the least objectionable.
I refer, my dear, to the men, of course. I do not know
anything that could make the women tolerable."

In less than a week Miss Mary had forgotten this episode, except that her afternoon walks took thereafter, al-

most unconsciously, another direction. She noticed, however, that every morning a fresh cluster of azalea blossoms appeared among the flowers on her desk. This was not strange, as her little flock were aware of her fondness for flowers, and invariably kept her desk bright with anemones, syringas, and lupines; but on questioning them, they one and all professed ignorance of the aza-leas. A few days later, Master Johnny Stidger, whose desk was nearest to the window, was suddenly taken with spasms of apparently gratuitous laughter that threatened the discipline of the school. All that Miss Mary could get from him was that someone had been "looking in the winder." Irate and indignant, she sallied from her hive to do battle with the intruder. As she turned the corner of the schoolhouse she came plump upon the quondam drunkard, now perfectly sober, and inexpressibly sheepish and guilty-looking.

These facts Miss Mary was not slow to take a feminine advantage of, in her present humor. But it was some-what confusing to observe, also, that the beast, despite some faint signs of past dissipation, was amiable-looking —in fact, a kind of blond Samson, whose corn-colored silken beard apparently had never yet known the touch of barber's razor or Delilah's shears. So that the cutting speech which quivered on her ready tongue died upon her lips, and she contented herself with receiving his stammering apology with supercilious eyelids and the gathered skirts of uncontamination. When she re-entered the schoolroom, her eyes fell upon the azaleas with a new sense of revelation; and then she laughed, and the little people all laughed, and they were all unconsciously very happy.

It was a hot day, and not long after this, that two short-legged boys came to grief on the threshold of the school with a pail of water, which they had laboriously brought from the spring, and that Miss Mary compassionately seized the pail and started for the spring herself. At the foot of the hill a shadow crossed her path, and a blue-shirted arm dexterously but gently relieved her of her burden. Miss Mary was both embarrassed and angry. "If you carried more of that for yourself," she said spitefully to the blue arm, without deigning to raise her lashes to its owner, "you'd do better." In the submissive silence that followed she regretted the speech, and thanked him so sweetly at the door that he stumbled. Which caused the children to laugh again—a laugh in which Miss Mary joined, until the color came faintly into her pale cheek. The next day a barrel was mysteriously placed beside the door, and as mysteriously filled with fresh spring-water every morning.

Nor was this superior young person without other quiet attentions. "Profane Bill," driver of the Slumgullion Stage, widely known in the newspapers for his "gallantry" in invariably offering the box seat to the fair sex, had excepted Miss Mary from this attention, on the ground that he had a habit of "cussin' on upgrades," and gave her half the coach to herself. Jack Hamlin, a gambler, having once silently ridden with her in the same coach, afterward threw a decanter at the head of a confederate for mentioning her name in a barroom. The over-dressed mother of a pupil whose paternity was doubtful had often lingered near this astute vestal's temple, never daring to enter its sacred precincts, but content to worship the priestess from afar.

With such unconscious intervals the monotonous procession of blue skies, glittering sunshine, brief twilights, and starlit nights passed over Red Gulch. Miss Mary grew fond of walking in the sedate and proper woods. Perhaps she believed, with Mrs. Stidger, that the balsamic odors of the firs "did her chest good," for certainly her slight cough was less frequent and her step was firmer; perhaps she had learned the unending lesson which the patient pines are never weary of repeating to heedful or listless ears. And so one day she planned a picnic on Buckeye Hill, and took the children with her. Away from the dusty road, the straggling shanties, the yellow ditches, the clamor of restless engines, the cheap finery of shop windows, the deeper glitter of paint and colored glass, and the thin veneering which barbarism takes upon itself in such localities, what infinite relief was theirs! The last heap of ragged rock and clay passed, the last unsightly chasm crossed—how the waiting woods opened their long files to receive them! How the children—perhaps because they had not yet grown quite away from the breast of the bounteous Mother—threw themselves face downward on her brown bosom with uncouth caresses, filling the air with their laughter; and how Miss Mary herself—felinely fastidious and intrenched as she was in the purity of spotless skirts, collar, and cuffs—forgot all, and ran like a crested quail at the head of her brood, until, romping, laughing, and panting, with a loosened braid of brown hair, a hat hanging by a knotted ribbon from her throat, she came suddenly and violently, in the heart of the forest, upon the luckless Sandy!

The explanations, apologies, and not overwise conversation that ensued need not be indicated here. It would seem, however, that Miss Mary had already established some acquaintance with this ex-drunkard. Enough that he was soon accepted as one of the party; that the children, with that quick intelligence which Providence gives the helpless, recognized a friend, and played with his blond beard and long silken mustache, and took other liberties—as the helpless are apt to do. And when he had built a fire against a tree, and had shown them other mysteries of woodcraft, their admiration knew no bounds. At the close of two such foolish, idle, happy hours he found himself lying at the feet of the schoolmistress, gazing dreamily in her face as she sat upon the sloping hillside weaving wreaths of laurel and syringa, in very much the same attitude as he had lain when first they met. Nor was the similitude greatly forced. The weakness of an easy, sensuous nature, that had found a dreamy exaltation in liquor, it is to be feared was now finding an equal intoxication in love.

I think that Sandy was dimly conscious of this himself. I know that he longed to be doing something—slaying a grizzly, scalping a savage, or sacrificing himself in some way for the sake of this sallow-faced, gray-eyed schoolmistress. As I should like to present him in an heroic attitude, I stay my hand with great difficulty at this moment, being only withheld from introducing such an episode by a strong conviction that it does not usually occur at such times. And I trust that my fairest reader, who remembers that in a real crisis it is always some uninteresting stranger or unromantic policeman, and not Adolphus, who rescues, will forgive the omission.

So they sat there undisturbed—the woodpeckers chattering overhead and the voices of the children coming pleasantly from the hollow below. What they said matters little. What they thought—which might have been interesting—did not transpire. The woodpeckers only learned how Miss Mary was an orphan; how she left her uncle's house to come to California for the sake of health and independence; how Sandy was an orphan too; how he came to California for excitement; how he had lived a wild life, and how he was trying to reform; and other details, which from a woodpecker's viewpoint undoubtedly must have seemed stupid and a waste of time. But even in such trifles was the afternoon spent; and when the children were again gathered, and Sandy, with a delicacy which the schoolmistress well understood, took leave of them quietly at the outskirts of the settlement, it had seemed the shortest day of her weary life.

As the long, dry summer withered to its roots, the school term of Red Gulch—to use a local euphuism—"dried up" also. In another day Miss Mary would be free, and for a season, at least, Red Gulch would know her no more. She was seated alone in the schoolhouse, her cheek resting on her hand, her eyes half closed in one of those daydreams in which Miss Mary, I fear, to the danger of school discipline, was lately in the habit of indulging. Her lap was full of mosses, ferns, and other woodland memories. She was so preoccupied with these and her own thoughts that a gentle tapping at the door passed unheard, or translated itself into the remembrance of far-off woodpeckers. When at last it asserted itself more distinctly, she started up with a flushed cheek and opened the door. On the threshold stood a woman, the self-assertion and audacity of whose dress were in singular contrast to her timid, irresolute bearing.

Miss Mary recognized at a glance the dubious mother of her anonymous pupil. Perhaps she was disappointed, perhaps she was only fastidious; but as she coldly invited her to enter, she half unconsciously settled her white cuffs and collar, and gathered closer her own chaste skirts. It was, perhaps, for this reason that the embarrassed stranger, after a moment's hesitation, left her gorgeous parasol open and sticking in the dust beside the

door, and then sat down at the farther end of a long
bench. Her voice was husky as she began—

"I heerd tell that you were goin' down to the Bay tomorrow, and I couldn't let you go until I came to thank
you for your kindness to my Tommy."

Tommy, Miss Mary said, was a good boy, and deserved
more than the poor attention she could give him.

"Thank you, miss; thank ye!" cried the stranger,
brightening even through the color which Red Gulch
knew facetiously as her "war paint," and striving, in her
embarrassment, to drag the long bench nearer the
schoolmistress. "I thank you, miss, for that; and if I am
his mother, there ain't a sweeter, dearer, better boy lives
than him. And if I ain't much as says it, thar ain't a
sweeter, dearer, angeler teacher lives than he's got."

Miss Mary, sitting primly behind her desk, with a ruler
over her shoulder, opened her gray eyes widely at this,
but said nothing.

"It ain't for you to be complimented by the like of me,
I know," she went on hurriedly. "It ain't for me to be
comin' here, in broad day, to do it, either; but I come to
ask a favor—not for me, miss—not for me, but for the
darling boy."

Encouraged by a look in the young schoolmistress's
eye, and putting her lilac-gloved hands together, the fingers downward, between her knees, she went on, in a low
voice:

"You see, miss, there's no one the boy has any claim
on but me, and I ain't the proper person to bring him up.
I thought some last year of sending him away to Frisco
to school, but when they talked of bringing a school-
ma'am here, I waited till I saw you, and then I knew it
was all right, and I could keep my boy a little longer.
And, oh! miss, he loves you so much; and if you could
hear him talk about you in his pretty way, and if he could
ask you what I ask you now, you couldn't refuse him.

"It is natural," she went on rapidly, in a voice that
trembled strangely between pride and humility—"it's natural that he should take to you, miss, for his father, when
I first knew him, was a gentleman—and the boy must
forget me, sooner or later—and so I ain't a-goin' to cry
about that. For I come to ask you to take my Tommy—

God bless him for the bestest, sweetest boy that lives—to—to—take him with you."

She had risen and caught the young girl's hand in her own, and had fallen on her knees beside her.

"I've money plenty, and it's all yours and his. Put him in some good school, where you can go and see him, and help him to—to—to forget his mother. Do with him what you like. The worst you can do will be kindness to what he will learn with me. Only take him out of this wicked life, this cruel place, this home of shame and sorrow. You will! I know you will—won't you? You will—you must not, you cannot say no! You will make him as pure, as gentle as yourself; and when he has grown up, you will tell him his father's name—the name that hasn't passed my lips for years—the name of Alexander Morton, whom they call here Sandy! Miss Mary!—do not take your hand away! Miss Mary, speak to me! You will take my boy? Do not put your face from me. I know it ought not to look on such as me. Miss Mary!—my God, be merciful!—she is leaving me!"

Miss Mary had risen, and in the gathering twilight, had felt her way to the open window. She stood there, leaning against the casement, her eyes fixed on the last rosy tints that were fading from the western sky. There was still some of its light on her pure young forehead, on her white collar, on her clasped white hands, but all fading slowly away. The suppliant had dragged herself, still on her knees, beside her.

"I know it takes time to consider. I will wait here all night; but I cannot go until you speak. Do not deny me now. You will!—I see it in your sweet face—such a face as I have seen in my dreams. I see it in your eyes, Miss Mary!—you will take my boy!"

The last red beam crept higher, suffused Miss Mary's eyes with something of its glory, flickered, and faded, and went out. The sun had set on Red Gulch. In the twilight and silence Miss Mary's voice sounded pleasantly.

"I will take the boy. Send him to me tonight."

The happy mother raised the hem of Miss Mary's skirts to her lips. She would have buried her hot face in its virgin folds, but she dared not. She rose to her feet.

"Does—this man—know of your intention?" asked Miss Mary suddenly.

"No, nor cares. He has never even seen the child to know it."

"Go to him at once—tonight—now! Tell him what you have done. Tell him I have taken his child, and tell him—he must never see—see—the child again. Wherever it may be, he must not come; wherever I may take it, he must not follow! There, go now, please—I'm weary, and —have much yet to do!"

They walked together to the door. On the threshold the woman turned.

"Good night!"

She would have fallen at Miss Mary's feet. But at the same moment the young girl reached out her arms, caught the sinful woman to her own pure breast for one brief moment, and then closed and locked the door.

It was with a sudden sense of great responsibility that Profane Bill took the reins of the Slumgullion stage the next morning, for the schoolmistress was one of his passengers. As he entered the highroad, in obedience to a pleasant voice from the "inside," he suddenly reined up his horses and respectfully waited, as Tommy hopped out at the command of Miss Mary.

"Not that bush, Tommy—the next."

Tommy whipped out his new pocketknife, and cutting a branch from a tall azalea bush, returned with it to Miss Mary.

"All right now?"

"All right!"

And the stage-door closed on the Idyl of Red Gulch.

Brown of
>>>->>>->>>->>>->>>->>>->>>->>>->>Calaveras->>>->>>->>>->>>

>>>->>>->>> A subdued tone of conversation, and the ab-
sence of cigar smoke and boot heels at the windows of
the Wingdam stagecoach, made it evident that one of the
inside passengers was a woman. A disposition on the part
of loungers at the stations to congregate before the window, and some concern in regard to the appearance of
coats, hats, and collars, further indicated that she was
lovely. All of which Mr. Jack Hamlin, on the box-seat,
noted with the smile of cynical philosophy. Not that he
depreciated the sex, but that he recognized therein a
deceitful element, the pursuit of which sometimes drew
mankind away from the equally uncertain blandishments
of poker—of which it may be remarked that Mr. Hamlin was a professional exponent.

So that when he placed his narrow boot on the wheel
and leaped down he did not even glance at the window
from which a green veil was fluttering, but lounged up
and down with that listless and grave indifference of his
class, which was, perhaps, the next thing to good breed-
ing. With his closely buttoned figure and self-contained
air he was a marked contrast to the other passengers,
with their feverish restlessness and boisterous emotion;
and even Bill Masters, a graduate of Harvard, with his
slovenly dress, his overflowing vitality, his intense appreciation of lawlessness and barbarism, and his mouth
filled with crackers and cheese, I fear cut but an unromantic figure beside this lonely calculator of chances,
with his pale Greek face and Homeric gravity.

The driver called "All aboard!" and Mr. Hamlin returned to the coach. His foot was upon the wheel, and
his face raised to the level of the open window, when, at
the same moment, what appeared to him to be the finest
eyes in the world suddenly met his. He quietly dropped

down again, addressed a few words to one of the inside passengers, effected an exchange of seats, and as quietly took his place inside. Mr. Hamlin never allowed his philosophy to interfere with decisive and prompt action.

I fear that this irruption of Jack cast some restraint upon the other passengers, particularly those who were making themselves most agreeable to the lady. One of them leaned forward, and apparently conveyed to her information regarding Mr. Hamlin's profession in a single epithet. Whether Mr. Hamlin heard it, or whether he recognized in the informant a distinguished jurist, from whom, but a few evenings before, he had won several thousand dollars, I cannot say. His colorless face betrayed no sign; his black eyes, quietly observant, glanced indifferently past the legal gentleman, and rested on the much more pleasing features of his neighbor. An Indian stoicism—said to be an inheritance from his maternal ancestor—stood him in good service, until the rolling wheels rattled upon the river gravel at Scott's Ferry, and the stage drew up at the International Hotel for dinner. The legal gentleman and a member of Congress leaped out, and stood ready to assist the descending goddess, while Colonel Starbottle of Siskiyou took charge of her parasol and shawl. In this multiplicity of attention there was a momentary confusion and delay. Jack Hamlin quietly opened the *opposite* door of the coach, took the lady's hand, with that decision and positiveness which a hesitating and undecided sex know how to admire, and in an instant had dexterously and gracefully swung her to the ground and again lifted her to the platform. An audible chuckle on the box, I fear, came from that other cynic, Yuba Bill, the driver. "Look keerfully arter that baggage, Kernel," said the expressman, with affected concern, as he looked after Colonel Starbottle, gloomily bringing up the rear of the triumphant procession to the waiting room.

Mr. Hamlin did not stay for dinner. His horse was already saddled and awaiting him. He dashed over the ford, up the gravelly hill, and out into the dusty perspective of the Wingdam road, like one leaving an unpleasant fancy behind him. The inmates of dusty cabins by the roadside shaded their eyes with their hands and looked after him, recognizing the man by his horse, and speculating what "was up with Comanche Jack." Yet much of this interest centered in the horse, in a community where the time made by "French Pete's" mare in his run from the Sheriff of Calaveras eclipsed all concern in the ultimate fate of that worthy.

The sweating flanks of his gray at length recalled him to himself. He checked his speed, and turning into a by-road sometimes used as a cutoff, trotted leisurely along, the reins hanging listlessly from his fingers. As he rode on, the character of the landscape changed and became more pastoral. Openings in groves of pine and sycamore disclosed some rude attempts at cultivation—a flowering vine trailed over the porch of one cabin, and a woman rocked her cradled babe under the roses of another. A little farther on, Mr. Hamlin came upon some barelegged children wading in the willowy creek, and so wrought upon them with a badinage peculiar to himself that they were emboldened to climb up his horse's legs and over his saddle, until he was fain to develop an exaggerated ferocity of demeanor, and to escape, leaving behind some kisses and coin. And then, advancing deeper into the woods, where all signs of habitation failed, he began to sing, uplifting a tenor so singularly sweet, and shaded by a pathos so subdued and tender, that I wot the robins and linnets stopped to listen. Mr. Hamlin's voice was not cultivated; the subject of his song was some sentimental lunacy, borrowed from the Negro minstrels; but there thrilled through all some occult quality of tone and expression that was unspeakably touching. Indeed, it was a wonderful sight to see this sentimental blackleg, with a pack of cards in his pocket and a revolver at his back, sending his voice before him through the dim woods with a plaint about his "Nelly's grave," in a way that over-flowed the eyes of the listener. A sparrow hawk, fresh from his sixth victim, possibly recognizing in Mr. Hamlin a kindred spirit, stared at him in surprise, and was fain to confess the superiority of man. With a superior predatory capacity *he* couldn't sing.

But Mr. Hamlin presently found himself again on the highroad and at his former pace. Ditches and banks of gravel, denuded hillsides, stumps, and decayed trunks of trees, took the place of woodland and ravine, and indicated his approach to civilization. Then a church steeple came in sight, and he knew that he had reached home. In a few moments he was clattering down the single narrow street that lost itself in a chaotic ruin of races, ditches, and tailings at the foot of the hill, and dismounted before the gilded windows of the Magnolia saloon. Passing through the long barroom, he pushed open a green baize door, entered a dark passage, opened another door with a passkey, and found himself in a dimly lighted room, whose furniture, though elegant and costly for the locality, showed signs of abuse. The inlaid center table was overlaid with stained disks that were not contemplated in the original design, the embroidered armchairs were discolored, and the green velvet lounge, on which Mr. Hamlin threw himself, was soiled at the foot with the red soil of Wingdam.

Mr. Hamlin did not sing in his cage. He lay still, looking at a highly colored painting above him, representing a young creature of opulent charms. It occurred to him then, for the first time, that he had never seen exactly that kind of a woman, and that, if he should, he would not probably fall in love with her. Perhaps he was thinking of another style of beauty. But just then someone knocked at the door. Without rising, he pulled a cord that apparently shot back a bolt, for the door swung open, and a man entered.

The newcomer was broad-shouldered and robust—a vigor not borne out in the face, which, though handsome, was singularly weak and disfigured by dissipation. He appeared to be, also, under the influence of liquor, for he started on seeing Mr. Hamlin, and said, "I thought Kate was here"; stammered, and seemed confused and embarrassed.

Mr. Hamlin smiled the smile which he had before worn on the Wingdam coach, and sat up, quite refreshed and ready for business.

"You didn't come up on the stage," continued the newcomer, "did you?"

"No," replied Hamlin; "I left it at Scott's Ferry. It isn't due for half an hour yet. But how's luck, Brown?"

"D—d bad," said Brown, his face suddenly assuming an

expression of weak despair. "I'm cleaned out again,
Jack," he continued, in a whining tone, that formed a
pitiable contrast to his bulky figure; "can't you help me
with a hundred till tomorrow's cleanup? You see I've
got to send money home to the old woman, and—you've
won twenty times that amount from me."

The conclusion was, perhaps, not entirely logical, but
Jack overlooked it, and handed the sum to his visitor.
"The old-woman business is about played out, Brown,"
he added, by way of commentary; "why don't you say
you want to buck ag'in' faro? You know you ain't married!"

"Fact, sir," said Brown, with a sudden gravity, as if the
mere contact of the gold with the palm of the hand had
imparted some dignity to his frame. "I've got a wife—a
d—d good one, too, if I do say it—in the States. It's
three years since I've seen her, and a year since I've writ
to her. When things is about straight, and we get down
to the lead, I'm going to send for her."

"And Kate?" queried Mr. Hamlin, with his previous
smile.

Mr. Brown of Calaveras essayed an archness of glance
to cover his confusion, which his weak face and
whiskey-muddled intellect but poorly carried out, and
said—

"D—n it, Jack, a man must have a little liberty, you
know. But come, what do you say to a little game? Give
us a show to double this hundred."

Jack Hamlin looked curiously at his fatuous friend.
Perhaps he knew that the man was predestined to lose
the money, and preferred that it should flow back into
his own coffers rather than any other. He nodded his
head, and drew his chair toward the table. At the same
moment there came a rap upon the door.

"It's Kate," said Mr. Brown.

Mr. Hamlin shot back the bolt and the door opened.
But, for the first time in his life, he staggered to his feet
utterly unnerved and abashed, and for the first time in
his life the hot blood crimsoned his colorless cheeks to
his forehead. For before him stood the lady he had lifted
from the Wingdam coach, whom Brown, dropping his
cards with a hysterical laugh, greeted as—

"My old woman, by thunder!"

They say that Mrs. Brown burst into tears and reproaches of her husband. I saw her in 1857 at Marysville, and disbelieve the story. And the *Wingdam Chronicle* of the next week, under the head of "Touching Reunion," said: "One of those beautiful and touching incidents peculiar to California life occurred last week in our city. The wife of one of Wingdam's eminent pioneers, tired of the effete civilization of the East and its inhospitable climate, resolved to join her noble husband upon these golden shores. Without informing him of her intention, she undertook the long journey, and arrived last week. The joy of the husband may be easier imagined than described. The meeting is said to have been indescribably affecting. We trust her example may be followed."

Whether owing to Mrs. Brown's influence, or to some more successful speculations, Mr. Brown's financial fortune from that day steadily improved. He bought out his partners in the "Nip and Tuck" lead, with money which was said to have been won at poker a week or two after his wife's arrival, but which rumor, adopting Mrs. Brown's theory that Brown had forsworn the gaming table, declared to have been furnished by Mr. Jack Hamlin. He built and furnished the Wingdam House, which pretty Mrs. Brown's great popularity kept overflowing with guests. He was elected to the Assembly, and gave largess to churches. A street in Wingdam was named in his honor.

Yet it was noted that in proportion as he waxed wealthy and fortunate, he grew pale, thin, and anxious. As his wife's popularity increased, he became fretful and impatient. The most uxorious of husbands, he was absurdly jealous. If he did not interfere with his wife's social liberty, it was because it was maliciously whispered that his first and only attempt was met by an outburst from Mrs. Brown that terrified him into silence. Much of this kind of gossip came from those of her own sex whom she had supplanted in the chivalrous attentions of Wingdam, which, like most popular chivalry, was devoted to an admiration of power, whether of masculine force or feminine beauty. It should be remembered, too, in her extenuation, that since her arrival she had been the unconscious priestess of a mythological worship, perhaps not more ennobling to her womanhood than that which distinguished an older Greek democracy. I think that Brown was dimly conscious of this. But his only confidant was Jack Hamlin, whose infelix reputation naturally precluded any open intimacy with the family, and whose visits were infrequent.

It was midsummer and a moonlit night, and Mrs. Brown, very rosy, large-eyed, and pretty, sat upon the piazza, enjoying the fresh incense of the mountain breeze, and, it is to be feared, another incense which was not so fresh nor quite as innocent. Beside her sat Colonel Starbottle and Judge Boompointer, and a later addition to her court in the shape of a foreign tourist. She was in good spirits.

"What do you see down the road?" inquired the gallant Colonel, who had been conscious for the last few minutes that Mrs. Brown's attention was diverted.

"Dust," said Mrs. Brown, with a sigh. "Only Sister Anne's 'flock of sheep.' "

The Colonel, whose literary recollections did not extend farther back than last week's paper, took a more practical view. "It ain't sheep," he continued; "it's a horseman. Judge, ain't that Jack Hamlin's gray?"

But the Judge didn't know; and as Mrs. Brown suggested the air was growing too cold for further investigations, they retired to the parlor.

Mr. Brown was in the stable, where he generally retired after dinner. Perhaps it was to show his contempt for his wife's companions; perhaps, like other weak natures, he found pleasure in the exercise of absolute power over inferior animals. He had a certain gratification in the training of a chestnut mare, whom he could beat or caress as pleased him, which he couldn't do with Mrs. Brown. It was here that he recognized a certain gray horse which had just come in, and looking a little farther on, found his rider. Brown's greeting was cordial and hearty; Mr. Hamlin's somewhat restrained. But, at Brown's urgent request, he followed him up the back stairs to a narrow corridor, and thence to a small room looking out upon the stable yard. It was plainly furnished with a bed, a table, a few chairs, and a rack for guns and whips.

"This yer's my home, Jack," said Brown with a sigh, as he threw himself upon the bed and motioned his companion to a chair. "Her room's t' other end of the hall. It's more'n six months since we've lived together, or met, except at meals. It's mighty rough papers on the head of the house, ain't it?" he said with a forced laugh. "But I'm glad to see you, Jack, d—d glad," and he reached from the bed, and again shook the unresponsive hand of Jack Hamlin.

"I brought ye up here, for I didn't want to talk in the stable; though, for the matter of that, it's all round town. Don't strike a light. We can talk here in the moonshine. Put up your feet on that winder and sit here beside me. Thar's whiskey in that jug."

Mr. Hamlin did not avail himself of the information. Brown of Calaveras turned his face to the wall, and continued—

"If I didn't love the woman, Jack, I wouldn't mind. But it's loving her, and seeing her day arter day goin' on at this rate, and no one to put down the brake; that's what gits me! But I'm glad to see ye, Jack, d—d glad."

In the darkness he groped about until he had found and wrung his companion's hand again. He would have detained it, but Jack slipped it into the buttoned breast of his coat, and asked listlessly, "How long has this been going on?"

"Ever since she came here; ever since the day she walked into the Magnolia. I was a fool then; Jack, I'm a fool now; but I didn't know how much I loved her till then. And she hasn't been the same woman since.

"But that ain't all, Jack; and it's what I wanted to see you about, and I'm glad you've come. It ain't that she doesn't love me any more; it ain't that she fools with every chap that comes along; for perhaps I staked her love and lost it, as I did everything else at the Magnolia; and perhaps foolin' is nateral to some women, and thar ain't no great harm done, 'cept to the fools. But, Jack, I think—I think she loves somebody else. Don't move, Jack! don't move; if your pistol hurts ye, take it off.

"It's been more'n six months now that she's seemed

unhappy and lonesome, and kinder nervous and scared-
like. And sometimes I've ketched her lookin' at me sort
of timid and pitying. And she writes to somebody. And
for the last week she's been gathering her own things—
trinkets, and furbelows, and jew'lry—and, Jack, I think
she's goin' off. I could stand all but that. To have her steal
away like a thief!" He put his face downward to the pillow, and for a few moments there was no sound but the
ticking of a clock on the mantel. Mr. Hamlin lit a cigar,
and moved to the open window. The moon no longer
shone into the room, and the bed and its occupant were
in shadow. "What shall I do, Jack?" said the voice
from the darkness.

The answer came promptly and clearly from the window side, "Spot the man, and kill him on sight."

"But, Jack"—

"He's took the risk!"

"But will that bring *her* back?"

Jack did not reply, but moved from the window towards
the door.

"Don't go yet, Jack; light the candle and sit by the
table. It's a comfort to see ye, if nothin' else."

Jack hesitated and then complied. He drew a pack of
cards from his pocket and shuffled them, glancing at the
bed. But Brown's face was turned to the wall. When
Mr. Hamlin had shuffled the cards, he cut them, and
dealt one card on the opposite side of the table towards
the bed, and another on his side of the table for himself.
The first was a deuce; his own card a king. He then
shuffled and cut again. This time "dummy" had a queen
and himself a four-spot. Jack brightened up for the third
deal. It brought his adversary a deuce and himself a
king again. "Two out of three," said Jack audibly.

"What's that, Jack?" said Brown.

"Nothing."

Then Jack tried his hand with dice; but he always threw
sixes and his imaginary opponent aces. The force of habit
is sometimes confusing.

Meanwhile some magnetic influence in Mr. Hamlin's
presence, or the anodyne of liquor, or both, brought sur-
cease of sorrow, and Brown slept. Mr. Hamlin moved his
chair to the window and looked out on the town of Wing-

dam, now sleeping peacefully, its harsh outlines softened and subdued, its glaring colors mellowed and sobered in the moonlight that flowed over all. In the hush he could hear the gurgling of water in the ditches and the sighing of the pines beyond the hill. Then he looked up at the firmament, and as he did so a star shot across the twinkling field. Presently another, and then another. The phenomenon suggested to Mr. Hamlin a fresh augury. If in another fifteen minutes another star should fall— He sat there, watch in hand, for twice that time, but the phenomenon was not repeated.

The clock struck two, and Brown still slept. Mr. Hamlin approached the table and took from his pocket a letter, which he read by the flickering candlelight. It contained only a single line, written in pencil, in a woman's hand—

"Be at the corral with the buggy at three."

The sleeper moved uneasily and then awoke. "Are you there, Jack?"

"Yes."

"Don't go yet. I dreamed just now, Jack—dreamed of old times. I thought that Sue and me was being married agin, and that the parson, Jack, was—who do you think?—you!"

The gambler laughed, and seated himself on the bed, the paper still in his hand.

"It's a good sign, ain't it?" queried Brown.

"I reckon! Say, old man, hadn't you better get up?"

The "old man," thus affectionately appealed to, rose, with the assistance of Hamlin's outstretched hand.

"Smoke?"

Brown mechanically took the proffered cigar.

"Light?"

Jack had twisted the letter into a spiral, lit it, and held it for his companion. He continued to hold it until it was consumed, and dropped the fragment—a fiery star—from the open window. He watched it as it fell, and then returned to his friend.

"Old man," he said, placing his hands upon Brown's shoulders, "in ten minutes I'll be on the road, and gone like that spark. We won't see each other agin; but, before I go, take a fool's advice: sell out all you've got, take your wife with you, and quit the country. It ain't no place for

you nor her. Tell her she must go; make her go if she
won't. Don't whine because you can't be a saint and she
ain't an angel. Be a man, and treat her like a woman.
Don't be a d——d fool. Good-by."

He tore himself from Brown's grasp and leaped down
the stairs like a deer. At the stable door he collared the
half-sleeping hostler, and backed him against the wall.
"Saddle my horse in two minutes, or I'll"—— The ellipsis
was frightfully suggestive.

"The missis said you was to have the buggy," stammered the man.

"D——n the buggy!"

The horse was saddled as fast as the nervous hands of
the astounded hostler could manipulate buckle and strap.

"Is anything up, Mr. Hamlin?" said the man, who, like
all his class, admired the *élan* of his fiery patron, and
was really concerned in his welfare.

"Stand aside!"

The man fell back. With an oath, a bound, and clatter,
Jack was into the road. In another moment, to the man's
half-awakened eyes, he was but a moving cloud of dust in
the distance, towards which a star just loosed from its
brethren was trailing a stream of fire.

But early that morning the dwellers by the Wingdam
turnpike, miles away, heard a voice, pure as a skylark's,
singing afield. They who were asleep turned over on their
rude couches to dream of youth, and love, and olden
days. Hard-faced men and anxious gold-seekers, already
at work, ceased their labors and leaned upon their picks
to listen to a romantic vagabond ambling away against the
rosy sunrise.

➤➤➤-➤➤➤-➤➤ We were eight including the driver. We had not spoken during the passage of the last six miles, since the jolting of the heavy vehicle over the roughening road had spoiled the Judge's last poetical quotation. The tall man beside the Judge was asleep, his arm passed through the swaying strap and his head resting upon it—altogether a limp, helpless looking object, as if he had hanged himself and been cut down too late. The French lady on the back seat was asleep too, yet in a half-conscious propriety of attitude, shown even in the disposition of the handkerchief which she held to her forehead and which partially veiled her face. The lady from Virginia City, traveling with her husband, had long since lost all individuality in a wild confusion of ribbons, veils, furs, and shawls. There was no sound but the rattling of wheels and the dash of rain upon the roof. Suddenly the stage stopped and we became dimly aware of voices. The driver was evidently in the midst of an exciting colloquy with someone in the road— a colloquy of which such fragments as "bridge gone," "twenty feet of water," "can't pass," were occasionally distinguishable above the storm. Then came a lull, and a mysterious voice from the road shouted the parting adjuration—

"Try Miggles's."

We caught a glimpse of our leaders as the vehicle slowly turned, of a horseman vanishing through the rain, and we were evidently on our way to Miggles's.

Who and where was Miggles? The Judge, our authority, did not remember the name, and he knew the country thoroughly. The Washoe traveler thought Miggles must keep a hotel. We only knew that we were stopped by high water in front and rear, and that Miggles was our rock of refuge. A ten minutes' splashing through a tangled byroad scarcely wide enough for the stage, and we drew up before a barred and boarded gate in a wide stone wall or fence about eight feet high. Evidently Miggles's, and evidently Miggles did not keep a hotel.

The driver got down and tried the gate. It was securely locked.

"Miggles! O Miggles!"

No answer.

"Migg-ells! You Miggles!" continued the driver, with rising wrath.

"Migglesy!" joined in the expressman persuasively. "O Miggy! Mig!"

But no reply came from the apparently insensate Miggles. The Judge, who had finally got the window down, put his head out and propounded a series of questions, which if answered categorically would have undoubtedly elucidated the whole mystery, but which the driver evaded by replying that "if we didn't want to sit in the coach all night we had better rise up and sing out for Miggles."

So we rose up and called on Miggles in chorus, then separately. And when we had finished, a Hibernian fellow passenger from the roof called for "Maygells!" whereat we all laughed. While we were laughing the driver cried, "Shoo!"

We listened. To our infinite amazement the chorus of "Miggles" was repeated from the other side of the wall, even to the final and supplemental "Maygells."

"Extraordinary echo!" said the Judge.

"Extraordinary d—d skunk!" roared the driver contemptuously. "Come out of that, Miggles, and show yourself! Be a man, Miggles! Don't hide in the dark; I wouldn't if I were you, Miggles," continued Yuba Bill, now dancing about in an excess of fury.

"Miggles!" continued the voice, "O Miggles!"

"My good man! Mr. Myghail!" said the Judge, softening the asperities of the name as much as possible. "Consider the inhospitality of refusing shelter from the inclemency of the weather to helpless females. Really, my dear sir"— But a succession of "Miggles," ending in a burst of laughter, drowned his voice.

Yuba Bill hesitated no longer. Taking a heavy stone from the road, he battered down the gate, and with the expressman entered the enclosure. We followed. Nobody was to be seen. In the gathering darkness all that we could distinguish was that we were in a garden—from the rose bushes that scattered over us a minute spray from their dripping leaves—and before a long, rambling wooden building.

"Do you know this Miggles?" asked the Judge of Yuba Bill.

"No, nor don't want to," said Bill shortly, who felt the Pioneer Stage Company insulted in his person by the contumacious Miggles.

"But, my dear sir," expostulated the Judge, as he thought of the barred gate.

"Lookee here," said Yuba Bill, with fine irony, "hadn't you better go back and sit in the coach till yer introduced? I'm going in," and he pushed open the door of the building.

A long room, lighted only by the embers of a fire that was dying on the large hearth at its farther extremity; the walls curiously papered, and the flickering firelight bringing out its grotesque pattern; somebody sitting in a large armchair by the fireplace. All this we saw as we crowded together into the room after the driver and expressman.

"Hello! be you Miggles?" said Yuba Bill to the solitary occupant.

The figure neither spoke nor stirred. Yuba Bill walked wrathfully toward it and turned the eye of his coach lantern upon its face. It was a man's face, prematurely old and wrinkled, with very large eyes, in which there was that expression of perfectly gratuitous solemnity which I had sometimes seen in an owl's. The large eyes wandered from Bill's face to the lantern, and finally fixed their gaze on that luminous object without further recognition.

Bill restrained himself with an effort.

"Miggles! be you deaf? You ain't dumb anyhow, you know," and Yuba Bill shook the insensate figure by the shoulder.

To our great dismay, as Bill removed his hand, the venerable stranger apparently collapsed, sinking into half his size and an undistinguishable heap of clothing.

"Well, dern my skin," said Bill, looking appealingly at us, and hopelessly retiring from the contest.

The Judge now stepped forward, and we lifted the mysterious invertebrate back into his original position. Bill was dismissed with the lantern to reconnoiter outside, for it was evident that from the helplessness of this solitary man there must be attendants near at hand, and we all drew around the fire. The Judge, who had regained his authority, and had never lost his conversational amiability —standing before us with his back to the hearth—charged us, as an imaginary jury, as follows:

"It is evident that either our distinguished friend here has reached that condition described by Shakespeare as 'the sere and yellow leaf,' or has suffered some premature abatement of his mental and physical faculties. Whether he is really the Miggles"—

Here he was interrupted by "Miggles! O Miggles! Miggle'sy! Mig!" and, in fact, the whole chorus of Miggles in very much the same key as it had once before been delivered unto us.

We gazed at each other for a moment in some alarm. The Judge, in particular, vacated his position quickly, as the voice seemed to come directly over his shoulder. The cause, however, was soon discovered in a large magpie who was perched upon a shelf over the fireplace, and who immediately relapsed into a sepulchral silence, which contrasted singularly with his previous volubility. It was undoubtedly his voice which we had heard in the road, and our friend in the chair was not responsible for the discourtesy. Yuba Bill, who re-entered the room after an unsuccessful search, was loath to accept the explanation, and still eyed the helpless sitter with suspicion. He had found a shed in which he had put up his horses, but he came back dripping and skeptical. "Thar ain't nobody but him within ten mile of the shanty, and that ar d—d old skeesicks knows it."

But the faith of the majority proved to be securely based. Bill had scarcely ceased growling before we heard a quick step upon the porch, the trailing of a wet skirt, the door was flung open, and with a flash of white teeth, a sparkle of dark eyes, and an utter absence of ceremony or diffidence, a young woman entered, shut the door, and, panting, leaned back against it.

"Oh, if you please, I'm Miggles!"

And this was Miggles! this bright-eyed, full-throated young woman, whose wet gown of coarse blue stuff could not hide the beauty of the feminine curves to which it clung; from the chestnut crown of whose head, topped by a man's oilskin sou'wester, to the little feet and ankles, hidden somewhere in the recesses of her boy's brogans, all was grace—this was Miggles, laughing at us, too, in the most airy, frank, offhand manner imaginable.

"You see, boys," said she, quite out of breath, and holding one little hand against her side, quite unheeding the speechless discomfiture of our party or the complete demoralization of Yuba Bill, whose features had relaxed into an expression of gratuitous and imbecile cheerfulness —"you see, boys, I was mor'n two miles away when you passed down the road. I thought you might pull up here, and so I ran the whole way, knowing nobody was home but Jim—and—and—I'm out of breath—and—that lets me out." And here Miggles caught her dripping oilskin hat from her head, with a mischievous swirl that scattered a shower of raindrops over us; attempted to put back her hair; dropped two hairpins in the attempt; laughed, and sat down beside Yuba Bill, with her hands crossed lightly on her lap.

The Judge recovered himself first and essayed an extravagant compliment.

"I'll trouble you for that ha'rpin," said Miggles gravely. Half a dozen hands were eagerly stretched forward; the missing hairpin was restored to its fair owner; and Miggles, crossing the room, looked keenly in the face of the invalid. The solemn eyes looked back at hers with an expression we had never seen before. Life and intelligence seemed to struggle back into the rugged face. Miggles laughed again—it was a singularly eloquent laugh—and turned her black eyes and white teeth once more towards us.

"This afflicted person is"—hesitated the Judge.

"Jim!" said Miggles.

"Your father?"

"No!"

"Brother?"

"No!"

"Husband?"

Miggles darted a quick, half-defiant glance at the two lady passengers, who I had noticed did not participate in the general masculine admiration of Miggles, and said gravely, "No, it's Jim!"

There was an awkward pause. The lady passengers moved closer to each other; the Washoe husband looked abstractedly at the fire, and the tall man apparently turned his eyes inward for self-support at this emergency. But Miggles's laugh, which was very infectious, broke the silence.

"Come," she said briskly, "you must be hungry. Who'll bear a hand to help me get tea?"

She had no lack of volunteers. In a few moments Yuba Bill was engaged like Caliban in bearing logs for this Miranda; the expressman was grinding coffee on the veranda; to myself the arduous duty of slicing bacon was assigned; and the Judge lent each man his good-humored and voluble counsel. And when Miggles, assisted by the Judge and our Hibernian "deck passenger," set the table with all the available crockery, we had become quite joyous in spite of the rain that beat against the windows, the wind that whirled down the chimney, the two ladies who whispered together in the corner, or the magpie, who uttered a satirical and croaking commentary on their conversation from his perch above. In the now bright, blazing fire we could see that the walls were papered with illustrated journals, arranged with feminine taste and discrimination. The furniture was extemporized and adapted from candleboxes and packing cases, and covered with gay calico or the skin of some animal. The armchair of the helpless Jim was an ingenious variation of a flour barrel. There was neatness, and even a taste for the picturesque, to be seen in the few details of the long, low room.

The meal was a culinary success. But more, it was a social triumph—chiefly, I think, owing to the rare tact of Miggles in guiding the conversation, asking all the questions herself, yet bearing throughout a frankness that rejected the idea of any concealment on her own part, so that we talked of ourselves, of our prospects, of the journey, of the weather, of each other—of everything but our host and hostess. It must be confessed that Miggles's conversation was never elegant, rarely grammatical, and that at times she employed expletives the use of which had generally been yielded to our sex. But they

were delivered with such a lighting up of teeth and eyes,
and were usually followed by a laugh—a laugh peculiar to Miggles—so frank and honest that it seemed to
clear the moral atmosphere.

Once during the meal we heard a noise like the rubbing
of a heavy body against the outer walls of the house. This
was shortly followed by a scratching and sniffling at the
door. "That's Joaquin," said Miggles, in reply to our
questioning glances; "would you like to see him?" Before
we could answer she had opened the door, and disclosed
a half-grown grizzly, who instantly raised himself on his
haunches, with his forepaws hanging down in the popular
attitude of mendicancy, and looked admiringly at Miggles,
with a very singular resemblance in his manner to Yuba
Bill. "That's my watchdog," said Miggles in explanation.
"Oh, he don't bite," she added, as the two lady passengers
fluttered into a corner. "Does he, old Toppy?" (the latter
remark being addressed directly to the sagacious Joaquin).
"I tell you what, boys," continued Miggles, after she had
fed and closed the door on Ursa Minor, "you were in big
luck that Joaquin wasn't hanging round when you dropped
in tonight."

"Where was he?" asked the Judge.

"With me," said Miggles. "Lord love you! he trots
round with me nights like as if he was a man."

We were silent for a few moments, and listened to the
wind. Perhaps we all had the same picture before us—of
Miggles walking through the rainy woods with her savage
guardian at her side. The Judge, I remember, said something about Una and her lion; but Miggles received it, as
she did other compliments, with quiet gravity. Whether
she was altogether unconscious of the admiration she
excited—she could hardly have been oblivious of Yuba
Bill's adoration—I know not; but her very frankness suggested a perfect sexual equality that was cruelly humiliating to the younger members of our party.

The incident of the bear did not add anything in Miggles's favor to the opinions of those of her own sex who
were present. In fact, the repast over, a chillness radiated
from the two lady passengers that no pine boughs brought
in by Yuba Bill and cast as a sacrifice upon the hearth
could wholly overcome. Miggles felt it; and suddenly de-

claring that it was time to "turn in," offered to show the ladies to their bed in an adjoining room. "You, boys, will have to camp out here by the fire as well as you can," she added, "for thar ain't but the one room."

Our sex—by which, my dear sir, I allude of course to the stronger portion of humanity—has been generally relieved from the imputation of curiosity or a fondness for gossip. Yet I am constrained to say that hardly had the door closed on Miggles than we crowded together, whispering, snickering, smiling, and exchanging suspicions, surmises, and a thousand speculations in regard to our pretty hostess and her singular companion. I fear that we even hustled that imbecile paralytic, who sat like a voiceless Memnon in our midst, gazing with the serene indifference of the past in his passionless eyes upon our wordy counsels. In the midst of an exciting discussion the door opened again and Miggles re-entered.

But not, apparently, the same Miggles who a few hours before had flashed upon us. Her eyes were downcast, and as she hesitated for a moment on the threshold, with a blanket on her arm, she seemed to have left behind her the frank fearlessness which had charmed us a moment before. Coming into the room, she drew a low stool beside the paralytic's chair, sat down, drew the blanket over her shoulders, and saying, "If it's all the same to you, boys, as we're rather crowded, I'll stop here tonight," took the invalid's withered hand in her own, and turned her eyes upon the dying fire. An instinctive feeling that this was only premonitory to more confidential relations, and perhaps some shame at our previous curiosity, kept us silent. The rain still beat upon the roof, wandering gusts of wind stirred the embers into momentary brightness, until, in a lull of the elements, Miggles suddenly lifted up her head, and throwing her hair over her shoulder, turned her face upon the group and asked—

"Is there any of you that knows me?"

There was no reply.

"Think again! I lived at Marysville in '53. Everybody knew me there, and everybody had the right to know me. I kept the Polka Saloon until I came to live with Jim. That's six years ago. Perhaps I've changed some."

The absence of recognition may have disconcerted her.

She turned her head to the fire again, and it was some seconds before she again spoke, and then more rapidly—

"Well, you see I thought some of you must have known me. There's no great harm done anyway. What I was going to say was this: Jim here"—she took his hand in both of hers as she spoke—"used to know me, if you didn't, and spent a heap of money upon me. I reckon he spent all he had. And one day—it's six years ago this winter—Jim came into my back room, sat down on my sofy, like as you see him in that chair, and never moved again without help. He was struck all of a heap, and never seemed to know what ailed him. The doctors came and said as how it was caused all along of his way of life,— for Jim was mighty free and wildlike—and that he would never get better, and couldn't last long anyway. They advised me to send him to Frisco to the hospital, for he was no good to anyone and would be a baby all his life. Perhaps it was something in Jim's eye, perhaps it was that I never had a baby, but I said 'No.' I was rich then, for I was popular with everybody—gentlemen like yourself, sir, came to see me—and I sold out my business and bought this yer place, because it was sort of out of the way of travel, you see, and I brought my baby here."

With a woman's intuitive tact and poetry, she had, as she spoke, slowly shifted her position so as to bring the mute figure of the ruined man between her and her audience, hiding in the shadow behind it, as if she offered it as a tacit apology for her actions. Silent and expressionless, it yet spoke for her; helpless, crushed, and smitten with the Divine thunderbolt, it still stretched an invisible arm around her.

Hidden in the darkness, but still holding his hand, she went on:

"It was a long time before I could get the hang of things about yer, for I was used to company and excitement. I couldn't get any woman to help me, and a man I dursn't trust; but what with the Indians hereabout, who'd do odd jobs for me, and having everything sent from the North Fork, Jim and I managed to worry through. The doctor would run up from Sacramento once in a while. He'd ask to see 'Miggles's baby,' as he called Jim, and when he'd go away, he'd say, 'Miggles, you're a trump—God bless you,' and it didn't seem so lonely after that. But the last time he was here he said, as he opened the door to go, 'Do you know, Miggles, your baby will grow up to be a man yet and an honor to his mother; but not here, Miggles, not here!' And I thought he went away sad—and—and"— and here Miggles's voice and head were somehow both lost completely in the shadow.

"The folks about here are very kind," said Miggles, after a pause, coming a little into the light again. "The men from the Fork used to hang around here, until they found they wasn't wanted, and the women are kind, and don't call. I was pretty lonely until I picked up Joaquin in the woods yonder one day, when he wasn't so high, and taught him to beg for his dinner; and then thar's Polly— that's the magpie—she knows no end of tricks, and makes it quite sociable of evenings with her talk, and so I don't feel like as I was the only living being about the ranch. And Jim here," said Miggles, with her old laugh again, and coming out quite into the firelight—"Jim—Why, boys, you would admire to see how much he knows for a man like him. Sometimes I bring him flowers, and he looks at 'em just as natural as if he knew 'em; and times, when we're sitting alone, I read him those things on the wall. Why, Lord!" said Miggles, with her frank laugh, "I've read him that whole side of the house this winter. There never was such a man for reading as Jim."

"Why," asked the Judge, "do you not marry this man to whom you have devoted your youthful life?"

"Well, you see," said Miggles, "it would be playing it rather low down on Jim to take advantage of his being so helpless. And then, too, if we were man and wife now, we'd both know that I was *bound* to do what I do now of my own accord."

"But you are young yet and attractive"—

"It's getting late," said Miggles gravely, "and you'd better all turn in. Good night, boys;" and throwing the blanket over her head, Miggles laid herself down beside Jim's chair, her head pillowed on the low stool that held his feet, and spoke no more. The fire slowly faded from the hearth; we each sought our blankets in silence; and presently there was no sound in the long room but the pattering of the rain upon the roof and the heavy breathing of the sleepers.

It was nearly morning when I awoke from a troubled dream. The storm had passed, the stars were shining, and through the shutterless window the full moon, lifting itself over the solemn pines without, looked into the room. It touched the lonely figure in the chair with an infinite compassion, and seemed to baptize with a shining flood the lowly head of the woman whose hair, as in the sweet old story, bathed the feet of him she loved. It even lent a kindly poetry to the rugged outline of Yuba Bill, half re-clining on his elbow between them and his passengers, with savagely patient eyes keeping watch and ward. And then I fell asleep and only woke at broad day, with Yuba Bill standing over me, and "All aboard" ringing in my ears.

Coffee was waiting for us on the table, but Miggles was gone. We wandered about the house and lingered long after the horses were harnessed, but she did not return. It was evident that she wished to avoid a formal leave-taking, and had so left us to depart as we had come. After we had helped the ladies into the coach, we re-turned to the house and solemnly shook hands with the paralytic Jim, as solemnly setting him back into position after each handshake. Then we looked for the last time around the long low room, at the stool where Miggles had sat, and slowly took our seats in the waiting coach. The whip cracked, and we were off!

But as we reached the highroad, Bill's dexterous hand laid the six horses back on their haunches, and the stage stopped with a jerk. For there, on a little emi-nence beside the road, stood Miggles, her hair flying, her eyes sparkling, her white handkerchief waving, and her white teeth flashing a last "good-by." We waved our hats in return. And then Yuba Bill, as if fearful of further fascination, madly lashed his horses forward, and we sank back in our seats.

We exchanged not a word until we reached the North Fork and the stage drew up at the Independence House. Then, the Judge leading, we walked into the barroom and took our places gravely at the bar.

"Are your glasses charged, gentlemen?" said the Judge, solemnly taking off his white hat.

They were.

"Well, then, here's to *Miggles*—GOD BLESS HER!"

Perhaps He had. Who knows?

How Santa Claus Came to
⋙⋙⋙⋙⋙⋙⋙⋙⋙⋙ Simpson's Bar ⋙⋙⋙⋙⋙

⋙⋙⋙⋙ It had been raining in the valley of the Sacramento. The North Fork had overflowed its banks, and Rattlesnake Creek was impassable. The few boulders that had marked the summer ford at Simpson's Crossing were obliterated by a vast sheet of water stretching to the foothills. The upstage was stopped at Granger's; the last mail had been abandoned in the tules, the rider swimming for his life. "An area," remarked the *Sierra Avalanche,* with pensive local pride, "as large as the State of Massachusetts is now under water."

Nor was the weather any better in the foothills. The mud lay deep on the mountain road; wagons that neither physical force nor moral objurgation could move from the evil ways into which they had fallen encumbered the track, and the way to Simpson's Bar was indicated by broken-down teams and hard swearing. And further on, cut off and inaccessible, rained upon and bedraggled, smitten by high winds and threatened by high water, Simpson's Bar, on the eve of Christmas Day, 1862, clung like a swallow's nest to the rocky entablature and splintered capitals of Table Mountain, and shook in the blast.

As night shut down on the settlement, a few lights gleamed through the mist from the windows of cabins on either side of the highway, now crossed and gullied by lawless streams and swept by marauding winds. Happily most of the population were gathered at Thompson's store, clustered around a red-hot stove, at which they silently spat in some accepted sense of social communion that perhaps rendered conversation unnecessary. Indeed, most methods of diversion had long since been exhausted on Simpson's Bar; high water had suspended the regular occupations on gulch and on river, and a con-

sequent lack of money and whiskey had taken the zest
from most illegitimate recreation. Even Mr. Hamlin was
fain to leave the Bar with fifty dollars in his pocket—the
only amount actually realized of the large sums won by
him in the successful exercise of his arduous profession.
"Ef I was asked," he remarked somewhat later— "ef I
was asked to pint out a purty little village where a retired sport as didn't care for money could exercise hisself, frequent and lively, I'd say Simpson's Bar; but for
a young man with a large family depending on his exer-
tions, it don't pay." As Mr. Hamlin's family consisted
mainly of female adults, this remark is quoted rather to
show the breadth of his humor than the exact extent of
his responsibilities.

Howbeit, the unconscious objects of this satire sat that
evening in the listless apathy begotten of idleness and
lack of excitement. Even the sudden splashing of hoofs
before the door did not arouse them. Dick Bullen alone
paused in the act of scraping out his pipe, and lifted his
head, but no other one of the group indicated any interest in, or recognition of, the man who entered.

It was a figure familiar enough to the company, and
known in Simpson's Bar as "The Old Man." A man of
perhaps fifty years; grizzled and scant of hair, but still
fresh and youthful of complexion. A face full of ready
but not very powerful sympathy, with a chameleonlike
aptitude for taking on the shade and color of contiguous
moods and feelings. He had evidently just left some hilarious companions, and did not at first notice the gravity of the group, but clapped the shoulder of the nearest
man jocularly, and threw himself into a vacant chair.

"Jest heard the best thing out, boys! Ye know Smiley,
over yar—Jim Smiley—funniest man in the Bar? Well,
Jim was jest telling the richest yarn about"—

"Smiley's a —— fool," interrupted a gloomy voice.

"A particular —— skunk," added another in sepulchral accents.

A silence followed these positive statements. The Old
Man glanced quickly around the group. Then his face
slowly changed. "That's so," he said reflectively, after a
pause, "certainly a sort of a skunk and suthin' of a fool.
In course." He was silent for a moment, as in painful con-

templation of the unsavoriness and folly of the unpopular Smiley. "Dismal weather, ain't it?" he added, now fully embarked on the current of prevailing sentiment. "Mighty rough papers on the boys, and no show for money this season. And tomorrow's Christmas."

There was a movement among the men at this announcement, but whether of satisfaction or disgust was not plain. "Yes," continued the Old Man in the lugubrious tone he had within the last few moments unconsciously adopted,—"yes, Christmas, and tonight's Christmas Eve. Ye see, boys, I kinder thought—that is, I sorter had an idee, jest passin' like, you know—that maybe ye'd all like to come over to my house tonight and have a sort of tear round. But I suppose, now, you wouldn't? Don't feel like it, maybe?" he added with anxious sympathy, peering into the faces of his companions.

"Well, I don't know," responded Tom Flynn with some cheerfulness. "P'r'aps we may. But how about your wife, Old Man? What does *she* say to it?"

The Old Man hesitated. His conjugal experience had not been a happy one, and the fact was known to Simpson's Bar. His first wife, a delicate, pretty little woman, had suffered keenly and secretly from the jealous suspicions of her husband, until one day he invited the whole Bar to his house to expose her infidelity. On arriving, the party found the shy, petite creature quietly engaged in her household duties, and retired abashed and discomfited. But the sensitive woman did not easily recover from the shock of this extraordinary outrage. It was with difficulty she regained her equanimity sufficiently to release her lover from the closet in which he was concealed, and escape with him. She left a boy of three years to comfort her bereaved husband. The Old Man's present wife had been his cook. She was large, loyal, and aggressive.

Before he could reply, Joe Dimmick suggested with great directness that it was the "Old Man's house," and that, invoking the Divine Power, if the case were his own, he would invite whom he pleased, even if in so doing he imperiled his salvation. The Powers of Evil, he further remarked, should contend against him vainly. All this delivered with a terseness and vigor lost in this necessary translation.

"In course. Certainly. Thet's it," said the Old Man with a sympathetic frown. "Thar's no trouble about thet. It's my own house, built every stick on it myself. Don't you be afeard o' her, boys. She *may* cut up a trifle rough —ez wimmin do—but she'll come round." Secretly the Old Man trusted to the exaltation of liquor and the power of courageous example to sustain him in such an emergency.

As yet, Dick Bullen, the oracle and leader of Simpson's Bar, had not spoken. He now took his pipe from his lips. "Old Man, how's that yer Johnny gettin' on? Seems to me he didn't look so peart last time I seed him on the bluff heavin' rocks at Chinamen. Didn't seem to take much interest in it. Thar was a gang of 'em by yar yesterday—drownded out up the river—and I kinder thought o' Johnny, and how he'd miss 'em! Maybe now, we'd be in the way ef he wus sick?"

The father, evidently touched not only by this pathetic picture of Johnny's deprivation, but by the considerate delicacy of the speaker, hastened to assure him that Johnny was better, and that a "little fun might 'liven him up." Whereupon Dick arose, shook himself, and saying, "I'm ready. Lead the way, Old Man: here goes," himself led the way with a leap, a characteristic howl, and darted out into the night. As he passed through the outer room he caught up a blazing brand from the hearth. The action was repeated by the rest of the partly, closely following and elbowing each other, and before the astonished proprietor of Thompson's grocery was aware of the intention of his guests, the room was deserted.

The night was pitchy dark. In the first gust of wind their temporary torches were extinguished, and only the red brands dancing and flitting in the gloom like drunken will-o'-the-wisps indicated their whereabouts. Their way led up Pine Tree Canyon, at the head of which a broad, low, bark-thatched cabin burrowed in the mountainside. It was the home of the Old Man, and the entrance to the tunnel in which he worked when he worked at all. Here the crowd paused for a moment, out of delicate deference to their host, who came up panting in the rear.

"P'r'aps ye'd better hold on a second out yer, whilst I go in and see that things is all right," said the Old Man, with an indifference he was far from feeling. The suggestion was graciously accepted, the door opened and closed on the host, and the crowd, leaning their backs against the wall and cowering under the eaves, waited and listened.

For a few moments there was no sound but the dripping of water from the eaves and the stir and rustle of wrestling boughs above them. Then the men became uneasy, and whispered suggestion and suspicion passed from the one to the other. "Reckon she's caved in his head the first lick!" "Decoyed him inter the tunnel and barred him up, likely." "Got him down and sittin' on him." "Prob'ly biling suthin' to heave on us: stand clear the door, boys!" For just then the latch clicked, the door slowly opened, and a voice said, "Come in out o' the wet."

The voice was neither that of the Old Man nor of his wife. It was the voice of a small boy, its weak treble broken by that preternatural hoarseness which only vagabondage and the habit of premature self-assertion can give. It was the face of a small boy that looked up at theirs—a face that might have been pretty, and even refined, but that it was darkened by evil knowledge from within, and dirt and hard experience from without. He had a blanket around his shoulders, and had evidently just risen from his bed. "Come in," he repeated, "and don't make no noise. The Old Man's in there talking to mar," he continued, pointing to an adjacent room which seemed to be a kitchen, from which the Old Man's voice came in deprecating accents. "Let me be," he added querulously to Dick Bullen, who had caught him up, blanket and all, and was affecting to toss him into the fire, "let go o' me, you d—d old fool, d'ye hear?"

Thus adjured, Dick Bullen lowered Johnny to the ground with a smothered laugh, while the men, entering quietly, ranged themselves around a long table of rough boards which occupied the center of the room. Johnny then gravely proceeded to a cupboard and brought out several articles, which he deposited on the table. "Thar's whiskey. And crackers. And red herons. And cheese." He took a bite of the latter on his way to the table. "And sugar." He scooped up a mouthful en route with a small and very dirty hand. "And terbacker. Thar's dried appils too on the shelf, but I don't admire 'em. Appils is swellin'. Thar," he concluded, "now wade in, and don't be afeard. *I* don't mind the old woman. She don't b'long to *me*. S'long."

He had stepped to the threshold of a small room, scarcely larger than a closet, partitioned off from the main apartment, and holding in its dim recess a small bed. He stood there a moment looking at the company, his bare feet peeping from the blanket, and nodded.

"Hello, Johnny! You ain't goin' to turn in agin, are ye?" said Dick.

"Yes, I are," responded Johnny decidedly.

"Why, wot's up, old fellow?"

"I'm sick."

"How sick?"

"I've got a fevier. And childblains. And roomatiz," returned Johnny, and vanished within. After a moment's pause, he added in the dark, apparently from under the bedclothes—"And biles!"

There was an embarrassing silence. The men looked at each other and at the fire. Even with the appetizing banquet before them, it seemed as if they might again fall into the despondency of Thompson's grocery, when the voice of the Old Man, incautiously lifted, came deprecatingly from the kitchen.

"Certainly! Thet's so. In course they is. A gang o' lazy, drunken loafers, and that ar Dick Bullen's the ornariest of all. Didn't hev no more *sabe* than to come round yar with sickness in the house and no provision. Thet's what I said: 'Bullen,' sez I, 'it's crazy drunk you are, or a fool,' sez I, 'to think o' such a thing.' 'Staples,' I sez, 'be you a man, Staples, and 'spect to raise h——ll under my roof and invalids lyin' round?' But they would come— they would. Thet's wot you must 'spect o' such trash as lays round the Bar."

A burst of laughter from the men followed this unfortunate exposure. Whether it was overheard in the kitchen, or whether the Old Man's irate companion had just then exhausted all other modes of expressing her contemptuous indignation, I cannot say, but a back door was suddenly slammed with great violence. A moment later and the Old Man reappeared, haply unconscious of the cause of the late hilarious outburst, and smiled blandly.

"The old woman thought she'd jest run over to Mrs. MacFadden's for a sociable call," he explained with jaunty indifference, as he took a seat at the board.

Oddly enough it needed this untoward incident to relieve the embarrassment that was beginning to be felt by the party, and their natural audacity returned with their host. I do not propose to record the convivialities of that evening. The inquisitive reader will accept the statement that the conversation was characterized by the same intellectual exaltation, the same cautious reverence, the same fastidious delicacy, the same rhetorical precision, and the same logical and coherent discourse somewhat later in the evening, which distinguish similar gatherings of the masculine sex in more civilized localities and under more favorable auspices. No glasses were broken in the absence of any; no liquor was uselessly spilt on the floor or table in the scarcity of that article.

It was nearly midnight when the festivities were interrupted. "Hush," said Dick Bullen, holding up his hand. It was the querulous voice of Johnny from his adjacent closet: "O dad!"

The Old Man arose hurriedly and disappeared in the closet. Presently he reappeared. "His rheumatiz is coming on agin bad," he explained, "and he wants rubbin'." He lifted the demijohn of whiskey from the table and shook it. It was empty. Dick Bullen put down his tin cup with an embarrassed laugh. So did the others. The Old Man examined their contents and said hopefully, "I reckon that's enough; he don't need much. You hold on all o' you for a spell, and I'll be back;" and vanished in the closet with an old flannel shirt and the whiskey. The door closed but imperfectly, and the following dialogue was distinctly audible:

"Now, sonny, whar does she ache worst?"

"Sometimes over yar and sometimes under yer; but it's most powerful from yer to yer. Rub yer, dad."

A silence seemed to indicate a brisk rubbing. Then Johnny:

"Hevin' a good time out yer, Dad?"

"Yes, sonny."

"Tomorrer's Chrismiss—ain't it?"

"Yes, sonny. How does she feel now?"

"Better. Rub a little furder down. Wot's Chrismiss, anyway? Wot's it all about?"

"Oh, it's a day."

This exhaustive definition was apparently satisfactory, for there was a silent interval of rubbing. Presently Johnny again:

"Mar sez that everywhere else but yer everybody gives things to everybody Chrismiss, and then she jist waded inter you. She sez thar's a man they call Sandy Claws, not a white man, you know, but a kind o' Chinemin, comes down the chimbley night afore Chrismiss and gives things to chillern—boys like me. Puts 'em in their butes! Thet's what she tried to play upon me. Easy now, pop, whar are you rubbin' to—thet's a mile from the place. She jest made that up, didn't she, jest to aggrewate me and you? Don't rub thar. . . . Why, Dad!"

In the great quiet that seemed to have fallen upon the house the sigh of the near pines and the drip of leaves without was very distinct. Johnny's voice, too, was lowered as he went on, "Don't you take on now, for I'm gettin' all right fast. Wot's the boys doin' out thar?"

The Old Man partly opened the door and peered through. His guests were sitting there sociably enough, and there were a few silver coins and a lean buckskin purse on the table. "Bettin' on suthin'—some little game or 'nother. They're all right," he replied to Johnny, and recommenced his rubbing.

"I'd like to take a hand and win some money," said Johnny reflectively after a pause.

The Old Man glibly repeated what was evidently a familiar formula, that if Johnny would wait until he struck it rich in the tunnel he'd have lots of money, etc., etc.

"Yes," said Johnny, "but you don't. And whether you strike it or I win it, it's about the same. It's all luck.

But it's mighty cur'o's about Chrismiss—ain't it? Why do they call it Chrismiss?"

Perhaps from some instinctive deference to the overhearing of his guests, or from some vague sense of incongruity, the Old Man's reply was so low as to be inaudible beyond the room.

"Yes," said Johnny, with some slight abatement of interest, "I've heard o' *him* before. Thar, that'll do, dad. I don't ache near so bad as I did. Now wrap me tight in this yer blanket. So. Now," he added in a muffled whisper, "sit down yer by me till I go asleep." To assure himself of obedience, he disengaged one hand from the blanket, and grasping his father's sleeve, again composed himself to rest.

For some moments the Old Man waited patiently. Then the unwonted stillness of the house excited his curiosity, and without moving from the bed he cautiously opened the door with his disengaged hand, and looked into the main room. To his infinite surprise it was dark and deserted. But even then a smoldering log on the hearth broke, and by the upspringing blaze he saw the figure of Dick Bullen sitting by the dying embers.

"Hello!"

Dick started, rose, and came somewhat unsteadily toward him.

"Whar's the boys?" said the Old Man.

"Gone up the canyon on a little *pasear*. They're coming back for me in a minit. I'm waitin' round for 'em. What are you starin' at, Old Man?" he added, with a forced laugh; "do you think I'm drunk?"

The Old Man might have been pardoned the supposition, for Dick's eyes were humid and his face flushed. He loitered and lounged back to the chimney, yawned, shook himself, buttoned up his coat, and laughed. "Liquor ain't so plenty as that, Old Man. Now don't you git up," he continued, as the Old Man made a movement to release his sleeve from Johnny's hand. "Don't you mind manners. Sit jest whar you be; I'm goin' in a jiffy. Thar, that's them now."

There was a low tap at the door. Dick Bullen opened it quickly, nodded "good night" to his host, and disappeared. The Old Man would have followed him but for

the hand that still unconsciously grasped his sleeve. He
could have easily disengaged it: it was small, weak, and
emaciated. But perhaps because it *was* small, weak, and
emaciated he changed his mind, and drawing his chair
closer to the bed, rested his head upon it. In this defense-
less attitude the potency of his earlier potations surprised
him. The room flickered and faded before his eyes, reappeared, faded again, went out, and left him—asleep.

Meantime Dick Bullen, closing the door, confronted his
companions. "Are you ready?" said Staples. "Ready,"
said Dick; "what's the time?" "Past twelve," was the
reply; "can you make it?—it's nigh on fifty miles, the
round trip hither and yon." "I reckon," returned Dick
shortly. "Whar's the mare?" "Bill and Jack's holdin' her at
the crossin'." "Let 'em hold on a minit longer," said Dick.

He turned and re-entered the house softly. By the light
of the guttering candle and dying fire he saw that the door
of the little room was open. He stepped toward it on tip-
toe and looked in. The Old Man had fallen back in his
chair, snoring, his helpless feet thrust out in a line with his
collapsed shoulders, and his hat pulled over his eyes.
Beside him, on a narrow wooden bedstead, lay Johnny,
muffled tightly in a blanket that hid all save a strip of
forehead and a few curls damp with perspiration. Dick
Bullen made a step forward, hesitated, and glanced over
his shoulder into the deserted room. Everything was
quiet. With a sudden resolution he parted his huge mustaches with both hands and stooped over the sleeping
boy. But even as he did so a mischievous blast, lying in
wait, swooped down the chimney, rekindled the hearth,
and lit up the room with a shameless glow from which
Dick fled in bashful terror.

His companions were already waiting for him at the
crossing. Two of them were struggling in the darkness
with some strange misshapen bulk, which as Dick came
nearer took the semblance of a great yellow horse.

It was the mare. She was not a pretty picture. From
her Roman nose to her rising haunches, from her arched
spine hidden by the stiff *machillas* of a Mexican saddle,
to her thick, straight bony legs, there was not a line of
equine grace. In her half-blind but wholly vicious white

eyes, in her protruding underlip, in her monstrous color, there was nothing but ugliness and vice.

"Now then," said Staples, "stand cl'ar of her heels, boys, and up with you. Don't miss your first holt of her mane, and mind ye get your off stirrup *quick*. Ready!"

There was a leap, a scrambling struggle, a bound, a wild retreat of the crowd, a circle of flying hoofs, two springless leaps that jarred the earth, a rapid play and jingle of spurs, a plunge, and then the voice of Dick somewhere in the darkness. "All right!"

"Don't take the lower road back onless you're hard pushed for time! Don't hold her in downhill! We'll be at the ford at five. G'lang! Hoopa! Mula! GO!"

A splash, a spark struck from the ledge in the road, a clatter in the rocky cut beyond, and Dick was gone.

Sing, O Muse, the ride of Richard Bullen! Sing, O Muse, of chivalrous men! the sacred quest, the doughty deeds, the battery of low churls, the fearsome ride and gruesome perils of the Flower of Simpson's Bar! Alack! she is dainty, this Muse! She will have none of this bucking brute and swaggering, ragged rider, and I must fain follow him in prose, afoot!

It was one o'clock, and yet he had only gained Rattlesnake Hill. For in that time Jovita had rehearsed to him all her imperfections and practiced all her vices. Thrice had she stumbled. Twice had she thrown up her Roman nose in a straight line with the reins, and resisting bit and spur, struck out madly across country. Twice had she reared, and rearing, fallen backward; and twice had the agile Dick, unharmed, regained his seat before she found her vicious legs again. And a mile beyond them, at the foot of a long hill, was Rattlesnake Creek. Dick knew that here was the crucial test of his ability to perform his enterprise, set his teeth grimly, put his knees well into her flanks, and changed his defensive tactics to brisk aggression. Bullied and maddened, Jovita began the descent of the hill. Here the artful Richard pretended to hold her in with ostentatious objurgation and well-feigned cries of alarm. It is unnecessary to add that Jovita instantly ran away. Nor need I state the time made in the descent; it is written in the chronicles of Simpson's Bar. Enough that in another moment, as it seemed to Dick, she was splashing on the overflowed banks of Rattlesnake Creek. As Dick expected, the momentum she had acquired carried her beyond the point of balking, and holding her well together for a mighty leap, they dashed into the middle of the swiftly flowing current. A few moments of kicking, wading, and swimming, and Dick drew a long breath on the opposite bank.

The road from Rattlesnake Creek to Red Mountain was tolerably level. Either the plunge in Rattlesnake Creek had dampened her baleful fire, or the art which led to it had shown her the superior wickedness of her rider, for Jovita no longer wasted her surplus energy in wanton conceits. Once she bucked, but it was from force of habit; once she shied, but it was from a new, freshly painted meetinghouse at the crossing of the county road. Hollows, ditches, gravelly deposits, patches of freshly springing grasses, flew from beneath her rattling hoofs. She began to smell unpleasantly, once or twice she coughed slightly, but there was no abatement of her strength or speed. By two o'clock he had passed Red Mountain and begun the descent to the plain. Ten minutes later the driver of the fast Pioneer coach was overtaken and passed by a "man on a pinto hoss,"—an event sufficiently notable for remark. At half past two Dick rose in his stirrups with a great shout. Stars were glittering through the rifted clouds, and beyond him, out of the plain, rose two spires, a flagstaff, and a straggling line of black objects. Dick jingled his spurs and swung his *riata,* Jovita bounded forward, and in another moment they swept into Tuttleville, and drew up before the wooden piazza of "The Hotel of All Nations."

What transpired that night at Tuttleville is not strictly a part of this record. Briefly I may state, however, that after Jovita had been handed over to a sleepy ostler, whom she at once kicked into unpleasant consciousness, Dick sallied out with the barkeeper for a tour of the sleeping town. Lights still gleamed from a few saloons and gambling houses; but avoiding these, they stopped before several closed shops, and by persistent tapping and judicious outcry roused the proprietors from their beds, and made them unbar the doors of their magazines and expose their wares. Sometimes they were met by curses, but oftener by interest and some concern in their needs, and the interview was invariably concluded by a drink. It was three o'clock before this pleasantry was given over, and with a small waterproof bag of India rubber strapped on his shoulders, Dick returned to the hotel. But here he was waylaid by Beauty—Beauty opulent in charms, affluent in dress, persuasive in speech, and Spanish in accent! In vain she repeated the invitation in "Excelsior," happily scorned by all Alpine-climbing youth, and rejected by this child of the Sierras—a rejection softened in this instance by a laugh and his last gold coin. And then he sprang to the saddle and dashed down the lonely street and out into the lonelier plain, where presently the lights, the black line of houses, the spires, and the flagstaff sank into the earth behind him again and were lost in the distance.

The storm had cleared away, the air was brisk and cold, the outlines of adjacent landmarks were distinct, but it was half-past four before Dick reached the meetinghouse and the crossing of the country road. To avoid the rising grade he had taken a longer and more circuitous road, in whose viscid mud Jovita sank fetlock deep at every bound. It was a poor preparation for a steady ascent of five miles more; but Jovita, gathering her legs under her, took it with her usual blind, unreasoning fury, and a half-hour later reached the long level that led to Rattlesnake Creek. Another half-hour would bring him to the creek. He threw the reins lightly upon the neck of the mare, chirruped to her, and began to sing.

Suddenly Jovita shied with a bound that would have unseated a less practiced rider. Hanging to her rein was a figure that had leaped from the bank, and at the same time from the road before her arose a shadowy horse and rider.

"Throw up your hands," commanded the second apparition, with an oath.

Dick felt the mare tremble, quiver, and apparently sink under him. He knew what it meant and was prepared.

"Stand aside, Jack Simpson. I know you, you d—d thief! Let me pass, or—"

He did not finish the sentence. Jovita rose straight in the air with a terrific bound, throwing the figure from her bit with a single shake of her vicious head, and charged with deadly malevolence down on the impediment before her. An oath, a pistol shot, horse and highwayman rolled over in the road, and the next moment Jovita was a hundred yards away. But the good right arm of her rider, shattered by a bullet, dropped helplessly at his side.

Without slacking his speed he shifted the reins to his left hand. But a few moments later he was obliged to halt and tighten the saddle girths that had slipped in the onset. This in his crippled condition took some time. He had no fear of pursuit, but looking up he saw that the eastern stars were already paling, and that the distant peaks had lost their ghostly whiteness and now stood out blackly against a lighter sky. Day was upon him. Then completely absorbed in a single idea, he forgot the pain of his wound, and mounting again dashed on toward Rattlesnake Creek. But now Jovita's breath came broken by gasps, Dick reeled in his saddle, and brighter and brighter grew the sky.

Ride, Richard; run, Jovita; linger, O day!

For the last few rods there was a roaring in his ears. Was it exhaustion from loss of blood, or what? He was dazed and giddy as he swept down the hill, and did not recognize his surroundings. Had he taken the wrong road, or was this Rattlesnake Creek?

It was. But the brawling creek he had swam a few hours before had risen, more than doubled its volume, and now rolled a swift and resistless river between him and Rattlesnake Hill. For the first time that night Richard's heart sank within him. The river, the mountain, the quickening east, swam before his eyes. He shut them to recover his self-control. In that brief interval, by some fantastic mental process, the little room at Simpson's Bar and the figures of the sleeping father and son rose upon him. He opened his eyes wildly, cast off his coat, pistol, boots, and saddle, bound his precious pack tightly to his shoulders, grasped the bare flanks of Jovita with his bared knees, and with a shout dashed into the yellow water. A cry rose from the opposite bank as the head of a man and horse struggled for a few moments against the battling current, and then were swept away amidst uprooted trees and whirling driftwood.

The Old Man started and woke. The fire on the hearth was dead, the candle in the outer room flickering in its socket, and somebody was rapping at the door. He opened it, but fell back with a cry before the dripping, half-naked figure that reeled against the doorpost.

"Dick?"

"Hush! Is he awake yet?"

"No; but, Dick—"

"Dry up, you old fool! Get me some whiskey, *quick!*" The Old Man flew and returned with—an empty bottle! Dick would have sworn, but his strength was not equal to the occasion. He staggered, caught at the handle of the door, and motioned to the Old Man.

"Thar's suthin' in my pack yer for Johnny. Take it off. I can't."

The Old Man unstrapped the pack, and laid it before the exhausted man.

"Open it, quick."

He did so with trembling fingers. It contained only a few poor toys—cheap and barbaric enough, goodness knows, but bright with paint and tinsel. One of them was broken; another, I fear, was irretrievably ruined by water, and on the third—ah me! there was a cruel spot.

"It don't look like much, that's a fact," said Dick ruefully. . . . "But it's the best we could do. . . . Take 'em, Old Man, and put 'em in his stocking, and tell him—tell him, you know—hold me, Old Man—" The Old Man caught at his sinking figure. "Tell him," said Dick, with a weak little laugh—"tell him Sandy Claus has come."

And even so, bedraggled, ragged, unshaven and unshorn, with one arm hanging helplessly at his side, Santa Claus came to Simpson's Bar and fell fainting on the first threshold. The Christmas dawn came slowly after, touching the remoter peaks with the rosy warmth of ineffable love. And it looked so tenderly on Simpson's Bar that the whole mountain, as if caught in a generous action, blushed to the skies.

Mrs. Skaggs's
⋙⋙⋙⋙⋙⋙⋙⋙Husbands⋙⋙⋙⋙⋙⋙⋙⋙

PART ONE
West

⋘⋘⋘ The sun was rising in the foothills. But for an hour the black mass of Sierra eastward of Angel's had been outlined with fire, and the conventional morning had come two hours before with the down coach from Placerville. The dry, cold, dewless California night still lingered in the long canyons and folded skirts of Table Mountain. Even on the mountain road the air was still sharp, and that urgent necessity for something to keep out the chill, which sent the barkeeper sleepily among his bottles and wine glasses at the station, obtained all along the road.

Perhaps it might be said that the first stir of life was in the barrooms. A few birds twittered in the sycamores at the roadside, but long before that glasses had clicked and bottles gurgled in the saloon of the Mansion House. This was still lit by a dissipated looking hanging lamp, which was evidently the worse for having been up all night, and bore a singular resemblance to a faded reveler of Angel's, who even then sputtered and flickered in *his* socket in an armchair below it——a resemblance so plain that when the first level sunbeam pierced the window-pane, the barkeeper, moved by a sentiment of consistency and compassion, put them both out together.

Then the sun came up haughtily. When it had passed the eastern ridge it began, after its habit, to lord it over Angel's, sending the thermometer up twenty degrees in as many minutes, driving the mules to the sparse shade of corrals and fences, making the red dust incandescent, and renewing its old imperious aggression on the spiked bosses of the convex shield of pines that defended Table Mountain. Thither by nine o'clock all coolness had retreated, and the "outsides" of the up stage plunged their hot faces in its aromatic shadows as in water.

It was the custom of the driver of the Wingdam coach to whip up his horses and enter Angel's at that remarkable pace which the woodcuts in the hotel barroom represented to credulous humanity as the usual rate of speed of that conveyance. At such times the habitual expression of disdainful reticence and lazy official severity which he wore on the box became intensified as the loungers gathered about the vehicle, and only the boldest ventured to address him. It was the Hon. Judge Beeswinger, Member of Assembly, who today presumed, perhaps rashly, on the strength of his official position.

"Any political news from below, Bill?" he asked, as the latter slowly descended from his lofty perch, without, however, any perceptible coming down of mien or manner.

"Not much," said Bill, with deliberate gravity. "The President o' the United States hezn't bin hisself sens you refoosed that seat in the Cabinet. The ginral feelin' in perlitical circles is one o' regret."

Irony, even of this outrageous quality, was too common in Angel's to excite either a smile or a frown. Bill slowly entered the barroom during a dry, dead silence, in which only a faint spirit of emulation survived.

"Ye didn't bring up that agint o' Rothschild's this trip?" asked the barkeeper slowly, by way of vague contribution to the prevailing tone of conversation.

"No," responded Bill, with thoughtful exactitude. "He said he couldn't look inter that claim o' Johnson's without first consultin' the Bank o' England."

The Mr. Johnson here alluded to being present as the faded reveler the barkeeper had lately put out, and as the alleged claim notoriously possessed no attractions whatever to capitalists, expectation naturally looked to him for some response to this evident challenge. He did so by simply stating that he would "take sugar" in his, and by walking unsteadily towards the bar, as if accepting a festive invitation. To the credit of Bill be it recorded that he did not attempt to correct the mistake,

but gravely touched glasses with him, and after saying
"Here's another nail in your coffin,"—a cheerful sentiment, to which "And the hair all off your head" was
playfully added by the others—he threw off his liquor
with a single dexterous movement of head and elbow,
and stood refreshed.

"Hello, old major!" said Bill, suddenly setting down
his glass. "Are *you* there?"

It was a boy, who, becoming bashfully conscious that
this epithet was addressed to him, retreated sideways to
the doorway, where he stood beating his hat against the
doorpost with an assumption of indifference that his
downcast but mirthful dark eyes and reddening cheek
scarcely bore out. Perhaps it was owing to his size, perhaps it was to a certain cherubic outline of face and
figure, perhaps to a peculiar trustfulness of expression,
that he did not look half his age, which was really fourteen.

Everybody in Angel's knew the boy. Either under the
venerable title bestowed by Bill, or as "Tom Islington,"
after his adopted father, his was a familiar presence in
the settlement, and the theme of much local criticism
and comment. His waywardness, indolence, and unac-
countable amiability—a quality at once suspicious and
gratuitous in a pioneer community like Angel's—had
often been the subject of fierce discussion. A large and
reputable majority believed him destined for the gallows; a minority not quite so reputable enjoyed his presence without troubling themselves much about his future;
to one or two the evil predictions of the majority possessed neither novelty nor terror.

"Anything for me, Bill?" asked the boy half mechanically, with the air of repeating some jocular formulary
perfectly understood by Bill.

"Anythin' for you!" echoed Bill, with an overacted
severity equally well understood by Tommy—"anythin'
for you? No! And it's my opinion there won't be anythin' for you ez long ez you hang around barrooms and
spend your valooable time with loafers and bummers.
Git!"

The reproof was accompanied by a suitable exaggera-
tion of gesture (Bill had seized a decanter), before

which the boy retreated still good-humoredly. Bill followed him to the door. "Dern my skin, if he hezn't gone off with that bummer Johnson," he added, as he looked down the road.

"What's he expectin', Bill?" asked the barkeeper.

"A letter from his aunt. Reckon he'll hev to take it out in expectin'. Likely they're glad to get shut o' him."

"He's leadin' a shiftless, idle life here," interposed the Member of Assembly.

"Well," said Bill, who never allowed anyone but himself to abuse his protégé, "seein' he ain't expectin' no offis from the hands of an enlightened constitooency, it *is* rayther a shiftless life." After delivering this Parthian arrow with a gratuitous twanging of the bow to indicate its offensive personality, Bill winked at the barkeeper, slowly resumed a pair of immense, bulgy buckskin gloves, which gave his fingers the appearance of being painfully sore and bandaged, strode to the door without looking at anybody, called out, "All aboard," with a perfunctory air of supreme indifference whether the invitation was heeded, remounted his box, and drove stolidly away.

Perhaps it was well that he did so, for the conversation at once assumed a disrespectful attitude toward Tom and his relatives. It was more than intimated that Tom's alleged aunt was none other than Tom's real mother, while it was also asserted that Tom's alleged uncle did not himself participate in this intimate relationship to the boy to an extent which the fastidious taste of Angel's deemed moral and necessary. Popular opinion also believed that Islington, the adopted father, who received a certain stipend ostensibly for the boy's support, retained it as a reward for his reticence regarding these facts. "He ain't ruinin' hisself by wastin' it on Tom," said the barkeeper, who possibly possessed positive knowledge of much of Islington's disbursements. But at this point exhausted nature languished among some of the debaters, and he turned from the frivolity of conversation to his severer professional duties.

It was also well that Bill's momentary attitude of didactic propriety was not further excited by the subsequent conduct of his protégé. For by this time Tom, half supporting the unstable Johnson, who developed a tend-

ency to occasionally dash across the glaring road, but
checked himself midway each time, reached the corral
which adjoined the Mansion House. At its farther extremity was a pump and horse trough. Here, without a
word being spoken, but evidently in obedience to some
habitual custom, Tom led his companion. With the boy's
assistance, Johnson removed his coat and neckcloth,
turned back the collar of his shirt, and gravely placed
his head beneath the pump spout. With equal gravity and
deliberation, Tom took his place at the handle. For a few
moments only the splashing of water and regular strokes
of the pump broke the solemnly ludicrous silence. Then
there was a pause in which Johnson put his hands to his
dripping head, felt it critically as if it belonged to somebody else, and raised his eyes to his companion. "That
ought to fetch *it*," said Tom in answer to the look. "Ef
it don't," replied Johnson doggedly, with an air of re-
lieving himself of all further responsibility in the mat-
er, "it's got to, thet's all!"

If "it" referred to some change in the physiognomy
of Johnson, "it" had probably been "fetched" by the process just indicated. The head that went under the pump
was large, and clothed with bushy, uncertain-colored
hair; the face was flushed, puffy, and expressionless, the
eyes injected and full. The head that came out from
under the pump was of smaller size and different shape,
the hair straight, dark, and sleek, the face pale and
hollow-cheeked, the eyes bright and restless. In the haggard, nervous ascetic that rose from the horse trough
there was very little trace of the Bacchus that had
bowed there a moment before. Familiar as Tom must
have been with the spectacle, he could not help looking
inquiringly at the trough, as if expecting to see some
traces of the previous Johnson in its shallow depths.

A narrow strip of willow, alder, and buckeye—a mere
dusty, raveled fringe of the green mantle that swept the
high shoulders of Table Mountain—lapped the edge of
the corral. The silent pair were quick to avail themselves of even its scant shelter from the overpowering
sun. They had not proceeded far, before Johnson, who
was walking quite rapidly in advance, suddenly brought

himself up, and turned to his companion with an interrogative "Eh?"

"I didn't speak," said Tommy quietly.

"Who said you spoke?" said Johnson, with a quick look of cunning. "In course you didn't speak, and I didn't speak neither. Nobody spoke. Wot makes you think you spoke?" he continued, peering curiously into Tommy's eyes.

The smile which habitually shone there quickly vanished as the boy stepped quietly to his companion's side, and took his arm without a word.

"In course you didn't speak, Tommy," said Johnson deprecatingly. "You ain't a boy to go for to play an ole soaker like me. That's wot I like you for. Thet's wot I seed in you from the first. I sez, 'Thet 'ere boy ain't going to play you, Johnson! You can go your whole pile on him, when you can't trust even a barkeep'.' Thet's wot I said. Eh?"

This time Tommy prudently took no notice of the interrogation, and Johnson went on: "Ef I was to ask you another question, you wouldn't go to play me neither—would you, Tommy?"

"No," said the boy.

"Ef I was to ask you," continued Johnson, without heeding the reply, but with a growing anxiety of eye and a nervous twitching of his lips—"ef I was to ask you, fur instance, ef that was a jackass rabbit that jest passed —eh?—you'd say it was or was not, ez the case may be. You wouldn't play the ole man on thet?"

"No," said Tommy quietly, "it *was* a jackass rabbit."

"Ef I was to ask you," continued Johnson, "ef it wore, say, fur instance, a green hat with yaller ribbons, you wouldn't play me, and say it did, onless"—he added, with intensified cunning—"onless it *did?*"

"No," said Tommy, "of course I wouldn't; but then, you see, *it did.*"

"It did?"

"It did!" repeated Tommy stoutly; "a green hat with yellow ribbons—and—and—a red rosette."

"I didn't get to see the ros-ette," said Johnson, with slow and conscientious deliberation, yet with an evident sense of relief; "but that ain't sayin' it wa'n't there, you know. Eh?"

Tommy glanced quietly at his companion. There were great beads of perspiration on his ashen-gray forehead, and on the ends of his lank hair; the hand which twitched spasmodically in his was cold and clammy, the other, which was free, had a vague, purposeless, jerky activity, as if attached to some deranged mechanism. Without any apparent concern in these phenomena, Tommy halted, and seating himself on a log, motioned his companion to a place beside him. Johnson obeyed without a word. Slight as was the act, perhaps no other incident of their singular companionship indicated as completely the dominance of this careless, half-effeminate, but self-possessed boy over this doggedly self-willed, abnormally excited man.

"It ain't the square thing," said Johnson, after a pause, with a laugh that was neither mirthful nor musical, and frightened away a lizard that had been regarding the pair with breathless suspense—"it ain't the square thing for jackass rabbits to wear hats, Tommy—is it, eh?"

"Well," said Tommy, with unmoved composure, "sometimes they do and sometimes they don't. Animals are mighty queer." And here Tommy went off in an animated, but, I regret to say, utterly untruthful and untrustworthy account of the habits of California fauna, until he was interrupted by Johnson.

"And snakes, eh, Tommy?" said the man, with an abstracted air, gazing intently on the ground before him.

"And snakes," said Tommy, "but they don't bite—at least not that kind you see. There!—don't move, Uncle Ben, don't move; they're gone now. And it's about time you took your dose."

Johnson had hurriedly risen as if to leap upon the log, but Tommy had as quickly caught his arm with one hand while he drew a bottle from his pocket with the other. Johnson paused and eyed the bottle. "Ef you say so, my boy," he faltered, as his fingers closed nervously around it; "say 'when,' then." He raised the bottle to his lips and took a long draught, the boy regarding him critically. "When," said Tommy suddenly. Johnson started, flushed, and returned the bottle quickly. But the color that had risen to his cheek stayed there, his eye grew less restless, and as they moved away again the hand that rested on Tommy's shoulder was steadier.

Their way lay along the flank of Table Mountain—a wandering trail through a tangled solitude that might have seemed virgin and unbroken but for a few oyster cans, yeast-powder tins, and empty bottles that had been apparently stranded by the "first low wash" of pioneer waves. On the ragged trunk of an enormous pine hung a few tufts of gray hair caught from a passing grizzly, but in strange juxtaposition at its foot lay an empty bottle of incomparable bitters—the chef-d'œuvre of a hygienic civilization, and blazoned with the arms of an all-healing republic. The head of a rattlesnake peered from a case that had contained tobacco, which was still brightly placarded with the high-colored effigy of a popular danseuse. And a little beyond this the soil was broken and fissured, there was a confused mass of roughly hewn timber, a straggling line of sluicing, a heap of gravel and dirt, a rude cabin, and the claim of Johnson.

Except for the rudest purposes of shelter from rain and cold, the cabin possessed but little advantage over the simple savagery of surrounding nature. It had all the practical directness of the habitation of some animal, without its comfort or picturesque quality; the very birds that haunted it for food must have felt their own superiority as architects. It was inconceivably dirty, even with its scant capacity for accretion; it was singularly stale, even in its newness and freshness of material. Unspeakably dreary as it was in shadow, the sunlight visited it in a blind, aching, purposeless way, as if despairing of mellowing its outlines or of even tanning it into color.

The claim worked by Johnson in his intervals of sobriety was represented by half a dozen rude openings in the mountainside, with the heaped-up débris of rock and gravel before the mouth of each. They gave very little evidence of engineering skill or constructive purpose, or indeed showed anything but the vague, successively abandoned essays of their projector. Today they served another purpose, for as the sun had heated the little cabin almost to the point of combustion, curling up the long dry shingles, and starting aromatic tears from the green pine beams, Tommy led Johnson into one of the larger openings, and with a sense of satisfaction threw himself panting upon its rocky floor. Here and there the grateful dampness was condensed in quiet pools of water, or in a monotonous and soothing drip from the rocks above. Without lay the staring sunlight—colorless, clarified, intense.

For a few moments they lay resting on their elbows in blissful contemplation of the heat they had escaped. "Wot do you say," said Johnson slowly, without looking at his companion, but abstractedly addressing himself to the landscape beyond—"wot do you say to two straight games fur one thousand dollars?"

"Make it five thousand," replied Tommy reflectively also to the landscape, "and I'm in."

"Wot do I owe you now?" said Johnson, after a lengthened silence.

"One hundred and seventy-five thousand, two hundred and fifty dollars," replied Tommy with businesslike gravity.

"Well," said Johnson after a deliberation commensurate with the magnitude of the transaction, "ef you win, call it a hundred and eighty thousand, round. War's the keerds?"

They were in an old tin box in a crevice of a rock above his head. They were greasy and worn with service. Johnson dealt, albeit his right hand was still uncertain—hovering, after dropping the cards, aimlessly about Tommy, and being only recalled by a strong nervous effort. Yet, notwithstanding this incapacity for even honest manipulation, Mr. Johnson covertly turned a knave from the bottom of the pack with such shameless inefficiency and gratuitous unskillfulness, that even Tommy was obliged to cough and look elsewhere to hide his embarrassment. Possibly for this reason the young gentleman was himself constrained, by way of correction, to add a valuable card to his own hand, over and above the number he legitimately held.

Nevertheless the game was unexciting and dragged listlessly. Johnson won. He recorded the fact and the amount with a stub of pencil and shaking fingers in wandering hieroglyphics all over a pocket diary. Then there was a long pause, when Johnson slowly drew something

from his pocket and held it up before his companion. It
was apparently a dull red stone.

"Ef," said Johnson slowly, with his old look of simple
cunning—"ef you happened to pick up sich a rock ez
that, Tommy, what might you say it was?"

"Don't know," said Tommy.

"Mightn't you say," continued Johnson cautiously,
"that it was gold or silver?"

"Neither," said Tommy promptly.

"Mightn't you say it was quicksilver? Mightn't you say
that ef thar was a friend o' yourn ez knew whar to go and
turn out ten ton of it a day, and every ton worth two
thousand dollars, that he had a soft thing, a very soft
thing—allowin', Tommy, that you used sich language,
which you don't?"

"But," said the boy, coming to the point with great
directness, *"do* you know where to get it? have you struck
it, Uncle Ben?"

Johnson looked carefully round. "I hev, Tommy. Listen.
I know whar thar's cartloads of it. But thar's only one
other specimen—the mate to this yer—thet's above
ground, and thet's in 'Frisco. Thar's an agint comin' up in
a day or two to look into it. I sent for him. Eh?"

His bright, restless eyes were concentrated on Tommy's
face now, but the boy showed neither surprise nor interest.
Least of all did he betray any recollection of Bill's ironical
and gratuitous corroboration of this part of the story.

"Nobody knows it," continued Johnson in a nervous
whisper—"nobody knows it but you and the agint in
'Frisco. The boys workin' round yar passes by and sees
the old man grubbin' away, and no signs o' color, not even
rotten quartz; the boys loafin' round the Mansion House
sees the old man lyin' round free in barrooms, and they
laughs and sez, 'Played out,' and spects nothin'. Maybe ye
think they spects suthin' now, eh?" queried Johnson suddenly, with a sharp look of suspicion.

Tommy looked up, shook his head, threw a stone at a
passing rabbit, but did not reply.

"When I fust set eyes on you, Tommy," continued
Johnson, apparently reassured, "the fust day you kem and
pumped for me, an entire stranger, and hevin' no call to
do it, I sez, 'Johnson, Johnson,' sez I, 'yer's a boy you kin

trust. Yer's a boy that won't play you; yer's a chap that's
white and square'—white and square, Tommy: them's the
very words I used."

He paused for a moment, and then went on in a confidential whisper, " 'You want capital, Johnson,' sez I, 'to
develop your resources, and you want a pardner. Capital
you can send for, but your pardner, Johnson—your pardner is right yer. And his name, it is Tommy Islington.'
Them's the very words I used."

He stopped and chafed his clammy hands upon his
knees. "It's six months ago sens I made you my pardner.
Thar ain't a lick I've struck sens then, Tommy, thar ain't
a han'ful o' yearth I've washed, thar ain't a shovelful o'
rock I've turned over, but I tho't o' you. 'Share, and share
alike,' sez I. When I wrote to my agint, I wrote ekal for
my pardner, Tommy Islington, he hevin' no call to know
ef the same was man or boy."

He had moved nearer the boy, and would perhaps have
laid his hand caressingly upon him, but even in his manifest affection there was a singular element of awed restraint and even fear—a suggestion of something withheld
even his fullest confidences, a hopeless perception of
some vague barrier that never could be surmounted. He
may have been at times dimly conscious that, in the eyes
which Tommy raised to his, there was thorough intellectual appreciation, critical good-humor, even feminine softness, but nothing more. His nervousness somewhat heightened by his embarrassment, he went on with an attempt
at calmness which his twitching white lips and unsteady
fingers made pathetically grotesque. "Thar's a bill o'
sale in my bunk, made out accordin' to law, of an ekal
ondivided half of the claim, and the consideration is two
hundred and fifty thousand dollars—gambling debts—
gambling debts from me to you, Tommy, you understand?"
—nothing could exceed the intense cunning of his eye at
this moment—"and then thar's a will."

"A will?" said Tommy in amused surprise.

Johnson looked frightened.

"Eh?" he said hurriedly, "wot will? Who said anythin'
'bout a will, Tommy?"

"Nobody," replied Tommy with unblushing calm.

Johnson passed his hand over his cold forehead, wrung

the damp ends of his hair with his fingers, and went on: "Times when I'm took bad ez I was today, the boys about yer sez—you sez, maybe, Tommy—it's whiskey. It ain't, Tommy. It's pizen—quicksilver pizen. That's what's the matter with me. I'm salivated! Salivated with merkery.

"I've heerd o' it before," continued Johnson, appealing to the boy, "and ez a boy o' permiskus reading, I reckon you hev too. Them men as works in cinnabar sooner or later gets salivated. It's bound to fetch 'em sometime. Salivated by merkery."

"What are you goin' to do for it?" asked Tommy.

"When the agint comes up, and I begins to realize on this yer mine," said Johnson contemplatively, "I goes to New York. I sez to the barkeep' o' the hotel, 'Show me the biggest doctor here.' He shows me. I sez to him, 'Salivated by merkery—a year's standin'—how much?' He sez, 'Five thousand dollars, and take two o' these pills at bedtime, and an ekil number o' powders at meals, and come back in a week.' And I goes back in a week, cured, and signs a certifikit to that effect."

Encouraged by a look of interest in Tommy's eye, he went on.

"So I gets cured. I goes to the barkeep', and I sez, 'Show me the biggest, fashionblest house thet's for sale yer.' And he sez, 'The biggest nat'rally b'longs to John Jacob Astor.' And I sez, 'Show him,' and he shows him. And I sez, 'Wot might you ask for this yer house?' And he looks at me scornful, and sez, 'Go 'way, old man; you must be sick.' And I fetches him one over the left eye and he apologizes, and I gives him his own price for the house. I stocks that house with mahogany furniture and pervisions, and thar we lives—you and me, Tommy, you and me!"

The sun no longer shone upon the hillside. The shadows of the pines were beginning to creep over Johnson's claim, and the air within the cavern was growing chill. In the gathering darkness his eyes shone brightly as he went on: "Then thar comes a day when we gives a big spread. We invites gov'ners, members o' Congress, gentlemen o' fashion, and the like. And among 'em I invites a Man as holds his head very high, a Man I once knew; but he doesn't know I knows him, and he doesn't remember me.

And he comes and he sits opposite me, and I watches
him. And he's very airy, this Man, and very chipper, and
he wipes his mouth with a white hankercher, and he
smiles, and he ketches my eye. And he sez, 'A glass o'
wine with you, Mr. Johnson;' and he fills his glass and I
fills mine, and we rises. And I heaves that wine, glass and
all, right into his damned grinnin' face. And he jumps for
me—for he is very game this Man, very game—but some
on 'em grabs him, and he sez, 'Who be you?' And I sez,
'Skaggs! Damn you, Skaggs! Look at me! Gimme back
my wife and child, gimme back the money you stole,
gimme back the good name you took away, gimme back
the health you ruined, gimme back the last twelve years!
Give 'em to me, damn you, quick, before I cuts your heart
out!' And naterally, Tommy, he can't do it. And so I cuts
his heart out, my boy; I cuts his heart out."

The purely animal fury of his eye suddenly changed
again to cunning. "You think they hangs me for it, Tommy, but they don't. Not much, Tommy. I goes to the
biggest lawyer there, and I says to him, 'Salivated by
merkery—you hear me—salivated by merkery.' And he
winks at me, and he goes to the judge, and he sez, 'This
yer unfortnet man isn't responsible—he's been salivated
by merkery.' And he brings witnesses; you comes, Tommy,
and you sez ez how you've seen me took bad afore; and
the doctor, he comes, and he sez as how he's seen me
frightful; and the jury, without leavin' their seats, brings
in a verdict o' justifiable insanity—salivated by merkery."

In the excitement of his climax he had risen to his feet,
but would have fallen had not Tommy caught him and led
him into the open air. In this sharper light there was an
odd change visible in his yellow-white face—a change
which caused Tommy to hurriedly support him, half leading, half dragging him toward the little cabin. When they
had reached it, Tommy placed him on a rude "bunk," or
shelf, and stood for a moment in anxious contemplation of
the tremor-stricken man before him. Then he said rapidly, "Listen, Uncle Ben. I'm goin' to town—to town, you
understand—for the doctor. You're not to get up or move
on any account until I return. Do you hear?" Johnson
nodded violently. "I'll be back in two hours." In another
moment he was gone.

For an hour Johnson kept his word. Then he suddenly sat up, and began to gaze fixedly at a corner of the cabin. From gazing at it he began to smile, from smiling at it he began to talk, from talking at it he began to scream, from screaming he passed to cursing and sobbing wildly. Then he lay quiet again.

He was so still that to merely human eyes he might have seemed asleep or dead. But a squirrel, that emboldened by the stillness had entered from the roof, stopped short upon a beam above the bunk, for he saw that the man's foot was slowly and cautiously moving towards the floor, and that the man's eyes were as intent and watchful as his own. Presently, still without a sound, both feet were upon the floor. And then the bunk creaked, and the squirrel whisked into the eaves of the roof. When he peered forth again, everything was quiet, and the man was gone.

An hour later two muleteers on the Placerville Road passed a man with disheveled hair, glaring, bloodshot eyes, and clothes torn with bramble and stained with the red dust of the mountain. They pursued him, when he turned fiercely on the foremost, wrested a pistol from his grasp, and broke away. Later still, when the sun had dropped behind Payne's Ridge, the underbrush on Deadwood Slope crackled with a stealthy but continuous tread. It must have been an animal whose dimly outlined bulk, in the gathering darkness, showed here and there in vague but incessant motion; it could be nothing but an animal whose utterance was at once so incoherent, monotonous, and unremitting. Yet, when the sound came nearer, and the chaparral was parted, it seemed to be a man, and that man Johnson.

Above the baying of phantasmal hounds that pressed him hard and drove him on, with never rest or mercy; above the lashing of a spectral whip that curled about his limbs, sang in his ears, and continually stung him forward; above the outcries of the unclean shapes that thronged about him—he could still distinguish one real sound, the rush and sweep of hurrying waters. The Stanislaus River! A thousand feet below him drove its yellowing current. Through all the vacillations of his unseated mind he had clung to one idea—to reach the river, to lave in it, to swim it if need be, but to put it forever between him and the harrying shapes, to drown forever in its turbid depths the thronging specters, to wash away in its yellow flood all stains and color of the past. And now he was leaping from boulder to boulder, from blackened stump to stump, from gnarled bush to bush, caught for a moment and withheld by clinging vines, or plunging downward into dusty hollows, until, rolling, dropping, sliding, and stumbling, he reached the riverbank, whereon he fell, rose, staggered forward, and fell again with outstretched arms upon a rock that breasted the swift current. And there he lay as dead.

A few stars came out hesitatingly above Deadwood Slope. A cold wind that had sprung up with the going down of the sun fanned them into momentary brightness, swept the heated flanks of the mountain, and ruffled the river. Where the fallen man lay there was a sharp curve in the stream, so that in the gathering shadows the rushing water seemed to leap out of the darkness and to vanish again. Decayed driftwood, trunks of trees, fragments of broken sluicing—the wash and waste of many a mile—swept into sight a moment, and were gone. All of decay, wreck, and foulness gathered in the long circuit of mining camp and settlement, all the dregs and refuse of a crude and wanton civilization, reappeared for an instant, and then were hurried away in the darkness and lost. No wonder that, as the wind ruffled the yellow waters, the waves seemed to lift their unclean hands toward the rock whereon the fallen man lay, as if eager to snatch him from it, too, and hurry him toward the sea.

It was very still. In the clear air a horn blown a mile away was heard distinctly. The jingling of a spur and a laugh on the highway over Payne's Ridge sounded clearly across the river. The rattling of harness and hoofs foretold for many minutes the approach of the Wingdam coach, that at last, with flashing lights, passed within a few feet of the rock. Then for an hour all again was quiet. Presently the moon, round and full, lifted herself above the serried ridge and looked down upon the river. At first the bared peak of Deadwood Hill gleamed white and skull-like. Then the shadows of Payne's Ridge cast on the slope slowly sank away, leaving the unshapely stumps, the dusty fissures, and clinging outcrop of Deadwood Slope to stand out in black and silver. Still stealing softly downward, the moonlight touched the bank and the rock, and then glittered brightly on the river. The rock was bare and the man was gone, but the river still hurried swiftly to the sea.

"Is there anything for me?" asked Tommy Islington, as, a week after, the stage drew up at the Mansion House, and Bill slowly entered the barroom. Bill did not reply, but turning to a stranger who had entered with him, indicated with a jerk of his finger the boy. The stranger turned with an air half of business, half of curiosity, and looked critically at Tommy. "Is there anything for me?" repeated Tommy, a little confused at the silence and scrutiny. Bill walked deliberately to the bar, and placing his back against it, faced Tommy with a look of demure enjoyment.

"Ef," he remarked slowly—"ef a hundred thousand dollars down and half a million in perspektive is ennything, Major, THERE IS!"

PART TWO

East

It was characteristic of Angel's that the disappearance of Johnson, and the fact that he had left his entire property to Tommy, thrilled the community but slightly in comparison with the astounding discovery that he had anything to leave. The finding of a cinnabar lode at Angel's absorbed all collateral facts or subsequent details. Prospectors from adjoining camps thronged the settlement; the hillside for a mile on either side of Johnson's claim was staked out and pre-empted; trade received a sudden stimulus; and, in the excited rhetoric of the *Weekly Record,* "a new era had broken upon Angel's." "On Thursday last," added that paper, "over five hundred dollars were taken in over the bar of the Mansion House."

Of the fate of Johnson there was little doubt. He had been last seen lying on a boulder on the riverbank by outside passengers of the Wingdam night coach, and when Finn of Robinson's Ferry admitted to have fired three shots from a revolver at a dark object struggling in the water near the ferry, which he "suspicioned" to be a bear, the question seemed to be settled. Whatever might have been the fallibility of his judgment, of the accuracy of his aim there could be no doubt. The general belief that Johnson, after possessing himself of the mule-teer's pistol, could have run amuck gave a certain retrib-utive justice to this story, which rendered it acceptable to the camp.

It was also characteristic of Angel's that no feeling of envy or opposition to the good fortune of Tommy Isling-ton prevailed there. That he was thoroughly cognizant, from the first, of Johnson's discovery, that his attentions to him were interested, calculating, and speculative, was, however, the general belief of the majority—a belief that, singularly enough, awakened the first feelings of genuine respect for Tommy ever shown by the camp. "He ain't no fool; Yuba Bill seed thet from the first," said the barkeep-er. It was Yuba Bill who applied for the guardianship of Tommy after his accession to Johnson's claim, and on whose bonds the richest men of Calaveras were represent-ed. It was Yuba Bill, also, when Tommy was sent East to finish his education, who accompanied him to San Fran-cisco, and before parting with his charge on the steamer's deck, drew him aside, and said, "Ef at enny time you want enny money, Tommy, over and 'bove your 'lowance, you kin write; but ef you'll take my advice," he added, with a sudden huskiness mitigating the severity of his voice, "you'll forget every derned ole spavined, string-halted bummer, as you ever met or knew at Angel's—ev'ry one, Tommy—ev'ry one! And so—boy—take care of yourself —and—and God bless ye, and pertikerly d—n me for a first-class A-1 fool." It was Yuba Bill, also, after this speech, who glared savagely around, walked down the crowded gangplank with a rigid and aggressive shoulder, picked a quarrel with his cabman, and after bundling that functionary into his own vehicle, took the reins himself, and drove furiously to his hotel. "It cost me," said Bill, recounting the occurrence somewhat later at Angel's — "it cost me a matter o' twenty dollars afore the jedge the next mornin'; but you kin bet high thet I taught them 'Frisco chaps suthin' new about drivin'. I didn't make it lively in Montgomery Street for about ten minutes—oh no!"

And so by degrees the two original locators of the great cinnabar lode faded from the memory of Angel's, and Calaveras knew them no more. In five years their very names had been forgotten; in seven the name of the town was changed; in ten the town itself was transported bodily to the hillside, and the chimney of the Union Smelting Works by night flickered like a corpse-light over the site of Johnson's cabin, and by day poisoned the pure spices of the pines. Even the Mansion House was dismantled, and the Wingdam stage deserted the highway for a shorter cut by Quicksilver City. Only the bared crest of Deadwood Hill, as of old, sharply cut the clear blue sky, and at its base, as of old, the Stanislaus River, unwearied and unresting, babbled, whispered, and hurried away to the sea.

A midsummer's day was breaking lazily on the Atlantic. There was not wind enough to move the vapors in the foggy offing, but when the vague distance heaved against a violet sky there were dull red streaks that, growing brighter, presently painted out the stars. Soon the brown rocks of Greyport appeared faintly suffused, and then the whole ashen line of dead coast was kindled, and the lighthouse beacons went out one by one. And then a hundred sail, before invisible, started out of the vapory horizon, and pressed toward the shore. It was morning, indeed, and some of the best society in Greyport, having been up all night, were thinking it was time to go to bed.

For as the sky flashed brighter it fired the clustering red roofs of a picturesque house by the sands that had all that night, from open lattice and illuminated balcony, given light and music to the shore. It glittered on the broad crystal spaces of a great conservatory that looked upon an exquisite lawn, where all night long the blended odors of sea and shore had swooned under the summer moon. But it wrought confusion among the colored lamps on the long veranda, and startled a group of ladies and gentlemen who had stepped from the drawing-room window to gaze upon it. It was so searching and sincere in its way, that as the carriage of the fairest Miss Gillyflower rolled away, that peerless young woman, catching sight of her face in

the oval mirror, instantly pulled down the blinds and nestling the whitest shoulders in Greyport against the crimson
cushions, went to sleep.

"How haggard everybody is! Rose, dear, you look almost intellectual," said Blanche Masterman.

"I hope not," said Rose simply. "Sunrises are very
trying. Look how that pink regularly puts out Mrs. Brown-
Robinson, hair and all!"

"The angels," said the Count de Nugat, with a polite
gesture toward the sky, "must have find these celestial
combinations very bad for the toilette."

"They're safe in white—except when they sit for their
pictures in Venice," said Blanche. "How fresh Mr.
Islington looks! It's really uncomplimentary to us."

"I suppose the sun recognizes in me no rival," said the
young man demurely. "But," he added, "I have lived
much in the open air and require very little sleep."

"How delightful!" said Mrs. Brown-Robinson in a low,
enthusiastic voice, and a manner that held the glowing
sentiment of sixteen and the practical experiences of
thirty-two in dangerous combination; "how perfectly delightful! What sunrises you must have seen, and in such
wild, romantic places! How I envy you! My nephew was
a classmate of yours, and has often repeated to me those
charming stories you tell of your adventures. Won't you
tell some now? Do! How you must tire of us and this
artificial life here, so frightfully artificial, you know" (in
a confidential whisper); "and then to think of the days
when you roamed the great West with the Indians, and
the bisons, and the grizzly bears! Of course, you have
seen grizzly bears and bisons?"

"Of course he has, dear," said Blanche a little pettishly,
throwing a cloak over her shoulders, and seizing her
chaperon by the arm; "his earliest infancy was soothed by
bisons, and he proudly points to the grizzly bear as the
playmate of his youth. Come with me, and I'll tell you all
about it. How good it is of you," she added, *sotto voce,*
to Islington as he stood by the carriage—"how perfectly good it is of you to be like those animals you tell us
of, and not know your full power. Think, with your experiences and our credulity, what stories you *might* tell!
And you are going to walk? Good night, then." A slim,

gloved hand was frankly extended from the window, and the next moment the carriage rolled away.

"Isn't Islington throwing away a chance there?" said Captain Merwin on the veranda.

"Perhaps he couldn't stand my lovely aunt's superadded presence. But then, he's the guest of Blanche's father, and I daresay they see enough of each other as it is."

"But isn't it a rather dangerous situation?"

"For him, perhaps; although he's awfully old, and very queer. For her, with an experience that takes in all the available men in both hemispheres, ending with Nugat over there, I should say a man more or less wouldn't affect her much, anyway. Of course," he laughed, "these are the accents of bitterness. But that was last year."

Perhaps Islington did not overhear the speaker; perhaps, if he did, the criticism was not new. He turned carelessly away, and sauntered out on the road to the sea. Thence he strolled along the sands toward the cliffs, where, meeting an impediment in the shape of a garden wall, he leaped it with a certain agile, boyish ease and experience, and struck across an open lawn toward the rocks again. The best society of Greyport were not early risers, and the spectacle of a trespasser in an evening dress excited only the criticism of grooms hanging about the stables, or cleanly housemaids on the broad verandas that in Greyport architecture dutifully gave upon the sea. Only once, as he entered the boundaries of Cliffwood Lodge, the famous seat of Renwyck Masterman, was he aware of suspicious scrutiny; but a slouching figure that vanished quickly in the lodge offered no opposition to his progress. Avoiding the pathway to the lodge, Islington kept along the rocks until, reaching a little promontory and rustic pavilion, he sat down and gazed upon the sea.

And presently an infinite peace stole upon him. Except where the waves lapped lazily the crags below, the vast expanse beyond seemed unbroken by ripple, heaving only in broad ponderable sheets, and rhythmically, as if still in sleep. The air was filled with a luminous haze that caught and held the direct sunbeams. In the deep calm that lay upon the sea, it seemed to Islington that all the tenderness of culture, magic of wealth, and spell of refinement that for years had wrought upon that favored shore had extended its gracious influence even here. What a pampered and caressed old ocean it was; cajoled, flattered, and fêted where it lay! An odd recollection of the turbid Stanislaus hurrying by the ascetic pines, of the grim outlines of Deadwood Hill, swam before his eyes, and made the yellow green of the velvet lawn and graceful foliage seem almost tropical by contrast. And, looking up, a few yards distant he beheld a tall slip of a girl gazing upon the sea—Blanche Masterman.

She had plucked somewhere a large fan-shaped leaf, which she held parasolwise, shading the blonde masses of her hair, and hiding her gray eyes. She had changed her festal dress, with its amplitude of flounce and train, for a closely fitting, half-antique habit whose scant outlines would have been trying to limbs less shapely, but which prettily accented the graceful curves and sweeping lines of this Greyport goddess. As Islington rose, she came toward him with a frankly outstretched hand and unconstrained manner. Had she observed him first? I don't know.

They sat down together on a rustic seat, Miss Blanche facing the sea and shading her eyes with the leaf.

"I don't really know how long I have been sitting here," said Islington, "or whether I have not been actually asleep and dreaming. It seemed too lovely a morning to go to bed. But you?"

From behind the leaf, it appeared that Miss Blanche, on retiring, had been pursued by a hideous four-winged insect which defied the efforts of herself and maid to dislodge. Odin, the Spitz dog, had insisted upon scratching at the door. And it made her eyes red to sleep in the morning. And she had an early call to make. And the sea looked lovely.

"I'm glad to find you here, whatever be the cause," said Islington, with his old directness. "Today, as you know, is my last day in Greyport, and it is much pleasanter to say good-by under this blue sky than even beneath your father's wonderful frescoes yonder. I want to remember you, too, as part of this pleasant prospect which belongs to us all, rather than recall you in anybody's particular setting."

"I know," said Blanche, with equal directness, "that houses are one of the defects of our civilization; but I don't think I ever heard the idea as elegantly expressed before. Where do you go?"

"I don't know yet. I have several plans. I may go to South America and become president of one of the republics—I am not particular which. I am rich, but in that part of America which lies outside of Greyport it is necessary for every man to have some work. My friends think I should have some great aim in life, with a capital A. But I was born a vagabond, and a vagabond I shall probably die."

"I don't know anybody in South America," said Blanche languidly. "There were two girls here last season, but they didn't wear stays in the house, and their white frocks never were properly done up. If you go to South America, you must write to me."

"I will. Can you tell me the name of this flower which I found in your greenhouse? It looks much like a California blossom."

"Perhaps it is. Father bought it of a half-crazy old man who came here one day. Do you know him?"

Islington laughed. "I am afraid not. But let me present this in a less businesslike fashion."

"Thank you. Remind me to give you one in return before you go—or will you choose yourself?"

They had both risen as by a common instinct.

"Good-by."

The cool, flowerlike hand lay in his for an instant.

"Will you oblige me by putting aside that leaf a moment before I go?"

"But my eyes are red, and I look like a perfect fright."

Yet, after a long pause, the leaf fluttered down, and a pair of very beautiful but withal very clear and critical eyes met his. Islington was constrained to look away. When he turned again she was gone.

"Mr. Hislington—sir!"

It was Chalker, the English groom, out of breath with running.

"Seein' you alone, sir—beg your pardon, sir—but there's a person—"

"A person! what the devil do you mean? Speak English —no, damn it, I mean don't," said Islington snappishly.

"I said a person, sir. Beg pardon—no offense—but not a gent, sir. In the lib'ry."

A little amused even through the utter dissatisfaction with himself and vague loneliness that had suddenly come upon him, Islington, as he walked toward the lodge, asked, "Why isn't he a gent?"

"No gent—beggin' your pardin, sir—'ud guy a man in sarvis, sir. Takes me 'ands so, sir, as I sits in the rumble at the gate, and puts 'em downd so, sir, and sez, 'Put 'em in your pocket, young man—or is it a road agint you expects to see that you 'olds hup your 'ands, hand crosses 'em like to that?' sez he. ' 'Old 'ard,' sez he, 'on the short curves, or you'll bust your precious crust,' sez he. And hasks for you, sir. This way, sir."

They entered the lodge. Islington hurried down the long Gothic hall and opened the library door.

In an armchair, in the center of the room, a man sat apparently contemplating a large, stiff, yellow hat with an enormous brim that was placed on the floor before him. His hands rested lightly between his knees, but one foot was drawn up at the side of his chair in a peculiar manner. In the first glance that Islington gave, the attitude in some odd, irreconcilable way suggested a brake. In another moment he dashed across the room, and holding out both hands, cried, "Yuba Bill!"

The man rose, caught Islington by the shoulders, wheeled him round, hugged him, felt of his ribs like a good-natured ogre, shook his hands violently, laughed, and then said somewhat ruefully, "And however did you know me?"

Seeing that Yuba Bill evidently regarded himself as in some elaborate disguise, Islington laughed, and suggested that it must have been instinct.

"And you?" said Bill, holding him at arm's length and surveying him critically—"you!—toe think—toe think—a little cuss no higher nor a trace, a boy as I've flicked outer the road with a whip time in agin, a boy ez never hed much clothes to speak of, turned into a sport!"

Islington remembered, with a thrill of ludicrous terror, that he still wore his evening dress.

"Turned," continued Yuba Bill severely—"turned into a

restyourant waiter—a garsong! Eh, Alfonse, bring me
a patty de foy grass and an omelet, demme!"

"Dear old chap!" said Islington, laughing, and trying to
put his hand over Bill's bearded mouth, "but you—*you*
don't look exactly like yourself! You're not well, Bill."
And indeed, as he turned toward the light, Bill's eyes appeared cavernous, and his hair and beard thickly streaked
with gray.

"Maybe it's this yer harness," said Bill a little anxiously. "When I hitches on this yer curb" (he indicated a massive gold watch chain with enormous links), "and mounts
this 'morning star'" (he pointed to a very large solitaire
pin which had the appearance of blistering his whole shirt
front), "it kinder weighs heavy on me, Tommy. Otherwise I'm all right, my boy—all right." But he evaded
Islington's keen eye and turned from the light.

"You have something to tell me, Bill," said Islington
suddenly and with almost brusque directness; "out with
it."

Bill did not speak, but moved uneasily toward his hat.

"You didn't come three thousand miles, without a
word of warning, to talk to me of old times," said Islington more kindly, "glad as I would have been to see you. It
isn't your way, Bill, and you know it. We shall not be disturbed here," he added, in reply to an inquiring glance
that Bill directed to the door, "and I am ready to hear
you."

"Firstly, then," said Bill, drawing his chair nearer Islington, "answer me one question, Tommy, fair and
square, and up and down."

"Go on," said Islington with a slight smile.

"Ef I should say to you, Tommy—say to you today,
right here, you must come with me—you must leave this
place for a month, a year, two years, maybe, perhaps
forever—is there anything that 'ud keep you—anything,
my boy, ez you couldn't leave?"

"No," said Tommy quietly; "I am only visiting here. I
thought of leaving Greyport today."

"But if I should say to you, Tommy, come with me on a
pasear to Chiny, to Japan, to South Ameriky, p'r'aps,
could you go?"

"Yes," said Islington after a slight pause.

"Thar isn't ennything," said Bill, drawing a little closer, and lowering his voice confidentially—"ennything in the way of a young woman—you understand, Tommy—ez would keep you? They're mighty sweet about here; and whether a man is young or old, Tommy, there's always some woman as is brake or whip to him!"

In a certain excited bitterness that characterized the delivery of this abstract truth, Bill did not see that the young man's face flushed slightly as he answered "No."

"Then listen. It's seven years ago, Tommy, thet I was working one o' the Pioneer coaches over from Gold Hill. Ez I stood in front o' the stage office, the sheriff o' the county comes to me, and he sez, 'Bill,' sez he, 'I've got a looney chap, as I'm in charge of, taking 'im down to the 'sylum in Stockton. He'z quiet and peaceable, but the insides don't like to ride with him. Hev you enny objection to give him a lift on the box beside you?' I sez, 'No; put him up.' When I came to go and get up on that box beside him, that man, Tommy—that man sittin' there, quiet and peaceable, was—Johnson!

"He didn't know me, my boy," Yuba Bill continued, rising and putting his hands on Tommy's shoulders—"he didn't know me. He didn't know nothing about you, nor Angel's, nor the quicksilver lode, nor even his own name. He said his name was Skaggs, but I knowed it was Johnson. Thar was times, Tommy, you might have knocked me off that box with a feather; thar was times when if the twenty-seven passengers o' that stage hed found theirselves swimming in the American River five hundred feet below the road, I never could have explained it satisfactorily to the company—never.

"The sheriff said," Bill continued hastily, as if to preclude any interruption from the young man—"the sheriff said he had been brought into Murphy's Camp three years before, dripping with water, and sufferin' from perkussion of the brain, and had been cared for generally by the boys 'round. When I told the sheriff I knowed 'im, I got him to leave him in my care; and I took him to 'Frisco, Tommy, to 'Frisco, and I put him in charge o' the best doctors there, and paid his board myself. There was nothin' he didn't have ez he wanted. Don't look that way, my dear boy, for God's sake don't!"

"O Bill!" said Islington, rising and staggering to the window, "why did you keep this from me?"

"Why?" said Bill, turning on him savagely—"why? because I wa'n't a fool. Thar was you winnin' your way in college; thar was *you* risin' in the world, and of some account to it. Yer was an old bummer, ez good ez dead to it—a man ez oughter been dead afore! a man ez never denied it! But you allus liked him better nor me," said Bill bitterly.

"Forgive me, Bill," said the young man, seizing both his hands. "I know you did it for the best; but go on."

"Thar ain't much more to tell, nor much use to tell it, as I can see," said Bill moodily. "He never could be cured, the doctors said, for he had what they called monomania—was always talking about his wife and darter that somebody had stole away years ago, and plannin' revenge on that somebody. And six months ago he was missed. I tracked him to Carson, to Salt Lake City, to Omaha, to Chicago, to New York—and here!"

"Here!" echoed Islington.

"Here! And that's what brings me here today. Whether he's crazy or well, whether he's huntin' you or lookin' up that other man, you must get away from here. You mustn't see him. You and me, Tommy, will go away on a cruise. In three or four years he'll be dead or missing, and then we'll come back. Come." And he rose to his feet.

"Bill," said Islington, rising also, and taking the hand of his friend with the same quiet obstinacy that in the old days had endeared him to Bill, "wherever he is, here or elsewhere, sane or crazy, I shall seek and find him. Every dollar that I have shall be his, every dollar that I have spent shall be returned to him. I am young yet, thank God, and can work; and if there is a way out of this miserable business, I shall find it."

"I knew," said Bill with a surliness that ill concealed his evident admiration of the calm figure before him—"I knew the partikler style of d—n fool that you was, and expected no better. Good-by, then—God Almighty! who's that?"

He was on his way to the open French window, but had started back, his face quite white and bloodless, and his eyes staring. Islington ran to the window and looked out.

A white skirt vanished around the corner of the veranda. When he returned, Bill had dropped into a chair.

"It must have been Miss Masterman, I think; but what's the matter?"

"Nothing," said Bill faintly; "have you got any whiskey handy?"

Islington brought a decanter and, pouring out some spirits, handed the glass to Bill. Bill drained it, and then said, "Who is Miss Masterman?"

"Mr. Masterman's daughter; that is, an adopted daughter, I believe."

"Wot name?"

"I really don't know," said Islington pettishly, more vexed than he cared to own at this questioning.

Yuba Bill rose and walked to the window, closed it, walked back again to the door, glanced at Islington, hesitated, and then returned to his chair.

"I didn't tell you I was married—did I?" he said suddenly, looking up in Islington's face with an unsuccessful attempt at a reckless laugh.

"No," said Islington, more pained at the manner than the words.

"Fact," said Yuba Bill. "Three years ago it was, Tommy —three years ago!"

He looked so hard at Islington that, feeling he was expected to say something, he asked vaguely, "Whom did you marry?"

"Thet's it!" said Yuba Bill; "I can't ezactly say; partikly, though a she-devil! generally, the wife of half a dozen other men."

Accustomed, apparently, to have his conjugal infelicities a theme of mirth among men, and seeing no trace of amusement on Islington's grave face, his dogged, reckless manner softened, and drawing his chair closer to Islington, he went on: "It all began outer this: we was coming down Watson's grade one night pretty free, when the expressman turns to me and says, 'There's a row inside, and you'd better pull up!' I pulls up, and out hops first a woman, and then two or three chaps swearin' and cursin', and tryin' to drag someone arter them. Then it 'peared, Tommy, thet it was this woman's drunken husband they was going to put out for abusin' her and strikin' her in the coach; and if it hadn't been for me, my boy, they'd have left that chap thar in the road. But I fixes matters up by putting her alongside o' me on the box, and we drove on. She was very white, Tommy—for the matter o' that, she was always one o' these very white women, that never got red in the face—but she never cried a whimper. Most women would have cried. It was queer, but she never cried. I thought so at the time.

"She was very tall, with a lot o' light hair meandering down the back of her head, as long as a deerskin whiplash, and about the color. She hed eyes thet'd bore ye through at fifty yards, and pooty hands and feet. And when she kinder got out o' that stiff, narvous state she was in, and warmed up a little, and got chipper, by G—d, sir, she was handsome—she was that!"

A little flushed and embarrassed at his own enthusiasm, he stopped, and then said carelessly, "They got off at Murphy's."

"Well," said Islington.

"Well, I used to see her often arter thet, and when she was alone she allus took the box seat. She kinder confided her troubles to me, how her husband got drunk and abused her; and I didn't see much o' him, for he was away in 'Frisco arter thet. But it was all square, Tommy—all square 'twixt me and her.

"I got a-going there a good deal, and then one day I sez to myself, 'Bill, this won't do,' and I got changed to another route. Did you ever know Jackson Filltree, Tommy?" said Bill, breaking off suddenly.

"No."

"Might have heerd of him, p'r'aps?"

"No," said Islington impatiently.

"Jackson Filltree ran the express from White's out to Summit, 'cross the North Fork of the Yuba. One day he sez to me, 'Bill, that's a mighty bad ford at the North Fork.' I sez, 'I believe you, Jackson.' 'It'll git me some day, Bill, sure,' sez he. I sez, 'Why don't you take the lower ford?' 'I don't know,' sez he, 'but I can't.' So ever after, when I met him, he sez, 'That North Fork ain't got me yet.' One day I was in Sacramento, and up comes Filltree. He sez, 'I've sold out the express business on account of the North Fork, but it's bound to get me yet,

Bill, sure'; and he laughs. Two weeks after they finds his body below the ford, whar he tried to cross, comin' down from the summit way. Folks said it was foolishness; Tommy, I sez it was Fate! The second day arter I was changed to the Placerville route thet woman comes outer the hotel above the stage office. Her husband, she said, was lying sick in Placerville; that's what she said; but it was Fate, Tommy, Fate. Three months afterward her husband takes an overdose of morphine for delirium tremens, and dies. There's folks ez sez she gave it to him, but it's Fate. A year after that I married her—Fate, Tommy, Fate!

"I lived with her jest three months," he went on, after a long breath—"three months! It ain't much time for a happy man. I've seen a good deal o' hard life in my day, but there was days in that three months longer than any day in my life—days, Tommy, when it was a tossup whether I should kill her or she me. But thar, I'm done. You are a young man, Tommy, and I ain't goin' to tell things thet, old as I am, three years ago I couldn't have believed."

When at last, with his grim face turned toward the window, he sat silently with his clenched hands on his knees before him, Islington asked where his wife was now.

"Ask me no more, my boy—no more. I've said my say." With a gesture as of throwing down a pair of reins before him, he rose, and walked to the window.

"You kin understand, Tommy, why a little trip around the world 'ud do me good. Ef you can't go with me, well and good. But go I must."

"Not before luncheon, I hope," said a very sweet voice, as Blanche Masterman suddenly stood before them. "Father would never forgive me if in his absence I permitted one of Mr. Islington's friends to go in this way. You will stay, won't you? Do! And you will give me your arm now; and when Mr. Islington has done staring, he will follow us into the dining room and introduce you."

"I have quite fallen in love with your friend," said Miss Blanche, as they stood in the drawing room looking at the figure of Bill, strolling with his short pipe in his mouth through the distant shrubbery. "He asks very queer questions, though. He wanted to know my mother's maiden name."

"He is an honest fellow," said Islington gravely.

"You are very much subdued. You don't thank me, I daresay, for keeping you and your friend here; but you couldn't go, you know, until father returned."

Islington smiled, but not very gaily.

"And then I think it much better for us to part here under these frescoes, don't you? Good-by."

She extended her long, slim hand.

"Out in the sunlight there, when my eyes were red, you were very anxious to look at me," she added in a dangerous voice.

Islington raised his sad eyes to hers. Something glittering upon her own sweet lashes trembled and fell.

"Blanche!"

She was rosy enough now, and would have withdrawn her hand, but Islington detained it. She was not quite certain but that her waist was also in jeopardy. Yet she could not help saying, "Are you sure that there isn't anything in the way of a young woman that would keep you?"

"Blanche!" said Islington in reproachful horror.

"If gentlemen will roar out their secrets before an open window, with a young woman lying on a sofa on the veranda reading a stupid French novel, they must not be surprised if she gives more attention to them than to her book."

"Then you know all, Blanche?"

"I know," said Blanche, "let's see—I know the partikler style of—ahem!—fool you was, and expected no better. Good-by." And, gliding like a lovely and innocent milk snake out of his grasp, she slipped away.

To the pleasant ripple of waves, the sound of music and light voices, the yellow midsummer moon again rose over Greyport. It looked upon formless masses of rock and shrubbery, wide spaces of lawn and beach, and a shimmering expanse of water. It singled out particular objects—a white sail in shore, a crystal globe upon the lawn, and flashed upon something held between the teeth of a crouching figure scaling the low wall of Cliffwood Lodge. Then, as a man and woman passed out from under the shadows of the foliage into the open moonlight of the garden path, the figure leaped from the wall, and stood erect and waiting in the shadow.

It was the figure of an old man, with rolling eyes, his trembling hand grasping a long, keen knife—a figure more pitiable than pitiless, more pathetic than terrible. But the next moment the knife was stricken from his hand, and he struggled in the firm grasp of another figure that apparently sprang from the wall beside him.

"D—n you, Masterman!" cried the old man hoarsely; "give me fair play, and I'll kill you yet!"

"Which my name is Yuba Bill," said Bill quietly, "and it's time this d—n fooling was stopped."

The old man glared in Bill's face savagely. "I know you. You're one of Masterman's friends—d—n you,— let me go till I cut his heart out—let me go! Where is my Mary?—where is my wife?—there she is! there!— there!—there! Mary!" He would have screamed, but Bill placed his powerful hand upon his mouth as he turned in the direction of the old man's glance. Distinct in the moonlight the figures of Islington and Blanche, arm in arm, stood out upon the garden path.

"Give me my wife!" muttered the old man hoarsely between Bill's fingers. "Where is she?"

A sudden fury passed over Yuba Bill's face. "Where is your wife?" he echoed, pressing the old man back against the garden wall, and holding him there as in a vise. "Where is your wife?" he repeated, thrusting his grim sardonic jaw and savage eyes into the old man's frightened face. "Where is Jack Adam's wife? Where is MY wife? Where is the she-devil that drove one man mad, that sent another to hell by his own hand, that eternally broke and ruined me? Where! Where! Do you ask where? In jail in Sacramento—in jail, do you hear?—in jail for murder, Johnson—murder!"

The old man gasped, stiffened, and then, relaxing, suddenly slipped, a mere inanimate mass at Yuba Bill's feet. With a sudden revulsion of feeling, Yuba Bill dropped at his side, and lifting him tenderly in his arms, whispered, "Look up, old man, Johnson! look up, for God's sake!— it's me—Yuba Bill! and yonder is your daughter, and—

Tommy—don't you know—Tommy, little Tommy Islington?"

Johnson's eyes slowly opened. He whispered, "Tommy! yes, Tommy! Sit by me, Tommy. But don't sit so near the bank. Don't you see how the river is rising and beckoning to me—hissing, and boilin' over the rocks? It's gittin' higher!—hold me, Tommy—hold me, and don't let me go yet. We'll live to cut his heart out, Tommy—we'll live—we'll—"

His head sank, and the rushing river, invisible to all eyes save his, leaped toward him out of the darkness, and bore him away, no longer to the darkness, but through it to the distant, peaceful, shining sea.

Wan Lee,
⋙⋙⋙⋙⋙⋙⋙⋙⋙ The Pagan ⋙⋙⋙⋙⋙

⋙⋙⋙ As I opened Hop Sing's letter there fluttered to the ground a square strip of yellow paper covered with hieroglyphics, which at first glance I innocently took to be the label from a pack of Chinese firecrackers. But the same envelope also contained a smaller strip of rice paper, with two Chinese characters traced in India ink, that I at once knew to be Hop Sing's visiting card. The whole, as afterwards literally translated, ran as follows:

> To the stranger the gates of my house are not closed;
>   the rice jar is on the left, and the sweetmeats on
>   the right, as you enter.
> Two sayings of the Master:
>   Hospitality is the virtue of the son and the wisdom
>   of the ancestor.
>   The superior man is lighthearted after the crop-
>   gathering; he makes a festival.
> When the stranger is in your melon patch observe him
>   not too closely; inattention is often the highest
>   form of civility.
>   Happiness, Peace, and Prosperity.
>   HOP SING

Admirable, certainly, as was this morality and proverbial wisdom, and although this last axiom was very characteristic of my friend Hop Sing, who was that most somber of all humorists, a Chinese philosopher, I must confess that even after a very free translation I was at a loss to make any immediate application of the message. Luckily I discovered a third enclosure in the shape of a little note in English and Hop Sing's own commercial hand. It ran thus:

The pleasure of your company is requested at No. —
Sacramento Street, on Friday evening at eight o'clock. A
cup of tea at nine—sharp.   HOP SING

This explained all. It meant a visit to Hop Sing's warehouse, the opening and exhibition of some rare Chinese
novelties and curios, a chat in the back office, a cup of
tea of a perfection unknown beyond these sacred precincts, cigars, and a visit to the Chinese Theater or
Temple. This was in fact the favorite program of Hop
Sing when he exercised his functions of hospitality as the
chief factor or superintendent of the Ning Foo Company.

At eight o'clock on Friday evening I entered the warehouse of Hop Sing. There was that deliciously com-
mingled mysterious foreign odor that I had so often
noticed; there was the old array of uncouth-looking objects, the long procession of jars and crockery, the same
singular blending of the grotesque and the mathematically
neat and exact, the same endless suggestions of frivolity
and fragility, the same want of harmony in colors that
were each, in themselves, beautiful and rare. Kites in the
shape of enormous dragons and gigantic butterflies; kites
so ingeniously arranged as to utter at intervals, when
facing the wind, the cry of a hawk; kites so large as to
be beyond any boy's power of restraint—so large that
you understood why kite-flying in China was an amusement for adults; gods of china and bronze so gratuitously
ugly as to be beyond any human interest or sympathy
from their very impossibility; jars of sweetmeats covered
all over with moral sentiments from Confucius; hats that
looked like baskets, and baskets that looked like hats;
silk so light that I hesitate to record the incredible number of square yards that you might pass through the
ring on your little finger—these and a great many other
indescribable objects were all familiar to me. I pushed
my way through the dimly lighted warehouse until I
reached the back office or parlor, where I found Hop
Sing waiting to receive me.

Before I describe him I want the average reader to
discharge from his mind any idea of a Chinaman that he
may have gathered from the pantomime. He did not wear
beautifully scalloped drawers fringed with little bells—I

never met a Chinaman who did; he did not habitually carry his forefinger extended before him at right angles with his body, nor did I ever hear him utter the mysterious sentence, "Ching a ring a ring chaw," nor dance under any provocation. He was, on the whole, a rather grave, decorous, handsome gentleman. His complexion, which extended all over his head except where his long pigtail grew, was like a very nice piece of glazed brown paper-muslin. His eyes were black and bright, and his eyelids set at an angle of 15°; his nose straight and delicately formed, his mouth small, and his teeth white and clean. He wore a dark blue silk blouse, and in the streets on cold days a short jacket of astrakhan fur. He wore also a pair of drawers of blue brocade gathered tightly over his calves and ankles, offering a general sort of suggestion that he had forgotten his trousers that morning, but that, so gentlemanly were his manners, his friends had forborne to mention the fact to him. His manner was urbane, although quite serious. He spoke French and English fluently. In brief, I doubt if you could have found the equal of this Pagan shopkeeper among the Christian traders of San Francisco.

There were a few others present: a judge of the federal court, an editor, a high government official, and a prominent merchant. After we had drunk our tea, and tasted a few sweetmeats from a mysterious jar that looked as if it might contain a preserved mouse among its other nondescript treasures, Hop Sing arose, and gravely beckoning us to follow him, began to descend to the basement. When we got there, we were amazed at finding it brilliantly lighted, and that a number of chairs were arranged in a half circle on the asphalt pavement. When he had courteously seated us, he said—

"I have invited you to witness a performance which I can at least promise you no other foreigners but yourselves have ever seen. Wang, the court juggler, arrived here yesterday morning. He has never given a performance outside of the palace before. I have asked him to entertain my friends this evening. He requires no theater, stage, accessories, or any confederate—nothing more than you see here. Will you be pleased to examine the ground yourselves, gentlemen."

Of course we examined the premises. It was the ordinary basement or cellar of the San Francisco storehouse, cemented to keep out the damp. We poked our sticks into the pavement and rapped on the walls to satisfy our polite host, but for no other purpose. We were quite content to be the victims of any clever deception. For myself, I knew I was ready to be deluded to any extent, and if I had been offered an explanation of what followed, I should have probably declined it.

Although I am satisfied that Wang's general performance was the first of that kind ever given on American soil, it has probably since become so familiar to many of my readers that I shall not bore them with it here. He began by setting to flight, with the aid of his fan, the usual number of butterflies made before our eyes of little bits of tissue paper, and kept them in the air during the remainder of the performance. I have a vivid recollection of the judge trying to catch one that had lit on his knee, and of its evading him with the pertinacity of a living insect. And even at this time Wang, still plying his fan, was taking chickens out of hats, making oranges disappear, pulling endless yards of silk from his sleeve, apparently filling the whole area of the basement with goods that appeared mysteriously from the ground, from his own sleeves, from nowhere! He swallowed knives to the ruin of his digestion for years to come; he dislocated every limb of his body; he reclined in the air, apparently upon nothing. But his crowning performance, which I have never yet seen repeated, was the most weird, mysterious, and astounding. It is my apology for this long introduction, my sole excuse for writing this article, the genesis of this veracious history.

He cleared the ground of its encumbering articles for a space of about fifteen feet square, and then invited us all to walk forward and again examine it. We did so gravely; there was nothing but the cemented pavement below to be seen or felt. He then asked for the loan of a handkerchief, and as I chanced to be nearest him, I offered mine. He took it and spread it open upon the floor. Over this he spread a large square of silk, and over this again a large shawl nearly covering the space he had cleared. He then took a position at one of the points of this rectangle, and began a monotonous chant, rocking his body to and fro in time with the somewhat lugubrious air.

We sat still and waited. Above the chant we could hear the striking of the city clocks, and the occasional rattle of a cart in the street overhead. The absolute watchfulness and expectation, the dim, mysterious half-light of the cellar, falling in a gruesome way upon the misshapen bulk of a Chinese deity in the background, a faint smell of opium smoke mingling with spice, and the dreadful uncertainty of what we were really waiting for, sent an uncomfortable thrill down our backs, and made us look at each other with a forced and unnatural smile. This feeling was heightened when Hop Sing slowly rose, and without a word, pointed with his finger to the center of the shawl.

There was something beneath the shawl! Surely—and something that was not there before. At first a mere suggestion in relief, a faint outline, but growing more and more distinct and visible every moment. The chant still continued, the perspiration began to roll from the singer's face, gradually the hidden object took upon itself a shape and bulk that raised the shawl in its center some five or six inches. It was now unmistakably the outline of a small but perfect human figure, with extended arms and legs. One or two of us turned pale; there was a feeling of general uneasiness, until the editor broke the silence by a gibe that, poor as it was, was received with spontaneous enthusiasm. Then the chant suddenly ceased, Wang arose, and with a quick, dexterous movement, stripped both shawl and silk away, and discovered, sleeping peacefully upon my handkerchief, a tiny Chinese baby!

The applause and uproar which followed this revelation ought to have satisfied Wang, even if his audience was a small one; it was loud enough to awaken the baby—a pretty little boy about a year old, looking like a Cupid cut out of sandalwood. He was whisked away almost as mysteriously as he appeared. When Hop Sing returned my handkerchief to me with a bow, I asked if the juggler was the father of the baby. "No sabe!" said the imperturbable Hop Sing, taking refuge in that Spanish form of noncommittalism so common in California.

"But does he have a new baby for every performance?"
I asked.

"Perhaps; who knows?"

"But what will become of this one?"

"Whatever you choose, gentlemen," replied Hop Sing,
with a courteous inclination; "it was born here—you are
its godfathers."

There were two characteristic peculiarities of any Californian assemblage in 1856: it was quick to take a hint,
and generous to the point of prodigality in its response to
any charitable appeal. No matter how sordid or avaricious
the individual, he could not resist the infection of sympathy. I doubled the points of my handkerchief into a
bag, dropped a coin into it, and without a word, passed
it to the judge. He quietly added a twenty-dollar gold
piece, and passed it to the next; when it was returned to
me it contained over a hundred dollars. I knotted the
money in the handkerchief, and gave it to Hop Sing.

"For the baby, from its godfathers."

"But what name?" said the judge. There was a running fire of "Erebus," "Nox," "Plutus," "Terra Cotta,"
"Antæus," etc., etc. Finally the question was referred to
our host.

"Why not keep his own name," he said quietly—"Wan
Lee?" And he did.

And thus was Wan Lee, on the night of Friday the
5th of March, 1856, born into this veracious chronicle.

The last form of the *Northern Star* for the 19th of
July, 1865—the only daily paper published in Klamath
County—had just gone to press, and at 3 A.M. I was
putting aside my proofs and manuscripts, preparatory to
going home, when I discovered a letter lying under some
sheets of paper which I must have overlooked. The envelope was considerably soiled, it had no postmark, but
I had no difficulty in recognizing the hand of my friend
Hop Sing. I opened it hurriedly, and read as follows:

MY DEAR SIR,—I do not know whether the bearer will
suit you, but unless the office of "devil" in your newspaper
is a purely technical one, I think he has all the qualities
required. He is very quick, active, and intelligent; under-

stands English better than he speaks it, and makes up for any defect by his habits of observation and imitation. You have only to show him how to do a thing once, and he will repeat it, whether it is an offense or a virtue. But you certainly know him already; you are one of his godfathers, for is he not Wan Lee, the reputed son of Wang the conjurer, to whose performances I had the honor to introduce you? But perhaps you have forgotten it.

I shall send him with a gang of coolies to Stockton, thence by express to your town. If you can use him there, you will do me a favor, and probably save his life, which is at present in great peril from the hands of the younger members of your Christian and highly civilized race who attend the enlightened schools in San Francisco.

He has acquired some singular habits and customs from his experience of Wang's profession, which he followed for some years, until he became too large to go in a hat, or be produced from his father's sleeve. The money you left with me has been expended on his education; he has gone through the triliteral classics, but, I think, without much benefit. He knows but little of Confucius, and absolutely nothing of Mencius. Owing to the negligence of his father, he associated, perhaps, too much with American children.

I should have answered your letter before, by post, but I thought that Wan Lee himself would be a better messenger for this.

Yours respectfully,
HOP SING

And this was the long-delayed answer to my letter to Hop Sing. But where was "the bearer"? How was the letter delivered? I summoned hastily the foreman, printers, and office boy, but without eliciting anything; no one had seen the letter delivered, nor knew anything of the bearer. A few days later I had a visit from my laundryman, Ah Ri.

"You wantee debbil? All lightee; me catchee him."

He returned in a few moments with a bright-looking Chinese boy, about ten years old, with whose appearance and general intelligence I was so greatly impressed that I engaged him on the spot. When the business was concluded, I asked his name.

"Wan Lee," said the boy.

"What! Are you the boy sent out by Hop Sing? What the devil do you mean by not coming here before, and how did you deliver that letter?"

Wan Lee looked at me and laughed. "Me pitchee in top side window."

I did not understand. He looked for a moment perplexed, and then, snatching the letter out of my hand, ran down the stairs. After a moment's pause, to my great astonishment, the letter came flying in at the window, circled twice around the room, and then dropped gently like a bird upon my table. Before I had got over my surprise Wan Lee reappeared, smiled, looked at the letter and then at me, said, "So, John," and then remained gravely silent. I said nothing further, but it was understood that this was his first official act.

His next performance, I grieve to say, was not attended with equal success. One of our regular paper-carriers fell sick, and, at a pinch, Wan Lee was ordered to fill his place. To prevent mistakes he was shown over the route the previous evening, and supplied at about daylight with the usual number of subscribers' copies. He returned after an hour, in good spirits and without the papers. He had delivered them all he said.

Unfortunately for Wan Lee, at about eight o'clock indignant subscribers began to arrive at the office. They had received their copies; but how? In the form of hard-pressed cannon balls, delivered by a single shot and a mere tour de force through the glass of bedroom windows. They had received them full in the face, like a baseball, if they happened to be up and stirring; they had received them in quarter sheets, tucked in at separate windows; they had found them in the chimney, pinned against the door, shot through attic windows, delivered in long slips through convenient keyholes, stuffed into ventilators, and occupying the same can with the morning's milk. One subscriber, who waited for some time at the office door to have a personal interview with Wan Lee (then comfortably locked in my bedroom), told me, with tears of rage in his eyes, that he had been awakened at five o'clock by a most hideous yelling below his windows; that on rising, in great agitation, he was startled by the sudden appearance of the *Northern Star*, rolled hard and bent into the form of a boomerang or East Indian club that sailed into the window, described a number of fiendish circles in the room, knocked over the light, slapped the baby's face, "took" him (the subscriber) "in the jaw," and then returned out of the window, and dropped helplessly in the area. During the rest of the day wads and strips of soiled paper, purporting to be copies of the *Northern Star* of that morning's issue, were brought indignantly to the office. An admirable editorial on "The Resources of Humboldt County," which I had constructed the evening before, and which, I have reason to believe, might have changed the whole balance of trade during the ensuing year, and left San Francisco bankrupt at her wharves, was in this way lost to the public.

It was deemed advisable for the next three weeks to keep Wan Lee closely confined to the printing office and the purely mechanical part of the business. Here he developed a surprising quickness and adaptability, winning even the favor and good will of the printers and foreman, who at first looked upon his introduction into the secrets of their trade as fraught with the gravest political significance. He learned to set type readily and neatly, his wonderful skill in manipulation aiding him in the mere mechanical act, and his ignorance of the language confining him simply to the mechanical effort—confirming the printer's axiom that the printer who considers or follows the ideas of his copy makes a poor compositor. He would set up deliberately long diatribes against himself, composed by his fellow printers, and hung on his hook as copy, and even such short sentences as "Wan Lee is the devil's own imp," "Wan Lee is a Mongolian rascal," and bring the proof to me with happiness beaming from every tooth and satisfaction shining in his huckleberry eyes.

It was not long, however, before he learned to retaliate on his mischievous persecutors. I remember one instance in which his reprisal came very near involving me in a serious misunderstanding. Our foreman's name was Webster, and Wan Lee presently learned to know and recognize the individual and combined letters of his name. It was during a political campaign, and the eloquent and fiery Colonel Starbottle of Siskiyou had delivered an effective speech, which was reported especially for the *Northern Star*. In a very sublime peroration Colonel Starbottle had said, "In the language of the godlike Webster, I repeat—" and here followed the quotation, which I have forgotten. Now, it chanced that Wan Lee, looking over the galley after it had been revised, saw the name of his chief persecutor, and, of course, imagined the quotation his. After the form was locked up, Wan Lee took advantage of Webster's absence to remove the quotation, and substitute a thin piece of lead of the same size as the type, engraved with Chinese characters, making a sentence which, I had reason to believe, was an utter and abject confession of the incapacity and offensiveness of the Webster family generally, and exceedingly eulogistic of Wan Lee himself personally.

The next morning's paper contained Colonel Starbottle's speech in full, in which it appeared that the "godlike" Webster had on one occasion uttered his thoughts in excellent but perfectly enigmatical Chinese. The rage of Colonel Starbottle knew no bounds. I have a vivid recollection of that admirable man walking into my office and demanding a retraction of the statement.

"But, my dear sir," I asked, "are you willing to deny, over your own signature, that Webster ever uttered such a sentence? Dare you deny that, with Mr. Webster's well-known attainments, a knowledge of Chinese might not have been among the number? Are you willing to submit a translation suitable to the capacity of our readers, and deny, upon your honor as a gentleman, that the late Mr. Webster ever uttered such a sentiment? If you are, sir, I am willing to publish your denial."

The Colonel was not, and left highly indignant.

Webster, the foreman, took it more coolly. Happily he was unaware that for two days after, Chinamen from the laundries, from the gulches, from the kitchens, looked in the front office door with faces beaming with sardonic delight; that three hundred extra copies of the *Star* were ordered for the wash-houses on the river. He only knew that during the day Wan Lee occasionally went off into convulsive spasms, and that he was obliged to kick him into consciousness again. A week after the occurrence I called Wan Lee into my office.

"Wan," I said gravely, "I should like you to give me, for my own personal satisfaction, a translation of that Chinese sentence which my gifted countryman, the late godlike Webster, uttered upon a public occasion." Wan Lee looked at me intently, and then the slightest possible twinkle crept into his black eyes. Then he replied, with equal gravity—

"Mishtel Webstel—he say: 'China boy makee me belly much foolee. China boy makee me heap sick.'" Which I have reason to think was true.

But I fear I am giving but one side, and not the best, of Wan Lee's character. As he imparted it to me, his had been a hard life. He had known scarcely any childhood— he had no recollection of a father or mother. The conjurer Wang had brought him up. He had spent the first seven years of his life in appearing from baskets, in dropping out of hats, in climbing ladders, in putting his little limbs out of joint in posturing. He had lived in an atmosphere of trickery and deception; he had learned to look upon mankind as dupes of their senses; in fine, if he had thought at all, he would have been a skeptic; if he had been a little older, he would have been a cynic; if he had been older still, he would have been a philosopher. As it was, he was a little imp! A good-natured imp it was, too—an imp whose moral nature had never been awakened, an imp up for a holiday, and willing to try virtue as a diversion. I don't know that he had any spiritual nature; he was very superstitious; he carried about with him a hideous little porcelain god, which he was in the habit of alternately reviling and propitiating. He was too intelligent for the commoner Chinese vices of stealing or gratuitous lying. Whatever discipline he practiced was taught by his intellect.

I am inclined to think that his feelings were not altogether unimpressible—although it was almost impossible to extract an expression from him—and I conscientiously believe he became attached to those that were good to him. What he might have become under more favorable

conditions than the bondsman of an overworked, under-
paid literary man, I don't know; I only know that the
scant, irregular, impulsive kindnesses that I showed him
were gratefully received. He was very loyal and patient—
two qualities rare in the average American servant. He
was like Malvolio, "sad and civil" with me; only once, and
then under great provocation, do I remember of his ex-
hibiting any impatience. It was my habit after leaving
the office at night to take him with me to my rooms, as
the bearer of any supplemental or happy afterthought in
the editorial way that might occur to me before the paper
went to press. One night I had been scribbling away past
the usual hour of dismissing Wan Lee, and had become
quite oblivious of his presence in a chair near my door,
when suddenly I became aware of a voice saying, in
plaintive accents, something that sounded like "Chy Lee."

I faced around sternly.

"What did you say?"

"Me say, 'Chy Lee.'"

"Well?" I said impatiently.

"You sabe, 'How do, John'?"

"Yes."

"You sabe, 'So long, John'?"

"Yes."

"Well, 'Chy Lee' allee same!"

I understood him quite plainly. It appeared that "Chy
Lee" was a form of "good night," and that Wan Lee was
anxious to go home. But an instinct of mischief which I
fear I possessed in common with him impelled me to act
as if oblivious of the hint. I muttered something about
not understanding him, and again bent over my work. In a
few minutes I heard his wooden shoes pattering pathetically over the floor. I looked up. He was standing
near the door.

"You no sabe, 'Chy Lee'?"

"No," I said sternly.

"You sabe muchee big foolee!—allee same!"

And with this audacity upon his lips he fled. The next
morning, however, he was as meek and patient as before,
and I did not recall his offense. As a probable peace-
offering, he blacked all my boots—a duty never required
of him—including a pair of buff deerskin slippers and

an immense pair of horseman's jack boots, on which he indulged his remorse for two hours.

I have spoken of his honesty as being a quality of his intellect rather than his principle, but I recall about this time two exceptions to the rule. I was anxious to get some fresh eggs as a change to the heavy diet of a mining town, and knowing that Wan Lee's countrymen were great poultry-raisers, I applied to him. He furnished me with them regularly every morning, but refused to take any pay, saying that the man did not sell them—a remarkable instance of self-abnegation, as eggs were then worth half a dollar apiece. One morning, my neighbor, Foster, dropped in upon me at breakfast, and took occasion to bewail his own ill fortune, as his hens had lately stopped laying, or wandered off in the bush. Wan Lee, who was present during our colloquy, preserved his characteristic sad taciturnity. When my neighbor had gone, he turned to me with a slight chuckle—"Flostel's hens—Wan Lee's hens—allee same!" His other offense was more serious and ambitious. It was a season of great irregularities in the mails, and Wan Lee had heard me deplore the delay in the delivery of my letters and newspapers. On arriving at my office one day, I was amazed to find my table covered with letters, evidently just from the post office, but unfortunately not one addressed to me. I turned to Wan Lee, who was surveying them with a calm satisfaction, and demanded an explanation. To my horror he pointed to an empty mailbag in the corner, and said, "Postman he say, 'No lettee, John—no lettee, John.' Postman plentee lie! Postman no good. Me catchee lettee last night—allee same!" Luckily it was still early; the mails had not been distributed; I had a hurried interview with the postmaster, and Wan Lee's bold attempt at robbing the U. S. mail was finally condoned, by the purchase of a new mailbag, and the whole affair thus kept a secret.

If my liking for my little pagan page had not been sufficient, my duty to Hop Sing was enough to cause me to take Wan Lee with me when I returned to San Francisco, after my two years' experience with the *Northern Star*. I do not think he contemplated the change with pleasure. I attributed his feelings to a nervous dread of crowded public streets—when he had to go across town for me on an errand, he always made a long circuit of the outskirts; to his dislike for the discipline of the Chinese and English school to which I proposed to send him; to his fondness for the free, vagrant life of the mines; to sheer willfulness! That it might have been a superstitious premonition did not occur to me until long after.

Nevertheless it really seemed as if the opportunity I had long looked for and confidently expected had come—the opportunity of placing Wan Lee under gently restraining influences, of subjecting him to a life and experience that would draw out of him what good my superficial care and ill-regulated kindness could not reach. Wan Lee was placed at the school of a Chinese missionary—an intelligent and kind-hearted clergyman, who had shown great interest in the boy, and who, better than all, had a wonderful faith in him. A home was found for him in the family of a widow, who had a bright and interesting daughter about two years younger than Wan Lee. It was this bright, cheery, innocent, and artless child that touched and reached a depth in the boy's nature that hitherto had been unsuspected—that awakened a moral susceptibility which had lain for years insensible alike to the teachings of society or the ethics of the theologian.

These few brief months, bright with a promise that we never saw fulfilled, must have been happy ones to Wan Lee. He worshiped his little friend with something of the same superstition, but without any of the caprice, that he bestowed upon his porcelain pagan god. It was his delight to walk behind her to school, carrying her books —a service always fraught with danger to him from the little hands of his Caucasian Christian brothers. He made her the most marvelous toys; he would cut out of carrots and turnips the most astonishing roses and tulips; he made lifelike chickens out of melon seeds; he constructed fans and kites, and was singularly proficient in the making of dolls' paper dresses. On the other hand she played and sang to him; taught him a thousand little prettinesses and refinements only known to girls; gave him a yellow ribbon for his pigtail, as best suiting his complexion; read to him; showed him wherein he was original and

valuable; took him to Sunday school with her, against
the precedents of the school, and small-womanlike, tri-
umphed. I wish I could add here that she effected his
conversion, and made him give up his porcelain idol,
but I am telling a true story, and this little girl was quite
content to fill him with her own Christian goodness, without letting him know that he was changed. So they got
along very well together—this little Christian girl, with
her shining cross hanging around her plump, white, little
neck, and this dark little pagan, with his hideous porcelain
god hidden away in his blouse.

There were two days of that eventful year which will
long be remembered in San Francisco—two days when a
mob of her citizens set upon and killed unarmed, de-
fenseless foreigners, because they were foreigners and of
another race, religion, and color, and worked for what
wages they could get. There were some public men so
timid that, seeing this, they thought that the end of the
world had come; there were some eminent statesmen,
whose names I am ashamed to write here, who began to
think that the passage in the Constitution which guaran-
tees civil and religious liberty to every citizen or for-
eigner was a mistake. But there were also some men who
were not so easily frightened, and in twenty-four hours
we had things so arranged that the timid men could wring
their hands in safety, and the eminent statesmen utter
their doubts without hurting anybody or anything. And in
the midst of this I got a note from Hop Sing, asking me
to come to him immediately.

I found his warehouse closed and strongly guarded by
the police against any possible attack of the rioters. Hop
Sing admitted me through a barred grating with his usual
imperturbable calm, but as it seemed to me, with more
than his usual seriousness. Without a word he took my
hand and led me to the rear of the room, and thence
downstairs into the basement. It was dimly lighted, but
there was something lying on the floor covered by a
shawl. As I approached, he drew the shawl away with a
sudden gesture, and revealed Wan Lee, the pagan, lying
there dead!

Dead, my reverend friends, dead! Stoned to death in
the streets of San Francisco, in the year of grace, eighteen

hundred and sixty-nine, by a mob of half-grown boys and Christian school children!

As I put my hand reverently upon his breast, I felt something crumbling beneath his blouse. I looked inquiringly at Hop Sing. He put his hand between the folds of silk, and drew out something with the first bitter smile I had ever seen on the face of that pagan gentleman.

It was Wan Lee's porcelain god, crushed by a stone from the hands of those Christian iconoclasts!

A Passage in the Life
>>>->>>->>>->>>->>>> of Mr. John Oakhurst >>>->>>

Gambler

>>>->>>->>>> He always thought it must have been Fate.
Certainly nothing could have been more inconsistent with
his habits than to have been in the Plaza at seven o'clock
of that midsummer morning. The sight of his colorless
face in Sacramento was rare at that season, and indeed
at any season, anywhere, publicly, before two o'clock in
the afternoon. Looking back upon it in after years, in
the light of a chanceful life, he determined, with the
characteristic philosophy of his profession, that it must
have been Fate.

Yet it is my duty as a strict chronicler of facts to state
that Mr. Oakhurst's presence there that morning was due
to a very simple cause. At exactly half past six, the bank
being then a winner to the amount of twenty thousand
dollars, he had risen from the faro table, relinquished
his seat to an accomplished assistant, and withdrawn
quietly, without attracting a glance from the silent, anxious faces bowed over the table. But when he entered
his luxurious sleeping room, across the passageway, he
was a little shocked at finding the sun streaming through
an inadvertently opened window. Something in the rare
beauty of the morning, perhaps something in the novelty
of the idea, struck him as he was about to close the
blinds, and he hesitated. Then, taking his hat from the
table, he stepped down a private staircase into the street.

The people who were abroad at that early hour were
of a class quite unknown to Mr. Oakhurt. There were
milkmen and hucksters delivering their wares, small
tradespeople opening their shops, housemaids sweeping
doorsteps, and occasionally a child. These Mr. Oakhurst
regarded with a certain cold curiosity, perhaps quite free
from the cynical disfavor with which he generally looked
upon the more pretentious of his race whom he was in the

habit of meeting. Indeed, I think he was not altogether displeased with the admiring glances which these humble women threw after his handsome face and figure, conspicuous even in a country of fine-looking men. While it is very probable that this wicked vagabond, in the pride of his social isolation, would have been coldly indifferent to the advances of a fine lady, a little girl who ran admiringly by his side in a ragged dress had the power to call a faint flush into his colorless cheek. He dismissed her at last, but not until she had found out—what sooner or later her large-hearted and discriminating sex inevitably did—that he was exceedingly free and openhanded with his money, and also—what perhaps none other of her sex ever did—that the bold black eyes of this fine gentleman were in reality of a brownish and even tender gray.

There was a small garden before a white cottage in a side street that attracted Mr. Oakhurst's attention. It was filled with roses, heliotrope, and verbena—flowers familiar enough to him in the expensive and more portable form of bouquets, but as it seemed to him then, never before so notably lovely. Perhaps it was because the dew was yet fresh upon them, perhaps it was because they were unplucked, but Mr. Oakhurst admired them, not as a possible future tribute to the fascinating and accomplished Miss Ethelinda, then performing at the Varieties, for Mr. Oakhurst's especial benefit, as she had often assured him; nor yet as a *douceur* to the enthralling Miss Montmorrissy, with whom Mr. Oakhurst expected to sup that evening, but simply for himself, and mayhap for the flowers' sake. Howbeit, he passed on, and so out into the open plaza, where, finding a bench under a cottonwood tree, he first dusted the seat with his handkerchief, and then sat down.

It was a fine morning. The air was so still and calm that a sigh from the sycamores seemed like the deep-drawn breath of the just awakening tree, and the faint rustle of its boughs as the outstretching of cramped and reviving limbs. Far away the Sierras stood out against a sky so remote as to be of no positive color—so remote that even the sun despaired of ever reaching it, and so expended its strength recklessly on the whole landscape, until it fairly glittered in a white and vivid contrast. With a very rare impulse, Mr. Oakhurst took off his hat, and half reclined on the bench, with his face to the sky. Certain birds who had taken a critical attitude on a spray above him apparently began an animated discussion regarding his possible malevolent intentions. One or two, emboldened by the silence, hopped on the ground at his feet, until the sound of wheels on the gravel walk frightened them away.

Looking up, he saw a man coming slowly towards him, wheeling a nondescript vehicle in which a woman was partly sitting, partly reclining. Without knowing why, Mr. Oakhurst instantly conceived that the carriage was the invention and workmanship of the man, partly from its oddity, partly from the strong, mechanical hand that grasped it, and partly from a certain pride and visible consciousness in the manner in which the man handled it. Then Mr. Oakhurst saw something more—the man's face was familiar. With that regal faculty of not forgetting a face that had ever given him professional audience, he instantly classified it under the following mental formula: "At 'Frisco, Polka Saloon. Lost his week's wages. I reckon seventy dollars—on red. Never came again." There was, however, no trace of this in the calm eyes and unmoved face that he turned upon the stranger, who, on the contrary, blushed, looked embarrassed, hesitated, and then stopped with an involuntary motion that brought the carriage and its fair occupant face to face with Mr. Oakhurst.

I should hardly do justice to the position she will occupy in this veracious chronicle by describing the lady now— if, indeed, I am able to do it at all. Certainly, the popular estimate was conflicting. The late Colonel Starbottle—to whose large experience of a charming sex I have before been indebted for many valuable suggestions—had, I regret to say, depreciated her fascinations. "A yellow-faced cripple, by dash—a sick woman, with mahogany eyes. One of your blanked spiritual creatures, with no flesh on her bones." On the other hand, however, she enjoyed later much complimentary disparagement from her own sex. Miss Celestina Howard, second leader in the ballet at the Varieties, had, with great alliterative directness, in after years, denominated her as an "aquiline asp." Mlle.

Brimborion remembered that she had always warned "Mr. Jack" that this woman would "empoison" him. But Mr. Oakhurst, whose impressions are perhaps the most important, only saw a pale, thin, deep-eyed woman, raised above the level of her companion by the refinement of long suffering and isolation, and a certain shy virginity of manner. There was a suggestion of physical purity in the folds of her fresh-looking robe, and a certain picturesque tastefulness in the details, that, without knowing why, made him think that the robe was her invention and handiwork, even as the carriage she occupied was evidently the work of her companion. Her own hand, a trifle too thin, but well-shaped, subtle-fingered, and gentlewomanly, rested on the side of the carriage, the counterpart of the strong mechanical grasp of her companion's.

There was some obstruction to the progress of the vehicle, and Mr. Oakhurst stepped forward to assist. While the wheel was being lifted over the curbstone, it was necessary that she should hold his arm, and for a moment her thin hand rested there, light and cold as a snowflake, and then—as it seemed to him—like a snowflake melted away. Then there was a pause, and then conversation—the lady joining occasionally and shyly.

It appeared that they were man and wife. That for the past two years she had been a great invalid, and had lost the use of her lower limbs from rheumatism. That until lately she had been confined to her bed, until her husband—who was a master carpenter—had bethought himself to make her this carriage. He took her out regularly for an airing before going to work, because it was his only time, and—they attracted less attention. They had tried many doctors, but without avail. They had been advised to go to the Sulphur Springs, but it was expensive. Mr. Decker, the husband, had once saved eighty dollars for that purpose, but while in San Francisco had his pocket picked—Mr. Decker was so senseless. (The intelligent reader need not be told that it is the lady who is speaking.) They had never been able to make up the sum again, and they had given up the idea. It was a dreadful thing to have one's pocket picked. Did he not think so?

Her husband's face was crimson, but Mr. Oakhurst's

countenance was quite calm and unmoved, as he gravely agreed with her, and walked by her side until they passed the little garden that he had admired. Here Mr. Oakhurst commanded a halt, and going to the door, astounded the proprietor by a preposterously extravagant offer for a choice of the flowers. Presently he returned to the carriage with his arms full of roses, heliotrope, and verbena, and cast them in the lap of the invalid. While she was bending over them with childish delight, Mr. Oakhurst took the opportunity of drawing her husband aside.

"Perhaps," he said in a low voice, and a manner quite free from any personal annoyance—"perhaps it's just as well that you lied to her as you did. You can say now that the pickpocket was arrested the other day, and you got your money back." Mr. Oakhurst quietly slipped four twenty-dollar gold pieces into the broad hand of the bewildered Mr. Decker. "Say that—or anything you like— but the truth. Promise me you won't say that!"

The man promised. Mr. Oakhurst quietly returned to the front of the little carriage. The sick woman was still eagerly occupied with the flowers, and as she raised her eyes to his, her faded cheek seemed to have caught some color from the roses, and her eyes some of their dewy freshness. But at that instant Mr. Oakhurst lifted his hat, and before she could thank him was gone.

I grieve to say that Mr. Decker shamelessly broke his promise. That night, in the very goodness of his heart and uxorious self-abnegation, he, like all devoted husbands, not only offered himself, but his friend and benefactor, as a sacrifice on the family altar. It is only fair, however, to add that he spoke with great fervor of the generosity of Mr. Oakhurst, and dealt with an enthusiasm quite common with his class on the mysterious fame and prodigal vices of the gambler.

"And now, Elsie, dear, say that you'll forgive me," said Mr. Decker, dropping on one knee beside his wife's couch. "I did it for the best. It was for you, dearey, that I put that money on them cards that night in 'Frisco. I thought to win a heap—enough to take you away, and enough left to get you a new dress."

Mrs. Decker smiled and pressed her husband's hand. "I do forgive you, Joe, dear," she said, still smiling, with eyes abstractedly fixed on the ceiling; "and you ought to be whipped for deceiving me so, you bad boy, and making me make such a speech. There, say no more about it. If you'll be very good hereafter, and will just now hand me that cluster of roses, I'll forgive you." She took the branch in her fingers, lifted the roses to her face, and presently said, behind their leaves—

"Joe!"

"What is it, lovey?"

"Do you think that this Mr.—what do you call him?—Jack Oakhurst would have given that money back to you if I hadn't made that speech?"

"Yes."

"If he hadn't seen me at all?"

Mr. Decker looked up. His wife had managed in some way to cover up her whole face with the roses, except her eyes, which were dangerously bright.

"No; it was you, Elsie—it was all along of seeing you that made him do it."

"A poor sick woman like me?"

"A sweet, little, lovely, pooty Elsie—Joe's own little wifey! How could he help it?"

Mrs. Decker fondly cast one arm around her husband's neck, still keeping the roses to her face with the other. From behind them she began to murmur gently and idiotically, "Dear, ole square Joey. Elsie's oney booful big bear." But, really, I do not see that my duty as a chronicler of facts compels me to continue this little lady's speech any further, and out of respect to the unmarried reader I stop.

Nevertheless, the next morning Mrs. Decker betrayed some slight and apparently uncalled-for irritability on reaching the plaza, and presently desired her husband to wheel her back home. Moreover, she was very much astonished at meeting Mr. Oakhurst just as they were returning, and even doubted if it were he, and questioned her husband as to his identity with the stranger of yesterday as he approached. Her manner to Mr. Oakhurst, also, was quite in contrast with her husband's frank welcome. Mr. Oakhurst instantly detected it. "Her husband has told her all, and she dislikes me," he said to himself, with that fatal appreciation of the half-truths of a woman's motives that causes the wisest masculine critic to stumble. He lingered only long enough to take the business address of the husband, and then, lifting his hat gravely, without looking at the lady, went his way. It struck the honest master carpenter as one of the charming anomalies of his wife's character that, although the meeting was evidently very much constrained and unpleasant, instantly afterward his wife's spirits began to rise. "You was hard on him—a leetle hard, wasn't you, Elsie?" said Mr. Decker deprecatingly. "I'm afraid he may think I've broke my promise." "Ah, indeed," said the lady indifferently. Mr. Decker instantly stepped round to the front of the vehicle. "You look like an A-1 first-class lady riding down Broadway in her own carriage, Elsie," said he; "I never seed you lookin' so peart and sassy before."

A few days later the proprietor of the San Isabel Sulphur Springs received the following note in Mr. Oakhurst's well-known dainty hand:

DEAR STEVE,—I've been thinking over your proposition to buy Nichols's quarter interest and have concluded to go in. But I don't see how the thing will pay until you have more accommodation down there, and for the best class—I mean *my* customers. What we want is an extension to the main building, and two or three cottages put up. I send down a builder to take hold of the job at once. He takes his sick wife with him, and you are to look after them as you would for one of us.

I may run down there myself after the races, just to look after things; but I sha'n't set upon any game this season.

Yours always,

JOHN OAKHURST

It was only the last sentence of this letter that provoked criticism. "I can understand," said Mr. Hamlin, a professional brother to whom Mr. Oakhurst's letter was shown—"I can understand why Jack goes in heavy and builds, for it's a sure spec, and is bound to be a mighty soft thing in time, if he comes here regularly. But why in blank he don't set up a bank this season and take the chance of getting some of the money back that he puts into circulation in building is what gets me. I wonder now," he mused deeply, "what *is* his little game."

The season had been a prosperous one to Mr. Oakhurst, and proportionally disastrous to several members of the legislature, judges, colonels, and others who had enjoyed but briefly the pleasure of Mr. Oakhurst's midnight society. And yet Sacramento had become very dull to him. He had lately formed a habit of early morning walks—so unusual and startling to his friends, both male and female, as to occasion the intensest curiosity. Two or three of the latter set spies upon his track, but the inquisition resulted only in the discovery that Mr. Oakhurst walked to the plaza, sat down upon one particular bench for a few moments, and then returned without seeing anybody, and the theory that there was a woman in the case was abandoned. A few superstitious gentlemen of his own profession believed that he did it for "luck." Some others, more practical, declared that he went out to "study points."

After the races at Marysville, Mr. Oakhurst went to San Francisco; from that place he returned to Marysville, but a few days after was seen at San José, Santa Cruz, and Oakland. Those who met him declared that his manner was restless and feverish, and quite unlike his ordinary calmness and phlegm. Colonel Starbottle pointed out the fact that at San Francisco, at the Club, Jack had declined to deal. "Hand shaky, sir—depend upon it; don't stimulate enough—blank him!"

From San José he started to go to Oregon by land with a rather expensive outfit of horses and camp equipage, but on reaching Stockton he suddenly diverged, and four hours later found him, with a single horse, entering the canyon of the San Isabel Warm Sulphur Springs.

It was a pretty triangular valley lying at the foot of three sloping mountains, dark with pines and fantastic with madroño and manzanita. Nestling against the mountainside, the straggling buildings and long piazza of the hotel glittered through the leaves; and here and there shone a white toylike cottage. Mr. Oakhurst was not an admirer of nature, but he felt something of the same novel satisfaction in the view that he experienced in his first morning walk in Sacramento. And now carriages began to

pass him on the road filled with gaily dressed women, and
the cold California outlines of the landscape began to take
upon themselves somewhat of a human warmth and color.
And then the long hotel piazza came in view, efflorescent
with the full-toileted fair. Mr. Oakhurst, a good rider
after the California fashion, did not check his speed as he
approached his destination, but charged the hotel at a
gallop, threw his horse on his haunches within a foot of
the piazza, and then quietly emerged from the cloud of
dust that veiled his dismounting.

Whatever feverish excitement might have raged within,
all his habitual calm returned as he stepped upon the
piazza. With the instinct of long habit he turned and faced
the battery of eyes with the same cold indifference with
which he had for years encountered the half-hidden sneers
of men and the half-frightened admiration of women. Only
one person stepped forward to welcome him. Oddly
enough, it was Dick Hamilton, perhaps the only one present who, by birth, education, and position, might have
satisfied the most fastidious social critic. Happily for Mr.
Oakhurst's reputation, he was also a very rich banker and
social leader. "Do you know who that is you spoke to?"
asked young Parker, with an alarmed expression. "Yes,"
replied Hamilton, with characteristic effrontery; "the
man you lost a thousand dollars to last week. *I* only
know him *socially*." "But isn't he a gambler?" queried the
youngest Miss Smith. "He is," replied Hamilton; "but I
wish, my dear young lady, that we all played as open and
honest a game as our friend yonder, and were as willing as he is to abide by its fortunes."

But Mr. Oakhurst was happily out of hearing of this
colloquy, and was even then lounging listlessly, yet watch-
fully, along the upper hall. Suddenly he heard a light foot-
step behind him, and then his name called in a familiar
voice that drew the blood quickly to his heart. He turned,
and she stood before him.

But how transformed! If I have hesitated to describe
the hollow-eyed cripple—the quaintly dressed artisan's
wife, a few pages ago—what shall I do with this graceful,
shapely, elegantly attired gentlewoman into whom she has
been merged within these two months? In good faith, she
was very pretty. You and I, my dear madam, would

have been quick to see that those charming dimples were misplaced for true beauty, and too fixed in their quality for honest mirthfulness; that the delicate lines around those aquiline nostrils were cruel and selfish; that the sweet, virginal surprise of those lovely eyes was as apt to be opened on her plate as upon the gallant speeches of her dinner partner; that her sympathetic color came and went more with her own spirits than yours. But you and I are not in love with her, dear madam, and Mr. Oakhurst is. And even in the folds of her Parisian gown, I am afraid this poor fellow saw the same subtle strokes of purity that he had seen in her homespun robe. And then there was the delightful revelation that she could walk, and that she had dear little feet of her own in the tiniest slippers of her French shoemaker, with such preposterous blue bows, and Chappell's own stamp, Rue de something or other, Paris, on the narrow sole.

He ran towards her with a heightened color and out-stretched hands. But she whipped her own behind her, glanced rapidly up and down the long hall, and stood looking at him with a half-audacious, half-mischievous admiration in utter contrast to her old reserve.

"I've a great mind not to shake hands with you at all. You passed me just now on the piazza without speaking, and I ran after you, as I suppose many another poor woman has done."

Mr. Oakhurst stammered that she was so changed.

"The more reason why you should know me. Who changed me? You. You have re-created me. You found a helpless, crippled, sick, poverty-stricken woman, with one dress to her back, and that her own make, and you gave her life, health, strength, and fortune. You did, and you know it, sir. How do you like your work?" She caught the side seams of her gown in either hand and dropped him a playful courtesy. Then, with a sudden, relenting gesture, she gave him both her hands.

Outrageous as this speech was, and unfeminine, as I trust every fair reader will deem it, I fear it pleased Mr. Oakhurst. Not but that he was accustomed to a certain frank female admiration; but then it was of the coulisses and not of the cloister with which he always persisted in associating Mrs. Decker. To be addressed in this way by an invalid Puritan, a sick saint, with the austerity of suffering still clothing her—a woman who had a Bible on the dressing table, who went to church three times a day, and was devoted to her husband, completely bowled him over. He still held her hands as she went on—

"Why didn't you come before? What were you doing in Marysville, in San José, in Oakland? You see I have followed you. I saw you as you came down the canyon, and knew you at once. I saw your letter to Joseph, and knew you were coming. Why didn't you write to me? You will sometime! Good evening, Mr. Hamilton."

She had withdrawn her hands, but not until Hamilton, ascending the staircase, was nearly abreast of them. He raised his hat to her with well-bred composure, nodded familiarly to Oakhurst, and passed on. When he had gone Mrs. Decker lifted her eyes to Mr. Oakhurst. "Some day I shall ask a great favor of you!"

Mr. Oakhurst begged that it should be now. "No, not until you know me better. Then, some day, I shall want you to—kill that man!"

She laughed, such a pleasant little ringing laugh, such a display of dimples—albeit a little fixed in the corners of her mouth—such an innocent light in her brown eyes, and such a lovely color in her cheeks, that Mr. Oakhurst—who seldom laughed—was fain to laugh too. It was as if a lamb had proposed to a fox a foray into a neighboring sheepfold.

A few evenings after this, Mrs. Decker arose from a charmed circle of her admirers on the hotel piazza, excused herself for a few moments, laughingly declined an escort, and ran over to her little cottage—one of her husband's creation—across the road. Perhaps from the sudden and unwonted exercise in her still convalescent state, she breathed hurriedly and feverishly as she entered her boudoir, and once or twice placed her hand upon her breast. She was startled on turning up the light to find her husband lying on the sofa.

"You look hot and excited, Elsie, love," said Mr. Decker; "you ain't took worse, are you?"

Mrs. Decker's face had paled, but now flushed again. "No," she said, "only a little pain here," as she again placed her hand upon her corsage.

"Can I do anything for you?" said Mr. Decker, rising with affectionate concern.

"Run over to the hotel and get me some brandy, quick!"

Mr. Decker ran. Mrs. Decker closed and bolted the door, and then putting her hand to her bosom, drew out the pain. It was folded foursquare, and was, I grieve to say, in Mr. Oakhurst's handwriting.

She devoured it with burning eyes and cheeks until there came a step upon the porch. Then she hurriedly replaced it in her bosom and unbolted the door. Her husband entered; she raised the spirits to her lips and declared herself better.

"Are you going over there again tonight?" asked Mr. Decker submissively.

"No," said Mrs. Decker, with her eyes fixed dreamily on the floor.

"I wouldn't if I was you," said Mr. Decker with a sigh of relief. After a pause he took a seat on the sofa, and drawing his wife to his side, said, "Do you know what I was thinking of when you came in, Elsie?" Mrs. Decker ran her fingers through his stiff black hair, and couldn't imagine.

"I was thinking of old times, Elsie; I was thinking of the days when I built that kerridge for you, Elsie—when I used to take you out to ride, and was both hoss and driver! We was poor then, and you was sick, Elsie, but we was happy. We've got money now, and a house, and you're quite another woman. I may say, dear, that you're a *new* woman. And that's where the trouble comes in. I could build you a kerridge, Elsie; I could build you a house, Elsie—but there I stopped. I couldn't build up *you.* You're strong and pretty, Elsie, and fresh and new. But somehow, Elsie, you ain't no work of mine!"

He paused. With one hand laid gently on his forehead and the other pressed upon her bosom as if to feel certain of the presence of her pain, she said sweetly and soothingly:

"But it was your work, dear."

Mr. Decker shook his head sorrowfully. "No, Elsie, not mine. I had the chance to do it once and I let it go. It's done now; but not by me."

Mrs. Decker raised her surprised, innocent eyes to his. He kissed her tenderly, and then went on in a more cheerful voice.

"That ain't all I was thinking of, Elsie. I was thinking that maybe you give too much of your company to that Mr. Hamilton. Not that there's any wrong in it, to you or him. But it might make people talk. You're the only one here, Elsie," said the master carpenter, looking fondly at his wife, "who isn't talked about; whose work ain't inspected or condemned."

Mrs. Decker was glad he had spoken about it. She had thought so, too, but she could not well be uncivil to Mr. Hamilton, who was a fine gentleman, without making a powerful enemy. "And he's always treated me as if I was a born lady in his own circle," added the little woman, with a certain pride that made her husband fondly smile. "But I have thought of a plan. He will not stay here if I should go away. If, for instance, I went to San Francisco to visit ma for a few days, he would be gone before I should return."

Mr. Decker was delighted. "By all means," he said; "go tomorrow. Jack Oakhurst is going down, and I'll put you in his charge."

Mrs. Decker did not think it was prudent. "Mr. Oakhurst is our friend, Joseph, but you know his reputation." In fact, she did not know that she ought to go now, knowing that he was going the same day; but with a kiss Mr. Decker overcame her scruples. She yielded gracefully. Few women, in fact, knew how to give up a point as charmingly as she.

She stayed a week in San Francisco. When she returned she was a trifle thinner and paler than she had been. This she explained as the result of perhaps too active exercise and excitement. "I was out-of-doors nearly all the time, as ma will tell you," she said to her husband, "and always alone. I am getting quite independent now," she added gaily. "I don't want any escort—I believe, Joey dear, I could get along even without you—I'm so brave!"

But her visit, apparently, had not been productive of her impelling design. Mr. Hamilton had not gone, but had remained, and called upon them that very evening. "I've thought of a plan, Joey, dear," said Mrs. Decker when he had departed. "Poor Mr. Oakhurst has a miserable room at the hotel—suppose you ask him when he returns from San Francisco to stop with us. He can have our spare room. I don't think," she added archly, "that Mr. Hamilton will call often." Her husband laughed, intimated that she was a little coquette, pinched her cheek, and complied. "The queer thing about a woman," he said afterwards confidentially to Mr. Oakhurst, "is that without having any plan of her own, she'll take anybody's and build a house on it entirely different to suit herself. And dern my skin, if you'll be able to say whether or not you didn't give the scale and measurements yourself. That's what gets me."

The next week Mr. Oakhurst was installed in the Deckers' cottage. The business relations of her husband and himself were known to all, and her own reputation was above suspicion. Indeed, few women were more popular. She was domestic, she was prudent, she was pious. In a country of great feminine freedom and latitude, she never rode or walked with anybody but her husband; in an epoch of slang and ambiguous expression, she was always precise and formal in her speech; in the midst of a fashion of ostentatious decoration she never wore a diamond, nor a single valuable jewel. She never permitted an indecorum in public; she never countenanced the familiarities of California society. She declaimed against the prevailing tone of infidelity and skepticism in religion. Few people who were present will ever forget the dignified yet stately manner with which she rebuked Mr. Hamilton in the public parlor for entering upon the discussion of a work on materialism, lately published; and some among them, also, will not forget the expression of amused surprise on Mr. Hamilton's face that gradually changed to sardonic gravity as he courteously waived his point. Certainly, not Mr. Oakhurst, who from that moment began to be uneasily impatient of his friend, and even—if such a term could be applied to any moral quality in Mr. Oakhurst—to fear him.

For, during this time, Mr. Oakhurst had begun to show symptoms of a change in his usual habits. He was seldom, if ever, seen in his old haunts, in a barroom, or with his old associates. Pink and white notes, in distracted handwriting, accumulated on the dressing table in his rooms at Sacramento. It was given out in San Francisco that he had some organic disease of the heart, for which his physician had prescribed perfect rest. He read more, he took long walks, he sold his fast horses, he went to church.

I have a very vivid recollection of his first appearance there. He did not accompany the Deckers, nor did he go into their pew, but came in as the service commenced, and took a seat quietly in one of the back pews. By some mysterious instinct his presence became presently known to the congregation, some of whom so far forgot themselves, in their curiosity, as to face around and apparently address their responses to him. Before the service was over it was pretty well understood that "miserable sinners" meant Mr. Oakhurst. Nor did this mysterious influence fail to affect the officiating clergyman, who introduced an allusion to Mr. Oakhurst's calling and habits in a sermon on the architecture of Solomon's Temple, and in a manner so pointed and yet labored as to cause the youngest of us to flame with indignation. Happily, however, it was lost upon Jack; I do not think he even heard it. His handsome, colorless face—albeit a trifle worn and thoughtful—was inscrutable. Only once, during the singing of a hymn, at a certain note in the contralto's voice, there crept into his dark eyes a look of wistful tenderness, so yearning and yet so hopeless that those who were watching him felt their own glisten. Yet I retain a very vivid remembrance of his standing up to receive the benediction, with the suggestion in his manner and tightly buttoned coat of taking the fire of his adversary at ten paces. After church he disappeared as quietly as he had entered, and fortunately escaped hearing the comments on his rash act. His appearance was generally considered as an impertinence—attributable only to some wanton fancy—or possibly a bet. One or two thought that the sexton was exceedingly remiss in not turning him out after discovering who he was; and a prominent pewholder remarked that if he couldn't take his wife and daughters to that church without exposing them to such an influence, he would try to find some church where he could. Another traced Mr. Oakhurst's presence to certain Broad Church radical tendencies, which he regretted to say he had lately noted in their pastor. Deacon Sawyer, whose delicately organized, sickly wife had already borne him eleven children, and died in an ambitious attempt to complete the dozen, avowed that the presence of a person of Mr. Oakhurst's various and indiscriminate gallantries was an insult to the memory of the deceased that, as a man, he could not brook.

It was about this time that Mr. Oakhurst, contrasting himself with a conventional world in which he had hitherto rarely mingled, became aware that there was something in his face, figure, and carriage quite unlike other men—something that if it did not betray his former career, at least showed an individuality and originality that was suspicious. In this belief he shaved off his long, silken mustache, and religiously brushed out his clustering curls every morning. He even went so far as to affect a negligence of dress, and hid his small, slim, arched feet in the largest and heaviest walking shoes. There is a story told that he went to his tailor in Sacramento, and asked him to make him a suit of clothes like everybody else. The tailor, familiar with Mr. Oakhurst's fastidiousness, did not know what he meant. "I mean," said Mr. Oakhurst savagely, "something *respectable*—something that doesn't exactly fit me, you know." But however Mr. Oakhurst might hide his shapely limbs in homespun and homemade garments, there was something in his carriage, something in the pose of his beautiful head, something in the strong and fine manliness of his presence, something in the perfect and utter discipline and control of his muscles, something in the high repose of his nature— a repose not so much a matter of intellectual ruling as of his very nature—that go where he would, and with whom, he was always a notable man in ten thousand. Perhaps this was never so clearly intimated to Mr. Oakhurst as when, emboldened by Mr. Hamilton's advice and assistance and his predilections, he became a San Francisco broker. Even before objection was made to his presence in the Board—the objection, I remember, was urged very eloquently by Watt Sanders, who was supposed to be the inventor of the "freezing out" system of disposing of poor stockholders, and who also enjoyed the reputation of having been the impelling cause of Briggs of Tuolumne's ruin and suicide—even before this formal protest of respectability against lawlessness, the aquiline suggestions of Mr. Oakhurst's mien and countenance not only prematurely fluttered the pigeons, but absolutely occasioned much uneasiness among the fish hawks, who circled below him with their booty. "Dash me! but he's as likely to go after us as anybody," said Joe Fielding.

It wanted but a few days before the close of the brief summer season at San Isabel Warm Springs. Already there had been some migration of the more fashionable, and there was an uncomfortable suggestion of dregs and lees in the social life that remained. Mr. Oakhurst was moody; it was hinted that even the secure reputation of Mrs. Decker could no longer protect her from the gossip which his presence excited. It is but fair to her to say that during the last few weeks of this trying ordeal she looked like a sweet, pale martyr, and conducted herself toward her traducers with the gentle, forgiving manner of one who relied not upon the idle homage of the crowd, but upon the security of a principle that was dearer than popular favor. "They talk about myself and Mr. Oakhurst, my dear," she said to a friend, "but Heaven and my husband can best answer their calumny. It never shall be said that my husband ever turned his back upon a friend in the moment of his adversity because the position was changed, because his friend was poor and he was rich." This was the first intimation to the public that Jack had lost money, although it was known generally that the Deckers had lately bought some valuable property in San Francisco.

A few evenings after this an incident occurred which seemed to unpleasantly discord with the general social harmony that had always existed at San Isabel. It was at dinner, and Mr. Oakhurst and Mr. Hamilton, who sat together at a separate table, were observed to rise in some agitation. When they reached the hall, by a common instinct they stepped into a little breakfast-room which was vacant, and closed the door. Then Mr. Hamilton turned, with a half-amused, half-serious smile, toward his friend, and said—

"If we are to quarrel, Jack Oakhurst—you and I—in the name of all that is ridiculous, don't let it be about a—"

I do not know what was the epithet intended. It was either unspoken or lost. For at that very instant Mr. Oakhurst raised a wine glass and dashed its contents into Hamilton's face.

As they faced each other the men seemed to have changed natures. Mr. Oakhurst was trembling with excitement, and the wine glass that he returned to the table shivered between his fingers. Mr. Hamilton stood there, grayish white, erect, and dripping. After a pause he said coldly—

"So be it. But remember! our quarrel commences here. If I fall by your hand, you shall not use it to clear her character; if you fall by mine, you shall not be called a martyr. I am sorry it has come to this, but amen!—the sooner now the better."

He turned proudly, dropped his lids over his cold steel-blue eyes, as if sheathing a rapier, bowed, and passed coldly out.

They met twelve hours later in a little hollow two miles from the hotel, on the Stockton road. As Mr. Oakhurst received his pistol from Colonel Starbottle's hands he said to him in a low voice, "Whatever turns up or down I shall not return to the hotel. You will find some directions in my room. Go there—" but his voice suddenly faltered, and he turned his glistening eyes away, to his second's intense astonishment. "I've been out a dozen times with Jack Oakhurst," said Colonel Starbottle afterwards, "and I never saw him anyways cut before. Blank me if I didn't think he was losing his sand, till he walked to position."

The two reports were almost simultaneous. Mr. Oakhurst's right arm dropped suddenly to his side, and his pistol would have fallen from his paralyzed fingers, but the discipline of trained nerve and muscle prevailed, and he kept his grasp until he had shifted it to the other hand, without changing his position. Then there was a silence that seemed interminable, a gathering of two or three dark figures where a smoke curl still lazily floated, and then the hurried, husky, panting voice of Colonel

Starbottle in his ear, "He's hit hard—through the lungs—
you must run for it!"

Jack turned his dark, questioning eyes upon his second,
but did not seem to listen; rather seemed to hear some
other voice, remoter in the distance. He hesitated, and
then made a step forward in the direction of the distant
group. Then he paused again as the figures separated, and
the surgeon came hastily toward him.

"He would like to speak with you a moment," said the
man. "You have little time to lose, I know; but," he
added in a lower voice, "it is my duty to tell you he has
still less."

A look of despair so hopeless in its intensity swept
over Mr. Oakhurst's usually impassive face that the surgeon started. "You are hit," he said, glancing at Jack's
helpless arm.

"Nothing—a mere scratch," said Jack hastily. Then he
added, with a bitter laugh, "I'm not in luck today. But
come! We'll see what he wants."

His long feverish stride outstripped the surgeon's, and
in another moment he stood where the dying man lay—
like most dying men—the one calm, composed, central
figure of an anxious group. Mr. Oakhurst's face was less
calm as he dropped on one knee beside him and took his
hand. "I want to speak with this gentleman alone," said
Hamilton, with something of his old imperious manner, as
he turned to those about him. When they drew back, he
looked up in Oakhurst's face.

"I've something to tell you, Jack."

His own face was white, but not so white as that which
Mr. Oakhurst bent over him—a face so ghastly, with
haunting doubts and a hopeless presentiment of coming
evil, a face so piteous in its infinite weariness and envy
of death, that the dying man was touched, even in the
languor of dissolution, with a pang of compassion, and
the cynical smile faded from his lips.

"Forgive me, Jack," he whispered more feebly, "for
what I have to say. I don't say it in anger, but only because it must be said. I could not do my duty to you—I
could not die contented until you knew it all. It's a miserable business at best, all around. But it can't be helped

now. Only I ought to have fallen by Decker's pistol and not yours."

A flush like fire came into Jack's cheek, and he would have risen, but Hamilton held him fast.

"Listen! in my pocket you will find two letters. Take them—there! You will know the handwriting. But promise you will not read them until you are in a place of safety. Promise me!"

Jack did not speak, but held the letters between his fingers as if they had been burning coals.

"Promise me," said Hamilton faintly.

"Why?" asked Oakhurst, dropping his friend's hand coldly.

"Because," said the dying man with a bitter smile—"because—when you have read them—you—will—go back—to capture—and death!"

They were his last words. He pressed Jack's hand faintly. Then his grasp relaxed, and he fell back a corpse.

It was nearly ten o'clock at night, and Mrs. Decker reclined languidly upon the sofa with a novel in her hand, while her husband discussed the politics of the country in the barroom of the hotel. It was a warm night, and the French window looking out upon a little balcony was partly open. Suddenly she heard a foot upon the balcony, and she raised her eyes from the book with a slight start. The next moment the window was hurriedly thrust wide and a man entered.

Mrs. Decker rose to her feet with a little cry of alarm.

"For Heaven's sake, Jack, are you mad? He has only gone for a little while—he may return at any moment. Come an hour later—tomorrow—any time when I can get rid of him—but go, now, dear, at once."

Mr. Oakhurst walked toward the door, bolted it, and then faced her without a word. His face was haggard, his coat sleeve hung loosely over an arm that was bandaged and bloody.

Nevertheless, her voice did not falter as she turned again toward him. "What has happened, Jack? Why are you here?"

He opened his coat, and threw two letters in her lap.

"To return your lover's letters—to kill you—and then

myself," he said in a voice so low as to be almost inaudible.

Among the many virtues of this admirable woman was invincible courage. She did not faint, she did not cry out. She sat quietly down again, folded her hands in her lap, and said calmly—

"And why should you not?"

Had she recoiled, had she shown any fear or contrition, had she essayed an explanation or apology, Mr. Oakhurst would have looked upon it as an evidence of guilt. But there is no quality that courage recognizes so quickly as courage, there is no condition that desperation bows before but desperation; and Mr. Oakhurst's power of analysis was not so keen as to prevent him from confounding her courage with a moral quality. Even in his fury he could not help admiring this dauntless invalid.

"Why should you not?" she repeated with a smile. "You gave me life, health, and happiness, Jack. You gave me your love. Why should you not take what you have given? Go on. I am ready."

She held out her hands with that same infinite grace of yielding with which she had taken his own on the first day of their meeting at the hotel. Jack raised his head, looked at her for one wild moment, dropped upon his knees beside her, and raised the folds of her dress to his feverish lips. But she was too clever not to instantly see her victory; she was too much of a woman, with all her cleverness, to refrain from pressing that victory home. At the same moment, as with the impulse of an outraged and wounded woman, she rose, and with an imperious gesture pointed to the window. Mr. Oakhurst rose in his turn, cast one glance upon her, and without another word passed out of her presence forever.

When he had gone, she closed the window and bolted it, and going to the chimney piece placed the letters, one by one, in the flame of the candle until they were consumed. I would not have the reader think that during this painful operation she was unmoved. Her hand trembled and—not being a brute—for some minutes (perhaps longer) she felt very badly, and the corners of her sensitive mouth were depressed. When her husband arrived it was with a genuine joy that she ran to him, and nestled against his broad breast with a feeling of security that thrilled the honest fellow to the core.

"But I've heard dreadful news tonight, Elsie," said Mr. Decker, after a few endearments were exchanged.

"Don't tell me anything dreadful, dear; I'm not well tonight," she pleaded sweetly.

"But it's about Mr. Oakhurst and Hamilton."

"Please!" Mr. Decker could not resist the petitionary grace of those white hands and that sensitive mouth, and took her to his arms. Suddenly he said, "What's that?"

He was pointing to the bosom of her white dress. Where Mr. Oakhurst had touched her there was a spot of blood.

It was nothing; she had slightly cut her hand in closing the window; it shut so hard! If Mr. Decker had remembered to close and bolt the shutter before he went out, he might have saved her this. There was such a genuine irritability and force in this remark that Mr. Decker was quite overcome by remorse. But Mrs. Decker forgave him with that graciousness which I have before pointed out in these pages, and with the halo of that forgiveness and marital confidence still lingering above the pair, with the reader's permission we will leave them and return to Mr. Oakhurst.

But not for two weeks. At the end of that time he walked into his rooms in Sacramento, and in his old manner took his seat at the faro table.

"How's your arm, Jack?" asked an incautious player.

There was a smile followed the question, which, however, ceased as Jack looked up quietly at the speaker.

"It bothers my dealing a little, but I can shoot as well with my left."

The game was continued in that decorous silence which usually distinguished the table at which Mr. John Oakhurst presided.

An Ingénue
⟫⟫⟫⟫⟫⟫⟫⟫⟫⟫⟫ of the Sierras ⟫⟫⟫⟫⟫⟫

ONE

⟫⟫⟫⟫⟫ We all held our breath as the coach rushed
through the semidarkness of Galloper's Ridge. The vehicle
itself was only a huge lumbering shadow; its side lights
were carefully extinguished, and Yuba Bill had just politely removed from the lips of an outside passenger even
the cigar with which he had been ostentatiously exhibit-
ing his coolness. For it had been rumored that the
Ramon Martinez gang of "road agents" were "laying"
for us on the second grade, and would time the passage
of our lights across Galloper's in order to intercept us
in the "brush" beyond. If we could cross the ridge without being seen, and so get through the brush before they
reached it, we were safe. If they followed, it would only
be a stern chase with the odds in our favor.

The huge vehicle swayed from side to side, rolled,
dipped, and plunged, but Bill kept the track, as if, in the
whispered words of the expressman, he could "feel and
smell" the road he could no longer see. We knew that at
times we hung perilously over the edge of slopes that
eventually dropped a thousand feet sheer to the tops of
the sugar pines below, but we knew that Bill knew it also.
The half visible heads of the horses, drawn wedgewise
together by the tightened reins, appeared to cleave the
darkness like a plowshare, held between his rigid hands.
Even the hoofbeats of the six horses had fallen into a
vague, monotonous, distant roll. Then the ridge was
crossed, and we plunged into the still blacker obscurity of
the brush. Rather we no longer seemed to move—it was
only the phantom night that rushed by us. The horses
might have been submerged in some swift Lethean stream;
nothing but the top of the coach and the rigid bulk of

Yuba Bill arose above them. Yet even in that awful moment our speed was unslackened; it was as if Bill cared no longer to *guide* but only to drive, or as if the direction of his huge machine was determined by other hands than his. An incautious whisperer hazarded the paralyzing suggestion of our "meeting another team." To our great astonishment Bill overhead it; to our greater astonishment he replied. "It 'ud be only a neck and neck race which would get to h—ll first," he said quietly. But we were relieved—for he had *spoken!* Almost simultaneously the wider turnpike began to glimmer faintly as a visible track before us; the wayside trees fell out of line, opened up, and dropped off one after another; we were on the broader tableland, out of danger, and apparently unperceived and unpursued.

Nevertheless in the conversation that broke out again with the relighting of the lamps, and the comments, congratulations, and reminiscences that were freely exchanged, Yuba Bill preserved a dissatisfied and even resentful silence. The most generous praise of his skill and courage awoke no response. "I reckon the old man waz just spilin' for a fight, and is feelin' disappointed," said a passenger. But those who knew that Bill had the true fighter's scorn for any purely purposeless conflict were more or less concerned and watchful of him. He would drive steadily for four or five minutes with thoughtfully knitted brows, but eyes still keenly observant under his slouched hat, and then, relaxing his strained attitude, would give way to a movement of impatience. "You ain't uneasy about anything, Bill, are you?" asked the expressman confidentially. Bill lifted his eyes with a slightly contemptuous surprise. "Not about anything ter *come*. It's what *hez* happened that I don't exackly *sabe*. I don't see no signs of Ramon's gang ever havin' been out at all, and ef they were out I don't see why they didn't go for us."

"The simple fact is that our ruse was successful," said an outside passenger. "They waited to see our lights on the ridge, and not seeing them, missed us until we had passed. That's my opinion."

"You ain't puttin' any price on that opinion, air ye?" inquired Bill politely.

"No."

" 'Cos thar's a comic paper in 'Frisco pays for them things, and I've seen worse things in it."

"Come off, Bill," retorted the passenger, slightly net-tled by the tittering of his companions. "Then what did you put out the lights for?"

"Well," returned Bill grimly, "it mout have been be-cause I didn't keer to hev you chaps blazin' away at the first bush you *thought* you saw move in your skeer, and bringin' down their fire on us."

The explanation, though unsatisfactory, was by no means an improbable one, and we thought it better to accept it with a laugh. Bill, however, resumed his ab-stracted manner.

"Who got in at the Summit?" he at last asked abruptly of the expressman.

"Derrick and Simpson of Cold Spring, and one of the 'Excelsior' boys," responded the expressman.

"And that Pike County girl from Dow's Flat, with her bundles. Don't forget her," added the outside passenger ironically.

"Does anybody here know her?" continued Bill, ignor-ing the irony.

"You'd better ask Judge Thompson; he was mighty attentive to her; gettin' her a seat by the off window, and lookin' after her bundles and things."

"Gettin' her a seat by the *window?*" repeated Bill.

"Yes, she wanted to see everything, and wasn't afraid of the shooting."

"Yes," broke in a third passenger, "and he was so d—d civil that when she dropped her ring in the straw, he struck a match agin all your rules, you know, and held it for her to find it. And it was just as we were crossin' through the brush, too. I saw the hull thing through the window, for I was hanging over the wheels with my gun ready for action. And it wasn't no fault of Judge Thomp-son's if his d—d foolishness hadn't shown us up, and got us a shot from the gang."

Bill gave a short grunt, but drove steadily on without further comment or even turning his eyes to the speaker.

We were now not more than a mile from the station at the crossroads where we were to change horses. The lights already glimmered in the distance, and there was a faint suggestion of the coming dawn on the summits of the ridge to the west. We had plunged into a belt of timber, when suddenly a horseman emerged at a sharp canter from a trail that seemed to be parallel with our own. We were all slightly startled, Yuba Bill alone preserving his moody calm.

"Hullo!" he said.

The stranger wheeled to our side as Bill slackened his speed. He seemed to be a "packer" or freight muleteer.

"Ye didn't get 'held up' on the Divide?" continued Bill cheerfully.

"No," returned the packer, with a laugh; *"I* don't carry treasure. But I see you're all right, too. I saw you crossin' over Galloper's."

"Saw us?" said Bill sharply. "We had our lights out."

"Yes, but there was suthin' white—a handkerchief or woman's veil, I reckon—hangin' from the window. It was only a movin' spot agin the hillside, but ez I was lookin' out for ye I knew it was you by that. Good night!"

He cantered away. We tried to look at each other's faces, and at Bill's expression in the darkness, but he neither spoke nor stirred until he threw down the reins when we stopped before the station. The passengers quickly descended from the roof; the expressman was about to follow, but Bill plucked his sleeve.

"I'm goin' to take a look over this yer stage and these yer passengers with ye, afore we start."

"Why, what's up?"

"Well," said Bill, slowly disengaging himself from one of his enormous gloves, "when we waltzed down into the brush up there I saw a man, ez plain ez I see you, rise up from it. I thought our time had come and the band was goin' to play, when he sorter drew back, made a sign, and we just scooted past him."

"Well?"

"Well," said Bill, "it means that this yer coach was *passed through free* tonight."

"You don't object to *that*—surely? I think we were deucedly lucky."

Bill slowly drew off his other glove. "I've been riskin' my everlastin' life on this d——d line three times a week," he said with mock humility, "and I'm allus thankful for small mercies. *But,*" he added grimly, "when it comes down to being passed free by some pal of a hoss thief, and thet called a speshal Providence, *I ain't in it!* No, sir, I ain't in it!"

TWO

It was with mixed emotions that the passengers heard that a delay of fifteen minutes to tighten certain screw bolts had been ordered by the autocratic Bill. Some were anxious to get their breakfast at Sugar Pine, but others were not averse to linger for the daylight that promised greater safety on the road. The expressman, knowing the real cause of Bill's delay, was nevertheless at a loss to understand the object of it. The passengers were all well-known; any idea of complicity with the road agents was wild and impossible, and even if there was a confederate of the gang among them, he would have been more likely to precipitate a robbery than to check it. Again, the discovery of such a confederate—to whom they clearly owed their safety—and his arrest would have been quite against the Californian sense of justice, if not actually illegal. It seemed evident that Bill's quixotic sense of honor was leading him astray.

The station consisted of a stable, a wagon shed, and a building containing three rooms. The first was fitted up with "bunks" or sleeping berths for the employees; the second was the kitchen; and the third and larger apartment was dining room or sitting room, and was used as general waiting room for the passengers. It was not a refreshment station, and there was no "bar." But a mysterious command from the omnipotent Bill produced a demijohn of whiskey, with which he hospitably treated the company. The seductive influence of the liquor loosened the tongue of the gallant Judge Thompson. He admitted to having struck a match to enable the fair Pike Countian to find her ring, which, however, proved to have fallen in her lap. She was "a fine, healthy young woman—a type of the Far West, sir; in fact, quite a prairie blossom! yet simple and guileless as a child." She was on her way to Marysville, he believed, "although she expected to meet friends—a friend, in fact—later on." It was her first visit to a large town—in fact, any civilized center—since she crossed the plains three years ago. Her girlish curiosity was quite touching, and her innocence irresistible. In fact, in a country whose tendency was to produce "frivolity and forwardness in young girls, he found her a most interesting young person." She was even then out in the stable yard watching the horses being harnessed, "preferring to indulge a pardonable healthy young curiosity than to listen to the empty compliments of the younger passengers."

The figure which Bill saw thus engaged, without being otherwise distinguished, certainly seemed to justify the Judge's opinion. She appeared to be a well-matured country girl, whose frank gray eyes and large laughing mouth expressed a wholesome and abiding gratification in her life and surroundings. She was watching the replacing of luggage in the boot. A little feminine start, as one of her own parcels was thrown somewhat roughly on the roof, gave Bill his opportunity. "Now there," he growled to the helper, "ye ain't carting stone! Look out, will yer! Some of your things, miss?" he added, with gruff courtesy, turning to her. "These yer trunks, for instance?"

She smiled a pleasant assent, and Bill, pushing aside the helper, seized a large square trunk in his arms. But from excess of zeal, or some other mischance, his foot slipped, and he came down heavily, striking the corner of the trunk on the ground and loosening its hinges and fastenings. It was a cheap, common-looking affair, but the accident discovered in its yawning lid a quantity of white, lace-edged feminine apparel of an apparently superior quality. The young lady uttered another cry and came quickly forward, but Bill was profuse in his apologies, himself girded the broken box with a strap, and declared his intention of having the company "make it good" to her with a new one. Then he casually accompanied her to the door of the waiting room, entered, made a place for her before the fire by simply lifting the nearest and most youthful passenger by the coat collar from the stool that he was occupying, and having installed the lady in it, displaced another man who was standing before the chimney, and drawing himself up to his full six feet of height in front of her, glanced down upon his fair passenger as he took his waybill from his pocket.

"Your name is down here as Miss Mullins?" he said.

She looked up, became suddenly aware that she and her questioner were the center of interest to the whole circle of passengers, and with a slight rise of color, returned, "Yes."

"Well, Miss Mullins, I've got a question or two to ask ye. I ask it straight out afore this crowd. It's in my rights to take ye aside and ask it—but that ain't my style; I'm no detective. I needn't ask it at all, but act as ef I knowed the answer, or I might leave it to be asked by others. Ye needn't answer it ef ye don't like; ye've got a friend over ther—Judge Thompson—who is a friend to ye, right or wrong, jest as any other man here is—as though ye'd packed your own jury. Well, the simple question I've got to ask ye is *this:* Did you signal to anybody from the coach when we passed Galloper's an hour ago?"

We all thought that Bill's courage and audacity had reached its climax here. To openly and publicly accuse a "lady" before a group of chivalrous Californians, and that lady possessing the further attractions of youth, good looks, and innocence, was little short of desperation. There was an evident movement of adhesion towards the fair stranger, a slight muttering broke out on the right, but the very boldness of the act held them in stupefied surprise. Judge Thompson, with a bland propitiatory smile began: "Really, Bill, I must protest on behalf of this young lady"—when the fair accused, raising her eyes to her accuser, to the consternation of everybody answered with the slight but convincing hesitation of conscientious truthfulness:

"*I did.*"

"Ahem!" interposed the Judge hastily, "er—that is—er—you allowed your handkerchief to flutter from the window—I noticed it myself—casually—one might say even playfully—but without any particular significance."

The girl, regarding her apologist with a singular mingling of pride and impatience, returned briefly:

"I signaled."

"Who did you signal to?" asked Bill gravely.

"The young gentleman I'm going to marry."

A start, followed by a slight titter from the younger passengers, was instantly suppressed by a savage glance from Bill.

"What did you signal to him for?" he continued.

"To tell him I was here, and that it was all right," returned the young girl, with a steadily rising pride and color.

"Wot was all right?" demanded Bill.

"That I wasn't followed, and that he could meet me on the road beyond Cass's Ridge Station." She hesitated a moment, and then, with a still greater pride, in which a youthful defiance was still mingled, said: "I've run away from home to marry him. And I mean to! No one can stop me. Dad didn't like him just because he was poor, and dad's got money. Dad wanted me to marry a man I hate, and got a lot of dresses and things to bribe me."

"And you're taking them in your trunk to the other feller?" said Bill grimly.

"Yes, he's poor," returned the girl defiantly.

"Then your father's name is Mullins?" asked Bill.

"It's not Mullins. I—I—took that name," she hesitated, with her first exhibition of self-consciousness.

"Wot *is* his name?"

"Eli Hemmings."

A smile of relief and significance went round the circle. The fame of Eli or "Skinner" Hemmings as a notorious miser and usurer had passed even beyond Galloper's Ridge.

"The step that you're taking, Miss Mullins, I need not tell you, is one of great gravity," said Judge Thompson, with a certain paternal seriousness of manner, in which, however, we were glad to detect a glaring affectation; "and I trust that you and your affianced have fully weighed it. Far be it from me to interfere with or question the natural affections of two young people, but may I ask you what you know of the—er—young gentleman for whom you are sacrificing so much, and perhaps imperiling your whole future? For instance, have you known him long?"

The slightly troubled air of trying to understand—not unlike the vague wonderment of childhood—with which Miss Mullins had received the beginning of this exordium, changed to a relieved smile of comprehension as she said quickly, "Oh yes, nearly a whole year."

"And," said the Judge, smiling, "has he a vocation—is he in business?"

"Oh yes," she returned; "he's a collector."

"A collector?"

"Yes; he collects bills, you know—money," she went on, with childish eagerness, "not for himself—*he* never has any money, poor Charley—but for his firm. It's dreadful hard work, too; keeps him out for days and nights, over bad roads and baddest weather. Sometimes, when he's stole over to the ranch just to see me, he's been so bad he could scarcely keep his seat in the saddle, much less stand. And he's got to take mighty big risks, too. Times the folks are cross with him and won't pay; once they shot him in the arm, and he came to me, and I helped do it up for him. But he don't mind. He's real brave—jest as brave as he's good." There was such a wholesome ring of truth in this pretty praise that we were touched in sympathy with the speaker.

"What firm does he collect for?" asked the Judge gently.

"I don't know exactly—he won't tell me; but I think it's a Spanish firm. You see—" she took us all into her confidence with a sweeping smile of innocent yet half-mischievous artfulness—"I only know because I peeped over a letter he once got from his firm, telling him he must hustle up and be ready for the road the next day; but I think the name was Martinez—yes, Ramon Martinez."

In the dead silence that ensued—a silence so profound that we could hear the horses in the distant stable yard rattling their harness—one of the younger "Excelsior" boys burst into a hysteric laugh, but the fierce eye of Yuba Bill was down upon him, and seemed to instantly stiffen him into a silent, grinning mask. The young girl, however, took no note of it. Following out, with loverlike diffusiveness, the reminiscences thus awakened, she went on:

"Yes, it's mighty hard work, but he says it's all for me, and as soon as we're married he'll quit it. He might have quit it before, but he won't take no money of me, nor what I told him I could get out of dad! That ain't his style. He's mighty proud—if he is poor—is Charley. Why, thar's all ma's money which she left me in the Savin's Bank that I wanted to draw out—for I had the right— and give it to him, but he wouldn't hear of it! Why, he wouldn't take one of the things I've got with me, if he knew it. And so he goes on ridin' and ridin', here and there and everywhere, and gettin' more and more played out and sad, and thin and pale as a spirit, and always so uneasy about his business, and startin' up at times when we're meetin' out in the South Woods or in the far clearin', and sayin': 'I must be goin' now, Polly,' and yet always tryin' to be chiffle and chipper afore me. Why, he must have rid miles and miles to have watched for me thar in the brush at the foot of Galloper's tonight, jest to see if all was safe; and Lordy! I'd have given him the signal and showed a light if I'd died for it the next minit. There! That's what I know of Charley—that's what I'm running away from home for—that's what I'm running to him for, and I don't care who knows it! And I only wish I'd done it afore—and I would—if—if—if—he'd only *asked me!* There now!" She stopped, panted, and choked. Then one of the sudden transitions of youthful emotion overtook the eager, laughing face; it clouded up with the swift change of childhood, a lightning quiver of expression broke over it, and—then came the rain!

I think this simple act completed our utter demoralization! We smiled feebly at each other with that assumption of masculine superiority which is miserably conscious of its own helplessness at such moments. We looked out of the window, blew our noses, said: "Eh— what?" and "I say," vaguely to each other, and were greatly relieved, and yet apparently astonished, when Yuba Bill, who had turned his back upon the fair speaker, and was kicking the logs in the fireplace, suddenly swept down upon us and bundled us all into the road, leaving Miss Mullins alone. Then he walked aside with Judge

Thompson for a few moments; returned to us, autocrat-
ically demanded of the party a complete reticence towards
Miss Mullins on the subject matter under discussion, re-
entered the station, reappeared with the young lady,
suppressed a faint idiotic cheer which broke from us at
the spectacle of her innocent face once more cleared and
rosy, climbed the box, and in another moment we were
under way.

"Then she don't know what her lover is yet?" asked
the expressman eagerly.

"No."

"Are *you* certain it's one of the gang?"

"Can't say *for sure*. It mout be a young chap from
Yolo who bucked again the tiger [1] at Sacramento, got
regularly cleaned out and busted, and joined the gang
for a flier. They say thar was a new hand in that job
over at Keeley's—and a mighty game one, too; and ez
there was some buckshot onloaded that trip, he might
hev got his share, and that would tally with what the girl
said about his arm. See! Ef that's the man, I've heered
he was the son of some big preacher in the States, and
a college sharp to boot, who ran wild in 'Frisco, and
played himself for all he was worth. They're the wust
kind to kick when they once get a foot over the traces.
For stiddy, comf'ble kempany," added Bill reflectively,
"give *me* the son of a man that was *hanged!*"

"But what are you going to do about this?"

"That depends upon the feller who comes to meet
her."

"But you ain't going to try to take him? That would be
playing it pretty low down on them both."

"Keep your hair on, Jimmy! The Judge and me are
only going to rastle with the sperrit of that gay young
galoot when he drops down for his girl—and exhort him
pow'ful! Ef he allows he's convicted of sin and will find
the Lord, we'll marry him and the gal offhand at the next
station, and the Judge will officiate himself for nothin'.
We're goin' to have this yer elopement done on the
square—and our waybill clean—you bet!"

---

[1] Gambled at faro.

"But you don't suppose he'll trust himself in your hands?"

"Polly will signal to him that it's all square."

"Ah!" said the expressman. Nevertheless in those few moments the men seemed to have exchanged dispositions. The expressman looked doubtfully, critically, and even cynically before him. Bill's face had relaxed, and something like a bland smile beamed across it, as he drove confidently and unhesitatingly forward.

Day, meantime, although full blown and radiant on the mountain summits around us, was yet nebulous and uncertain in the valleys into which we were plunging. Lights still glimmered in the cabins and few ranch buildings which began to indicate the thicker settlements. And the shadows were heaviest in a little copse, where a note from Judge Thompson in the coach was handed up to Yuba Bill, who at once slowly began to draw up his horses. The coach stopped finally near the junction of a small crossroad. At the same moment Miss Mullins slipped down from the vehicle, and with a parting wave of her hand to the Judge, who had assisted her from the steps, tripped down the crossroad, and disappeared in its semiobscurity. To our surprise the stage waited, Bill holding the reins listlessly in his hands. Five minutes passed— an eternity of expectation, and as there was that in Yuba Bill's face which forbade idle questioning, an aching void of silence also! This was at last broken by a strange voice from the road:

"Go on—we'll follow."

The coach started forward. Presently we heard the sound of other wheels behind us. We all craned our necks backward to get a view of the unknown, but by the growing light we could only see that we were followed at a distance by a buggy with two figures in it. Evidently Polly Mullins and her lover! We hoped that they would pass us. But the vehicle, although drawn by a fast horse, preserved its distance always, and it was plain that its driver had no desire to satisfy our curiosity. The expressman had recourse to Bill.

"Is it the man you thought of?" he asked eagerly.

"I reckon," said Bill briefly.

"But," continued the expressman, returning to his former skepticism, "what's to keep them both from levanting together now?"

Bill jerked his hand towards the boot with a grim smile. "Their baggage."

"Oh!" said the expressman.

"Yes," continued Bill. "We'll hang on to that gal's little frills and fixin's until this yer job's settled and the ceremony's over, jest as ef we waz her own father. And, what's more, young man," he added, suddenly turning to the expressman, *"you'll* express them trunks of hers *through to Sacramento* with your kempany's labels, and hand her the receipts and checks for them so she *can get 'em there.* That'll keep *him* outer temptation and the reach o' the gang, until they get away among white men and civilization again. When your hoary-headed ole grandfather, or to speak plainer, that partikler old whiskeysoaker known as Yuba Bill, wot sits on this box," he continued, with a diabolical wink at the expressman, "waltzes in to pervide for a young couple jest startin' in life, thar's nothin' mean about his style, you bet. He fills the bill every time! Speshul Providences take a back seat when he's around."

When the station hotel and straggling settlement of Sugar Pine, now distinct and clear in the growing light, at last rose within rifleshot on the plateau, the buggy suddenly darted swiftly by us, so swiftly that the faces of the two occupants were barely distinguishable as they passed, and keeping the lead by a dozen lengths, reached the door of the hotel. The young girl and her companion leaped down and vanished within as we drew up. They had evidently determined to elude our curiosity, and were successful.

But the material appetites of the passengers, sharpened by the keen mountain air, were more potent than their curiosity, and as the breakfast bell rang out at the moment the stage stopped, a majority of them rushed into the dining room and scrambled for places without giving much heed to the vanished couple or to the Judge and Yuba Bill, who had disappeared also. The through coach to Marysville and Sacramento was likewise waiting, for Sugar Pine was the limit of Bill's ministration, and the coach which we had just left went no farther. In the course of twenty minutes, however, there was a slight and somewhat ceremonious bustling in the hall and on the veranda, and Yuba Bill and the Judge reappeared. The latter was leading, with some elaboration of manner and detail, the shapely figure of Miss Mullins, and Yuba Bill was accompanying her companion to the buggy. We all rushed to the windows to get a good view of the mysterious stranger and probable ex-brigand whose life was now linked with our fair fellow passenger. I am afraid, however, that we all participated in a certain impression of disappointment and doubt. Handsome and even cultivated-looking, he assuredly was—young and vigorous in appearance. But there was a certain half-shamed, half-defiant suggestion in his expression, yet coupled with a watchful lurking uneasiness which was not pleasant and hardly becoming in a bridegroom—and the possessor of such a bride. But the frank, joyous, innocent face of Polly Mullins, resplendent with a simple, happy confidence, melted our hearts again, and condoned the fellow's shortcomings. We waved our hands; I think we would have given three rousing cheers as they drove away if the omnipotent eye of Yuba Bill had not been upon us. It was well, for the next moment we were summoned to the presence of that soft-hearted autocrat.

We found him alone with the Judge in a private sitting room, standing before a table on which there were a decanter and glasses. As we filed expectantly into the room and the door closed behind us, he cast a glance of hesitating tolerance over the group.

"Gentlemen," he said slowly, "you was all present at the beginnin' of a little game this mornin', and the Judge thar thinks that you oughter be let in at the finish. *I* don't see that it's any of *your* d—d business—so to speak; but ez the Judge here allows you're all in the secret, I've called you in to take a partin' drink to the health of Mr. and Mrs. Charley Byng—ez is now comf'ably off on their bridal tower. What *you* know or what *you* suspects of the young galoot that's married the gal ain't worth shucks to anybody, and I wouldn't give it to a yaller pup to play with, but the Judge thinks you ought all to promise right here that you'll keep it dark. That's his opinion. Ez far as my opinion goes, gen'l'men," continued Bill, with greater blandness and apparent cordiality, "I wanter simply remark, in a keerless, offhand gin'ral way, that ef I ketch any God-forsaken, lop-eared, chuckle-headed blatherin' idjet airin' *his* opinion——"

"One moment, Bill," interposed Judge Thompson with a grave smile; "let me explain. You understand, gentlemen," he said, turning to us, "the singular, and I may say affecting, situation which our good-hearted friend here has done so much to bring to what we hope will be a happy termination. I want to give here, as my professional opinion, that there is nothing in his request which, in your capacity as good citizens and law-abiding men, you may not grant. I want to tell you, also, that you are condoning no offense against the statutes; that there is not a particle of legal evidence before us of the criminal antecedents of Mr. Charles Byng, except that which has been told you by the innocent lips of his betrothed, which the law of the land has now sealed forever in the mouth of his wife, and that our own actual experience of his acts has been in the main exculpatory of any previous irregularity—if not incompatible with it. Briefly, no judge would charge, no jury convict, on such evidence. When I add that the young girl is of legal age, that there is no evidence of any previous undue influence, but rather of the reverse, on the part of the bridegroom, and that I was content, as a magistrate, to perform the ceremony, I think you will be satisfied to give your promise, for the sake of the bride, and drink a happy life to them both."

I need not say that we did this cheerfully, and even extorted from Bill a grunt of satisfaction. The majority of the company, however, who were going with the through coach to Sacramento, then took their leave, and as we accompanied them to the veranda, we could see that Miss Polly Mullins's trunks were already transferred to the other vehicle under the protecting seals and labels of the all-potent Express Company. Then the whip cracked, the coach rolled away, and the last traces of the adventurous young couple disappeared in the hanging red dust of its wheels.

But Yuba Bill's grim satisfaction at the happy issue of the episode seemed to suffer no abatement. He even exceeded his usual deliberately regulated potations, and standing comfortably with his back to the center of the now deserted barroom, was more than usually loquacious with the expressman. "You see," he said, in bland reminiscence, "when your old Uncle Bill takes hold of a job like this, he puts it straight through without changin' hosses. Yet thar was a moment, young feller, when I thought I was stompt! It was when we'd made up our mind to make that chap tell the gal fust all what he was! Ef she'd rared or kicked in the traces, or hung back only ez much ez that, we'd hev given him jest five minits' law to get up and get and leave her, and we'd hev toted that gal and her fixin's back to her dad again! But she jest gave a little scream and start, and then went off inter hysterics, right on his buzzum, laughin' and cryin' and sayin' that nothin' should part 'em. Gosh! if I didn't think *he* woz more cut up than she about it; a minit it looked as ef *he* didn't allow to marry her arter all, but that passed, and they was married hard and fast—you bet! I reckon he's had enough of stayin' out o' nights to last him, and ef the valley settlements hevn't got hold of a very shinin' member, at least the foothills hev got shut of one more of the Ramon Martinez gang."

"What's that about the Ramon Martinez gang?" said a quiet potential voice.

Bill turned quickly. It was the voice of the Divisional Superintendent of the Express Company—a man of eccentric determination of character, and one of the few whom the autocratic Bill recognized as an equal—who had just entered the barroom. His dusty pongee cloak and soft hat indicated that he had that morning arrived on a round of inspection.

"Don't care if I do, Bill," he continued, in response to Bill's invitatory gesture, walking to the bar. "It's a little raw out on the road. Well, what were you saying about Ramon Martinez gang? You haven't come across one of 'em, have you?"

"No," said Bill, with a slight blinking of his eye, as he ostentatiously lifted his glass to the light.

"And you *won't*," added the Superintendent, leisurely sipping his liquor. "For the fact is, the gang is about played out. Not from want of a job now and then, but from the difficulty of disposing of the results of their

work. Since the new instructions to the agents to identify
and trace all dust and bullion offered to them went into
force, you see, they can't get rid of their swag. All the
gang are spotted at the offices, and it costs too much for
them to pay a fence or a middleman of any standing.
Why, all that flaky river gold they took from the Excelsior Company can be identified as easy as if it was
stamped with the company's mark. They can't melt it
down themselves; they can't get others to do it for them;
they can't ship it to the mint or assay offices in Marysville and 'Frisco, for they won't take it without our certifi-
cate and seals; and *we* don't take any undeclared freight
within the lines that we've drawn around their beat, except from people and agents known. Why, *you* know that
well enough, Jim," he said, suddenly appealing to the
expressman, "don't you?"

Possibly the suddenness of the appeal caused the expressman to swallow his liquor the wrong way, for he
was overtaken with a fit of coughing, and stammered
hastily as he laid down his glass, "Yes—of course—certainly."

"No, sir," resumed the Superintendent cheerfully,
"they're pretty well played out. And the best proof of it
is that they've lately been robbing ordinary passengers'
trunks. There was a freight wagon 'held up' near Dow's
Flat the other day, and a lot of baggage gone through. I
had to go down there to look into it. Darned if they hadn't
lifted a lot o' woman's wedding things from that rich
couple who got married the other day out at Marysville.
Looks as if they were playing it rather low-down, don't
it? Coming down to hardpan and the bedrock—eh?"

The expressman's face was turned anxiously towards
Bill, who, after a hurried gulp of his remaining liquor,
still stood staring at the window. Then he slowly drew
on one of his large gloves. "Ye didn't," he said, with a
slow, drawling, but perfectly distinct, articulation, "happen to know old 'Skinner' Hemmings when you were over
there?"

"Yes."

"And his daughter?"

"He hasn't got any."

"A sort o' mild, innocent, guileless child of nature?"

persisted Bill, with a yellow face, a deadly calm, and Satanic deliberation.

"No. I tell you he *hasn't* any daughter. Old man Hemmings is a confirmed old bachelor. He's too mean to support more than one."

"And you didn't happen to know any o' that gang, did ye?" continued Bill, with infinite protraction.

"Yes. Knew 'em all. There was French Pete, Cherokee Bob, Kanaka Joe, One-eyed Stillson, Softy Brown, Spanish Jack, and two or three Greasers."

"And ye didn't know a man by the name of Charley Byng?"

"No," returned the Superintendent, with a slight suggestion of weariness and a distraught glance towards the door.

"A dark, stylish chap, with shifty black eyes and a curled-up merstache?" continued Bill, with dry, colorless persistence.

"No. Look here, Bill, I'm in a little bit of a hurry—but I suppose you must have your little joke before we part. Now, what *is* your little game?"

"Wot you mean?" demanded Bill, with sudden brusqueness.

"Mean? Well, old man, you know as well as I do. You're giving me the very description of Ramon Martinez himself, ha! ha! No—Bill! you didn't play me this time. You're mighty spry and clever, but you didn't catch on just then."

He nodded and moved away with a light laugh. Bill turned a stony face to the expressman. Suddenly a gleam of mirth came into his gloomy eyes. He bent over the young man, and said in a hoarse, chuckling whisper:

"But I got even after all!"

"How?"

"He's tied up to that lying little she-devil, hard and fast!"

A Protégée of
➤➤➤➤➤➤➤➤➤➤➤➤ Jack Hamlin's ➤➤➤➤➤➤➤

ONE

➤➤➤➤➤➤ The steamer Silveropolis was sharply and steadily cleaving the broad, placid shallows of the Sacramento
River. A large wave like an eagre, diverging from its
bow, was extending to either bank, swamping the tules
and threatening to submerge the lower levees. The great
boat itself—a vast but delicate structure of airy stories,
hanging galleries, fragile colonnades, gilded cornices, and
resplendent frescoes—was throbbing throughout its whole
perilous length with the pulse of high pressure and the
strong monotonous beat of a powerful piston. Floods of
foam pouring from the high paddle boxes on either side
and reuniting in the wake of the boat left behind a track
of dazzling whiteness, over which trailed two dense black
banners flung from its lofty smokestacks.

Mr. Jack Hamlin had quietly emerged from his stateroom on deck and was looking over the guards. His
hands were resting lightly on his hips over the delicate
curves of his white waistcoat, and he was whistling
softly, possibly some air to which he had made certain
card-playing passengers dance the night before. He was
in comfortable case, and his soft brown eyes under their
long lashes were veiled with gentle tolerance of all
things. He glanced lazily along the empty hurricane deck
forward; he glanced lazily down to the saloon deck below
him. Far out against the guards below him leaned a young
girl. Mr. Hamlin knitted his brows slightly.

He remembered her at once. She had come on board
that morning with one Ned Stratton, a brother gambler,
but neither a favorite nor intimate of Jack's. From certain
indications in the pair, Jack had inferred that she was
some foolish or reckless creature whom "Ed" had "got

on a string," and was spiriting away from her friends and family. With the abstract morality of this situation Jack was not in the least concerned. For himself he did not indulge in that sort of game; the inexperience and vacillations of innocence were apt to be bothersome, and besides, a certain modest doubt of his own competency to make an original selection had always made him prefer to confine his gallantries to the wives of men of greater judgment than himself who had. But it suddenly occurred to him that he had seen Stratton quickly slip off the boat at the last landing stage. Ah! that was it; he had cast away and deserted her. It was an old story. Jack smiled. But he was not greatly amused with Stratton.

She was very pale, and seemed to be clinging to the network railing, as if to support herself, although she was gazing fixedly at the yellow glancing current below, which seemed to be sucked down and swallowed in the paddle box as the boat swept on. It certainly was a fascinating sight—this sloping rapid, hurrying on to bury itself under the crushing wheels. For a brief moment Jack saw how they would seize anything floating on that ghastly incline, whirl it round in one awful revolution of the beating paddles, and then bury it, broken and shattered out of all recognition, deep in the muddy undercurrent of the stream behind them.

She moved away presently with an odd, stiff step, chafing her gloved hands together as if they had become stiffened, too, in her rigid grasp of the railing. Jack leisurely watched her as she moved along the narrow strip of deck. She was not at all to his taste—a rather plump girl with a rustic manner and a great deal of brown hair under her straw hat. She might have looked better had she not been so haggard. When she reached the door of the saloon she paused, and then, turning suddenly, began to walk quickly back again. As she neared the spot where she had been standing her pace slackened, and when she reached the railing she seemed to relapse against it in her former helpless fashion. Jack became lazily interested. Suddenly she lifted her head and cast a quick glance around and above her. In that momentary lifting of her face Jack saw her expression. Whatever it was, his own changed instantly; the next moment there was a crash on

the lower deck. It was Jack who had swung himself over
the rail and dropped ten feet, to her side. But not before
she had placed one foot in the meshes of the netting and
had gripped the railing for a spring.

The noise of Jack's fall might have seemed to her
bewildered fancy as a part of her frantic act, for she fell
forward vacantly on the railing. But by this time Jack had
grasped her arm as if to help himself to his feet.

"I might have killed myself by that foolin', mightn't I?"
he said cheerfully.

The sound of a voice so near her seemed to recall to
her dazed sense the uncompleted action his fall had arrested. She made a convulsive bound towards the railing,
but Jack held her fast.

"Don't," he said in a low voice—"don't, it won't pay.
It's the sickest game that ever was played by man or
woman. Come here!"

He drew her towards an empty stateroom whose door
was swinging on its hinges a few feet from them. She
was trembling violently; he half led, half pushed her into
the room, closed the door, and stood with his back against
it as she dropped into a chair. She looked at him vacantly; the agitation she was undergoing inwardly had
left her no sense of outward perception.

"You know Stratton would be awfully riled," continued
Jack easily. "He's just stepped out to see a friend and got
left by the fool boat. He'll be along by the next steamer,
and you're bound to meet him in Sacramento."

Her staring eyes seemed suddenly to grasp his meaning.
But to his surprise she burst out with a certain hysterical
desperation, "No! no! Never! *never* again! Let me pass!
I must go," and struggled to regain the door. Jack, albeit
singularly relieved to know that she shared his private
sentiments regarding Stratton, nevertheless resisted her.
Whereat she suddenly turned white, reeled back, and sank
in a dead faint in the chair.

The gambler turned, drew the key from the inside of
the door, passed out, locking it behind him, and walked
leisurely into the main saloon.

"Mrs. Johnson," he said gravely, addressing the stewardess, a tall mulatto, with his usual winsome su-
premacy over dependents and children, "you'll oblige me

if you'll corral a few smelling salts, vinaigrettes, hairpins, and violet powder, and unload them in deck stateroom No. 257. There's a lady—"

"A lady, Marse Hamlin?" interrupted the mulatto, with an archly significant flash of her white teeth.

"A lady," continued Jack with unabashed gravity, "in a sort of conniption fit. A relative of mine; in fact, a niece, my only sister's child. Hadn't seen each other for ten years, and it was too much for her."

The woman glanced at him with a mingling of incredulous belief but delighted obedience, hurriedly gathered a few articles from her cabin, and followed him to No. 257. The young girl was still unconscious. The stewardess applied a few restoratives with the skill of long experience, and the young girl opened her eyes. They turned vacantly from the stewardess to Jack with a look of half recognition and half frightened inquiry.

"Yes," said Jack, addressing the eyes, although ostentatiously speaking to Mrs. Johnson, "she'd only just come by steamer to 'Frisco and wasn't expecting to see me, and we dropped right into each other here on the boat. And I haven't seen her since she was so high. Sister Mary ought to have warned me by letter; but she was always a slouch at letter writing. There, that'll do, Mrs. Johnson. She's coming round; I reckon I can manage the rest. But you go now and tell the purser I want one of those inside staterooms for my niece—*my niece,* you hear—so that you can be near her and look after her."

As the stewardess turned obediently away the young girl attempted to rise, but Jack checked her.

"No," he said, almost brusquely; "you and I have some talking to do before she gets back, and we've no time for foolin'. You heard what I told her just now! Well, it's got to be as I said, you sabe. As long as you're on this boat you're my niece, and my sister Mary's child. As I haven't got any sister Mary, you don't run any risk of falling foul of her, and you ain't taking anyone's place. That settles that. Now, do you or do you not want to see that man again? Say yes, and if he's anywhere above ground I'll yank him over to you as soon as we touch shore." He had no idea of interfering with his colleague's amours, but he had determined to make Stratton pay for the bother their slovenly sequence had caused him. Yet he was relieved and astonished by her frantic gesture of indignation and abhorrence. "No?" he repeated grimly. "Well, that settles that. Now, look here; quick, before she comes—do you want to go back home to your friends?"

But here occurred what he had dreaded most and probably thought he had escaped. She had stared at him, at the stewardess, at the walls, with abstracted, vacant, and bewildered, but always undimmed and unmoistened eyes. A sudden convulsion shook her whole frame, her blank expression broke like a shattered mirror, she threw her hands over her eyes, and fell forward with her face to the back of her chair in an outburst of tears.

Alas for Jack! with the breaking up of those sealed fountains came her speech also, at first disconnected and incoherent, and then despairing and passionate. No! she had no longer friends or home! She had lost and disgraced them! She had disgraced *herself!* There was no home for her but the grave. Why had Jack snatched her from it? Then bit by bit, she yielded up her story—a story decidedly commonplace to Jack, uninteresting, and even irritating to his fastidiousness. She was a schoolgirl (not even a convent girl, but the inmate of a Presbyterian female academy at Napa. Jack shuddered as he remembered to have once seen certain of the pupils walking with a teacher), and she lived with her married sister. She had seen Stratton while going to-and-fro on the San Francisco boat; she had exchanged notes with him, had met him secretly, and finally consented to elope with him to Sacramento, only to discover when the boat had left the wharf the real nature of his intentions. Jack listened with infinite weariness and inward chafing. He had read all this before in cheap novelettes, in the police reports, in the Sunday papers; he had heard a street preacher declaim against it, and warn young women of the serpentlike wiles of tempters of the Stratton variety. But even now Jack failed to recognize Stratton as a serpent, or indeed anything but a blundering cheat and clown, who had left his dirty 'prentice work on his (Jack's) hands. But the girl was helpless and, it seemed, homeless, all through a certain desperation of feeling which, in spite of her tears, he could not but respect. That momentary shadow of death had exalted her. He stroked his mustache, pulled down his white waistcoat, and let her cry, without saying anything. He did not know that this most objectionable phase of her misery was her salvation and his own.

But the stewardess would return in a moment.

"You'd better tell me what to call you," he said quietly. "I ought to know my niece's first name."

The girl caught her breath, and between two sobs said, "Sophonisba."

Jack winced. It seemed only to need this last sentimental touch to complete the idiotic situation.

"I'll call you Sophy," he said hurriedly and with an effort. "And now look here! You are going in that cabin with Mrs. Johnson where she can look after you, but I can't. So I'll have to take your word, for I'm not going to give you away before Mrs. Johnson, that you won't try that foolishness—you know what I mean—before I see you again. Can I trust you?"

With her head still bowed over the chair back, she murmured slowly somewhere from under her disheveled hair: "Yes."

"Honest Injin?" adjured Jack gravely.

"Yes."

The shuffling step of the stewardess was heard slowly approaching.

"Yes," continued Jack abruptly, slightly lifting his voice, as Mrs. Johnson opened the door—"yes, if you'd only had some of those spearmint drops of your aunt Rachel's that she always gave you when these fits came on you'd have been all right inside of five minutes. Aunty was no slouch of a doctor, was she? Dear me, it only seems yesterday since I saw her. You were just playing round her knee like a kitten on the back porch. How time does fly! But here's Mrs. Johnson coming to take you in. Now rouse up, Sophy, and just hook yourself on to Mrs. Johnson on that side, and we'll toddle along."

The young girl put back her heavy hair, and with her face still averted submitted to be helped to her feet by the kindly stewardess. Perhaps something homely sympathetic and nurselike in the touch of the mulatto gave her assurance and confidence, for her head lapsed quite naturally against the woman's shoulder, and her face was partly hidden as she moved slowly along the deck. Jack accompanied them to the saloon and the inner stateroom door. A few passengers gathered curiously near, as much attracted by the unusual presence of Jack Hamlin in such a procession as by the girl herself.

"You'll look after her specially, Mrs. Johnson," said Jack, in unusually deliberate terms. "She's been a good deal petted at home, and my sister perhaps has rather spoilt her. She's pretty much of a child still, and you'll have to humor her. Sophy," he continued, with ostentatious playfulness, directing his voice into the dim recesses of the stateroom, "you'll just think Mrs. Johnson's your old nurse, won't you? Think it's old Katy, hey?"

To his great consternation the girl approached tremblingly from the inner shadow. The faintest and saddest of smiles for a moment played around the corners of her drawn mouth and tear-dimmed eyes as she held out her hand and said:

"God bless you for being so kind."

Jack shuddered and glanced quickly round. But luckily no one heard this crushing sentimentalism, and the next moment the door closed upon her and Mrs. Johnson.

It was past midnight, and the moon was riding high over the narrowing yellow river, when Jack again stepped out on deck. He had just left the captain's cabin, and a small social game with the officers, which had served to some extent to vaguely relieve his irritation and their pockets. He had presumably quite forgotten the incident of the afternoon, as he looked about him, and complacently took in the quiet beauty of the night.

The low banks on either side offered no break to the uninterrupted level of the landscape, through which the river seemed to wind only as a race track for the rushing boat. Every fiber of her vast but fragile bulk quivered under the goad of her powerful engines. There was no other movement but hers, no other sound but this monstrous beat and panting; the whole tranquil landscape seemed to breathe and pulsate with her; dwellers in the tules, miles away, heard and felt her as she passed, and it seemed to Jack, leaning over the railing, as if the whole river swept like a sluice through her paddle boxes.

Jack had quite unconsciously lounged before that part of

the railing where the young girl had leaned a few hours ago. As he looked down upon the streaming yellow mill-race below him he noticed—what neither he nor the girl had probably noticed before—that a space of the top bar of the railing was hinged, and could be lifted by withdrawing a small bolt, thus giving easy access to the guards. He was still looking at it, whistling softly, when footsteps approached.

"Jack," said a lazy voice, "how's sister Mary?"

"It's a long time since you've seen her only child, Jack, ain't it?" said a second voice; "and yet it sort o' seems to me somehow that I've seen her before."

Jack recognized the voice of two of his late companions at the card table. His whistling ceased; so also dropped every trace of color and expression from his handsome face. But he did not turn, and remained quietly gazing at the water.

"Aunt Rachel, too, must be getting on in years, Jack," continued the first speaker, halting behind Jack.

"And Mrs. Johnson does not look so much like Sophy's old nurse as she used to," remarked the second, following his example. Still Jack remained unmoved.

"You don't seem to be interested, Jack," continued the first speaker. "What are you looking at?"

Without turning his head the gambler replied, "Looking at the boat; she's booming along, just chawing up and spitting out the river, ain't she? Look at that sweep of water going under her paddle wheels," he continued, unbolting the rail and lifting it to allow the two men to peer curiously over the guards as he pointed to the murderous incline beneath them; "a man wouldn't stand much show who got dropped into it. How these paddles would just snatch him bald-headed, pick him up, and slosh him round and round, and then sling him out down there in such a shape that his own father wouldn't know him."

"Yes," said the first speaker, with an ostentatious little laugh, "but all that ain't telling us how sister Mary is."

"No," said the gambler, slipping into the opening with a white and rigid face in which nothing seemed living but the eyes—"no; but it's telling you how two d—d fools who didn't know when to shut their mouths might get them shut once and forever. It's telling you what might

happen to two men who tried to 'play' a man who didn't
care to be 'played,'—a man who didn't care much what
he did, when he did it, or how he did it, but would do
what he'd set out to do—even if in doing it he went to
hell with the men he sent there."

He had stepped out on the guards, beside the two men,
closing the rail behind him. He had placed his hands on
their shoulders; they had both gripped his arms; yet,
viewed from the deck above, they seemed at that moment
an amicable, even fraternal group, albeit the faces of the
three were dead white in the moonlight.

"I don't think I'm so very much interested in sister
Mary," said the first speaker quietly, after a pause.

"And I don't seem to think so much of aunt Rachel as
I did," said his companion.

"I thought you wouldn't," said Jack, coolly reopening
the rail and stepping back again. "It all depends upon the
way you look at those things. Good night."

"Good night."

The three men paused, shook each other's hands silently, and separated, Jack sauntering slowly back to his stateroom.

TWO

The educational establishment of Mrs. Mix and Madame Bance, situated in the best quarter of Sacramento
and patronized by the highest state officials and members
of the clergy, was a pretty if not an imposing edifice. Although surrounded by a high white picket fence and
entered through a heavily boarded gate, its balconies fes-
tooned with jasmine and roses, and its spotlessly
draped windows as often graced with fresh, flowerlike
faces, were still plainly and provokingly visible above
the ostentatious spikes of the pickets. Nevertheless, Mr.
Jack Hamlin, who had six months before placed his niece,
Miss Sophonisba Brown, under its protecting care, felt a
degree of uneasiness, even bordering on timidity, which
was new to that usually self-confident man. Remembering
how his first appearance had fluttered this dovecot

and awakened a severe suspicion in the minds of the two
principals, he had discarded his usual fashionable attire
and elegantly fitting garments for a rough homespun
suit, supposed to represent a homely agriculturist, but
which had the effect of transforming him into an adorable
Strephon, infinitely more dangerous in his rustic shep-
herdlike simplicity. He had also shaved off his silken mustache for the same prudential reasons, but had only
succeeded in uncovering the delicate lines of his handsome mouth, and so absurdly reducing his apparent years
that his avuncular pretensions seemed more preposterous
than ever; and when he had rung the bell and was admitted by a severe Irish waiting maid, his momentary hesitation and half-humorous diffidence had such an unexpected effect upon her that it seemed doubtful if he would
be allowed to pass beyond the vestibule.

"Shure, miss," she said in a whisper to an underteach-
er, "there's wan at the dhure who calls himself 'Mister'
Hamlin, but av it is not a young lady maskeradin' in her
brother's clothes oim very much mistaken; and av it's a
boy, one of the pupil's brothers, shure ye might put a
dhress on him when you take the others out for a walk,
and he'd pass for the beauty of the whole school."

Meantime the unconscious subject of this criticism was
pacing somewhat uneasily up and down the formal reception room into which he had been finally ushered. Its
farther end was filled by an enormous parlor organ, a
number of music books, and a cheerfully variegated globe.
A large presentation Bible, an equally massive illustrated
volume on the Holy Land, a few landscapes in cold, bluish
milk and water colors, and rigid heads in crayons—the
work of pupils—were presumably ornamental. An imposing mahogany sofa and what seemed to be a disproportionate excess of chairs somewhat coldly furnished
the room. Jack had reluctantly made up his mind that if
Sophy was accompanied by anyone he would be obliged
to kiss her to keep up his assumed relationship. As she
entered the room with Miss Mix, Jack advanced and sob-
erly saluted her on the cheek. But so positive and apparent was the gallantry of his presence, and perhaps so suggestive of some pastoral flirtation, that Miss Mix, to

Jack's surprise, winced perceptibly and became stony. But he was still more surprised that the young lady herself shrank half uneasily from his lips, and uttered a slight exclamation. It was a new experience to Mr. Hamlin.

But this somewhat mollified Miss Mix, and she slightly relaxed her austerity. She was glad to be able to give the best accounts of Miss Brown, not only as regarded her studies, but as to her conduct and deportment. Really, with the present freedom of manners and laxity of home discipline in California, it was gratifying to meet a young lady who seemed to value the importance of a proper decorum and behavior, especially towards the opposite sex. Mr. Hamlin, although her guardian, was perhaps too young to understand and appreciate this. To this inexperience she must also attribute the indiscretion of his calling during school hours and without preliminary warning. She trusted, however, that this informality could be overlooked after consultation with Madame Bance, but in the meantime, perhaps for half an hour, she must withdraw Miss Brown and return with her to the class. Mr. Hamlin could wait in this public room, reserved especially for visitors, until they returned. Or, if he cared to accompany one of the teachers in a formal inspection of the school, she added doubtfully, with a glance at Jack's distracting attractions, she would submit this also to Madame Bance.

"Thank you, thank you," returned Jack hurriedly, as a depressing vision of the fifty or sixty scholars rose before his eyes, "but I'd rather not. I mean, you know, I'd just as lief stay here *alone*. I wouldn't have called anyway, don't you see, only I had a day off—and—and—I wanted to talk with my niece on family matters."

He did not say that he had received a somewhat distressful letter from her asking him to come; a new instinct made him cautious.

Considerably relieved by Jack's unexpected abstention, which seemed to spare her pupils the distraction of his graces, Miss Mix smiled more amicably and retired with her charge. In the single glance he had exchanged with Sophy he saw that, although resigned and apparently self-controlled, she still appeared thoughtful and melancholy. She had improved in appearance and seemed more

refined and less rustic in her school dress, but he was
conscious of the same distinct separation of her personality (which was uninteresting to him) from the sentiment that had impelled him to visit her. She was possibly
still hankering after that fellow Stratton, in spite of her
protestations to the contrary; perhaps she wanted to go
back to her sister, although she had declared she would
die first, and had always refused to disclose her real
name or give any clue by which he could have traced her
relations. She would cry, of course; he almost hoped that
she would not return alone; he half regretted he had
come. She still held him only by a single quality of her
nature—the desperation she had shown on the boat; that
was something he understood and respected.

He walked discontentedly to the window and looked
out; he walked discontentedly to the end of the room and
stopped before the organ. It was a fine instrument; he
could see that with an admiring and experienced eye.
He was alone in the room; in fact, quite alone in that part
of the house which was separated from the classrooms.
He would disturb no one by trying it. And if he did, what
then? He smiled a little recklessly, slowly pulled off his
gloves, and sat down before it.

He played cautiously at first, with the soft pedal down.
The instrument had never known a strong masculine hand
before, having been fumbled and frivoled over by softly
incompetent, feminine fingers. But presently it began to
thrill under the passionate hand of its lover, and carried
away by his one innocent weakness, Jack was launched
upon a sea of musical reminiscences. Scraps of church
music, Puritan psalms of his boyhood, dying strains from
sad, forgotten operas, fragments of oratorios and sym-
phonies, but chiefly phrases from old masses heard at the
missions of San Pedro and Santa Isabel, swelled up from
his loving and masterful fingers. He had finished an Agnus
Dei; the formal room was pulsating with divine aspiration;
the rascal's hands were resting listlessly on the keys, his
brown lashes, lifted, in an effort of memory, tenderly towards the ceiling.

Suddenly, a subdued murmur of applause and a slight
rustle behind him recalled him to himself again. He
wheeled his chair quickly round. The two principals of the

school and half a dozen teachers were standing gravely
behind him, and at the open door a dozen curled and
frizzled youthful heads peered in eagerly, but half restrained by their teachers. The relaxed features and
apologetic attitude of Madame Bance and Miss Mix
showed that Mr. Hamlin had unconsciously achieved a
triumph.

He might not have been as pleased to know that his
extraordinary performance had solved a difficulty, effaced
his other graces, and enabled them to place him on the
moral pedestal of a mere musician, to whom these ec-
centricities were allowable and privileged. He shared the
admiration extended by the young ladies to their music
teacher, which was always understood to be a sexless enthusiasm and a contagious juvenile disorder. It was also a
fine advertisement for the organ. Madame Bance smiled
blandly, improved the occasion by thanking Mr. Hamlin
for having given the scholars a gratuitous lesson on the
capabilities of the instrument, and was glad to be able to
give Miss Brown a half-holiday to spend with her accomplished relative. Miss Brown was even now upstairs putting on her hat and mantle. Jack was relieved. Sophy
would not attempt to cry on the street.

Nevertheless, when they reached it and the gate closed
behind them, he again became uneasy. The girl's clouded
face and melancholy manner were not promising. It also
occurred to him that he might meet someone who knew
him and thus compromise her. This was to be avoided at
all hazards. He began with forced gaiety:

"Well, now, where shall we go?"

She slightly raised her tear-dimmed eyes.

"Where you please—I don't care."

"There isn't any show going on here, is there?"

He had a vague idea of a circus or menagerie—himself behind her in the shadow of the box.

"I don't know of any."

"Or any restaurant—or cake shop?"

"There's a place where the girls go to get candy on
Main Street. Some of them are there now."

Jack shuddered; this was not to be thought of.

"But where do you walk?"

"Up and down Main Street."

"Where everybody can see you?" said Jack, scandalized.

The girl nodded.

They walked on in silence for a few moments. Then a bright idea struck Mr. Hamlin. He suddenly remembered that in one of his many fits of impulsive generosity and largess he had given to an old Negro retainer—whose wife had nursed him through a dangerous illness—a house and lot on the river bank. He had been told that they had opened a small laundry or wash house. It occurred to him that a stroll there and a call upon "Uncle Hannibal and Aunt Chloe" combined the propriety and respectability due to the young person he was with, and the requisite secrecy and absence of publicity due to himself. He at once suggested it.

"You see she was a mighty good woman, and you ought to know her, for she was my old nurse"—

The girl glanced at him with a sudden impatience.

"Honest Injin," said Jack solemnly; "she did nurse me through my last cough. I ain't playing old family gags on you now."

"Oh, dear," burst out the girl impulsively, "I do wish you wouldn't ever play them again. I wish you wouldn't pretend to be my uncle; I wish you wouldn't make me pass for your niece. It isn't right. It's all wrong. Oh, don't you know it's all wrong, and can't come right any way? It's just killing me. I can't stand it. I'd rather you'd say what I am and how I came to you and how you pitied me."

They had luckily entered a narrow side street, and the sobs which shook the young girl's frame were unnoticed. For a few moments Jack felt a horrible conviction stealing over him, that in his present attitude towards her he was not unlike that hound Stratton, and that, however innocent his own intent, there was a sickening resemblance to the situation on the boat in the base advantage he had taken of her friendlessness. He had never told her that he was a gambler like Stratton, and that his peculiar infelix reputation among women made it impossible for him to assist her, except by stealth or the deception he had practiced, without compromising her. He who had for years faced the sneers and half-frightened opposition of the world dared not tell the truth to this girl, from whom he expected nothing and who did not interest him. He felt he was almost slinking at her side. At last he said desperately:

"But I snatched them bald-headed at the organ, Sophy, didn't I?"

"Oh, yes," said the girl, "you played beautifully and grandly. It was so good of you, too. For I think, somehow, Madame Bance had been a little suspicious of you, but that settled it. Everybody thought it was fine, and some thought it was your profession. Perhaps," she added timidly, "it is."

"I play a good deal, I reckon," said Jack, with a grim humor which did not, however, amuse him.

"I wish *I* could, and make money by it," said the girl eagerly. Jack winced, but she did not notice it as she went on hurriedly: "That's what I wanted to talk to you about. I want to leave the school and make my own living. Anywhere where people won't know me and where I can be alone and work. I shall die here among these girls—with all their talk of their friends and their—sisters—and their questions about you."

"Tell 'em to dry up," said Jack indignantly. "Take 'em to the cake shop and load 'em up with candy and ice cream. That'll stop their mouths. You've got money—you got my last remittance, didn't you?" he repeated quickly. "If you didn't here's—"; his hand was already in his pocket when she stopped him with a despairing gesture.

"Yes, yes, I got it all. I haven't touched it. I don't want it. For I can't live on you. Don't you understand—I want to work. Listen—I can draw and paint. Madame Bance says I do it well; my drawing master says I might in time take portraits and get paid for it. And even now I can retouch photographs and make colored miniatures from them. And," she stopped and glanced at Jack half timidly, "I've—done some already."

A glow of surprised relief suffused the gambler. Not so much at this astonishing revelation as at the change it seemed to effect in her. Her pale blue eyes, made paler by tears, cleared and brightened under their swollen lids like wiped steel; the lines of her depressed mouth straight-ened and became firm. Her voice had lost its hopeless monotone.

"There's a shop in the next street—a photographer's —where they have one of mine in their windows," she went on, reassured by Jack's unaffected interest. "It's only round the corner, if you care to see."

Jack assented; a few paces farther brought them to the corner of a narrow street, where they presently turned into a broader thoroughfare and stopped before the window of a photographer. Sophy pointed to an oval frame, containing a portrait painted on porcelain. Mr. Hamlin was startled. Inexperienced as he was, a certain artistic inclination told him it was good, although it is to be feared he would have been astonished even if it had been worse. The mere fact that this headstrong country girl, who had run away with a cur like Stratton, should be able to do anything else took him by surprise.

"I got ten dollars for that," she said hesitatingly, "and I could have got more for a larger one, but I had to do that in my room during recreation hours. If I had more time and a place where I could work—" She stopped timidly and looked tentatively at Jack. But he was already indulging in a characteristically reckless idea of coming back after he had left Sophy, buying the miniature at an extravagant price, and ordering half a dozen more at extraordinary figures. Here, however, two passersby, stopping ostensibly to look in the window, but really attracted by the picturesque spectacle of the handsome young rustic and his schoolgirl companion, gave Jack such a fright that he hurried Sophy away again into the side street.

"There's nothing mean about that picture business," he said cheerfully; "it looks like a square kind of game," and relapsed into thoughtful silence.

At which Sophy, the ice of restraint broken, again burst into passionate appeal. If she could only go away somewhere—where she saw no one but the people who would buy her work, who knew nothing of her past nor cared to know who were her relations! She would work hard; she knew she could support herself in time. She would keep the name he had given her—it was not distinctive enough to challenge any inquiry—but nothing more. She need not assume to be his niece; he would always be her kind friend, to whom she owed everything, even her miserable life. She trusted still to his honor never to seek to know her real name, nor ever to speak to her of that man if he ever met him. It would do no good to her or to them; it might drive her, for she was not yet quite sure of herself, to do that which she had promised him never to do again.

There was no threat, impatience, or acting in her voice, but he recognized the same dull desperation he had once heard in it, and her eyes, which a moment before were quick and mobile, had become fixed and set. He had no idea of trying to penetrate the foolish secret of her name and relations; he had never had the slightest curiosity, but it struck him now that Stratton might at any time force it upon him. The only way that he could prevent it was to let it be known that, for unexpressed reasons, he would shoot Stratton "on sight." This would naturally restrict any verbal communication between them. Jack's ideas of morality were vague, but his convictions on points of honor were singularly direct and positive.

THREE

Meantime Hamlin and Sophy were passing the outskirts of the town; the open lots and cleared spaces were giving way to grassy stretches, willow copses, and groups of cottonwood and sycamore; and beyond the level of yellowing tules appeared the fringed and raised banks of the river. Half tropical-looking cottages with deep verandas —the homes of early Southern pioneers—took the place of incomplete blocks of modern houses, monotonously alike. In these sylvan surroundings Mr. Hamlin's picturesque rusticity looked less incongruous and more Arcadian; the young girl had lost some of her restraint with her confidences, and lounging together side by side, without the least consciousness of any sentiment in their words or actions, they nevertheless contrived to impress the spectator with the idea that they were a charming pair of pastoral lovers. So strong was this impression that, as they approached Aunt Chloe's laundry, a pretty rose-covered cottage with an enormous whitewashed barnlike extension in the rear, the black proprietress herself, standing at the door, called to her husband to come and look at them, and flashed her white teeth in such unqualified commendation and patronage that Mr. Hamlin, withdrawing himself from Sophy's side, instantly charged down upon them.

"If you don't slide the lid back over that grinning box of dominoes of yours and take it inside, I'll just carry Hannibal off with me," he said in a quick whisper, with a half-wicked, half-mischievous glitter in his brown eyes. "That young lady's—*a lady*—do you understand? No riffraff friend of mine, but a regular *nun*—a saint—do you hear? So you just stand back and let her take a good look round, and rest herself until she wants you." "Two black idiots, Miss Brown," he continued cheerfully in a higher voice of explanation, as Sophy approached, "who think because one of 'em used to shave me and the other saved my life they've got a right to stand at their humble cottage door and frighten horses!"

So great was Mr. Hamlin's ascendency over his former servants that even this ingenious pleasantry was received with every sign of affection and appreciation of the humorist, and of the profound respect for his companion. Aunt Chloe showed them effusively into her parlor, a small but scrupulously neat and sweet-smelling apartment, inordinately furnished with a huge mahogany center-table and chairs, and the most fragile and meretricious china and glass ornaments on the mantel. But the three jasmine-edged lattice windows opened upon a homely garden of old-fashioned herbs and flowers, and their fragrance filled the room. The cleanest and starchiest of curtains, the most dazzling and whitest of tidies and chair covers, bespoke the adjacent laundry; indeed, the whole cottage seemed to exhale the odors of lavender soap and freshly ironed linen. Yet the cottage was large for the couple and their assistants.

"Dar was two front rooms on de next flo' dat dey never used," explained Aunt Chloe; "friends allowed dat dey could let 'em to white folks, but dey had always been

done kep' for Marse Hamlin, ef he ever wanted to be wid
his old niggers again."

Jack looked up quickly with a brightened face, made a
sign to Hannibal, and the two left the room together.

When he came through the passage a few moments
later, there was a sound of laughter in the parlor. He
recognized the full, round, lazy, chuckle of Aunt Chloe,
but there was a higher girlish ripple that he did not
know. He had never heard Sophy laugh before. Nor,
when he entered, had he ever seen her so animated.
She was helping Chloe set the table, to that lady's intense delight at "Missy's" girlish housewifery. She was
picking the berries fresh from the garden, buttering the
Sally Lunn, making the tea, and arranging the details of
the repast with apparently no trace of her former discontent and unhappiness in either face or manner. He
dropped quietly into a chair by the window, and, with
the homely scents of the garden mixing with the honest
odors of Aunt Chloe's cookery, watched her with an
amusement that was as pleasant and grateful as it was
strange and unprecedented.

"Now, den," said Aunt Chloe to her husband, as she
put the finishing touch to the repast in the plate of
doughnuts as exquisitely brown and shining as Jack's
eyes were at that moment, "Hannibal, you just come
away, and let dem two white quality chillens have dey
tea. Dey's done starved, shuah." And with an approving
nod to Jack, she bundled her husband from the room.

The door closed; the young girl began to pour out the
tea, but Jack remained in his seat by the window. It was
a singular sensation which he did not care to disturb. It
was no new thing for Mr. Hamlin to find himself at a
tête-à-tête repast with the admiring and complaisant
fair; there was a cabinet particulier in a certain San
Francisco restaurant which had listened to their various
vanities and professions of undying faith; he might have
recalled certain festal rendezvous with a widow whose
piety and impeccable reputation made it a moral duty
for her to come to him only in disguise; it was but a
few days before that he had been let privately into the
palatial mansion of a high official for a midnight supper
with a foolish wife. It was not strange, therefore, that he

should be alone here, secretly, with a member of that indirect, loving sex. But that he should be sitting there in a cheap Negro laundry with absolutely no sentiment of any kind towards the heavy-haired, freckled-faced country schoolgirl opposite him, from whom he sought and expected nothing, and *enjoying* it without scorn of himself or his companion, to use his own expression, "got him." Presently he rose and sauntered to the table with shining eyes.

"Well, what do you think of Aunt Chloe's shebang?" he asked smilingly.

"Oh, it's so sweet and clean and homelike," said the girl quickly.

At any other time he would have winced at the last adjective. It struck him now as exactly the word.

"Would you like to live here, if you could?"

Her face brightened. She put the teapot down and gazed fixedly at Jack.

"Because you can. Look here. I spoke to Hannibal about it. You can have the two front rooms if you want to. One of 'em is big enough and light enough for a studio to do your work in. You tell that nigger what you want to put in 'em, and he's got my orders to do it. I told him about your painting; said you were the daughter of an old friend, you know. Hold on, Sophy; d——n it all, I've got to do a little gilt-edged lying; but I let you out of the niece business this time. Yes, from this moment I'm not longer your uncle. I renounce the relationship. It's hard," continued the rascal, "after all these years and considering sister Mary's feelings; but, as you seem to wish it, it must be done."

Sophy's steel-blue eyes softened. She slid her long brown hand across the table and grasped Jack's. He returned the pressure quickly and fraternally, even to that half-shamed, half-hurried evasion of emotion peculiar to all brothers. This was also a new sensation; but he liked it.

"You are too, too good, Mr. Hamlin," she said quietly.

"Yes," said Jack cheerfully, "that's what's the matter with me. It isn't natural, and if I keep it up too long it brings on my cough."

Nevertheless, they were happy in a boy and girl fash-

ion, eating heartily, and, I fear, not always decorously;
scrambling somewhat for the strawberries, and smacking
their lips over the Sally Lunn. Meantime, it was arranged
that Mr. Hamlin should inform Miss Mix that Sophy would
leave school at the end of the term, only a few days
hence, and then transfer herself to lodgings with some old
family servants, where she could more easily pursue her
studies in her own profession. She need not make her
place of abode a secret, neither need she court publicity.
She would write to Jack regularly, informing him of her
progress, and he would visit her whenever he could. Jack
assented gravely to the further proposition that he was
to keep a strict account of all the moneys he advanced
her, and that she was to repay him out of the proceeds
of her first pictures. He had promised also, with a slight
mental reservation, not to buy them all himself, but to
trust to her success with the public. They were never to
talk of what had happened before; she was to begin life
anew. Of such were their confidences, spoken often together at the same moment, and with their mouths full.
Only one thing troubled Jack: he had not yet told her
frankly who he was and what was his reputation. He
had hitherto carelessly supposed she would learn it, and
in truth had cared little if she did; but it was evident
from her conversation that day that by some miracle she
was still in ignorance. Unable to tell her himself, he had
charged Hannibal to break it to her casually after he
was gone.

"You can let me down easy if you like, but you'd better
make a square deal of it while you're about it. And,"
Jack had added cheerfully, "if she thinks after that she'd
better drop me entirely, you just say that if she wishes
to *stay*, you'll see that I don't ever come here again. And
you keep your word about it too, you black nigger, or
I'll be the first to thrash you."

Nevertheless, when Hannibal and Aunt Chloe returned
to clear away the repast, they were a harmonious party;
albeit Mr. Hamlin seemed more content to watch them
silently from his chair by the window, a cigar between
his lips, and the pleasant distraction of the homely
scents and sounds of the garden in his senses. Allusion
having been made again to the morning performance of

the organ, he was implored by Hannibal to diversify his talent by exercising it on an old guitar which had passed into that retainer's possession with certain clothes of his master's when they separated. Mr. Hamlin accepted it dubiously; it had twanged under his volatile fingers in more pretentious but less innocent halls. But presently he raised his tenor voice and soft brown lashes to the humble ceiling and sang.

"Way down upon the Swanee River,"

discoursed Jack plaintively—

"Far, far away,
Thar's whar my heart is turning ever,
Thar's whar the old folks stay."

The two dusky scions of an emotional race, that had been wont to sweeten its toils and condone its wrongs with music, sat wrapt and silent, swaying with Jack's voice until they could burst in upon the chorus. The jasmine vines trilled softly with the afternoon breeze; a slender yellow hammer, perhaps emulous of Jack, swung himself from an outer spray and peered curiously into the room; and a few neighbors, gathering at their doors and windows, remarked that "after all, when it came to real singing, no one could beat those d—d niggers."

The sun was slowly sinking in the rolling gold of the river when Jack and Sophy started leisurely back through the broken shafts of light and across the far-stretching shadows of the cottonwoods. In the midst of a lazy silence they were presently conscious of a distant monotonous throb, the booming of the up boat on the river. The sound came nearer—passed them, the boat itself hidden by the trees; but a trailing cloud of smoke above cast a momentary shadow upon their path. The girl looked up at Jack with a troubled face. Mr. Hamlin smiled reassuringly; but in that instant he had made up his mind that it was his moral duty to kill Mr. Edward Stratton.

FOUR

For the next two months Mr. Hamlin was professionally engaged in San Francisco and Marysville, and the transfer of Sophy from the school to her new home was effected without his supervision. From letters received by him during that interval, it seemed that the young girl had entered energetically upon her new career, and that her artistic efforts were crowned with success. There were a few Indian-ink sketches, studies made at school and expanded in her own "studio," which were eagerly bought as soon as exhibited in the photographer's window—notably by a florid and inartistic bookkeeper, an old Negro woman, a slangy stableboy, a gorgeously dressed and painted female, and the bearded second officer of a river steamboat, without hesitation and without comment. This, as Mr. Hamlin intelligently pointed out in a letter to Sophy, showed a general and diversified appreciation on the part of the public. Indeed, it emboldened her in the retouching of photographs to offer sittings to the subjects, and to undertake even large crayon copies, which had resulted in her getting so many orders that she was no longer obliged to sell her drawings, but restricted herself solely to profitable portraiture. The studio became known; even its quaint surroundings added to the popular interest, and the originality and independence of the young painter helped her to a genuine success. All this she wrote to Jack. Meantime Hannibal had assured him that he had carried out his instructions by informing "Missy" of his old master's real occupation and reputation, but that the young lady hadn't "took no notice." Certainly there was no allusion to it in her letters, nor any indication in her manner. Mr. Hamlin was greatly, and it seemed to him properly, relieved. And he looked forward with considerable satisfaction to an early visit to old Hannibal's laundry.

It must be confessed, also, that another matter, a simple affair of gallantry, was giving him an equally unusual, unexpected, and absurd annoyance, which he had never

before permitted to such trivialities. In a recent visit to a
fashionable watering place he had attracted the attention
of what appeared to be a respectable, matter-of-fact
woman, the wife of a recently elected rural senator. She
was, however, singularly beautiful, and as singularly cold.
It was perhaps this quality, and her evident annoyance at
some unreasoning prepossession which Jack's fascinations
exercised upon her, that heightened that reckless desire
for risk and excitement which really made up the greater
part of his gallantry. Nevertheless, as was his habit, he
had treated her always with a charming unconsciousness
of his own attentions, and a frankness that seemed inconsistent with any insidious approach. In fact, Mr. Hamlin
seldom made love to anybody, but permitted it to be
made to him with good-humored deprecation and cheerful skepticism. He had once, quite accidentally, while
riding, come upon her when she had strayed from her
own riding party, and had behaved with such unexpected
circumspection and propriety, not to mention a certain
thoughtful abstraction—it was the day he had received
Sophy's letter—that she was constrained to make the first
advances. This led to a later innocent rendezvous, in
which Mrs. Camperly was impelled to confide to Mr. Hamlin the fact that her husband had really never understood
her. Jack listened with an understanding and sympathy
quickened by long experience of such confessions. If
anything had ever kept him from marriage it was this
evident incompatibility of the conjugal relations with a
just conception of the feminine soul and its aspirations.

And so eventually this yearning for sympathy dragged
Mrs. Camperly's clean skirts and rustic purity after Jack's
heels into various places and various situations not so
clean, rural, or innocent; made her miserably unhappy
in his absence, and still more miserably happy in his
presence; impelled her to lie, cheat, and bear false witness;
forced her to listen with mingled shame and admiration to
narrow criticism of his faults, from natures so palpably
inferior to his own that her moral sense was confused and
shaken; gave her two distinct lives, but so unreal and
feverish that, with a recklessness equal to his own, she
was at last ready to merge them both into his. For the first
time in his life Mr. Hamlin found himself bored at the

beginning of an affair, actually hesitated, and suddenly disappeared from San Francisco.

He turned up a few days later at Aunt Chloe's door, with various packages of presents and quite the air of a returning father of a family, to the intense delight of that lady and to Sophy's proud gratification. For he was lost in a profuse, boyish admiration of her pretty studio, and in wholesome reverence for her art and her astounding progress. They were also amused at his awe and evident alarm at the portraits of two ladies, her latest sitters, that were still on the easels, and in consideration of his half-assumed, half-real bashfulness, they turned their faces to the wall. Then his quick, observant eye detected a photograph of himself on the mantel.

"What's that?" he asked suddenly.

Sophy and Aunt Chloe exchanged meaning glances. Sophy had, as a surprise to Jack, just completed a handsome crayon portrait of himself from an old photograph furnished by Hannibal, and the picture was at that moment in the window of her former patron—the photographer.

"Oh, dat! Miss Sophy jus' put it dar fo' de lady sitters to look at to gib 'em a pleasant 'spresshion," said Aunt Chloe, chuckling.

Mr. Hamlin did not laugh, but quietly slipped the photograph into his pocket. Yet, perhaps it had not been recognized.

Then Sophy proposed to have luncheon in the studio; it was quite "Bohemian" and fashionable, and many artists did it. But to her great surprise Jack gravely objected, preferring the little parlor of Aunt Chloe, the vine-fringed windows, and the heavy respectable furniture. He thought it was profaning the studio, and then—anybody might come in. This unusual circumspection amused them, and was believed to be part of the boyish awe with which Jack regarded the models, the draperies, and the studies on the walls. Certain it was that he was much more at his ease in the parlor, and when he and Sophy were once more alone at their meal, although he ate nothing, he had regained all his old naïveté. Presently he leaned forward and placed his hand fraternally on her arm. Sophy looked up with an equally frank smile.

"You know I promised to let bygones be bygones, eh?
Well, I intended it, and more—I intended to make 'em so.
I told you I'd never speak to you again of that man who
tried to run you off, and I intended that no one else
should. Well, as he was the only one who could talk—that
meant him. But the cards are out of my hands; the game's
been played without me. For he's dead!"

The girl started. Mr. Hamlin's hand passed caressingly
twice or thrice along her sleeve with a peculiar gentleness
that seemed to magnetize her.

"Dead," he repeated slowly. "Shot in San Diego by
another man, but not by me. I had him tracked as far as
that, and had my eyes on him, but it wasn't my deal. But
there," he added, giving her magnetized arm a gentle
and final tap as if to awaken it, "he's dead, and so is the
whole story. And now we'll drop it forever."

The girl's downcast eyes were fixed on the table.

"But there's my sister," she murmured.

"Did she know you went with him?" asked Jack.

"No; but she knows I ran away."

"Well, you ran away from home to study how to be an
artist, don't you see? Someday she'll find out you *are one;*
that settles the whole thing."

They were both quite cheerful again when Aunt Chloe
returned to clear the table, especially Jack, who was in the
best spirits, with preternaturally bright eyes and a somewhat rare color on his cheeks. Aunt Chloe, who had
noticed that his breathing was hurried at times, watched
him narrowly, and when later he slipped from the room,
followed him into the passage. He was leaning against
the wall. In an instant the negress was at his side.

"De Lawdy Gawd, Marse Jack, not *agin?*"

He took his handkerchief, slightly streaked with blood,
from his lips and said faintly, "Yes, it came on—on the
boat; but I thought the d—d thing was over. Get me out
of this, quick, to some hotel, before she knows it. You can
tell her I was called away. Say that—" but his breath
failed him, and when Aunt Chloe caught him like a child
in her strong arms he could make no resistance.

In another hour he was unconscious, with two doctors
at his bedside, in the little room that had been occupied
by Sophy. It was a sharp attack, but prompt attendance

and skillful nursing availed; he rallied the next day, but it would be weeks, the doctors said, before he could be removed in safety. Sophy was transferred to the parlor, but spent most of her time at Jack's bedside with Aunt Chloe, or in the studio with the door open between it and the bedroom. In spite of his enforced idleness and weakness, it was again a singularly pleasant experience to Jack; it amused him to sometimes see Sophy at her work through the open door, and when sitters came—for he had insisted on her continuing her duties as before, keeping his invalid presence in the house a secret—he had all the satisfaction of a mischievous boy in rehearsing to Sophy such of the conversation as could be overheard through the closed door, and speculating on the possible wonder and chagrin of the sitters had they discovered him. Even when he was convalescent and strong enough to be helped into the parlor and garden, he preferred to remain propped up in Sophy's little bedroom. It was evident, however, that this predilection was connected with no suggestion nor reminiscence of Sophy herself. It was true that he had once asked her if it didn't make her "feel like home." The decided negative from Sophy seemed to mildly surprise him. "That's odd," he said; "now all these fixings and things," pointing to the flowers in a vase, the little hanging shelf of books, the knickknacks on the mantel shelf, and the few feminine ornaments that still remained, "look rather like home to me."

So the days slipped by, and although Mr. Hamlin was soon able to walk short distances, leaning on Sophy's arm, in the evening twilight along the river bank, he was still missed from the haunts of dissipated men. A good many people wondered, and others, chiefly of the more irrepressible sex, were singularly concerned. Apparently one of these, one sultry afternoon, stopped before the shadowed window of a photographer's; she was a handsome, well-dressed woman, yet bearing a certain countrylike simplicity that was unlike the restless smartness of the more urban promenaders who passed her. Nevertheless she had halted before Mr. Hamlin's picture, which Sophy had not yet dared to bring home and present to him, and was gazing at it with rapt and breathless attention. Suddenly she shook down her veil and entered the shop.

Could the proprietor kindly tell her if that portrait was the work of a local artist?

The proprietor was both proud and pleased to say that *it was!* It was the work of a Miss Brown, a young girl student; in fact, a mere schoolgirl, one might say. He could show her others of her pictures.

Thanks. But could he tell her if this portrait was from life?

No doubt; the young lady had a studio, and he himself had sent her sitters.

And perhaps this was the portrait of one that he had sent her?

No; but she was very popular and becoming quite the fashion. Very probably this gentleman, who, he understood, was quite a public character, had heard of her, and selected her on that account.

The lady's face flushed slightly. The photographer continued. The picture was not for sale; it was only there on exhibition; in fact it was to be returned tomorrow.

To the sitter?

He couldn't say. It was to go back to the studio. Perhaps the sitter would be there.

And this studio? Could she have its address?

The man wrote a few lines on his card. Perhaps the lady would be kind enough to say that he had sent her. The lady, thanking him, partly lifted her veil to show a charming smile, and gracefully withdrew. The photographer was pleased. Miss Brown had evidently got another sitter, and from that momentary glimpse of her face, it would be a picture as beautiful and attractive as the man's. But what was the odd idea that struck him? She certainly reminded him of someone! There was the same heavy hair, only this lady's was golden, and she was older and more mature. And he remained for a moment with knitted brows musing over his counter.

Meantime the fair stranger was making her way towards the river suburb. When she reached Aunt Chloe's cottage, she paused, with the unfamiliar curiosity of a newcomer, over its quaint and incongruous exterior. She hesitated a moment also when Aunt Chloe appeared in the doorway, and, with a puzzled survey of her features, went upstairs to announce a visitor. There was the sound of hurried shutting of doors, of the moving of furniture, quick footsteps across the floor, and then a girlish laugh that startled her. She ascended the stairs breathlessly to Aunt Chloe's summons, found the negress on the landing, and knocked at a door which bore a card marked "Studio." The door opened; she entered; there were two sudden outcries that might have come from one voice.

"Sophonisba!"

"Marianne!"

"Hush."

The woman had seized Sophy by the wrist and dragged her to the window. There was a haggard look of desperation in her face akin to that which Hamlin had once seen in her sister's eyes on the boat, as she said huskily: "I did not know *you* were here. I came to see the woman who had painted Mr. Hamlin's portrait. I did not know it was *you*. Listen! Quick! answer me one question. Tell me—I implore you—for the sake of the mother who bore us both!—tell me—is this the man for whom you left home?"

"No! No! A hundred times no!"

Then there was a silence. Mr. Hamlin from the bedroom heard no more.

An hour later, when the two women opened the studio door, pale but composed, they were met by the anxious and tearful face of Aunt Chloe.

"Lawdy Gawd, Missy—but dey done gone!—bofe of 'em!"

"Who is gone?" demanded Sophy, as the woman beside her trembled and grew paler still.

"Marse Jack and dat fool nigger, Hannibal."

"Mr. Hamlin gone?" repeated Sophy incredulously. "When? Where?"

"Jess now—on de down boat. Sudden business. Didn't like to disturb yo' and yo' friend. Said he'd write."

"But he was ill—almost helpless," gasped Sophy.

"Dat's why he took dat old nigger. Lawdy, Missy, bress yo' heart. Dey both knows aich udder, shuah! It's all right. Dar now, dar dey are; listen."

She held up her hand. A slow pulsation that might have been the dull, labored beating of their own hearts was making itself felt throughout the little cottage. It came nearer—a deep regular inspiration that seemed slowly to fill and possess the whole tranquil summer twilight. It was nearer still—was abreast of the house—passed—grew fainter—and at last died away like a deep-drawn sigh. It was the down boat that was now separating Mr. Hamlin and his protégée, even as it had once brought them together.

SELECTED BIBLIOGRAPHY

OTHER WORKS BY BRET HARTE

Condensed Novels and Other Papers, 1867   Satire

*The Lost Galleon and
  Other Tales in Verse,* 1867   Poems

The Heathen Chinee, 1870   Poem

The Little Drummer, 1872   Story

Tales of the Argonauts, 1875   Stories

Echoes of the Foot-Hills, 1875   Poems

Two Men of Sandy Bar, 1876   Play

Gabriel Conroy, 1876   Novel

Ah Sin, 1877 (with Mark Twain) Play based on
  The Heathen Chinee

The Twins of Table Mountain, 1879   Story

The Postmistress of Laurel Run, 1892   Story

The Bell-Ringer of Angel's, 1894   Story

Barker's Luck and Other Stories, 1896   Stories

Tales of Trail and Town, 1898   Stories

Under the Redwoods, 1901   Story

Sketches of the Sixties (with Mark Twain), 1927

SELECTED BIOGRAPHY AND CRITICISM

Harte, Geoffrey Bret (ed.) *The Letters of Bret Harte.* Boston:
Houghton, Mifflin Company, 1926.

Merwin, Henry Childs. *The Life of Bret Harte, with some Account of the California Pioneers.* Boston: Houghton, Mifflin
Company, 1911.

O'Brien, Edward J. "Bret Harte and Mark Twain" in *The Advance of the American Short Story.* New York: Dodd, Mead
and Company, 1923.

Pattee, Fred Lewis. "Bret Harte" in *The Development of the
American Short Story.* New York: Harper and Brothers,
1923.

Pemberton, Thomas Edgar. *The Life of Bret Harte.* London: C.
Arthur Pearson, Ltd., 1903.
———. *Bret Harte: A Treatise and a Tribute.* New York:
Greening & Co., Ltd., 1900.

Quinn, Arthur Hobson. *American Fiction.* New York: D. Appleton-Century Co., 1936, pp. 232-42.

Stewart, George R. *Bret Harte: Argonaut and Exile.* Boston:
Houghton, Mifflin Co., 1931.

Walker, Franklin. *San Francisco's Literary Frontier.* New York:
Alfred A. Knopf, Inc., 1939.

A NOTE ON THE TEXT

The text of this edition follows *The Writings of Bret Harte,* Standard Library Edition. Boston: Houghton, Mifflin and Company, 1896-1904. The Standard Library Edition represented an attempt by the publishers, with the aid of Mr. Harte, to make a "uniform and orderly presentation of the results of more than thirty years of genial industry."

![Signet logo]

SIGNET CLASSICS of American Literature

Other SIGNET CLASSICS of American Literature

𝒞

More American SIGNET CLASSICS